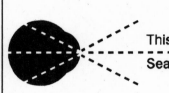

INDULGENCE IN DEATH

J. D. ROBB

WHEELER PUBLISHING
A part of Gale, Cengage Learning

GALE
CENGAGE Learning

Detroit • New York • San Francisco • New Haven, Conn • Waterville, Maine • London

GALE
CENGAGE Learning™

Wheeler Publishing Large Print Hardcover.
The text of this Large Print edition is unabridged.
Other aspects of the book may vary from the original edition.
Set in 16 pt. Plantin.

LIBRARY OF CONGRESS CATALOGING-IN-PUBLICATION DATA

Robb, J. D., 1950–
    Indulgence in death / by J. D. Robb.
        p. cm.
    ISBN-13: 978-1-4104-3164-6
    ISBN-10: 1-4104-3164-9
    1. Dallas, Eve (Fictitious character)—Fiction. 2. Policewomen—New York (State)—New York—Fiction. 3. Serial murderers—Fiction. 4. Rich people—Fiction. 5. Contests—Fiction. 6. Successful people—Crimes against—Fiction. 7. Service industries workers—Crimes against—Fiction. 8. New York (N.Y.)—Fiction. 9. Large type books. I. Title.
    PS3568.O243I53 2010b
    813'.54—dc22   2010031103

Published in 2010 by arrangement with G. P. Putnam's Sons, a member of Penguin Group (USA) Inc.

Printed in the United States of America
1 2 3 4 5 6 7 14 13 12 11 10

Thou shalt not covet; but tradition
Approves all forms of competition.
— ARTHUR HUGH CLOUGH

It is the wretchedness of being rich that
you have to live with rich people.
— LOGAN PEARSALL SMITH

1

The road was a killer, hardly wider than a decent stream of spit and snaking like a cobra between giant bushes loaded with strange flowers that resembled drops of blood.

She had to remind herself that the trip had been her idea — love was another killer — but how could she have known driving in western Ireland meant risking life and limb at every curve?

Rural Ireland, she thought, holding her breath as they zipped around the next turn on the Journey of Death. Where the towns were barely a hiccup on the landscape, and where she was pretty damn sure the cows outnumbered the people. And the sheep outnumbered the cows.

And why didn't that cause anyone concern? she wondered. Didn't people consider what could happen if armies of farm animals united in revolt?

When Murder Road finally carved its way out of the blood-drop bushes, the world opened up into fields and hills, green, green, eerily green against a sky stacked with clouds that couldn't decide if they wanted to rain or just sit there ominously. And she knew those dots all over the green were sheep and cows.

Probably discussing war strategy.

She'd actually seen them hanging around those weird — and okay, a little bit fascinating — stone ruins. Towering, tumbling places that had maybe been castles or forts. A good place for armies of farm animals to plot their revolt.

Maybe it was beautiful in a hang-the-painting-on-your-wall kind of way, but it just wasn't natural. No, it was too natural, she corrected. That was the deal, too much nature, too much open. Even the houses scattered over the endless landscape insisted on decking themselves out with flowers. Everything blooming, colors smashed against colors, shapes against shapes.

She'd even seen clothes hanging on lines like executed prisoners. It was 2060, for God's sake. Didn't people out here own drying units?

And speaking of that — yeah, speaking of that — where was all the air traffic? She'd barely spotted a handful of airtrams, and not a single ad blimp lumbered overhead blasting out its hype on sales.

No subway, no glide carts, no tourists blissfully providing marks for street thieves, no maxibuses farting, no Rapid Cab drivers cursing.

God, she missed New York.

She couldn't even risk driving to take her mind off it, as for some cruel, inexplicable reason people over here insisted on driving on the wrong side of the road.

Why?

She was a cop, sworn to protect and serve, so she could hardly get behind the wheel on these death-trap roads where she'd probably end up mowing down innocent civilians. And maybe some farm animals while she was at it.

She wondered if they'd ever get where they were going, and what the odds were of getting there in one piece.

Maybe she should run some probabilities.

The road narrowed again, boxed in again, and Lieutenant Eve Dallas, veteran murder cop, pursuer of psychopaths, serial killers, homicidal deviants, fought to hold back a squeal as her side of the car lightly kissed the hedges.

Her husband of two years — and the

reason she'd suggested this leg of their vacation — took his hand off the wheel to pat her thigh. "Relax, Lieutenant."

"Watch the road! Don't look at me, look at the road. Except it's not really a road. It's a track. What are these damn bushes, and why are they here?"

"It's fuchsia. Lovely, aren't they?"

They made her think of blood spatter, possibly resulting from a massacre by a battalion of farm animals.

"They ought to move them away from the stupid road."

"I imagine they were here first."

Ireland wound through his voice a lot more appealingly than the road wound through the countryside.

She risked a glance in his direction. He looked happy, she realized. Relaxed, happy, at ease in a thin leather jacket and T-shirt, his black hair swept back from that amazing face (another killer), his eyes so rich a blue it made the heart ache.

She remembered they'd nearly died together a few weeks before, and he'd been badly wounded. She'd thought — she could still remember that breathless instant when she'd thought she'd lost him.

And here he was, alive and whole. So maybe she'd forgive him for being amused at her expense.

Maybe.

Besides, it was her own fault. She'd suggested they take part of their vacation, their anniversary celebration, here so he could visit the family he'd only recently discovered. She'd been here before, after all.

Of course, that trip she'd taken in a jet-copter.

When he slowed as they entered what could very loosely be called a town, she breathed a little easier.

"Nearly there now," he told her. "This is Tulla. Sinead's farm is a few kilometers from the village."

Okay, they'd made it this far. Ordering herself to settle down, she scooped a hand through her choppy cap of brown hair.

"Look there. The sun's breaking through."

She studied the miserly opening in the gray, and the watery beam that struggled through. "Wow, the light. It's blinding."

He laughed, reached out to smooth a hand over the hair she'd just ruffled. "We're out of our element, Lieutenant. Maybe it's good for us to be out of the norm now and again."

She knew her norm. Death, investigation, the insanity of a city that ran instead of walked, the smells of a cop shop, the rush and the burden of command.

Some of that had become Roarke's norm in the last couple years, she mused. He juggled that with his own world, which was buying, selling, owning, creating pretty much every freaking thing in the known universe.

His beginnings had been as dark and ugly as hers. Dublin street rat, she thought, thief, conniver, survivor of a brutal, murderous father. The mother he'd never known hadn't been so lucky.

From that, he'd built an empire — not always on the sunny side of the law.

And she, cop to the bone, had fallen for him despite the shadows — or maybe because of them. But there was more to him than either of them had known, and the more lived on a farm outside of the little village of Tulla in County Clare.

"We could've taken a copter from the hotel," she said to him.

"I like the drive."

"I know you mean that, so it makes me wonder about you, pal."

"We'll take a shuttle when we leave for Florence."

"No argument."

"And we'll have a candlelight dinner in our suite." He glanced toward her with that relaxed, happy smile. "The best pizza in the city."

"Now you're talking."

"It means a lot to them that we'd come like this — together — for a couple of days."

"I like them," she said of his mother's family. "Sinead, the rest. Vacations are good. I just have to work myself into the mode and stop thinking about what's going on back at Central. What do people do here, anyway?"

"They work, farm, run shops, tend homes and families, go to the pub for a pint and community. Simple doesn't mean unfulfilled."

She let out a little snort. "You'd go crazy here."

"Oh, within a week. We're urban creatures, you and I, but I can appreciate those who make this way their own, who value and support community. *Comhar*," he added, "that's the Irish word for it. It's particular to the west counties."

There were woods now, sort of looming back from the road, and pretty — if you went for that kind of thing — stretches of fields divided by low walls of rock she imagined had been mined from the pretty fields.

She recognized the house when Roarke

turned. It managed to be sprawling and tidy at the same time, fronted with flowers in what Roarke had told her they called a *dooryard*. If buildings sent off an aura, she supposed this one would be content.

Roarke's mother had grown up here before she'd run off to the bright lights of Dublin. There, young, naive, trusting, she'd fallen in love with Patrick Roarke, had borne his child. And had died trying to save that child.

Now her twin sister ran the house, helped run the farm with the man she'd married, with their children and siblings, parents — the whole brood seemed to root here, in the green.

Sinead stepped out of the house, telling Eve she'd been watching for them. Her gilded red hair framed her pretty face where green eyes warmed in welcome.

It wasn't the connection of blood kin that put that affection on her face, or in the arms she stretched out. It was family. Blood, Eve knew, didn't always mean warmth and welcome.

Sinead caught Roarke in a solid, swaying hug, and as her murmured greeting was in Irish, Eve couldn't understand the words. But the emotion translated.

This was love, open and accepting.

When she turned, Eve found herself

caught in the same full-on embrace. It widened her eyes, shifted her balance.

"*Fáilte abhaile.* Welcome home."

"Thanks. Ah . . ."

"Come in, come in. We're all in the kitchen or out the back. We've enough food to feed the army we are, and thought we'd have a picnic, as you've brought such nice weather."

Eve cast a glance up at the sky, and supposed there were degrees of nice weather, depending where you stood on the planet.

"I'll have one of the boys fetch your bags and take them up to your room. Oh, it's good to see your faces. We're all here now. We're all home."

They were fed and feted, surrounded and questioned. Eve managed the names and faces by imagining them all as suspects on a murder board — even the ones who toddled and crawled.

Especially the one who kept toddling over and trying to claw its way into her lap.

"Our Devin's a lady's man." His mother — Maggie — laughed as she hauled him up, and in the way of some women, lodged him effortlessly on her hip. "Da says you're off to Italy next. Connor and I splurged on our honeymoon and went to Venice. It was brilliant."

The kid on her hip babbled something and bounced.

"All right, my man, since we're having a holiday. I'm after getting him another biscuit. Would you like one?"

"No, thanks. I'm good."

A moment later, Eve felt an itch between her shoulder blades. Shifting, she saw a boy staring at her. She recognized him — the Brody family green eyes, the solar system of freckles — from when the family had come to New York the previous Thanksgiving.

"What's the deal?" she demanded.

"I'm wondering if you've got your stunner."

She hadn't worn the harness, but she'd strapped her clutch piece to her ankle. Old habits die hard, she supposed, just as she supposed Sinead and the rest of the females wouldn't appreciate her showing the kid the weapon at a family picnic.

"Why? Somebody need to go down?"

He grinned at that. "My sister, if you wouldn't mind."

"What's the offense?"

"Being a git. That should be enough."

She knew the gist of the meaning from Roarke's use of the word when he lapsed into his native slang. "Not in New York, ace. The city's full of gits."

16

"I think I'll be a cop and blast the bad guys. How many've you blasted?"

Bloodthirsty little bastard, Eve thought. She liked him. "No more than my share. Putting them in a cage is more satisfying than blasting them."

"Why?"

"It lasts longer."

He considered that. "Well now, I'll blast them first, then put them in a cage."

When she laughed, he shot out another grin. "We don't get bad guys around here, and that's a pity. Maybe I'll come to New York again, and you can show me some of yours."

"Maybe."

"That'll be frosted!" he said, and bolted off.

The minute he did, someone plopped down beside her and pushed a fresh pint into her hand. Seamus, she identified, Sinead's oldest son. She was pretty sure.

"So, how're you finding Ireland then?"

"We went east from New York. Green," she added when he chuckled and gave her a friendly elbow in the ribs. "With a lot of sheep. And good beer."

"Every shepherd deserves a pint of an evening. You've made my mother very happy, taking this time to come, be with

17

family. She thinks of Roarke as hers now, in her sister's place. What you're doing for her, and for him, it matters."

"It doesn't take much effort to sit around and drink good beer."

He patted her thigh. "It's a long way to travel for a pint. Added to it, you've thrilled my boy to pieces."

"Sorry?"

"My Sean, who was just here interrogating you."

"Oh. It's hard to figure who's whose."

"Sure it is. Since we visited you last year, he's given up his dream of being a space pirate in favor of being a cop and blasting bad guys for his living."

"He mentioned it."

"Truth be known he's wishing desperately for a murder while you're about. Something gruesome and mysterious."

"Get a lot of those around here?"

He sat back, took a contemplative sip of beer. "The last I recall was when old Mrs. O'iley broke her husband's head with a skillet when he, once again, came home pissed and smelling of another woman's perfume. I suppose it was gruesome enough, but not altogether mysterious. That would be about a dozen years back."

"Not much action in the area for a murder cop."

"Sadly for Sean, no. He likes to follow your cases, searching out tidbits on his computer. This last? The hologames murder gave him endless thrills."

"Oh." She glanced over to where Roarke stood with Sinead, her arm around his waist. And thought of the blade slicing into his side.

"We've a parental lock on, so he can't get the juicier details."

"Yeah, that's probably a good thing."

"How bad was he hurt, my cousin? The media didn't have much on that — which is, I suppose, how he wanted it."

His blood, warm, sliding through her shaking fingers. "Bad enough."

Seamus nodded, lips pursed as he studied Roarke. "He's not at all his father's son, is he then?"

"Not where it counts."

Irish picnics, Eve discovered, went on for hours, as did the Irish summer day, and included music, dancing, and general carryings-on till well after the stars winked on.

"We've kept you up late." Sinead walked them upstairs, this time wrapping an arm around Eve's waist.

Eve never knew exactly what to do when people looped their arms around her — unless it was combat, or Roarke.

"After all your travels, too. Barely giving you time to unpack, and none at all to settle in."

"It was a nice party."

"It was, it was, yes. And now my Seamus talked Roarke into going out in the field in the morning." She gave Eve a little squeeze. At the signal, Eve glanced back at Roarke.

"Seriously. In the field, like farm field?" Eve said.

"I'll enjoy it. I've never driven a tractor."

"I hope you say the same when we're dragging you out of bed at half-six."

"He hardly sleeps anyway," Eve commented. "He's like a droid."

Sinead laughed, opened the door to their bedroom. "Well, I hope you'll be comfortable for the time you have." She looked around the room with its simple furniture, its soft colors, and white lace at the windows under the slant of the ceiling.

Flowers, a charm of colors and shapes, stood in a squat pot on the dresser.

"If you need a thing, anything at all, I'm just down the hall."

"We'll be fine." Roarke turned to her, kissed her cheek. "More than."

"I'll see you at breakfast then. Sleep well."
She slipped out, shut the door.

"Why," Eve asked, "do you want to drive a tractor?"

"I have no idea, but it seems like the thing to do." Idly, he pulled off his shoes. "I'll get out of it if you don't want to be left on your own in the morning."

"It's no problem for me. I plan on sleeping off a year's worth of beer anyway."

He came to her smiling, brushed a hand over her hair. "A lot of people for you to deal with at one time."

"They're okay. At least after you figure out what they're talking about. What they talk about, a lot, is you."

"I'm the new element." He kissed her forehead. "We're the new element, as they're fairly fascinated by my cop." He drew her in so they stood holding each other in the center of the pretty farmhouse bedroom with the night breeze wafting through the window to stir the fragrance of the flowers through the air. "It's a different life entirely here. A world away."

"The last murder was about a dozen years ago."

He drew back, shook his head. Just laughed. "Trust you."

"I didn't bring it up. Do you hear that?"

"What?"

"Nothing. See, it's really quiet, and it's really dark," she added with a glance at the window. "Dead quiet, dead dark. So you'd think there'd be more murders."

"Looking for a busman's holiday?"

"I know what that means even though it doesn't make any sense. And no. I'm good with the quiet. Mostly." She ran a hand up his side, laid it on the wound. "Okay?"

"Well enough. In fact . . ." He leaned down, took her mouth with his, and let his own hand roam.

"Okay, hold it. That's just weird."

"It feels very natural to me."

"Your aunt's just — what is it — down the hall. You know damn well this place isn't soundproofed."

"You'll just have to be quiet." He gave her ribs a deliberate tickle that made her jump and yelp. "Or not."

"Didn't I bang you already today, twice this morning?"

"Darling Eve, you're a pathetic romantic." He backed her toward the bed she'd already noted was less than half the size of the one at home.

"At least turn on the screen or something. For cover noise."

He brushed his lips over her cheek, his

hand over the taut muscles of her ass. "There's no screen in here."

"No screen?" She nudged him away, scanned the walls. "Seriously? What kind of place is this?"

"The sort where people use bedrooms for sex and sleep, which is exactly what I have in mind." To prove it, he tumbled her onto the bed.

It squeaked.

"What is that? Did you hear that? Is there a farm animal in here?"

"I'm fairly certain they keep those outside. It's the bed." He tugged her shirt over her head.

Testing, she lifted her hips, let them fall. "Oh, for God's sake. We can't do this on a talking bed. Everybody in the house will know what's going on in here."

Enjoying himself, he nuzzled at her throat. "I believe they already suspect we have sex."

"Maybe, but that's different than having the bed yell out, 'Whoopee!' "

Was it any wonder he adored her? he thought.

Watching her face, he trailed a finger over her breast. "We'll have quiet, dignified sex."

"If sex is dignified it's not being done right."

"There's a point." He smiled down at her,

cupping her breasts now, laying his lips lightly on hers. "Look at you," he murmured, "all mine for two more lovely weeks."

"Now you're just trying to soften me up." And softened, she reached out to comb her fingers through his hair.

All hers, she thought in turn.

"It's good, being here." She took his shirt by the hem, drew it over his head. Once again laid her palm on the healing wound. "Getting here, we'll forget all about that. But being here, it's good."

"It's been an interesting journey altogether."

"I wouldn't have missed a single mile." She framed his face now, lifted until their lips met. "Even the rocky ones."

When he lowered to her, she drew him in, and sighed.

Eyes closed, she ran her hands over the good, strong muscles of his back, let the shape and scent of him seep into those places inside her that always waited. Always opened, always welcomed.

She turned her head, found his lips again. Longer, deeper into a drift as easy and sweet as the night air.

The bed gave another rusty squeak, made her laugh. Then another as she shifted to him. "We should try the floor."

"Next time," he suggested, and made her laugh again. Made her sigh again. Made all those waiting, welcoming places warm.

And when they curled together, sated and sleepy, she nuzzled in and said, "Whoopee."

She woke in the gray, shot straight up in bed.

"What was that? Did you hear that?" Naked, she leaped out of bed to grab the clutch piece she'd left on the little bedside table.

"There! There it is again! What language is that?"

From the bed, Roarke shifted. "I believe it's known as rooster."

With the weapon at her side, she stared at him, slack-jawed. "Are you fucking kidding me?"

"Not a bit. It's morning, more or less, and that's a cock signaling the dawn."

"A cock?"

"I'd say. I don't think Sinead and her man want you to stun their rooster, but I have to say, Lieutenant, you make a fascinating picture."

She heaved out a breath, set her weapon down. "Jesus Christ, we may as well be on another planet." She slid back into bed.

"And if your cock gets any ideas about signaling the day, remember I've got a weapon."

"As charming an idea as that is, I think that's my wake-up call. Though I'd rather be riding my wife instead of a tractor, they're expecting me."

"Have fun." Eve rolled over and put the pillow over her head.

Screaming cocks, she thought, squeezing her eyes tight. And, good God, was that a cow? Actually mooing? Just how close were those bastards to the house?

She lifted the pillow an inch, squinted to assure herself her weapon was at hand.

How the hell was a person supposed to sleep with all that mooing and cockadoodle-dooing, and only God knew what else was going on out there? It was just plain creepy, that's what it was. What were they saying to each other? And why?

Wasn't the window open? Maybe she should get up and . . .

The next thing she knew she awoke to yellow sunlight.

She'd slept after all, even if she'd had an unsettling farm animal dream where they were all decked out in military fatigues.

Her first thought was coffee before she remembered where she was and barely muttered a curse. They drank tea over here, and she didn't know how the hell she was supposed to deal with the day she had ahead of her without a hit.

She dragged herself up, looked blearily around. And spotted the robe at the foot of the bed, and the memo cube sitting on it. She reached for the cube, flicked it on.

"Good morning, Lieutenant. In case you're still half asleep, the shower's straight down the hall to the left. Sinead says to come down for breakfast whenever you're up and about. Apparently I'm to meet you about noon. Sinead will take you wherever we're supposed to be. Take care of my cop.

"No bad guys, remember?"

She put on her robe, and after a moment's deliberation, stuffed her weapon in its pocket. Better on her, she decided, than left in the room.

And mourning coffee, she walked down to wake herself up in the shower.

2

The bed was made and the room tidied when she finished her shower. Did they have droids? she wondered, and decided she'd been smart to take her weapon with her.

If they had droids, why not an AutoChef in the bedroom — one with coffee on the menu? Or a screen so she could scan the international crime news to see what was happening at home.

Adapt, she ordered herself as she dressed while some species of bird went cuckoo — literally — over and over again outside the window. This wasn't New York, or even a close facsimile. And surely she was racking up good wife points every minute.

She raked her fingers through her damp hair — no drying tube in the facilities — and considered herself as ready for the day as she was going to get.

Halfway down the steps she heard more singing, a pretty and bright human voice lilting away about love. And on the turn for the kitchen, she swore she caught the siren's scent of coffee.

Hope shimmered even as she told herself it was likely just sense memory. But the scent snagged her and drew her like a fish-hook the rest of the way.

"Oh, thank God." She hadn't realized she'd spoken out loud until Sinead turned from the stove and smiled at her.

"Good morning to you. I hope you slept well."

"Great, thanks. Is that really coffee?"

"It is, yes. Roarke had it sent, special, the sort you like particularly. I remembered you've a fondness for it."

"It's more a desperate need."

"I need a strong cup of tea in the morning before I'm human." Sinead handed Eve a thick brown mug. She wore trim oatmeal-colored pants and a bright blue shirt with the sleeves cuffed at the elbows. Some sort of hinged pin scooped her hair back from her face and fastened it at the back of her head.

"Have a seat, get the gears moving."

"Thanks. Really."

"The men are off looking at machinery, so you can have a peaceful breakfast. Roarke said you'd go for a full Irish."

"Ah . . ."

"What we'll call a civilized portion," Sinead said with a quick grin. "Not the heaps the men manage to consume."

"I'm really fine with coffee. You don't have to bother."

"I'd like to bother. It pleases me. Meats already done so I've got it warming. It won't take but a minute or two to cook up the rest. It's nice to have company in the kitchen," she added as she turned back to the stove.

Odd, Eve thought, very odd to sit down and actually watch somebody cook. She imagined Summerset, Roarke's majordomo, did a lot of it as he stocked the AutoChefs.

But hanging out in the kitchen, especially with Summerset, was on her list of top-ten nightmares.

"I hear the cock woke you up."

Eve choked on her coffee. "What?"

"Not that kind of cock." Sinead sent a sparkling look over her shoulder. "Though if that's true as well, good for you. I meant the rooster."

"Oh, right. Yeah. It does that every morning?"

"Fair or foul, though I'm too used to it to hear him go off most days." She broke eggs into the skillet. "It would be like traffic noises to you, I suppose. Just part of the world you live in."

She glanced back again as food sizzled. "I'm so glad you're staying another night, and we've got such a fine, bright day shining on your gift to Roarke. I thought I'd take you over there a bit early, so you could have a look before Seamus brings him."

"The pictures you sent gave me the gist, but it'd be good to see it firsthand. I appreciate all you did there, Sinead."

"It means the world to me and mine. It's more than a grand anniversary gift, Eve. Much, much more."

She took a plate out of the oven, added the eggs, fried potatoes, a small half tomato. "And here's brown bread fresh this morning," she said, putting the plate and a crock of butter in front of Eve, then taking a cloth off a half round of bread.

"Smells great."

With a smile, Sinead topped off Eve's coffee, then brought a mug of tea to the table. Waited while Eve sampled.

"Tastes even better, and I've gotten spoiled when it comes to breakfast."

"That's grand then. I like feeding people, tending to them. I like thinking I've a talent for it."

"I'd say you do."

"We should all be lucky enough to do what we like, and what we've a talent for. Your work gives you that."

"Yeah."

"I can't imagine doing what you do any more than I think you can imagine my life here. Yet here we are, sitting together at the kitchen table sharing the morning. Fate's an odd thing, and in this case a generous one. I have to thank you for coming this way, spending these precious days of your holiday with us."

"I'm eating a really good breakfast and drinking terrific coffee. It's not exactly a sacrifice."

Sinead reached across the table, touched Eve's hand briefly. "You have power over a powerful man. His love for you gives you the power, though I suspect there are times the two of you fight like cats."

"More than a few."

"He's here now, likely driving a tractor around a field instead of lounging on some brilliant terrace in some exotic place, and drinking champagne for breakfast because you wanted it for him. Because you know he needs this connection, and needs just as much for you to share it with him."

"You gave him something he didn't know he wanted or needed. If you hadn't, we wouldn't be sitting together at the kitchen table sharing the morning."

"I miss my sister every day."

She looked away for a moment. "Twins," she murmured. "It's a bond more intimate than I can explain. Now, with Roarke, I have a part of her I never thought to claim, and I stand as his mother now. He has my heart, as I know he has yours. I want us to be friends, you and I. I want to think that you'll come back now and then, or we'll come to you. That this connection will only grow stronger, truer — and that what there is between you and me won't only be because of the man we both love."

Eve said nothing for a moment as she tried to order her thoughts. "A lot of people would have blamed him."

"He was a baby."

Eve shook her head. "In my world people blame, hurt, maim, kill for all kinds of illogical reasons. His father murdered your sister. Patrick Roarke used her, abused her, betrayed her, and finally killed her — took her from you. And some would twist that into looking at Roarke as the only thing left from that loss, even the reason for the loss. When he learned what had happened, when he found out about his mother after a lifetime of believing a lie, he came to you.

You didn't turn him away, you didn't blame him or punish him. You brought him into your home, and you gave him comfort when he needed it.

"I don't make friends easily. I'm not very good at it. But for that reason alone you'd be mine, so between us I guess we've got the elements for friendship."

"He's lucky to have you."

Eve shoveled in more eggs. "Damn right."

Sinead held her mug in both hands as she laughed. "She'd have liked you. Siobhan."

"Really?"

"She would, yes. She liked the bright and the bold." Shifting, Sinead leaned forward. "Now tell me, while it's just us two, all the nasty details of this last murder you solved. The sorts they don't talk about in the media."

Shortly before noon, Eve stood in the little park, hands on hips, studying the equipment. She didn't know dick-all about kids' playgrounds, but this looked like a pretty good one. Surrounding the stuff they'd swing on, climb on, tunnel through, and whatever the hell kids did, ran pretty rivers of flowers, young, green trees.

A cherry tree, a young version of the one Sinead had planted at her farm in memory of her sister, stood graceful and sweet near a little pavilion. Benches sat here and there where she imagined parents could take a load off while kids ran wild.

A pretty stone fountain gurgled near a pint-sized house complete with scaled-down furniture on a covered porch. Nearby ranged what Sinead called a football pitch, some bleachers, a kind of hut for serving snacks, a larger building where players could suit up.

Paths wound here and there, though some went nowhere for the moment. Work wasn't quite done, but she had to give Sinead and the family major credit for what had been accomplished already.

"It completely rocks."

Sinead let out a long breath. "I was so nervous it wouldn't be all you wanted."

"It's more than I could've thought of or done." She stepped closer to the swings, stopped, looked down as she pumped her boot in the spongy ground.

"It's safety material. Children fall and tumble, and it protects them."

"Excellent. It looks . . . fun," Eve decided. "It's pretty and nicely designed, but mostly it looks like fun."

"We brought some of our young ones out to test it, and I can promise you that's what they had."

The steady breeze ruffled the hair Sinead had unclipped as she — hands on hips — turned a circle. "The village is full of talk about it. It's a lovely thing altogether. Just a lovely thing."

"If he doesn't like it, I'll kick his ass."

"I'll hold your coat. Ah well now, here they come." Sinead lifted her chin as she spotted the truck. "I'm going to take my group off a ways so you can give Roarke his gift in private."

"Appreciate it."

She wasn't comfortable with gifts — giving or receiving — most of the time anyway. And in this case she was a little nervous she'd taken on too much. What had seemed like a good idea at the time — the past November during Sinead's visit — had become more complicated and complex, and she worried maybe not altogether appropriate.

Presents, anniversaries, family — limited experience all around.

She watched him walking toward her, long and lanky in jeans and boots, a faded blue shirt rolled up to his elbows, the thick black silk of his hair pulled back in work mode. Two years married, she thought, and he could still make her heart hum.

"So, giving it all up for farming?" she called out.

"I think not, though I did have fun at it for a few hours. They've horses." He stopped, leaned down to kiss her when he reached her. "You could try a ride." He skimmed a fingertip down the dent in her chin when she gave him a bland stare. "You might enjoy it, more than that recent holoride into battle."

She remembered the speed and power of the hologram horse, and thought she actually might. But she had a different agenda for the moment.

"They're bigger than cows, but don't look as weird."

"There's that." He glanced around, and her nerves started to jingle. "Are you after another picnic? It's a perfect place for it."

"You like it?"

"It's charming." He took her hand, and she caught the scent of the field on him. The green of it. "Want a push on the swing?"

"Maybe."

"Neither of us got much of that, did we, when we were children?" With her hand in his he began to walk. "I didn't realize there was a park here. A nice spot, near enough to the village, and just out enough to make

37

it an adventure. The trees are young, so I suppose it's new, and still being done," he added, noting the digging equipment and tarped supplies.

"Yeah, still needs some work." She guided him around, as subtly as she could, beyond the little house to the gurgling fountain.

"A fine day like this, I'm surprised it's not packed with kids."

"It's not actually officially open for business."

"All to ourselves then? Sean's along with us. He'd likely enjoy a romp through."

"Yeah, maybe . . ." She'd thought he'd look at the fountain, but should've known he'd be more interested in the equipment, probably speculating on what was left to be done. "So, there's this thing."

"Hmmm?" He glanced back at her.

"Jeez." Frustrated, she turned him around and all but shoved his face into the plaque on the fountain.

SIOBHAN BRODY MEMORIAL PARK
DEDICATED BY HER SON

When he said nothing, she shoved her hands in her pockets. "So, well . . . happy anniversary a few days early."

He looked at her then, just stared at her

with those wonderful wild blue eyes. Just said her name. Just "Eve."

"I got the idea when the Irish invaded last fall and walked it by Sinead. She and the rest of them ran with it. Mostly I just sent money. Hell, your money since it's what you dumped in that account for me when we got married. So —"

"Eve," he repeated, and drew her in, hard, pressed his face to her hair.

She heard him draw a breath, long and quiet, release it as his arms tightened around her.

"So it's good."

He didn't speak for a moment, only ran his hand up and down her back. "What a woman you are," he murmured, and she heard the emotion in it, the way the Irish thickened just a bit in his voice. And saw it in those vivid eyes when he drew back. "That you would think of this. That you would do this."

"Sinead and the rest did the heavy lifting. I just —"

He shook his head, kissed her. Like the breath, long and quiet.

"I can't thank you enough. There isn't enough thanks. I can't say what this means to me, even to you. I don't have the words for it." He took her hands, brought them both to his lips. "*A ghra.* You stagger me."

"So it's good."

He framed her face now, touched his lips to her brow. Then looked in her eyes and spoke in Irish.

"Come again?"

When he smiled now it lit her up. "I said, you're the beat of my heart, the breath in my body, the light in my soul."

Moved to melting, she took his wrists. "Even when I'm the pain in your ass?"

"Particularly then." He turned to study the plaque. "It's lovely. Simple and lovely."

"Well, you're a simple guy."

He laughed as she'd wanted him to. "I've come to know her a little through the family. This would mean a great deal to her. A safe place for children to play," he said, looking around again. "For families to come. Young people sitting on the grass, doing schoolwork, listening to music. Practicing on the football pitch."

"I don't get why they call it a pitch when it's football, which isn't actually football at all but killer soccer. It's not baseball, that's for sure. People over here don't have two clues about real baseball, which is just too bad for them."

He laughed again, took her hand, gave it a swing. "We should call the rest in, and you can show me around."

"Sure."

The kid bolted for the playground the second he got the signal and set to scrambling up ladders, hanging from bars, swinging on poles like a freckle-faced monkey.

Eve supposed it was a solid endorsement.

Before long, Sinead and more of the family who came along set up food on picnic tables where dogs were shooed away.

When Sinead walked over to sit on the lip of the fountain, Roarke followed, sat beside her. She took his hand, sat for a moment in silence.

"It's good to know my grandchildren and those that come after will play here, and laugh and fight and run. It's good something lasting and kind can come out of the sorrow and loss. Your wife knows your heart, and that makes you a rich man."

"It does. You put in a great deal of time on this."

"Oh, I've some to spare, and it was a gift to me, too. To my brothers, to all of us. Our mother cried when I told her what Eve wanted to do. Good tears. All of us shed too many sorrowful ones for Siobhan, so good tears wash clean. Your woman knows death and sorrow. They sit on her, move in her, and have made her sensitive." She

41

glanced at him. "She has a gift, a touch of sight that doesn't come through the eyes, but the heart and the belly."

"She'd call it instinct, training, cop sense."

"Hardly matters what it's called, does it? Ah now, look here." She laughed, drew him to his feet. "Here's a friend come to play with you."

Puzzled, he looked around. Grinned. "Well, it's Brian, come from Dublin."

"I thought you'd enjoy a childhood friend on such a day. Go on then, as it looks as if he's making time with your wife."

Brian Kelly's grin stretched across his wide, ruddy face as he pulled Eve into a hug. "Ah, Lieutenant darling." He crushed an enthusiastic kiss to her mouth. "The minute you're ready to toss Roarke aside, I'll be there."

"Always good to have backup."

He barked out a laugh, then draped an arm over her shoulders as Roarke strode toward them. "I'll fight you for her. And fight dirty."

"Who could blame you?"

He chuckled, releasing Eve to give Roarke the same greeting — a crushing hug and kiss. "You always were a lucky bastard."

"It's good to see you, Brian."

"Your aunt was kind enough to ask me."

He eased back to look around the pretty little park. "Well, isn't this a thing now. Isn't this a fine thing?"

Eve looked down when Sean tugged on her hand. "What?"

"The dogs've run off in the woods over there."

"Okay."

"They won't come back when I call, just go on barking."

"And?"

He rolled his eyes at her. "Well, you're a detective, aren't you? I'm not allowed to go in on my own, so you'll have to come with me to find them."

"I will?"

"Aye, of course," he said matter-of-factly. "They might've found something. Like a treasure, or a clue to a mystery."

"Or a squirrel."

He gazed at her darkly. "You can't know until you know."

Brian spoke up. "I could use a bit of a walk to stretch my legs after the drive from Dublin. I could use some treasure as well."

Sean beamed at Brian. "We'll go then, but she has to come. She'd be in charge as she's a lieutenant."

"Fair enough. Up for a bit of search and rescue?" he asked Roarke.

"I'll show you the way!" The boy raced ahead.

"Come on, Lieutenant." Roarke took her hand. "You're in charge. How are things at the pub, Brian?"

"Oh, much the same. I pull the pints, listen to the gossip and the woes." He winked over Eve's head at his friend. "It's the quiet life for me now."

"How do you say *bullshit* in Irish?" Eve wondered.

"Now, Lieutenant darling, I'm a reformed man since this one led me onto the wayward path in my youth. You come to Dublin again soon, see for yourself. I'll stand you both to all you can drink."

They walked easily, though the boy raced back and forth urging them to hurry. Eve heard the dogs now, high, excited, insistent barking.

"Why are dogs always running off to find something to sniff at, pee on, or chase?"

"Every day's a holiday when you're a dog," Brian observed. "Especially when there's a boy in the mix."

When they reached the verge of the trees she resigned herself to tromping through nature — a dangerous bitch in her opinion.

Moss grew green on rock and tree with sunlight filtering with a greenish hue through the leaves. Gnarled branches twisted themselves into strange shapes as they rose up or spread out.

"Mind the faeries," Brian said with a grin. "Christ, it's been years since I stepped into a country wood. Roarke, do you remember when we skinned those Germans in the hotel, then hid out for two days with travelers in the wood down in Wexford till the heat was off?"

"Jesus, I'm standing right here," Eve pointed out. "Cop."

"There was that girl," Brian continued, unabashed. "Ah, the sultry beauty. And no matter how I tried to charm her, she only had eyes for you."

"Again, right here. Married."

"It was long ago and far away."

"You lost half your take at dice before we were done there," Roarke reminded him.

"I did, yes, but had a fine time."

"Where's the kid?" Eve stopped a moment.

"He's just run ahead a bit," Roarke said. "He's having an adventure."

They heard him call out. "There you are, you great stupids!"

"And he's got the dogs."

"Good, he can bring them back or whatever." She stood where she was, scanning.

"Is it creepy in here, or is it just me?"

"Just you, darling." Roarke started to call Sean back, when he heard the sound of running. "Here he comes."

The boy flew down the path, the freckles standing out starkly on his white face, his eyes huge. "You have to come."

"Is one of the dogs hurt?" Roarke moved forward, but the boy shook his head, grabbed Eve's arm.

"Hurry. You have to see."

"See what?"

"Her. The dogs found her." He pulled and dragged. "Please. She's awfully dead."

Eve started to snap something, but the look in Sean's eyes killed annoyance, awoke instinct. The kid wasn't having a harmless adventure now. "Show me."

"An animal," Brian began, "or a bird. Dogs will find the dead."

But Eve let Sean guide her off the rough path, through the thickets, over moss-coated rocks to where the dogs sat, quiet now, quivering.

"There."

Sean pointed, but she'd already seen.

The body lay belly down, one high-heeled shoe tipping loosely off the right foot. The face, livid with bruising, was turned toward her, eyes filmed, sightless as the pale green

46

light showered down.

The kid was right, she thought. That was awfully dead.

"No." She yanked him back when he took another step forward. "That's close enough. Keep those dogs away. They've already compromised the scene."

Her hand automatically reached up for the recorder that wasn't on her lapel. So, she etched the scene in her mind.

"I don't know who the hell to call in around here."

"I'll see to it." Roarke pulled out his pocket 'link. "Brian, take Sean and the dogs back, would you?"

"No. I'm staying." Sean dug in, hands fisted at his sides. "I found her, so I should stay with her. Someone killed her. Someone killed her and left her alone. I found her so I have to look after her now."

Before Roarke could object, Eve turned to the boy. She'd thought to dismiss him, but something on that young, freckled face changed her mind. "If you stay, you have to do what you're told."

"You're in charge."

"That's right." Until the locals got there. "Did you touch her? Don't lie, it's important."

"I didn't. I swear. I saw the dogs, and I

47

ran up. Then I saw her, and I tried to yell, but . . ." He flushed a little. "I couldn't make anything come out. I made the dogs come away from her, and sit, and stay."

"You did just right. Do you know her?"

He shook his head, slowly, solemnly, from side to side. "What do we do?"

"You already secured the scene, so we keep it secured until the police come."

"You're the police."

"I don't have authority here."

"Why?"

"Because it's not New York. How far is this from a road?"

"It's not far that way to the road that goes right by my school." He pointed. "We cut through sometimes, if I was with some of the older cousins, when they were putting up the playground and such."

"Who else comes in here?"

"I don't know. Anyone who wants to."

"Garda's coming," Roarke told her.

"Sean, do me a solid and walk Roarke to the road you told me about. I'll stay with her," she assured him before he could object. "I want to know how long it takes to walk it."

"Is it a clue?"

"It might be."

When they were out of earshot, Eve said, "Fuck."

"Aye," Brian agreed. "She's young, I think."

"Early twenties. About five-five and a hundred and twenty. Mixed race female, blond with blue and red streaks, brown eyes, tats on inner left ankle — small bird — and back of right shoulder — flaming sun. Pierced eyebrow and nose, multiple ear piercings. She's city. She's still wearing the rings and studs, rings on three fingers."

"Well, I can't say I noticed all of that, but see it right enough now. How did she die?"

"Best guess, from the bruising, strangulation with some smacking around prior. She's fully dressed, but there could have been sexual assault."

"Poor child. A hard end to a short life."

Eve said nothing, but thought murder was always a hard end however short or long the life. She turned as she heard Roarke and the boy come back.

"It's no more than a two-minute walk to the road, and the path's clear enough. Street lighting would come on at dusk, as it's near the school." He waited a moment. "I could put together a makeshift field kit without too much trouble."

She itched for it. "It's not my place, not

49

my case."

"We found her," Sean argued, with considerable stubborn in his tone.

"That makes us witnesses."

Once again she heard rustling, footsteps. A uniformed cop came into view on the path. Young, she thought, and nearly sighed. As young as the dead with the open, pink-cheeked face of innocence.

"I'd be Officer Leary," he began. "You reported a bit of trouble? What . . ." He trailed off, turned the same pale green as the light, when he saw the body.

Eve grabbed his arm, turned him away. "Soldier up, Leary. You've got a DB, and don't want to compromise the scene by booting on the vic."

"I'm sorry?"

"You would be if you puked. Where's your superior?"

"I — my — ah — Sergeant Duffy's in Ballybunion with his family on holiday. He only left this morning. Who are you? Are you the Yank cop from New York City? Roarke's cop?"

"I'm Lieutenant Dallas, NYPSD. Put your damn recorder on, Leary," she muttered.

"Yes. Sorry. I've never . . . we don't. I'm not quite sure what I'm about."

"You're about to take a witness report,

50

secure this scene, then call in whoever it is around here who investigates homicides."

"There really isn't anyone — that is, not right around here. I'll have to contact the sergeant. We just don't have this happen here. Not here." He looked at her. "Would you help me? I don't want to make a mistake."

"Names. You have mine. That's Roarke. This is Brian Kelly, a friend from Dublin. This is Sean Lannigan."

"Yeah, I know Sean here. How's it all going then?"

"I found her."

"Are you doing all right there, lad?"

"Sean, tell the officer what you know, what you did."

"Well, see, we were all over at the park there, having another picnic, and the dogs ran off in here. They wouldn't come back and were barking like the mad. So I asked my lieutenant cousin to come find them with me. We all came in the wood, and I went on ahead to where the dogs were barking. And I saw her there, the dead girl, and I ran back and brought our cop to see."

"That's a good lad." Leary looked appealingly at Eve.

"We've remained here since the discovery.

Roarke and Sean walked to the road and back. The dogs have been all over the scene, as you can see from their prints in the softer ground. You can also observe shoe prints, which would most likely belong to whoever put her here, as none of us have gone closer than we are now."

"Shoe prints. Aye, I see. All right. I can't say I recognize her."

"She's not from around here." Eve dug for patience. "She's city. Multiple tats and piercings, neon polish, fingers and toes. Look at the shoe. She didn't walk in here wearing those. This is a dump site."

"You're meaning she wasn't killed here, but put here, as you said before."

"There's no sign of struggle here. No bruising on her wrists or ankles, so she wasn't restrained. Somebody punches you in the face a few times, chokes you to death, you generally put up a fight. You need to record her, call in your ME, forensics. You need to ID her and determine time of death. The animals haven't been at her, so she can't have been here very long."

He nodded, kept nodding, then pulled an ID pad out of his pocket. "I've got this, but I've never used it."

Eve walked him through it.

"She's Holly Curlow. Lives in — lived in

— Limerick."

Eve tipped her head to read the data. Twenty-two, single, bar waitress, a couple of illegals pops. Next of kin, mother from someplace called Newmarket-on-Fergus.

Where did they get these names?

"I'll, ah, need to get the other equipment — and I'll contact the sergeant. Would you mind staying, to secure the scene? To keep it that way, I'm meaning. This is a bleeding mess, and I want to do right by her."

"I'll wait. You're doing okay."

"Thanks for that. I'll be back quick as I can."

She turned to Sean. "We've got her now, okay? I'll stay with her, but you need to go back. You and Brian need to go back, take the dogs. Leave this to me now."

"She has a name. She's Holly. I'll remember it."

"You stood up, Sean. You stood up for her. That's the first thing a cop has to do."

With a ghost of a smile, he turned to the dogs. "Let's go, lads."

"I'll look after him." Brian laid a hand on Sean's shoulder and walked with him.

Eve turned, looked at Roarke. "There are always bad guys."

"It's a hard lesson to learn that young."

"It's hard anytime."

She took Roarke's hand and stood over the dead, as she had countless times before.

3

A green cop, a dead body, and no legitimate authority added up to frustration. Leary tried, she gave him that, but he was struggling to navigate through what was for him completely uncharted territory.

When he confided to Eve that the only dead person he'd ever seen was his granny at her wake, she couldn't decide whether to pat his head or boot his ass.

"They'll send down a team from Limerick," he told her, shifting from foot to foot as the doctor who served as the ME examined the body. "And my sergeant will come back if he's needed, but for now I'm supposed to . . . proceed."

"Okay."

"Maybe you could help me. Just give me a pointer or two."

Eve continued to study the body. She didn't need the ME to give her cause of death, not from the pattern of bruising around the throat. Manual strangulation, she thought, and her instincts pointed her toward violent argument, crime of the moment, desperate cover-up.

Too soon, not enough data.

"Get the ME's opinion on cause of death, time of death."

The ME, who with his lion's mane of snowy hair and eyes she thought would have been described as merry under other circumstances, glanced up.

"She was throttled, good and proper. Beaten a bit about the face first, then . . ." He demonstrated by lifting his hands, curling his fingers in a choke hold. "She's some skin and blood under her nails, so I'd say she got a piece of him before she went down. And she died just after two this morning, rest her soul. Not here," he added. "Not from the way the blood settled. I'll take her in, of course, when you're ready for that, and do the rest of it."

"Ask him if he's calling it homicide."

"Sure and it's murder, no question there. Someone brought her here after, miss, and left her."

"Lieutenant," Eve said automatically.

"Um, if she scraped the skin off him, it'd show, wouldn't it?" Leary asked. "Seems she'd go for his face or his hands, wouldn't

56

she? So he'd have marks on him that show."

He's thinking now, Eve decided. Trying to see it.

"And wouldn't bringing her here this way, without even trying to bury her, mean it was all done paniclike?"

"Well, I'm not a detective, Jimmy, but that seems logical enough. Would you say, Lieutenant?"

"Even a shallow grave would've bought him time, and the ground's soft so it wouldn't have taken that much effort. She's listed a Limerick address, but that's miles from here according to my data. Panic and stupidity probably merged on this, but not enough for me to buy the killer drove a dead woman all this way."

"So . . ." Leary's brow creased. "They were nearby when he killed her."

"I'd say the probability's high. You should run that. She's dressed for a party or a fancy night out. So you try to run down where she might've gone, with whom. You show her ID picture around, check to see if anyone knows her or saw her. And when you notify next of kin, you ask about boyfriends."

"Notify . . ." He didn't turn green this time around but sheet white. "I'm to do that? To tell her mother?"

"You're currently primary of this investigation. They'll run the skin and blood under her nails, and with any luck you'll get an ID through the DNA bank."

She hesitated, then shrugged. "Look, whoever did this isn't very bright, and it's botched so badly it was probably a first kill. Your ME's going to check for sexual assault, but she's fully dressed, underwear's in place, so it's not saying rape to me. It's going to be a boyfriend or somebody who wanted to be, somebody who used to be. You have the data — where she worked, lived, went to school. You run it down. Either she or the killer had some sort of a connection with the area."

"Tulla?"

"That or the surrounding area, one of the towns within, most likely, an hour's drive. Run the probabilities, connect the data, use the data. You've probably got your killer with what's under her nails, but until you have an ID, and a suspect to bring in to interview, you work the case."

"Well, her mother lives in Newmarket-on-Fergus, that's not far at all."

"Start there," Eve advised.

"Go to her mother and tell her . . ." Leary glanced at the body again. "You've done that before."

"Yeah."

"Can you tell me how, the best way?"

"Quick. Take a grief counselor, or," she said, remembering where she was, "maybe a priest. Maybe the mother has a priest you could take with you. Then you say it, get it done, because when she sees a cop and a priest, she knows it's bad news. You identify yourself — rank, name, division, or whatever it is around here. You're sorry to inform her that her daughter, Holly Curlow, has been murdered."

Leary looked at the body again, shook his head. "Just like that?"

"There's no good way. Get her to tell you all she can, and tell her as little as you can. When did she last see or speak to Holly, did she have a boyfriend, who did she hang with, what did she do. You have to have a feel for it, you have to guide her through it."

"Christ save us," he murmured.

"Use the priest or the counselor, offer to contact someone to come be with her. She'll likely ask you how, and you tell her that's being determined. She'll ask why, and you tell her you and the investigative team will do everything possible to find out, and to identify the person who hurt her. That's the only comfort you can give, and your job is to get information."

"I wonder if I could ask if you —"

"I can't go with you," she said, anticipating him. "I can get away with what I'm doing here because I'm a wit who also happens to be a cop. It makes me, unofficially maybe, an expert consultant. But I can't investigate or interview or notify next of kin. It's over the line."

She stuck her hands in her pockets. "Look, you can contact me after you get some of this done, some of it lined up. Maybe I can give you some angles if you need them. It's all I can do."

"It's been a great deal already."

"You've got my contact information. I'm due to leave for Italy tomorrow."

"Oh." He looked pained.

"You get an ID from what's under her nails, Leary, and you'll have a suspect before nightfall. I've got to get back." She took one last look at the dead. "You'll do all right by her."

"I hope I do. Thank you."

She started back to the park, a little uneasy about walking through that green wood — not of killers or maniacs, but of fauna and the stupid faeries she didn't even believe in.

So she pulled out her 'link to contact

Roarke. She'd asked him to go on back rather than wait.

"There you are," he said when his face came on-screen.

"I'm heading back. I can't do any more here."

"Difficult."

"On a lot of levels. The local's okay. Not much confidence but a decent brain. She has trace under her nails, blood and skin. If he's in the bank, they'll ID him quick enough. Leary's got to notify the mother, and with any luck she'll give him a name or two. It has the smell of a slam-dunk to me — impulse, stupidity, panic. The killer may try to run, but they'll get him. He's as green at this as Leary is."

She scanned the area as she walked, just in case something four-legged and furry made an appearance. "Got some cops coming down from where she was living. I expect they'll knock on some doors first, get a sense of her."

"What's your sense?"

"Young, maybe a little wild, more tats showed up when the ME started his exam. More piercings. Sexy panties, but they were still on her so I'm doubting sexual assault. But I'm betting the murder had its roots there. She left with the wrong guy, or she flirted with somebody, and the guy she was with didn't like it. Argue, slap, scratch, punch, passion and fury, he chokes her out of that fury or to shut her the hell up — and kills her before he pulls it together again. Panic. This can't be happening to me. Self-preservation. Get rid of her, get away from her. Go home and hide."

"Did you run probabilities?"

"Maybe." She smiled just a little. "To pass the time. I guess this kind of screwed up the day."

"It certainly did for Holly Curlow."

"You've got that right. If you come pick me up, we can go back and do whatever it is we're supposed to do with the rest of it."

"Happy to."

When she stepped out of the woods seconds later — with only the slightest shudder of relief — she saw him. He sat on the lip of the fountain, looking toward her.

"You made pretty good time," she said into her 'link.

"No reason to dawdle."

"What's a dawdle exactly? Is it more than a pause, less than procrastination?"

Now he smiled. "Somewhere in that vicinity."

She shut off the 'link, slipped it into her pocket as she approached. "People should be able to dawdle when they're on vacation."

"So they should." He took her hand, drew her down to sit beside him. "This is a fine spot for dawdling."

"It didn't spoil it?"

"No." He draped an arm over her shoulders, pressed a kiss to her temple. "Who knows better than we that death happens even in good places? You wish you could finish it for her."

"I can't. She's Leary's. Technically," she added when he kissed her again.

"Then know that she was lucky you were here. And that if it doesn't go as you think it will, we can easily spend a few more days in Clare."

Part of her wanted to agree, to hold him to the offer. But the rest, what had evolved between them, had her shaking her head. "No. This isn't my case, and this is our time. Let's go back to the farm. I think I could use a pint."

Leary contacted her three times, with information and for advice. She tried to be discreet about it, easing her way out of the room to take the transmission. And she kept the updates to herself even though the family — including Sean, who'd wheedled his way into an overnight — stared at her on her return.

By moonrise, he was on the doorstep.

"Good evening to you, Mrs. Lannigan. Sorry to disturb you, but I wonder if I could just have a word with the lieutenant."

"Come in, Jimmy. How's your ma doing then?"

"She's well, thanks."

"How about a cup of tea?"

"Sure I could use one."

"Come on back to the kitchen." Without looking around, she pointed a finger at Sean when he got to his feet. "Sit where you are, lad."

"But, Gran, I —"

"And not a word out of you. Eve, why don't you come on back? You and Jimmy can have a cup and talk in private."

Removing his uniform hat, Jimmy stepped in, looked around. "How's it all going then?"

"Well enough," Aidan Brody told him. "You've had a hard day, lad. Go have your tea."

Sinead fussed a little, setting out the tea, adding a plate of the cookies they called — for reasons that eluded Eve — biscuits. She gave Leary a motherly pat on the shoulder.

"Take all the time you need. I'll keep that lot out of your way."

"Thanks for that." Leary added sugar and milk to his tea, then with eyes closed took a long sip. "Missed my supper," he told Eve and grabbed a cookie.

He looked tired, and considerably less green — in complexion and experience — than he had that afternoon. "Murder usually trumps food."

"I know that now, that's for certain. We have him." He let out a little breath, almost a surprised laugh. "We have the one who killed Holly Curlow. I wanted to tell you in person."

"Boyfriend?"

He nodded. "Or one who thought he ought to be the one and only for her, and who she'd decided to shake off. They'd been at a party in Ennis last night, got into a bit of a spat. They'd come, it seems, as a kind of reunion for her with some mates from that neck. They'd — Kevin Donahue is his name — been seeing each other for a few months with him more serious about the thing than she. I went up to Limerick myself when we got the DNA, and they'd picked him up. She's scored both his cheeks like a cat would, and good for her, I say about that."

He took another sip of tea. "It just tumbled down from there, you could say.

65

They had me sit in on the interview, but it was quick. Three minutes in and he's bawling like a baby and telling all."

He sighed now, and Eve said nothing, asked no questions, let him gather it up in his head.

"They'd fought again in the car," Leary went on, "and she'd told him she was good and done and to take her on to her ma's, or just let her out. They'd been drinking, the both of them, and probably that added to the temper of it. He said he pulled over, and they shouted at each other more. It got physical. Him slapping, her scratching, then he said he just snapped. Hit her with his fists, and she kicked and hit and screamed. He claims he doesn't remember putting his hands around her throat, and it might be the truth. But he came back to himself, and she was dead."

Leary shook his head at the waste of it, scooted up a bit to hunch over his tea. "He told how he tried to bring her back somehow, how he just drove around a bit, trying to make it all not so. Then he pulled off at the wood, you see, carried her in — her other shoe was still in his car when they picked him up. He says he said a prayer over her and left her.

"He's very sorry for it," Leary added, with

a hard bitterness in the tone that told Eve he'd lost a lot of his innocence that day. "He said, more than once, as if that would make it all right and tight again. He was very sorry for choking the life out of the girl because she didn't want him. Bloody gobshite."

He flushed a little. "Beg your pardon."

"I'd say that's a pretty good description." *Gobshite,* she thought. She had to remember that one. "You did good work."

"If I did, it was because you told me how." His gaze lifted to hers. "The worst of it all was standing on her mother's doorstep, saying what you'd told me to say. Watching that woman break apart that way. Knowing, even though it wasn't you who'd done what was done, you brought that pain to her."

"Now you've given her and her daughter justice. You did the job, and that's all you can do."

"Aye. Well, I could live my life easy with never having to break a mother's heart again. But the rest . . ."

"Felt good."

"It did, yes. And does. Does it still for you when you've done it?"

"If it didn't, I don't think I could knock on another mother's door."

He sat another moment, nodding to himself. "All right then." He rose, held out a hand. "Thank you for all your help."

"You're welcome." She shook.

"If you don't mind, I'll just go out the back and not disturb your family again. Would you tell them good night for me?"

"Yeah, sure."

"It was fine meeting you, Lieutenant, even under the circumstances."

He went out the back, and Eve shoved aside the tea she had no desire for. Like Leary she sat for a moment in silence. Then she pushed to her feet and went back to where the family gathered. The music stopped.

She walked to Sean, waited while he stood up.

"His name is Kevin Donahue. They'd come this way to go to a party, and had a fight. In the car after they'd left, they had a bigger fight and he killed her in what he claims and probably was what we call a moment of passion."

"Just . . . just because he was mad at her?"

"More or less, yes. Then he got scared and sorry, but it was too late for sorry. Too late for *I didn't mean to* or *I wish I hadn't*. He's weak and stupid and selfish, so he took her into the woods and left her there, and ran away. You found her less than twelve hours

68

after he'd done that. Because you did, the police were able to find him, arrest him. He'll be punished for what he did."

"They'll put him in a cage."

"He's in one now."

"For how long?"

Jesus, Eve thought, kids were merciless. "I don't know. Sometimes it doesn't seem long enough, but it's what we've got."

"I hope they coshed him first, good and proper."

Eve struggled back a grin. "Kid, if you want to be a cop, you have to learn not to say that out loud. Bad guy's in a cage. Case closed. Have some cake or something."

"A fine idea." Sinead moved in to take Sean's hand. "Help me slice up what's left of it, that's a good lad." She sent Eve a quick smile. "Eemon, get that fiddle going. Our Yank will think we don't know how to have a ceili."

Eve started to sit as the music flew out again, but Brian grabbed her, gave her a swing. "I'll have a dance, Lieutenant darling."

"I don't do that. The dance thing."

"You do tonight."

Apparently she did. And so did everyone else until the middle of the night, when her

69

legs were rubber and barely carried her to bed.

Where the rooster woke her at dawn.

They said some good-byes over breakfast. Good-byes included a great many hugs, a lot of kissing. Or, in the case of Brian, being lifted right off her feet.

"I'll come courting the minute you're done with that one."

What the hell, she thought, and kissed him back. "Okay, but he's got some miles in him yet."

He laughed, turned to slap hands with Roarke. "Lucky bastard. Take care of yourself, and her."

"The best I can."

"I'm walking you to the car." Sinead took Roarke's hand. "I'm going to miss you." She smiled at Eve as they walked through misting rain. "Both of you."

"Come for Thanksgiving." Roarke squeezed her hand.

"Oh . . ."

"We'd like all of you to come again, as you did last year. I can make the arrangements."

"I know you can. I would love it. I think I'd be safe in saying we'd all love it." She sighed, just leaned into Roarke for a moment. Then she drew back, kissed his cheek.

"From your mother," she murmured, then kissed the other. "From me." Then laid her lips lightly to his. "And from all of us."

She repeated the benediction on Eve before blinking her damp eyes.

"Go on now, go enjoy your holiday. Safe journey." She grabbed Roarke's hand another moment, spoke in Irish, then backed up, waving them away.

"What did she say?" Eve asked when they got into the car.

"Here's love, she said, to hold until next we meet and I give you more."

He watched her in the rearview until they'd turned out of sight.

In the silence Eve stretched out her legs. "I guess you are a pretty lucky bastard."

It made him smile; he sent her a quick, cocky look. "As they come," he agreed.

"Eyes on the road, Lucky Bastard."

She tried not to hold her breath all the way to the airport.

4

It was good to be home. Driving downtown to Cop Central through ugly traffic, blasting horns, hyping ad blimps, belching maxibuses just put her in a cheerful mood.

Vacations were great, but to Eve's mind New York had it all and a bag of soy chips.

The temperature might have been as brutal as a tax audit, with sweaty waves of heat bouncing off concrete and steel, but she wouldn't trade her city for any place on or off planet.

She was rested, revved, and ready for work.

She rode the elevator up from the garage, shuffling over as more cops squeezed in on every floor. When she felt the oxygen supply depleting, she pried her way out to take the glides the rest of the way up.

It smelled like home, she thought — cop, criminal, the pissed off, the unhappy, the resigned. Sweat and bad coffee merged together in an aroma she wasn't sure could be found anywhere but a cop shop.

And that was fine with her.

She listened to a beanpole of a man in restraints mutter his mantra as a pair of uniforms muscled him up the glide.

Fucking cops, fucking cops, fucking cops.

It was music to her ears.

She stepped off, angled toward Homicide, and spotted Jenkinson, one of her detectives, studying the offerings at Vending with a hopeless expression.

"Detective."

He brightened slightly. "Hey, Lieutenant, good to see you."

He looked as if he'd slept in his clothes for a couple days.

"You pull a double?"

"Caught one late, me and Reineke." He settled on something that looked like a cheese Danish if you were blind in one eye. "Just wrapping it up. Vic's in a titty bar over on Avenue A, getting himself a lap dance. Asshole comes in, starts it up. The titty doing the lap dance is his ex. Gives her a couple smacks. The guy with the hard-on clocks him. Asshole gets hauled out. He goes home, gets his souvenir Yankees baseball bat, lays in wait. Vic comes out, and the asshole jumps him. Beat the holy shit out of

73

him and left his brains on the sidewalk."

"High price for a lap dance."

"You're telling me. Asshole's stupid, but slippery." Jenkinson ripped the wrapping off the sad-looking Danish, took a resigned bite. "Leaves the bat and runs. We got wits falling out of our pockets, got his prints, got his name, his address. Slam-fucking-dunk. He doesn't go home and make our lives easier, but what he does, a couple hours after, is go to the ex's. Brings her freaking flowers he dug up out of a sidewalk planter deal. Dirt's still falling off the roots."

"Classy guy," Eve observed.

"Oh, yeah." He downed the rest of the Danish. "She won't let him in — stripper's got more sense — but calls it in while he's crying and banging on the door, and dumping flower dirt all over the hallway. We get there to pick him up, and what does he do? He jumps out the freaking window end of the hall. Four flights up. Still holding the damn flowers and trailing dirt all the way."

He shifted to order coffee with two hits of fake sugar. "Got the luck of God 'cause he lands on a couple chemi-heads doing a deal down below — killed one of them dead, other's smashed up good. But they broke his fall."

Deeply entertained, Eve shook her head.

74

"You can't make this shit up."

"Gets better," Jenkinson told her, slurping coffee. "Now we got to chase his ass. I go down the fire escape — and let me tell you smashed chemi-heads make one hell of a mess — Reineke goes out the front. He spots him. Asshole runs through the kitchen of an all-night Chinese place, and people are yelling and tumbling like dice. This fucker is throwing shit at us, pots and food and Christ knows. Reineke slips on some moo goo something, goes down. Hell no, you can't make this shit up, LT."

He grinned now, slurped more coffee. "He heads for this sex joint, but the bouncer sees this freaking blood-covered maniac coming and blocks the door. The bouncer's built like a tank — so the asshole just bounces off him like a basketball off the rim, goes airborne for a minute and plows right into me. Jesus. Now I've got blood and chemi-head brains on me, and Reineke's hauling ass over, and he's covered with moo goo. And this asshole starts yelling police brutality. Took some restraint not to give him some.

"Anyway." He blew out a breath. "We're wrapping it up."

Was it any wonder she loved New York?

"Good work. Do you want me to take you

75

off the roll?"

"Nah. We'll flex a couple hours, grab some sleep up in the crib once the asshole's processed. You look at the big picture, boss? All that, over a pair of tits."

"Love screws you up."

"Fucking A."

She turned into the bullpen, acknowledged "heys" from cops finishing up the night tour. She walked into her office, left the door open. Detective Sergeant Moynahan had, as she'd expected, left her desk pristine. Everything was exactly as it had been when she'd walked out her office door three weeks before, except cleaner. Even her skinny window sparkled, and the air smelled vaguely — not altogether unpleasantly — like the woods she'd walked through in Ireland.

Minus the dead body.

She programmed coffee from her Auto-Chef and, with a satisfied sigh, sat at her desk to read over the reports and logs generated during her absence.

Murder hadn't taken a holiday during hers, she noted, but her division had run pretty smooth. She moved through closed and open cases, requests for leave, overtime, personal time, reimbursements.

She heard the muffled clump that was

Peabody's summer air boots, and glanced up as her partner stepped into the open doorway.

"Welcome home! How was it? Was it just mag?"

"It was good."

Peabody's square face sported a little sun-kiss, which reminded Eve her partner had taken a week off with her squeeze, Electronic Detectives Division ace McNab. She had her dark hair pulled back in a short, but jaunty tail, and wore a thin, buff-colored jacket over cargo trousers a few shades darker. Her tank matched the air boots in a bright cherry red.

"It looks like DS Moynahan kept things oiled while I was gone."

"Yeah. He sure dots every 'i,' but he's easy to work with. He's solid, and he knows how to ride a desk. He steers clear of field work, but he had a good sense of how to run the ship. So, what did you get?"

"A pile of reports."

"No, come on, for your anniversary. I know Roarke had to come up with something total. Come on," Peabody insisted when Eve just sat there. "I came in early just for this. I figure we've got nearly five before we're officially on the clock."

True enough, Eve thought, and since

Peabody's brown eyes pleaded like a puppy's, she held up her arm, displayed the new wrist unit she wore.

"Oh."

The reaction, Eve thought, was perfect. Baffled surprise, severe disappointment, the heroic struggle to mask both.

"Ah, that's nice. It's a nice wrist unit."

"Serviceable." Eve turned her wrist to admire the simple band, the flat, silver-toned face.

"Yeah, it looks it."

"It's got a couple of nice features," she added as she fiddled with it.

"It's nice," Peabody said again, then drew her beeping communicator out of her pocket. "Give me a sec, I . . . hey, it's you." Mouth dropping, Peabody jerked her head up. "It's got a micro-com in it? That's pretty mag. Usually they're all fuzzy, but this is really clean."

"Nano-com. You know how the vehicle he rigged up for me looks ordinary?"

"Ordinary leaning toward ugly," Peabody corrected. "But nobody gives it a second look or knows that it's loaded, so . . . same deal?"

Automatically Peabody dug out her 'link when it signaled, then paused. "Is that you? It's got full communication capability? In a wrist unit that size?"

"Not only that, it's got navigation, full data capabilities. Total data and communications — he programmed it with all my stuff. If I had to, I could access my files on it. Waterproof, shatterproof, voice-command capabilities. Gives me the ambient temp. Plus it tells time."

Not to mention he'd given her a second with the exact same specs — only fired with diamonds. Something she'd wear when she suited up for fancy.

"That is so utterly iced. How does it —"

Eve snatched her wrist away. "No playing with it. I haven't figured it all out myself yet."

"It's just like the perfect thing for you. The abso perfect thing. He really gets it. And you got to go to Ireland and Italy and finish it up at that island he's got. Nothing but romance and relaxation."

"That's about it, except for the dead girl."

"Yeah, and McNab and I had a really good time — what? What dead girl?"

"If I had more coffee I might be inclined to tell you."

Peabody sprang toward the AutoChef.

Minutes later, she polished off her own cup and shook her head. "Even on vacation you investigated a homicide."

"I didn't investigate, the Irish cop did. I consulted — unofficially. Now my serviceable yet frosty wrist unit tells me we're on duty. Scram."

"I'm scramming, but I want to tell you about how McNab and I took scuba lessons, and —"

"Why?"

"I don't know, but I liked it. And how I did these interviews on Nadine's book, which is still number one in case you haven't been checking. If we don't catch a case, maybe we can have lunch. I'll buy."

"Maybe. I've got to catch up."

Alone, she considered it. She wouldn't mind hanging for lunch, she realized. It would be a kind of bridge between vacation and the job, screwing around and the routine of work.

She didn't have any meetings scheduled, no actives on her plate. She'd need to go over some of the open cases with the teams assigned, touch base with Moynahan mostly to thank him for his service. Other than that —

She scanned the next report, answering her 'link. "Lieutenant Dallas, Homicide."

Dispatch, Dallas, Lieutenant Eve.

So much, she thought, for bridges.

Jamal Houston died with his chauffeur's hat on behind the wheel of a limo of glittery gold, long and sleek as a snake. The limo had been tidily parked in a short-term slot at LaGuardia.

Since the crossbow bolt angled through Jamal's neck and into the command pad of the wheel, Eve assumed Jamal had done the parking.

With her hands and boots sealed, Eve studied the entry wound. "Even if you're pissed off you missed your transpo, this is a little over the top."

"A crossbow?" Peabody studied the body from the other side of the limo. "You're sure?"

"Roarke has a couple in his weapons collection. One of them fires these bolts like this. One question is just why someone had a loaded crossbow in a limo to begin with."

Houston, Jamal, she mused, going over the data they'd already accessed, black male, age forty-three, co-owner of Gold Star transportation service. Married, two offspring. No adult criminal. Sealed juvie. He'd been six feet one and one-ninety and wore a smart and crisp black suit, white shirt, red tie. His shoes were shined like mirrors.

He wore a wrist unit as gold as the limo and a gold star lapel pin with a diamond winking in the center.

"From the angle, it looks like he was shot from the right rear."

"Passenger area is pristine," Peabody commented. "No trash, no luggage, no used glasses or cups or bottles, and all the slots for the glassware are filled, so the killer and/or passenger didn't take any with him. Everything gleams, and there are fresh — real — white roses in these little vases between the windows. A selection of viewing and audio and reading discs all organized by alpha and type in a compartment, and they don't look like they've been touched. There are three full decanters of different types of alcohol, a fridge stocked with cold drinks, and a compact AutoChef. The log there says it was stocked about sixteen hundred, and it hasn't been accessed since."

"The passenger must not have been thirsty, and didn't want a snack while he didn't listen to music, read, or catch some screen. We'll have the sweepers go over it."

She circled the car, slid in beside the body. "Wedding ring, pricey wrist unit, gold star with diamond pin, single gold stud in his earlobe." She worked her hand under the body, tugged out a wallet.

"He's got plastic, and about a hundred fifty cash, small bills. It sure as hell wasn't robbery." She tried to access the dash comp. "It's passcoded." She had better luck with the 'link, and listened to his last transmission, informing his dispatcher he'd arrived at LaGuardia with his passenger for the pickup, and suggesting the dispatcher call it a night.

"He was supposed to pick up a second passenger." Eve considered. "Picked up the first, second passenger coming in, transpo on time according to this communication. So he parks, and before he can get out to open the door for passenger one, he takes one in the neck. Time of death and the 'link log are only a few minutes apart."

"Why does somebody hire a driver to go to the airport, then kill him?"

"There's got to be a record of who hired the service, where they were picked up. One shot," Eve murmured. "No muss, but a lot of fuss. Add in what you'd call an exotic weapon."

She took a memo book from his pocket, his personal 'link, breath mints, a cotton handkerchief. "He's got a pickup listed here at the Chrysler Building, ten-twenty P.M. AS to LTC. Passenger initials. No full name, no full addy. This is just his backup. Let's see if we can find anyone who saw anything — ha ha — get crime scene in here. We'll go check in with the company first."

Gold Star ran its base out of Astoria. Peabody relayed the salient data as they drove. Houston and his partner, Michael Chin, had started the business fourteen years before with a single secondhand limo, and had run it primarily out of Houston's home, with his wife serving as dispatcher, office dogsbody, and bookkeeper.

In less than fifteen years, they'd expanded to a fleet of twelve — all gold, high-end luxury limos with premier amenities, and had earned a five-diamond rating every year for nearly a decade.

They employed eight drivers, and an office and administrative staff of six. Mamie Houston continued to keep the books, and Chin's wife of five years served as head mechanic. Houston's son and daughter were listed as part-time employees.

When Eve pulled up in front of the streamlined building with its mammoth garage, a man of about forty in a business suit was watering a long window box full of

84

red and white flowers. He paused, turned his pleasant face toward them with an easy smile.

"Good morning."

"We're looking for Michael Chin."

"You've found me. Please come in, out of the heat. Barely nine in the morning and already sweltering."

Cool air and the scent of flowers greeted them. A counter held the flowers and a compact data-and-communications unit. On a table glossy brochures fanned out. A couple of cozy scoop chairs ranged beside it while a gold sofa and a couple more chairs formed a conference area.

"Can I get you something cold to drink?"

"No, thanks. Mr. Chin, I'm Lieutenant Dallas, and this is Detective Peabody. We're with the NYPSD."

"Oh." His smile remained pleasant, but edged toward puzzled. "Is there a problem?"

"I regret to inform you your partner, Jamal Houston, was found dead this morning."

His face went blank, like a switch turned off. "I'm sorry, what?"

"He was found in one of the vehicles registered to this company."

"An accident." He took a step back, bumped into one of the chairs. "An accident? Jamal had an accident?"

"No, Mr. Chin. We believe Mr. Houston was murdered at approximately ten-twenty-five last night."

"But no, no. Oh, I see. I see, there's been a mistake. I spoke with Jamal myself shortly before that time. Minutes before that time. He was at the airport, at LaGuardia, driving a client, and picking up the client's wife."

"There's no mistake. We've identified Mr. Houston. He was found in the limo, parked at LaGuardia, early this morning."

"Wait." This time Chin gripped the back of the chair, swayed a little. "You're telling me Jamal is dead? Murdered? But how, how? Why?"

"Mr. Chin, why don't you sit down?" Peabody eased him into the chair. "Can I get you some water?"

He shook his head, kept shaking it as his eyes, a brilliant green behind a forest of black lashes, filled. "Someone killed Jamal. My God, my sweet God. They tried to steal the car? Was that it? We're supposed to cooperate in a jacking. It's firm company policy. No car is worth a life. Jamal."

"I know this is a shock," Eve began, "and it's very difficult, but we need to ask you some questions."

"We're having dinner tonight. We're all having dinner tonight. A cookout."

"You were here last night. You were running dispatch?"

"Yes. No. Oh, God." He pressed the heels of his hands to those wet, brilliant eyes. "I was home, running dispatch from home. He had this late run, you see. He took it because Kimmy had two night runs in a row, and West was on an early one this morning, and it was Peter's son's birthday, and . . . it doesn't matter. We flipped a coin, winner chooses dispatch or the run. He took the run."

"When was it booked?"

"Just that afternoon."

"Who was the client?"

"I . . . I'll look it up. I don't remember. I can't think." He dropped his head into his hands, then jerked it up again. "Mamie, the children. Oh, God, oh, God. I have to go. I have to get my wife. We have to go to Mamie."

"Soon. The most important thing you can do for Jamal right now is give us information. We believe whoever was in the car with him killed him or knows who did. Who was in the car, Mr. Chin?"

"Wait." He rose, went to the unit on the counter. "It doesn't make sense. I know it was a new client, but he just wanted to surprise his wife by picking her up in style at the airport, then taking her out to a late supper. I remember that. Here, here it is. Augustus Sweet. The pickup was in front of the Chrysler Building. He was going to work late, and wanted to be picked up at his office. I have his credit card information. We always take that information in advance. I have everything here."

"Can you make me a copy?"

"Yes, yes. But he was going to pick up his wife at the airport. He did request our best driver, but he didn't even know Jamal, so I don't understand. I could have been driving. Any of us could have. It was just . . ."

The flip of a coin, Eve thought.

He fell apart when Eve allowed him to call his wife in. Sobbed in her arms. She was six inches taller with flaming red hair, and was hugely pregnant.

Eve watched tears run down her cheeks, but she held together.

"We need to go with you," she said to Eve. "She shouldn't hear this from strangers. I'm sorry, that's what you are. She needs family with her. We're family."

"That's fine. Can you tell us the last time you saw or spoke with Mr. Houston?"

"Yesterday, about five, I guess. I'd gone

88

over to Mamie's because she was watching Tige — our son. His babysitter needed the day off. He came in just as we were leaving. He had that run later, and he went home for a few hours first. And I guess you need to know, because that's the way it is. Michael got home about six-thirty, and we had dinner with our boy. Michael gave him his bath and put him to bed just before eight, because I was tired. He ran the dispatch from home. He came to bed about eleven. I know because I was still awake. I was tired," she added, rubbing her belly. "The baby wasn't. I don't know the exact times, but that's close."

Eve ran them through a few more routine questions, but she already had the picture, had a sense.

The Houstons had a large and pretty suburban house with big windows, a rolling lawn, and a front garden that made Eve think of Ireland. Mamie Houston, a wide-brimmed straw hat protecting her face from the sun, stood snipping long-stemmed blooms and putting them in a wide, flat basket.

She turned, started to smile, to wave. Then the smile froze, and her hand dropped slowly to her side.

She knows something's wrong, Eve

89

thought. She's wondering why her friends, her partners would drive to her house with a couple of strangers.

She dropped the basket. Flowers spilled out on the green lawn as she began to run.

"What's wrong? What's happened?"

"Mamie." Michael's voice cracked. "Jamal. It's Jamal."

"Has there been an accident? Who are you?" she demanded of Eve. "What's happened?"

"Mrs. Houston, I'm Lieutenant Dallas with the NYPSD." As Eve spoke, Kimmy Chin moved to Mamie's side, put an arm around her. "I regret to inform you your husband was killed last night."

"That's not possible. That can't be true. He's out for his run, or at the gym. I . . ." She patted her gardening pants. "I don't have my 'link. I always forget my 'link when I come out to work in the garden. Michael, use yours, will you? He's just gone out for his run."

"He came home?"

"Of course he came home." She snapped it at Michael, then bit her lip. "I . . ."

"Mrs. Houston, why don't we go inside?"

She rounded on Eve. "I don't want to go inside. I want to talk to my husband."

"When's the last time you did?"

"I . . . When he left last night for work, but —"

"Weren't you concerned when he didn't come home?"

"But he must have. It was late. He was going to be late and said I shouldn't wait up, so I went to bed. And he got up early, that's all. He got up early to take his run and go by the gym. We have a gym in the house, but he likes to go there, to socialize. You know how he likes to take his run, then go to the gym to gossip, Kimmy."

"I know, honey. I know. Let's go inside. Come on now, we're going inside."

Inside, Kimmy sat beside her, holding her close in a sun-washed living area. Mamie stared at Eve, eyes glassy and unfocused.

"I don't understand."

"We're going to do everything we can to find out what happened. You can help us. Do you know anyone who'd want to cause your husband harm?"

"No. He's a good man. Tell her, Kimmy."

"A very good man," Kimmy soothed.

"Any trouble with employees?"

"No. We've kept it small. Exclusive. That . . . that was the whole point."

"Has anything been troubling him?"

"No. Nothing."

"Any money problems?"

"No. We have a good life, the business has given us a good life. We like the work — that's why he still drives, why I keep the books. He's always wanted to be his own boss, and the business is everything we wanted. He's proud of what we've all built. We have two children in college, but we planned for it, so . . . the children. What will I tell the children?"

"Where are your children, Mrs. Houston?"

"Benji's taking summer classes. He's going to be a lawyer. He'll be our lawyer. Lea's at the beach for a couple days with friends. What should I tell them?" She turned to weep on Kimmy's shoulder. "How can I tell them?"

Eve kept at it a while longer, but — for now at least — there was nothing here but shock and grief.

Stepping out into the drenching heat was a relief.

"Let's check out the business financials, get a background on the partner and his wife, the rest of the employees. We'll check this gym, verify his early-morning habit."

"I've got it started. Doesn't feel like it's there," Peabody commented. "They really do seem like family."

"We closed a case recently where everybody was friends and partners with the dead guy."

"Yeah." Peabody sighed. "It can sure make you cynical."

"Did you run this Augustus Sweet?"

"Yeah. He's a senior VP, internal security, Dudley and Son, pharmaceuticals. Chrysler Building HQ."

"Let's go pay him a visit."

5

Dudley and son spread over five prime floors of the landmark building, with its lobby areas done in what Eve thought of as swanky urban excess. The steel and glass counters meant that none of the half dozen working reception could forget to keep their knees together, while the polished silver wall behind them shot out reflections and shimmered with light zeroing in from a multitude of windows.

Weird glass sculptures hung from the ceiling over a high-gloss floor in unrelieved black.

Visitors could bide their time on long, backless benches padded with black gel cushions and watch a wall of screens hype the company's self-proclaimed innovations and history.

Eve chose a receptionist who looked bored, and laid her badge on the glass counter. "Augustus Sweet."

"Name, please."

Eve laid a finger on the badge.

"One moment." She danced her fingers on a screen behind the counter. "Mr. Sweet is in meetings until two. If you'd like to make an appointment, I'd be —"

Eve tapped her badge again. "That's my appointment. You're going to want to interrupt Mr. Sweet and tell him the cops are here. Oh, and one more thing? If you send his admin or some other minion out here to ask me what my business is, I'm going to take it the wrong way, and I'm going to take that wrong way out on you."

"There's no reason to get snippy."

Eve merely smiled. "You haven't seen snippy yet. Get Sweet, then we can both do our jobs."

She got Sweet. It took nearly ten minutes, but he walked through a set of glass doors. He wore a dark suit, dark tie, and an expression that said he probably wasn't a fun guy.

His hair, a pewter gray, was cut short and bristling around a tough, square-jawed face. His eyes, hard and blue, held Eve's as he walked.

"I assume this is important enough to interrupt my schedule."

"I think so, but then I rank murder pretty high on the list."

She'd projected just enough to draw attention. Sweet's jaw tightened as he turned, gave Eve an impatient come-with-me gesture, then strode back to the glass doors. She followed with Peabody down a wide hallway that opened into a secondary lobby. He turned, eating up the ground beyond offices to a corner space with an important desk ranged in front of an important view of the city.

He closed the door, folded his arms over his chest. "Identification."

Both Eve and Peabody took out their ID. He took out a pocket scanner, verified them.

"Lieutenant Dallas. I know your reputation."

"Handy."

"Who's been murdered?"

"Jamal Houston."

"That name's not familiar to me." Now he drew out a communicator. "Mitchell, check my files for any information on a Houston, Jamal. He doesn't work in my department," he said to Eve. "I know the names of everyone who works in my department."

"He didn't work here. He's the co-owner of a limousine service, one you booked last night for transport to LaGuardia."

"I didn't book any transportation last

night. I used the company service."

"For what?"

"For transportation to and from a dinner meeting. Intermezzo, eight o'clock, party of six. I left here at seven-thirty, arrived at the restaurant at seven-fifty-three. I left the restaurant at ten-forty-six, and arrived home at eleven. I had no business at LaGuardia last night."

"Picking up your wife?"

He smiled, sourly. "My wife and I separated four months ago. I wouldn't pick her up off the floor, much less at the airport. In any case, as far as I know she's spending the summer in Maine. You have the wrong man."

"Maybe. Your name, address, and credit card were used to book the service. The driver picked up the passenger at this location." Wanting his reaction, she pulled out the hard copy Chin had given her, offered it.

And watched his eyes, saw them widen. He pulled out the communicator again. "Mitchell, cancel all my credit cards, initiate a search on the accounts, and arrange for temporary secure replacements. ASAP," he snapped. "I want Gorem to do a sniff on all my electronics, and for Lyle to do an all-level sweep. Now."

"Who'd have access to your information?" Eve asked when he shoved the communicator back in his pocket.

"I'm in the business of security. No one should've been able to access that credit information. That's a company card. How was this booked?"

"Via 'link."

"The sweep will include a check of all 'link logs in this department."

"The Electronic Detectives Division will be doing a sweep of its own, which will include your personal 'links."

She didn't think it was possible, but his jaw tightened a few more notches. "You'll need a warrant."

"No problem."

"What is this about? I need to take care of this breach of security immediately."

"It's about murder, Mr. Sweet, which may prove to be connected to your security problem, but still ranks higher on the food chain. The driver's body was found early this morning, in his ride, at LaGuardia."

"Killed by someone who used my name, my information."

"It appears."

"I'll give you the names and contact of everyone at the meeting last night, and every one of them can and will verify my presence. I only use company vehicles and drivers, again for security. To my knowledge I don't know this Jamal Houston, and I don't appreciate having my data compromised this way. Or having my personal logs and electronics sniffed over by the police."

"I think Jamal's probably even more pissed off."

"I don't know him."

"Your PA, some of your staff, would have your information, and probable access to that card number."

"A handful, yes, who hold the necessary level of security clearance."

"I'll want the names of that handful," Eve told him.

She split the interviews with Peabody and took Mitchell Sykes, the PA, first. He was thirty-four and looked slick and efficient in what she thought of as an FBI-lite suit.

"I coordinate Mr. Sweet's schedule." He had a prissy, I-am-efficient-and-educated voice and kept his hands folded on his left knee. "I confirmed the reservation for the dinner meeting last night, and arranged for Mr. Sweet's transportation to and from."

"And when did you do all that?"

"Two days ago, with follow-ups yesterday afternoon. Mr. Sweet left his office at seven-thirty. I left at seven-thirty-eight. It's in the logs."

"I bet. You have access to Mr. Sweet's company credit card?"

"I do, of course."

"What do you use that for?"

"Expenses incurred by company business, at Mr. Sweet's direction. All use is logged and screened. If I use it, the expense must include a purchase order or signed request, and also includes my passcode."

"Anything in the log about its use last night?"

"I looked, as requested. There's no entry. If there had been a charge against the account, it would have sent up an auto notice, but as it was simply used to hold a reservation, there's no flag. The security code on the account is changed every three days, again automatically. Without the code, even a hold would be denied."

"So someone had the code. You'd have that?"

"Yes. As Mr. Sweet's personal assistant I have Level Eight clearance. Only executives at Mr. Sweet's level have higher."

"Why don't you tell me where you were last night, between nine and midnight?"

His lip curled. "As I said, I left the office — verified by our logs — at seven-thirty-eight. I walked home. That's one block north, two and three-quarters blocks east. I arrived at approximately seven-fifty. My cohabitation partner is out of town on business. I spoke with her via 'link from eight-oh-five until eight-seventeen. I had dinner in, and remained in my apartment for the evening."

"Alone."

"Yes, alone. As I didn't expect to be interrogated by the police this morning, I saw no reason to secure a proper alibi." This time he managed to curl his lip and look down his nose simultaneously. "You'll simply have to take my word for it."

Eve smiled. "Will I? How long have you worked here?"

"I've been employed by Dudley and Son for eight years, the last three as Mr. Sweet's PA."

"Ever use Gold Star?"

"I have not. Nor am I acquainted in any way with the unfortunate Mr. Houston. My only concern in this incident is the fraudulent use of Mr. Sweet's name, information, and credit data. This department provides the company with the very finest security in the corporate aegis."

"Think so? Funny, then, how a little thing like — alleged — identity theft slipped through."

It was small of her, no doubt, but she got some satisfaction at the sour look that put on his face.

With the interviews done, she hooked up with Peabody to ride back down to street level.

"The two I interviewed, Sweet's head of security and the accountant, cooperated. The accountant's alibi — birthday party for his mother, twelve people attending, hosted at his home with his wife from eight to eleven or so. Security guy's a little spongier. He's married, but his wife went out with friends for the evening, and he stayed in and watched the ball game. She didn't get home until around midnight. He's got home security that would log the comings and goings, but being as he's in the business, he could probably tweak that. Thing is, he's former military, decorated, solid record, married fourteen years, one kid — who's in summer camp at this time. He's worked for Dudley a dozen years. He really strikes me as straight up."

"What's his military?"

"Army, communications and security."

She squeezed into traffic. "The PA doesn't have an alibi, and he's a snot. Nearly went cross-eyed looking down his nose at me. It's an arrogant crime, to my way of thinking. He's an arrogant little bastard. So's Sweet."

"Would either of them be stupid enough to use Sweet's name and data?"

"Or would either of them be smart enough to do just that because it comes off stupid?" Eve countered. "Something to think about. Let's go see Jamal."

She didn't expect any surprises in the morgue, but it was a task that required checking off. In any case, sessions with Morris, the ME, often served to confirm her basic theories or open up new ones.

She found him at work, a protective cloak over his sharp suit. The midnight blue color rather than the severe black he'd worn since his lover's murder told her he'd gone to the next phase of grief. For the first time since spring, he'd added a bright touch with a tie of strong, vibrant red. He'd braided his hair with a cord of the same color, drawing it back from his striking face.

He worked to music, she noted, another good sign. A low and smoky female voice wafted through the cool, sterile air like a warm, perfumed breeze.

Morris's long, dark eyes met Eve's, smiled. "How was your holiday?"

"Pretty damn good. Found a body."

"They turn up everywhere. Anyone we know?"

"Nope. A dumped-boyfriend bash. Locals handled it."

"And you've hit the ground running at home," he observed. "How are you, Peabody?"

"Excellent. Had some beach time. Didn't find a body."

"Ah well, better luck next time." He shifted his attention to the body on the steel table, opened by Morris's careful and precise V-cut.

"And here we have Jamal Houston, a man who kept in shape, tended his appearance. His hands are really quite beautiful. His scans show several old injuries. Breaks."

Morris brought the scans on-screen. "The right forearm, and the shoulder there — what I see is consistent with twisting. Ribs — two broken. Left wrist as well. All injuries would have been suffered during childhood and adolescence, while the bones were still forming."

"Abuse."

"I can only speculate, but that would be first on my list. Accident or injury wouldn't cause this damage to the shoulder."

"Grab the arm, twist, pull," Eve concluded.

"Yes. Violently. As it didn't heal properly, I doubt it was properly treated. And I expect it troubled him still from time to time, particularly in damp weather. None of these, of course, relate to cause of death. I believe the bolt through his neck gave you a clue on that."

"Yeah, it got me thinking."

"Otherwise, he was a healthy, and very fit, man in his early forties. No trace of drugs or alcohol in his tox. Stomach contents show his last meal was about seven last evening. Whole grain pasta with mixed vegetables, a light white sauce, water, and a coffee substitute. He also ingested breath mints. The body's clean but for the killing wound."

"Guy eats a nice healthy dinner, knocks back some fake coffee because it's going to be a long night and he wants to pump in a little caffeine. He grabs a shower, puts on a fresh suit, the chauffeur's cap. Takes his 'link, his memo book — he's got books on the 'link, according to the wife, to read while he waits for his clients. Pops the breath mints, kisses wife good-bye. About ninety minutes later, he's dead."

"But with clean, fresh breath," Morris added. "The barb of the bolt entered here." Gently, he turned the body to reveal the insult. "Slightly right of center, angling left and down as it pierced through."

"Killer's sitting in the back, right side, shoots at that slight angle. The bolt went right through, stuck in the control pad of the wheel."

"He'd need a good angle," Peabody commented, "to keep from hitting the seatback."

"One shot, and a pretty good one if he hit what he was aiming for." Eve brought the vehicle into her head, the interior with its long, plush passenger area, the open privacy screen to the driver's cab.

"And it's dark," she concluded, "lights on in the limo, but it's not optimum light. Still, it has to be dark or somebody might notice, even through the tinted windows, some guy sitting at the wheel of a limo with a bolt through his neck. Maybe he had a scope," she speculated, "or a target gauge. Put the little red dot where you want it, fire. Score."

She blew out a breath. "Well, I guess that's all he's got to tell me. His widow wants to see him, probably the kids, too."

"Yes, I'll arrange it once I've closed him."

Since they hadn't managed Peabody's hopes of a sit-down lunch, Eve sprang for soy dogs and fries from the corner glide cart, and put the vehicle on auto to eat on the way to the lab.

"How many people," she speculated, "own crossbows much less actually know how to use one with any accuracy? You'd need a collector's license to own a weapon like that, possibly a recreational use permit — if you acquired it legit. And I just don't see somebody going black or gray market to get one specifically for this. A lot of easier ways to kill. This feels like showing off, or at least showy."

"It wasn't target specific," Peabody added, "since the killer couldn't have known for sure who'd be driving. If he'd wanted Houston specifically, he could've requested him. Easy enough to blow smoke there. I've heard he's an excellent driver, blah blah."

"The target could be the business itself. Could be an inside deal, but it doesn't have that feel. It feels random, at least at this stage. At the same time, the Sweet connection isn't random."

"Maybe somebody decides to kill Houston, or whoever takes the job, to put pressure on Sweet. Top security man for an important corporation gets pulled into a homicide investigation, has to explain how his data could be compromised. It doesn't look good, even if you're innocent, and could have repercussions on the job."

"Yeah, some people are sick or ambitious

enough to try something that convoluted. We'll check and see who might be up for his position if he gets the ax. Or who he's axed in the last few months. I don't like the PA," Eve added with her own curl of the lip. "Not sure he'd have the stomach to kill somebody, but I don't like him. Want a closer look there."

The lab meant dealing with Dick Berenski, not so affectionately known as Dickhead. Eve understood he was brilliant at his work, but it didn't make him less of a dick.

He considered bribes his due for expediting work on a hot investigation, juggled the women who actually agreed to go out with him — she expected he paid for most of them — like bowling pins and often held small orgies in his office after hours.

She walked to his station, the long white counter where he slid from comp to scope to gauge on his stool, squatting on it like a bug, she thought, with his weird head like a shiny egg plastered with thin, boot-black hair.

He glanced up, shot her a smile that put a hitch in her stride. It resembled an actual human expression.

"Yo, Dallas, looking good. How's it hanging, Peabody?" The weirdly human smile remained in place, and made the back of

Eve's neck itch. "First day back, and you got a DB. Fancy one, too. We don't get many crossbow bolts through here."

"Okay. Tell me about the bolt."

"Top of the line. Carbon with a titanium core and barb. Front two-thirds of it's weighted heavier for increased penetration, with the back third lighter. It's got a specialized coating that helps you pull the bastard out of whatever you shot. It's twenty inches long. Brand name's Firestrike, manufacturer's Stelle Weaponry. You gotta have a license and permit to purchase, and there's an auto-check on that. Bastard costs a hundred through legit outlets."

For a moment Eve said nothing, wasn't certain she could. She hadn't threatened, insulted, bribed, or even snarled, and he'd given her more data in one shot than she usually beat out of him in a full meet.

"Okay . . . That's good to know."

"No prints, no trace but the vic's. But I got the code, manufacturer codes them in case of defect and whatnot. It was made in April of last year, shipped to New York from Germany. Only two outlets in the city. I got those." He offered her a disc. "All the data's in there."

"Did you get bashed on the head recently?"

"What?"

"Never mind. Anything out of the vehicle?"

"We got the 'link transes and the trip log. We're still processing the rest. It's a damn big bastard. Prelim doesn't turn up prints or trace, not even a loose hair, except for the driver's. Cleanest damn car I've ever seen, if you don't count the blood in the front."

"Okay," she said for a third time, at a loss. "Good work."

"That's what we do around here," he said so cheerfully her stomach threatened to curdle. "You go catch the bad guy."

"Right." Eve slid a glance at Peabody as they left. "What the fuck was that? Is it like that vid, with the people and the pods and the dupes?"

"Oh, that's a scary one. It's sort of like that. He's in love."

"What with?"

"Who," Peabody said with a laugh. "Apparently he met somebody a few weeks ago, and he's in love. He's happy."

"He's fucking creepy, that's what he is. I think I like him better when he's a dick. He kept smiling."

"Happy makes you smile."

"It's unnatural."

Still, she had a constructive chunk of data to work with. Back at Central she closed herself in her office to open her murder book, set up her murder board, and write up her initial report while Peabody contacted the two outlets to try to track down the bolt.

She tagged Cher Reo in the PA's office.

"How was your vacation?"

Eve resigned herself to answering the question all day. "Good. Listen, I caught a case this morning."

"Already?"

"Crime marches on. The vic's got a sealed juvie. I need to unseal it."

Reo sat back, pushed a hand through her fluffy blond hair. "You believe the juvie's pertinent to the case?"

"I don't know, that's why I need to see it. Guy's a successful business owner, husband, father, big fancy house in the burbs. No trouble on the surface, so far. The scan in autopsy shows multiple old wounds, mostly breaks. Might be abuse, might be from fighting. The past can come back to haunt you, right?"

"So they say. It shouldn't be a problem for the primary on a homicide to view the records of the victim. I'll make the request."

"Appreciate it."

111

"How'd he die?"

"Crossbow."

Reo's bright blue eyes widened. "Never a dull moment. I'll get back to you."

Eve programmed coffee, put her boots on her desk, and studied the board.

Moments later, Peabody gave a cursory knock and stepped in. "I've got a customer list for that particular batch of bolts. It's a couple of dozen worldwide, with a handful off planet. There's only one with a New York residence. I ran her, and she's clean, but you have to be to get the license and permit."

"We'll look at her. Why Gold Star?" she wondered. "Small, exclusive company, small fleet, small staff, and if their hype's to be believed, premium class, personal service. Top of the line," she murmured, "like the weapon. Expensive. Connect to Sweet, high-level exec for a high-level company. If there's no connection between Houston or his company and Sweet and his, then the only common denominator is they're both successful men with specialized skills."

"Maybe it's totally random."

"If it is, Houston may or may not be the first, but he won't be the last. Listen to Houston's transmissions." She ordered the computer to play it.

"Hey, Michael. I'm pulling up to the pickup now. Traffic's not too bad, considering. I'll check back when I've got the Person on Board."

"I'll be here."

"How's Kimmy doing?"

"She's beat. She's gone on to bed. I'm going to carry the portable with me when I check on her and our boy."

"Couple more weeks, you'll be a daddy again. You get some rest, too. I think I see the client. I'll come back."

"Time lapse to next trans," Eve said, "three minutes, ten."

"POB," Jamal said, his voice quieter now, brisker. "En route to LaGuardia, commercial transpo area for pickup, Supreme Airlines, Flight six-two-four out of Atlanta. ETA, ten-twenty."

"Copy that."

"Go to bed, Michael." Jamal's voice was barely a whisper now. "Take the portable with you if you're going to be a stickler. I'll come back to you if I need to. It's a long run, no point in both of us getting a short night. I've got a book. I'll entertain myself when the clients have their late supper."

"Come back when you get to the airport, then I'll go to bed."

"Deal. The client's excited about this

surprise for his wife," Jamal added. "He's sitting back there grinning. Just keeps grinning. I have a feeling I'll be using the privacy window before the night's over."

Michael chuckled. "Client's king."

"Last transmission," Eve said.

Jamal relayed his arrival, said good night to Michael.

"Within five minutes, he's dead. There's no worry, no tension in his voice. Just the opposite. No sense of threat from the passenger, no worries. The killer's not nervous, not if Houston's read him right, and somebody who does what he did for a living should have a good sense. His passenger's excited, happy, he's anticipating the kill."

"*He* — which lets out Iris Quill — the bolt buyer."

"She could've provided the weapon, been the 'wife.' We'll look at her. The transmissions tell me Houston didn't recognize the client. Could be wearing a disguise, could be somebody he hasn't seen in a long time. But a stranger says something else."

"Random again," noted Peabody.

"Even random has a pattern. We find the pattern. Get me this Quill woman's address. I'll take her on the way home. I'm going to work there. Do a secondary on everyone who bought that make of bolt, and on the

114

owners and employees of the outlets."

"Jeez."

"Send me the list, and I'll take half."

"Yay."

"Do a standard on Mitchell's financials, copy me. Add Sweet's to that. We'll see if money takes us anywhere."

Iris Quill lived in a sturdy townhome in Tribeca. The exterior spoke of no nonsense, no fuss. She hadn't troubled to deck it out with flowers or plants in a neighborhood that seemed to love them. She hadn't stinted on security, however, and Eve went through the routine with the palm plate, the scanner, the computer's demand for her name, her badge, her business.

The woman who opened the door hit about five foot two, weighed in at maybe a hundred pounds with a short straight skull-cap of shining silver hair and sharp blue eyes. She wore brown shorts that showed off short but exceptionally toned legs and a skin tank that showcased strong, defined arms.

Eve judged her to clock in at about seventy-five.

"Ms. Quill."

"That's right, and what can I do for you, Dallas, Lieutenant Eve? Last thing I killed was a black bear, and that was up in Canada."

"Did you use a crossbow?"

"A Trident 450 long-barrel." She cocked her head. "Crossbow?"

"Can I come in?"

"Why not? I recognized your name with the badge scan. I keep up with city crime, mostly watch Furst on Seventy-five."

In a tidy foyer, sparsely furnished with what looked like quality antiques, Iris gestured to a small, equally tidy living area. "Have a seat."

"I'm investigating a homicide. A crossbow bolt is the murder weapon."

"Hard way to go."

"Do you own a crossbow, Ms. Quill?"

"I own two. Both properly licensed and registered," she added with a gleam in her eye that told Eve the woman understood that information was already confirmed. "I like to hunt. I travel, and indulge my hobby. I enjoy testing myself against the prey with a variety of weapons. A crossbow takes skill and steady hands."

"Records show you purchased six Fire-strike bolts last May."

"I imagine I did. They're the best, in my opinion. Excellent penetration. I don't want the prey to suffer, so that's an important factor in a bolt or an arrow. And they're designed for reasonably easy extraction. I also don't want to waste my ammo. Have to replace the barbs, of course, but the shafts are durable."

"Have you sold, given, or lent any of your bolts to anyone?"

"Why the hell would I do that? First, I expect you know as well as I do it's illegal, unless it's a gift or a documented loan to another licensed individual. Second, I don't trust anybody with my equipment. And last, those suckers ran me ninety-six-fifty each."

"I thought they ran a hundred."

Quill's eyebrow cocked up with her smile. "I bought a half-dozen bolts and a dozen extra barbs and I know how to bargain."

"Can you tell me where you were last night, between nine and midnight."

"Sure I can. I was right here. I got back from a two-week safari in Kenya day before yesterday. I'm still a little turned around with my internal clock. I stayed home, wrote — I'm writing a book on my experiences — and was in bed by eleven. I'm a suspect." She smiled a little. "That's so interesting. Who am I suspected of killing?"

Since the media would be running with the story, Eve relayed the basics. "Jamal Houston. He was forty-three. He had a wife and two children."

She nodded slowly as even the ghost of a smile faded. "That's a pity. I never married, never had children, but I loved a man once. He was killed in the Urban Wars. People hunted people then. I suppose they still do or you wouldn't have a job, would you? Personally, I prefer animals. I'm sorry for his family."

"Do you use a limo service?"

"Of course. Streamline." The smile twinkled back. "It's your husband's, and it's the best in the city. When I pay for something, I want the best for my money. I have a record of the bolts — all my ammo — I've purchased. Also a record of what I've used in hunts, what remains in my inventory. Would you like copies?"

Hardly necessary, Eve thought, but it never hurt to take more than you needed. "I'd appreciate that."

"I've only been using that type of bolt for two years — when they first started making them. So I'll copy from there. Otherwise you'd have reams to go through. I've been hunting for sixty-six years. My mother taught me."

"Do you know anyone else who uses them, specifically? Someone you've hunted with or talked crossbows with?"

"Certainly. I could probably give you a list of names. Would that help?"

"It couldn't hurt. Can I just ask you, just personal curiosity: After you kill something, what do you do with it?"

"Since I'm not interested in trophies, I donate the kill to Hunters Against Hunger. Whatever can be used from the animal is processed and distributed to those in need. HAH's an excellent global organization."

Eve said, "HAH."

6

As with Central, Eve felt pleased to drive through the gates of home. A different atmosphere, certainly, than her professional house, but like Central it was hers now.

Rich summer green grass spread, a luxuriant carpet for leafy trees, sumptuous blankets of flowers, and madly blooming shrubs. Through the banquet of color, of green, of cooling shade the drive wound through to Roarke's elegant jewel.

Maybe the house was huge — so huge she wasn't sure she'd been in all the rooms — but it had dignity and style with its stone towers and turrets, its big and generous windows and terraces. What he'd built out of guile and need and vision held both the warmth and welcome they'd both lived most of their lives without.

It could, she supposed, swallow a dozen or more Brody farmhouses, but now that she'd experienced both she understood, at the core, they offered the same.

Welcome, stability, continuity.

She parked, gathered what she needed for the night's work, and walked past the flowers into her home.

Where Summerset materialized in the foyer like fog over a headstone. Bony in black, with the fat cat at his feet, he gave Eve the beady eye.

"Your first day back and you manage to come home without dripping blood on the floor. Shall I open champagne to commemorate?"

"Skip it, because I think about dripping blood on the floor. But it's always yours."

Insults exchanged, she thought as she headed upstairs with the cat padding after her. Now she was officially home.

She went to the bedroom first to strip off her jacket, change her boots for skids. Galahad wound in and out, in and out of her legs like an engorged ribbon.

"I think you gained weight." She sat on the floor, hauled the bulk of him into her lap. "You're a disgrace. You're like a cat and a half in a one-cat package." She gave him a good scratch while he stared at her with his bicolored eyes. "No point giving me the look, pal. You are officially on a diet. Maybe we'll get you one of those pet workout things."

"He'd just sleep on it," Roarke said as he came in.

"We could hang food at the end, rig it so he can't get it until he puts in the time."

"He's always been . . . big boned," Roarke said with a smile.

"He's got more pudge than he had when we left." She poked the cat's belly to demonstrate. "Summerset spoiled him."

"Probably." Still in his business suit, Roarke joined her on the floor. Galahad immediately switched laps. "But then, so do we."

"Look how he's cozying up to you because I was talking about diet and exercise, and he doesn't want to hear it."

Stroking the cat into locomotive purrs, he leaned in, kissed his wife. "I missed you today. I've gotten used to having you all to myself."

"You missed all the sex."

"Absolutely, but I missed that face of yours as well. And how was your day?"

"Limo driver meets crossbow bolt. Bolt wins."

"And here I thought my day was interesting."

"What planet did you buy?"

"Which would you like?"

"I'll take Saturn," she decided. "It's got pizzazz."

"I'll see what I can do."

She gave his tie a tug. "I thought you were going to stop wearing so many clothes."

"They frown on less at global business meetings."

"What do they know?" She unknotted his tie. "I think you should be naked."

"Oddly, I was just thinking the same about you." Reaching out, he hit the release on her weapon harness. The cat gave him a head butt, obviously annoyed the stroking had stopped. "I'll get back to you," Roarke promised, and nudged Galahad aside.

Eve took Galahad's place, wrapped her legs around Roarke's waist, her arms around his neck. "Maybe I missed your face."

"Maybe you missed the sex."

"I guess it can be both." She laid her lips on his, sank in. "Yeah," she murmured. "It can definitely be both."

While the cat stalked away in disgust, she shoved the jacket off Roarke's shoulders, tugged it off. He simply pulled the sleeveless tank she wore over her head.

"See how much easier mine are? You've got all these buttons." She attacked them while he let his hands roam.

123

He loved the feel of her, long and lean with that supple core of muscle. Hers was a warrior's body, agile and strong, and she gave it to him without reservation.

Her fingers, impatient and quick, dealt with buttons, pulled open his shirt. Their eyes met, hers that gilded brown, and aware. Watching her, he cupped her breasts, slid his thumbs back and forth over her until that awareness deepened.

When he took her mouth again, she pressed against him, center to center.

The beat of his blood quickened to a fierce and primal rhythm, driving, driving the need to possess. But when he would have pushed her back to the floor, she shifted her weight, and took him down.

Her breath, already unsteady, feathered over his lips. "Sometimes you've just gotta take it." She caught his bottom lip in her teeth, tugged.

She used her teeth again, on his throat, on his shoulder while her hand snaked between them to open his trousers.

She felt his muscles coil and release. All the power, she thought, under her. All that he was, hers for the taking. The thrill of that rode inside her while she helped herself, stirred him as she wanted him stirred until that power quivered for her.

He was hard and smooth, and she used her hands, her mouth to pleasure and to torment. Used her body to tease and arouse until her own needs nearly swallowed her.

He rolled, pinned her, his eyes fiercely blue.

"Now you'll take it," he said, and proceeded to destroy her.

She cried out once as those hands that had so coolly stroked the cat now used her, ruthlessly. He drenched her, saturated her with sensations that robbed her breath, shuddered through her body in choppy, drowning waves.

When she trembled, he hiked up her hips and plunged into her.

Filled and surrounded, caught and found. Craved. Power merged with power now as they drove each other.

Once again their eyes met, and he saw that deep and gilded brown. And now let himself fall into them.

A damn good welcome home, Eve decided as she dressed. She glanced over at Roarke. "I've got some work to get to."

"Limo driver, crossbow. I figured as much. This would be the driver from Gold Star."

She frowned a little, knowing he often checked the crime reports. "How much does the media have? I didn't have time to monitor."

"That's about it. You've been stingy with the details."

"They probably have the rest by now. Driver and co-owner, husband, father of two. Not a lot there to make too many ripples mediawise, until they get the crossbow angle. That'll ripple some."

"I expect it will." She left off weapon and jacket, he noted, and slipped her feet back into her skids. Her comfortable work mode.

The murder might not ripple overmuch in the media, he thought, but for Eve it would be a drowning pool until she closed the case.

He had a bit more work to catch up on, but nothing, he decided, that couldn't wait.

"Why don't we have a meal in here and you can fill me in before you get to it?"

"That'll work. I don't want much. I took pity on Peabody and sprang for dogs and fries this afternoon."

"Some cold pasta?"

"As long as it doesn't come with a light white sauce. Vic's last meal."

"We'll go for a light white wine instead."

They ate in the sitting area of the bedroom while she relayed the basics.

"Are you convinced the killer didn't know who'd be at the wheel?"

126

"It plays," she said. "We'll still look at the vic, the company, the employees, but it feels like the partner, the wife are telling it straight. The vic took the ride on a coin toss. When you listen to the transmissions during the ride, it's easy, business as usual with casual personal stuff mixed in. I don't, at this point, see Houston as a specific target. The company, maybe, but not him."

"Add in the security expert. It's interesting." As he tore a hunk of olive bread, handed her a share, Roarke considered it. "Dudley and Son is an old company, with a long reach and very deep pockets. I'd expect a man in Sweet's position to have been well vetted."

"He was pissed. It felt real. Then again." She shrugged and stabbed some curly pasta. "If he'd set it up, he'd be ready to make it feel real."

"The question would be why."

"Why Houston, why Sweet, why that company, why that method. Sweet's PA's off a little. Something off there," she considered. "I want a closer look at that little bastard. Thinks a lot of himself. Whoever did this thinks a lot of himself. The method matters, the whole, elaborate setup. If you don't know who you're going to kill, then it's about the killing, not the victim. When

127

you go to this much fuss, it's about *how* a lot more than *who*."

"You've looked into who bought that particular make of bolt?"

"Yeah. I interviewed one of them on my way home. Iris Quill."

"I know of her." Roarke lifted his wineglass. "She's got quite a reputation. A very serious hunter, and one of the founders of Hunters Against Hunger."

"HAH."

"An unfortunate acronym from the animal's viewpoint, I imagine. Still, they do good work."

"She struck me as solid. Gave me all her records on that weapon, even let me do a count of the bolts she has. And they add up. She also gave me a list of people she knows who use the same type. You don't hunt."

"No. It doesn't appeal to me."

"Mostly I don't get why people want to tramp around the jungle or the woods, or wherever in the stone bitch of nature just to kill some stupid animal who's just hanging around where it lives. You want meat, you can buy a dog on the street."

"That's not meat."

"Not technically."

"Not in any reasonable sense. I expect it's

the primal charge with hunting, the pitting yourself against the stone bitch of nature and so on."

"Yeah, but you'd be the one with the weapon." She frowned a moment. "Maybe this is kind of the same deal. Houston — or whoever might've been driving — is in his natural habitat, so to speak. You're sitting in his space, maybe it's the back of a fancy limo, but you're hunting. Primal charge, maybe."

"But hardly sporting," Roarke pointed out. "He shot an unarmed man from behind. Most animals have what you could term a weapon at least. Tooth and fang — and the advantage, to some extent, of instinct and speed."

"I don't think he's worried about being fair. Maybe a hunter, maybe, and maybe a little bored with shooting four-legged mammals. Trying for bigger game? Something to think about."

She thought about it in her home office while she set up a second murder board. She programmed coffee, glanced at the door that joined her office with Roarke's. He had work to catch up on, she knew, and it felt homey in their own strange way to be working in connecting rooms.

She set up her computer to start runs, and

while it worked began to add to her case notes.

Hunter. Bigger game. Thrill kill. Unusual weapon, elaborate setup = attention. Attention = trophy? Who has access to Sweet's data and hunts? Motive for involving Sweet?

She paused, glancing over at an incoming transmission. "Reo comes through," she murmured, and called the incoming file, now unsealed, on-screen.

Vandalism, shoplifting, illegals possession, truancy, she read. Two stints in juvie, with another illegals pop for dealing and destruction of private property in between. Mandatory counseling, all before Houston hit sixteen.

Tipping back in her chair, she read social workers' reports, counselors' reports, judges' opinions. Basically they'd labeled him a wild child, a troublemaker, a chronic offender with a taste for street drugs.

Until somebody'd bothered to dig a little deeper, somebody'd bothered to take a good look at his medicals.

Broken bones, blackened eyes, bruised kidneys — all attributed to accidents or fighting. Until just before his seventeenth birthday he'd beaten his father unconscious and taken off.

Her stomach shuddered with memory, with sympathy. She knew what it was to be broken and battered, knew what it was to finally fight back.

"They went after you, didn't they? Yeah, hunted you down, tossed you in a cage for a while. But somebody finally took a good, hard look."

She read his mother's statement, read the fear and the shame in it, but felt no sympathy there. A mother was meant to protect the child, wasn't she? No matter what. This one had hidden all those breaks and bruises out of that shame and fear, until the right cop, the right moment, and they'd pulled it out of her.

Supervised halfway house, more counseling — that, she thought, and maybe the power of finally fighting back had turned a teenage boy around, and helped build him into a man.

And last night, someone had taken that from him.

"His juvenile record," Roarke said from the doorway.

"Yeah."

"The system worked for him, maybe not as soon as it should have, but it worked for him." He came to her, kissed the top of her head. "And so will you. How can I help?"

"You said you had work."

"I've caught up with some, and have a few things running that can go on their own for a bit."

He thought of her, she understood, when he read the file. And he thought of himself, too — of being kicked and punched, broken and battered by his father.

It connected him — she understood that as well — to a man he'd never met.

"It's grunt work now, mostly. I'm doing runs on a portion of the staff at Dudley, and the transpo company's employees. I'm going to cross-reference those with any membership in hunting clubs or that kind of travel, licenses and permits for crossbows. And I want to dig on Sweet's PA's financials, just because the little bastard is off somewhere."

"Why don't I take the financials? I can do them faster."

"Show-off."

"But I do it so well." He pulled her in for a moment. "Take that down now." He studied the data on-screen as she did. "It reminds you, and that upsets and distracts you."

She shook her head. "Not until I do a

search for the father. Maybe he wanted pay-back after all these years. Maybe he got enough money for some sort of hit, or . . . I have to cross it off."

"All right. I'll look into the money on the little bastard."

It made her laugh. "Thanks."

She did the grunt work, sorted through runs, sieved the data, ran probabilities until a low-grade headache brewed behind her eyes.

"I can't find one person in the mix with a hunting connection, at least not that shows. No permits, no licenses, no purchases of that nature. I tried crossing with sporting — people do the damnedest things, and there's competitions for archery and shit. Legal ones. Nothing there, either."

"Well, I had better luck."

"I knew it." Eve slapped a fist on her desk. "I knew that little bastard was wrong. What did you find?"

"An account he'd buried under a few lay-ers. Not a bad job of it, really, and it would likely have remained buried if no one had a reason to dig. You'll note, as I did," Roarke continued, "he's been careful not to give anyone a reason to dig. Clean record, bills paid in a timely fashion, taxes all right and tight. I transferred the account data to your machine. Computer," he ordered, "display Mitchell Sykes's financials on screen two."

Acknowledged . . .

When the data flashed on, Eve picked up her coffee, narrowed her eyes. "That's a nice chunk. Heading toward half a million." But she frowned. "Am I reading this right? Deposits in increments over — what? — a two-year period."

"Nearly three, actually."

"Doesn't smell like payoff for a murder, unfortunately. The last deposit was a little over a week ago, in the amount of twenty-three-thousand dollars and fifty-three cents. That's a weird number."

"All the deposits are uneven amounts, and all under twenty-five thousand."

"Blackmail, maybe, and he deposits odd amounts to try to stay under the radar, which he has."

"Possibly."

"Or some corporate espionage, selling Dudley data to competitors. He's PA for one of the top security guys, so he'd have some access there."

"Another possibility."

"They're pretty regular, aren't they?" Hands in pockets, eyes narrowed, she studied the figures. "Every four or six weeks, another little bump in the nest egg. Withdrawals are few and far between, and pretty light. Living within his means, using a little extra here and there no one would blink at. Still, the amounts are . . . Wait, he's got a cohab, double the amount of deposits and it makes more sense." She glanced over. "And you've already gone there."

"As it happens. Computer, secondary financials, split screen."

"Karolea Prinz, nearly the same amounts, nearly the same dates. Now we've got something. She works for Dudley," Eve added. "I ran her. Pharmaceutical rep." She sipped her coffee. "So, I'll tell you what you've already figured out. They're skimming drug supplies, which she'd have access to, and selling them on the street or to a supplier. Every month or so."

"It reads that way to me."

"Nothing to do with Houston. In fact, this bumps them down below bottom, unless I find out Houston or someone connected was a customer. But the fact is, using his boss's data would bring just this sort of attention. Why go there when you've got such a nice sideline? You don't want to shine any lights."

"They've been successful, so I'd agree,

135

bringing the cops to their own doorstep would be monumentally stupid."

"Too bad, but it'll be fun to get him in the box and sweat the snot out of him." In fact, remembering his curled lip and down-the-nose smirk, it gave her a warm little thrill.

"Between this and the use of Sweet's data, it doesn't look like that arm of Dudley's is as secure as it should be." And that, she thought, was interesting, too. "Where there's one hole, there's probably another. Houston's killer's in one of those holes."

"Nothing on the victim's family connections?" Roarke asked her.

"The father's dead. Beat some neighbor kid, got a stretch in the Tombs. Picked the wrong con to mess with inside, and ended up bleeding out in the showers, thanks to the shiv in his gut. The mother moved back to Tennessee where her family's from. There's nothing there."

She puffed out her cheeks, blew out the breath. "I've run the partner, the partner's wife, the vic's wife, even the vic's kids back, forth, sideways. There's no buzz, no pop. The wife gets Houston's share of the business, but essentially she already had it. This killing just wasn't about Houston particularly. And nothing about the company, so

136

far, brings up any questions. If there's a connection, Dudley's the most likely source. Even then . . ."

She shook her head.

"Even then?"

"It's playing more and more like it was for the thrill. Just for the rush. And if that's the way it is, he's already looking for the next thrill."

The scream ripped out of the shadows, high and wild. Behind it chased a gurgle of maniacal laughter. For a moment, Ava Crampton caught a glimpse of her reflection in a smoky mirror before the ghoul burst out of the false glass, claws dripping blood.

Her squeal was quick and unplanned, but her pivot toward her date, the urgent press of her body to his, was calculated.

She knew her job.

At thirty-three she'd clocked over twelve years' experience as a licensed companion, and had worked her way steadily up the levels to the pinnacle.

She invested in herself, folding her profits back into her face, her body, her education, her style. She could speak conversationally in three languages, and was diligently working on a fourth. She kept her five foot six inch frame rigorously toned, was, in fact, an advanced yogini — the practice not only kept her centered but gave her a superb flexibility that pleased her clients.

She considered her mixed-race heritage a gift that had provided her with dusky skin (which she tended as rigorously as she did her body), cut-glass cheekbones, full lips, and crystalline blue eyes. She kept her hair long, curled, artfully tumbled in a caramel brown that set off that skin, those eyes.

Her investment paid off. She was one of the highest-rated LCs on the East Coast, routinely commanding a cool ten thousand an evening — double that for an overnight. She'd trained and tested and was licensed for a menu of extras and specialties to suit the varied whims of her clients.

Her date tonight was a first-timer, but had passed her strict and scrupulous screening. He was wealthy, healthy, and boasted a clean criminal record. He'd been married for twelve years, divorced for eight months. His young daughter attended an excellent private school.

He owned a brownstone in the city and a vacation home in Aruba.

Though his looks struck her as dead average, he'd grown a trendy goatee since his last ID shot, had grown out his hair. He'd also put on a few pounds, but she considered him still in good shape.

Trying on a new look with the little beard and longer hair, she thought, as men often did after a divorce.

She could feel his nerves. He'd confessed, charmingly she thought, that he'd never dated a professional before.

At his request, she'd met him at Coney Island — he'd provided a limo. Since he'd steered her almost immediately to the House of Horrors, she assumed he wanted the adrenaline rush, and a female who'd gasp and cling.

So she gasped, and she clung, and remembered to tremble when he worked up the nerve to kiss her.

"It all seems so real!"

"It's a favorite of mine," he whispered in her ear.

Something howled in the dark, and with it, on a rattle of chains, something shambled closer.

"It's coming!"

"This way." He tugged her along, keeping her close as overhead came the flutter of bat wings. The wind from them stirred her hair.

A holo-image of a monster wielding a bloodied ax leaped forward and she felt the air from the strike shiver by her shoulder.

He yanked her through a door that clanged shut behind them. On a yelp of surprise and disgust, she swiped at cobwebs. Caught up, she spun to try to escape them, and came face-to-face with a severed head on a spike.

Her scream, completely genuine, ripped out as she stumbled back. She managed a nervous laugh.

"God, who thinks of this stuff?"

She thought fleetingly that her last date had been a romp on silk sheets with a follow-up in an indoor wave pool. But no one knew better than Ava that it took all kinds.

And this kind got his kicks in the torture chamber of an amusement park.

The light fluttered, a dozen guttering candles with the red glow of a fire where a hooded man, stripped to the waist, heated an iron spike.

The air stank, she thought. They'd made it just a little too real, so it reeked of sweat and piss and what she thought was blood. The scream and prayers of the tortured and the damned crowded the room where stones dripped and the eyes of rats glowed in the corners.

A woman begged for mercy as her body stretched horribly on the rack. A man shrieked at the lash of a barbed whip.

And her date for the evening watched her with avid eyes.

Okay, she thought, she got the drift.

"You want to hurt me? Do you want me to like it?"

He smiled a little shyly as he came toward her. But the pace of his breathing had increased. "Don't fight."

"You're stronger. I'd never win." Playing the game, she let him back her into a shadowy corner behind a figure moaning as it turned on a spit. "I'll do anything you want." She worked some fear into her voice. "Anything. I'm your prisoner."

"I paid for you."

"And your slave." She watched pleasure darken his eyes, kept her voice low, throaty. "What do you want me to do?" Let her breath catch. "What are you going to do to me?"

"What I brought you here to do. Now be very still."

He pressed against her as he reached in his pocket, into the sheath hugging his thigh.

He kissed her once, squeezed his free hand on her breast to feel her heart pump against his palm.

She heard something, a slide, a click. "What's that?"

"Death," he said, and stepping back drove the blade into that pumping heart.

7

With her mind crowded with data and theories, Eve crawled into bed. Her body clock yearned to be wound down, turned off, and rebooted after a solid downtime. She curved into Roarke as his arm came around her, felt everything in her give in, relax.

She closed her eyes.

Her 'link signaled.

"Hell. Lights on, ten percent. Block video." She shoved herself up, answered. "Dallas."

Dispatch, Dallas, Lieutenant Eve. See the officer, Coney Island, House of Horrors, main entrance. Possible homicide.

"Acknowledged. Contact Peabody, Detective Delia. Probability of connection with Houston investigation?"

Unclear, but flagged.

"On my way. Shit," she said as she cut transmission.

"I'll drive." Roarke stood, shook his head when she frowned. "I've a business interest in the park, as you know. I'll be contacted —" He broke off when his 'link signaled. "Now, I'd say."

She didn't argue. He'd probably be handy.

She dressed, programmed a couple of coffees to go.

And said nothing when he chose one of his topless toys to zing them through the warm summer night. The wind and the caffeine would clear her brain and reboot the body clock a few hours ahead of schedule.

"What kind of security's on that place?" she asked him.

"Minimal as it's an amusement. Standard scanners at the entrances to the park, a network of cams and alarms throughout. Security personnel do routine sweeps."

"A night like this, it's probably packed."

"From a business standpoint, one hopes. We've had very little trouble since we opened, and that on the minor side." He flicked a glance in her direction. "I'm no happier to have a dead body there than you are."

"Dead body's less happy than both of us."

"No doubt." But it troubled him on an elemental level, not only because it was primarily his, but because it was meant to be a place for fun, for families, for children to be dazzled and entertained.

It was meant to be safe and, of course, he knew no place was really safe. Not a pretty Irish wood, not an amusement park.

"Security's duping the discs now," he told her. "You'll have the originals, and they'll scan the copies. They'll be enhanced, as the lighting in that amusement is deliberately low, and there are sections with fog or other effects. We use droids, anitrons, and holos," he said before she could ask. "There's no live performers."

"The stuff runs on a timer?"

"No. It's motion activated, programmed to follow the customer's movements. As for timing, there's a feature that funnels customers in their groups, or individually if they come in alone, into different areas to enhance and personalize the experience."

"So the victim and killer, if they came in together, could and would have been alone — at least for a portion of the ride, or whatever it is."

"Sensory experience. There are sections inaccessible to minors under fifteen to conform with codes."

"You've been through it."

"Yes, several times during the design and construction stages. It's appropriately gruesome and terrifying."

"Won't scare me. I have the gruesome and the terrifying greet me at the door every freaking day." She smiled to herself, thinking it was too bad Summerset wasn't around to hear her get that one off.

The lights shimmered and sparkled against the night sky, and music vied with the happy screams of people zooming on the curves and loops of the coasters, spinning on wheels that flashed and boomed.

She didn't much see the appeal of paying for something that tore screams out of your throat.

On the midway, people paid good money to try to win enormous stuffed animals or big-eyed dolls she considered less appealing than rides that tore screams out of the throat. They shot, tossed, blasted, and hammered with abandon or strolled around with soy dogs or cream cones or sleeves of fries and whopping drinks.

It smelled a little like candy-coated sweat.

The House of Horrors was just that, a huge, spooky-looking house with lights flickering in the windows where the occasional ghoul, ghost, or ax murderer would pop out to snarl or howl.

A big, burly uniform and a skinny civilian secured the entrance.

"Officer."

"Lieutenant. We've got the building secured. One officer, one park security inside with the DB. We've got a guard on every egress. Did an e-scan. No civilians left inside."

"Why is it still running?" she asked, studying the door knocker in the form of a bat with shivering, papery wings and glowing red eyes.

"I didn't want to make the determination to shut down, considering you might have wanted to go through as the vic had."

It was a reasonable call. "We'll do a replay when and if. For now, shut it down."

"I can do that from the box." The skinny guy glanced at Eve, then sent Roarke a sorrowful look. "Sir. I have no idea how this could've happened."

"We'll want to find that out. For now, shut it down."

"I need to go inside," the civilian said to Eve. "Just inside to the box."

"Show me." She nodded to the uniform, who uncoded the door.

It creaked ominously.

Cobwebs draped the shadowy foyer like shawls over a body back. Light, such as it was, came from the flickering glow of ornate candelabras and a swaying chandelier where a very lifelike rat perched.

Something breathed heavily to the left, and made her fingers itch for her weapon. Shadows seemed to swoop and dive from the ceiling. Up a long curve of steps a door groaned like a man in pain, then slammed.

The skinny guy moved to a panel on the wall, aimed his little handheld. The panel slid open to reveal a keypad. He coded something in.

Lights flashed on, movement and sound died.

Glancing around, she decided it was a little creepier in the bright and the still. Anitrons stood frozen on the floor, in the air, on the stairs. In a mirror a face held in midscream while a severed hand holding a twobladed ax hung suspended.

"Where's the body?"

"Subsection B. Torture Chamber," the skinny guy told her.

"Who are you?"

"I'm Gumm. Ah, I'm Electronics and Effects."

"Okay. Lead the way."

"Do you want to go by the amusement

route or employee?"

"The most direct."

"This way." He walked to a bookcase —
why was it always a bookcase? Eve wondered
— and engaging another hidden mechanism, opened the doorway.

"We have a series of connecting passages
and monitoring stations throughout the
amusement." He guided them through a
brightly lit, white-walled passage, past
controls and screens.

"It's all automated?"

"Yes, state of the art. To give the customers the full experience, we're able to funnel
them in various directions rather than have
them all follow the same route and crowd
together. It's more personal. They can, if
they choose, interact with the effects. Speak
to them, ask questions, give chase or attempt to evade. There's no danger, of
course, though we have had some customers pass out. A loss of consciousness trig-
gers an alarm in Medical."

"How about death?"

"Well . . ." He made a turn, paused.
"Technically, a loss of heartbeat should have
triggered an alarm. There was a glitch, a
kind of blip at twenty-three-fifty-two. A kind
of blip. We're looking into it, sir," he said to
Roarke.

He opened the door into the Torture Chamber. There was the faint memory of stench, as if something hadn't been thoroughly cleaned. Over it smeared the smell of death.

The officer holding the scene came to attention. Eve gave him a nod.

The body slumped against the fake stone wall, legs spread, chin on chest. As if the woman had fallen asleep. The mass of curling brown hair hid most of her face, but one wide blue eye stared out from a part in that curtain, almost flirtatiously.

Sparkling stones glittered at her throat, her wrists, on her fingers. She wore a white dress in a summery fabric, cut low on the breasts. Blood stained it in a thin line where the blade pierced her heart.

Eve opened her field kit, used Seal-It to cover her hands and boots before tossing the can to Roarke. She'd already engaged her recorder.

"Victim is mixed-race female, looks early thirties, brown and blue. She has a small, jeweled bag on the belt at her waist, and is wearing considerable jewelry. Single stab wound," she said as she stepped over and crouched. "Heart shot, and it looks dead-on, with a knife still in the body. The blade has some sort of mechanism, like a socket, on the grip."

"It's a bayonet," Roarke said from behind her. "It would fit on a rifle or other firearm, or can be removed, as it is now, for use as a sidearm."

"A bayonet," she murmured. "Something else you don't see every day." She opened the little bag. "About two-fifty in cash, breath spray, lip dye, credit card and ID card, both in the name of Ava Crampton, Upper East Side addy. And it lists her as a top-level LC on her ID."

She checked fingerprints to verify.

"Who found her?"

"Ah, I did." With a look of apology on his face — Eve wondered if it was situational or permanent — Gumm raised his hand. "We ran down the source of the glitch to this sector, and I came down to do an on-site check. She was . . . just there."

"Did you touch her?"

"No. I could see . . . It was clear." He swallowed. "I called Security, and they notified the police. We cleared the amusement. I'm afraid there had been several people through here between the glitch and the . . . discovery."

Eve simply stared at him. "Customers tromped through the crime scene?"

"We — they — no one knew there'd been

a crime. She was probably taken as part of the amusement. The exhibits are very life-like."

"Crap. I need the security discs."

"We're putting them together for you now. There is a bit of a wrinkle."

Eve paused as she reached for her gauge. Glitch, blip, wrinkle, she thought. What other cute term would he find for cluster-fuck? "Define wrinkle."

"There are sections on the discs from various areas that appear to be blank."

"Appear to be."

"I'm having them analyzed. Sir." He addressed Roarke now. "My first thought is someone entered and toured while carrying a sophisticated jammer. A pinpoint device of considerable strength. In order to bypass the security walls, and only for moments at a time, it had to be extreme, and in my opinion, the user had to know the locations of the cameras and alarms. He had to know the system. The route, as far as we can tell from the first run, leads here, then out through Sector D, which would be the nearest exit. I'm afraid whoever did this" — he glanced at the body — "periodically jammed our system so as to go undetected."

"Did you kill her, Gumm?"

His head jerked on his bony shoulder as

he gaped at Eve. "No! No, of course not. I don't even know her. I've never —"

"She's winding you up, Gumm," Roarke said mildly, but Eve heard the anger under the surface.

"Finish the analysis, and get the lieutenant the discs," he began when they heard footsteps coming down the passage.

Peabody popped out seconds before the love of her life, EDD ace McNab.

"This place rocks even when it's turned off. McNab and I came in for the spooks a couple weeks ago. It's total."

"Glad you're enjoying yourself. Seal up," Eve ordered. "Not you," she added pointing a finger at McNab. "This is Gumm. Go with him and do e-crap."

"Sure." McNab, skinny of build, bony of ass, looked positively robust compared to Gumm. He offered a smile as sunny as the hair he'd pulled back into a long tail. "Live to serve."

Because he was amenable, and as good as they come, Eve ignored the fact he wore red maxi cargo with multicolored pockets and a short-sleeved yellow jacket over a tank that looked like he'd soaked it in a rainbow.

"Go live. TOD, twenty-three-fifty-two." She looked at Roarke. "There's your blip. Her heart stopped, and whatever he was jamming it with gave you the blip instead of the alarm. He came prepared. Weapon, jammer, knew the route and the system if Gumm is to be believed."

"He is. He's skilled and reliable."

"I'll want a list of people who know the system, anyone who's been fired or written up."

"You'll have it."

"Peabody, contact the usual, and let's get this place processed. Spookville's shut down for the foreseeable."

"What kind of knife is that?" Peabody asked as she pulled out her 'link.

"Bayonet. Vic is a high-priced LC. From a visual exam on the clothes, the state of the body, it doesn't look like sexual assault — and really what would be the point? She's got jewelry, cash, and credit still on her, so that ditches robbery — and again, why haul her in here, bringing a jammer and a freaking bayonet, if you just wanted sex and glitters?

"Limo driver, crossbow, transpo station parking. Pricey LC, bayonet, amusement park. Luxury items, unusual weapons, semi-public places. He's got a system, and right now he's two for two."

She stood up. "Officer —"

"Milway."

"Milway, see if you can find out how she got here. Personal transpo, private, public. Round up entrance security. Let's see if he jammed that, too. Talk to park employees, find out if anyone saw her. She's a looker. If they noticed her, they may have noticed who she was with."

She waited until the uniform stepped out. "How do you figure he got that through the scanners?" she asked, gesturing to the bayonet.

"The smartest way would be to have it on him, in a sheath or holder lined with magnetic fiber that would block the reading."

Eve nodded, continued to study the body, the room. "An LC of that level has to have solid experience as well as skill and a clean bill. Her hair's still perfect. Her dress, except for the blood, isn't messed up. No bruises, no sign she tried to evade or fight. She didn't see it coming. Didn't get any kind of buzz he was off."

"Neither did Houston," Roarke pointed out. "A driver would be good at reading clients."

"Should be. She comes in here with him. We'll get the route from the glitches, the blips, whatever Gumm wants to call them, and then she ends up here. Must be gruesome when it's running."

"It's meant to be."

"People are fucked up," she said half to herself. "Can you get them to turn on this sector? Just this sector. I want to see how it played."

"Give me a moment." He took out his 'link, stepped away.

"Sweepers dispatched, morgue team's heading in."

Nodding at Peabody, Eve considered. "She doesn't have a memo book on her, but you can bet someone at her level has perfect records. She'll have this guy listed. But he'd know that."

"If it's the same killer, you're thinking he faked his ID again."

"I'm thinking he'd cover himself, play the same pattern. If so, it means she didn't know him. A first round. Wouldn't she run him? Make sure she's not dating a psycho — not that it did her any good. But wouldn't she? I want to talk to Charles about that," she said referring to their mutual friend, a retired LC.

"Charles might've known her," Peabody added. "They would've run in the same circles, same social strata."

She jumped as if her air skids were springs at the bloodcurdling scream.

"Nerves of steel," Eve muttered while

156

moans and stench and eerie light filled the chamber. She watched an anitron score another anitron's face with a glowing poker.

"The torture methods in play are historically accurate," Roarke told her. "The instruments are carefully crafted replicas of those used."

"Yeah, seriously fucked up. Is there another entrance?"

"To the public, no. That one would channel the customers in here, through the maze of the place, then move them out again over there to the next sector."

"Okay." She moved to the entrance, ignoring cobwebs, skittering rats. "Is the smell authentic, too?"

"Or a close approximation."

"And people pay for this." She shook her head. "They come in here. Does it excite him, all the screams, the smell of blood and piss, the realism? I bet it does. He didn't just decide to do it here, he planned it. Here in this replica of misery, cruelty, fear, despair. Maybe she's playing the part, shivering, cringing, holding on to him. Or she's going the other way, aroused, excited — whichever she thinks the client's after.

"But they moved around." She began to walk through. "Getting a closer look. Had to get to the kill zone. Shadows are deeper there. Maybe he maneuvers her, or she goes that way and plays into his hands. Up against the wall, braced against the wall, that's how he did her. She thinks he wants a little sample of what's coming, and he gets her against the wall so she doesn't fall on anything, knock anything. Jamming the cameras, the sensors, but if she falls and knocks anything over, that could get through. He wants a little time to get out, get away. He leaves, the jamming stops. But she's on the floor, in the shadows, and the show goes on."

She walked over to a doorway that resembled the mouth of a cave. "Out here. Where does this go?"

"Here." Roarke held out his PPC. "That's the layout of this area. Depending on the route and timing of anyone ahead of you, the program would take you out into one of these three sectors. There are appropriately mocking signs here, here, here, for those who want to end their tour. This is where Gumm believes he exited."

"Let's have a look. Peabody, stay with the body, set up the sweepers when they're on scene."

"Ah, could we maybe lose the effects?"

"Coward."

But Roarke winked at her, ordered them

shut down.

The security lights illuminated a narrow corridor with torches on the walls. They followed its left fork into a wide cavern with what appeared to be a deep pool of water. On it sat a boat where men in dingy pirate garb were frozen in mid–sword fight. A couple of decaying corpses lay piled under jutting rocks. The topmost had a crow on its belly, beak buried in torn flesh.

"Nice."

"You get what you pay for. When running there's head severing, disemboweling, a bit of keel hauling, and the skeletal spirits of the damned. It's fairly impressive."

"I bet." She studied the sign on an arched door fashioned to replicate planks.

IF THE PIRATE'S BLADE YOU FEAR,
TAKE THIS CHANCE TO ESCAPE
FROM HERE.

"The exit." She tried the door. It opened into the bright lights and sounds of the park. "He'd be out and gone in two minutes, easily. With the heart jab, he shouldn't have gotten any blood on him. Or if he did, it's easily cleaned off before he leaves. Stroll right out. He could buy a fucking soy dog to celebrate. He'd look ordinary, forgettable.

But she doesn't, that's the thing. She's the type people notice, so maybe somebody noticed him, too."

She shut the door. "I'm going to take another walk through. Maybe you could give Gumm and McNab a kick. I want whatever they've got, and we'll see what EDD can do with it. And yeah," she said before he could speak, "you're on as expert consultant, civilian, if you want to be. I know this is your place, and you're pissed."

"Not entirely mine, but, yes, I'm pissed. It's good security here," he added, looking around, "but it's a playground. Families, children, people looking for a bit of fun. I don't suppose we were as stringent in that area as we might have been."

"Nobody's going to monitor an amusement spook house the way they do the UN. And he knew what he was doing, just how to do it." She frowned. "I want a list of other investors, partners, whatever they are. The money people who'd know what went into this place. He has money, or he wants it. The kind that buys gold limos and expensive LCs."

She went out the exit, circled around to the front. This time she wanted to retrace the killer's route. She tagged McNab. "Guide me through this place, by the blips on the security."

"Can do. Let me get a fix on your 'link."

She followed his directions, winding through a vampire's lair, a graveyard with zombies dragging themselves out of the ground. She could imagine the lighting, the sounds, the movements well enough.

What if the program had taken them another way? she wondered. He'd had alternatives set up. Other kill zones with easily accessed exits. And the vic had played along, doing what she'd been paid to do.

She stopped, narrowed her eyes. Paid. An LC in her league would get a hefty deposit. She needed to consult with Charles, get a solid opinion on the practice and procedure.

By the time she reached Peabody she had the route mapped in her head. "He probably made it here with her in under twenty. Probability's high this was his first stop, and her last."

"I did a run on her. She had over a dozen years in, not a single citation. Clean and regular health checks, paid her fees on time, worked her way up the chain. She's diamond level, and if I remember what Charles said that means she earns about ten thousand for a four-hour date. She's certified for male and female, groups, bondage, submissive or dominant. Name it, she's licensed.

There are only half a dozen LCs in the city at her level. Only one other female."

"He wants or needs exclusive." She turned as Officer Milway came back in.

"Lieutenant. She didn't book transpo, but I checked for private going to her address tonight. There was a pickup for that address, her name, booked at twenty-two-thirty. Elegant Transportation. The driver, Wanda Fickle, dropped her off at the main entrance at twenty-three-ten. The car was ordered by and paid for by a Foster M. Urich. He's got an address in the Village."

"Good work."

"Yes, sir. We're asking around. We found a couple of people who think they saw her. With a male, but they're vague and contradictory on the male. We'll keep on it."

"If you get anything solid there, I want to know ASAP."

"Yes, sir."

She pulled out her 'link. "I've got to go to the Village."

"Take the car," Roarke told her. "McNab and I will get ourselves and the discs into Central."

Since suggesting he go home and get some sleep first would be a waste of time, she didn't bother. "I'll see you there."

"Morgue's in the house." Peabody tucked

away her communicator. "Sweepers right behind them."

"Good, let's get things wrapped here, and go see Foster M. Urich. Do a run."

"Already on it. Forty-three, Caucasian male, recently divorced, one child — daughter, age eight. CEO of Intelicore. Minor bust for zoner at age twenty. Nothing else on his record."

"What's Intelicore?"

"Data gathering and storing services. Major player globally and off planet. Three generations in."

"Interesting," Eve murmured. "That's another two for two."

8

The minute she spotted the car Peabody wiggled her hips and swung her arms in the air. "Hot-diggity damn!"

"Stop that."

"It's so pretty." She settled for wiggling her shoulders. "It's so sexy. It's so frosty. It's so Roarke."

"Keep it up and you'll be taking public transportation to the Village."

"I'll be good, I'll be good. I'll be especially good if we can have the top down. Can we? Please, please?"

"You're embarrassing yourself." Eve uncoded the locks.

"Not even close. It's all smooth and shiny." She purred as she stroked fingertips along the hood.

"Your ass'll be all smooth and shiny when I'm finished kicking it. I'm putting the top down." Eve's snarl and pointed finger cut off Peabody's squeal. It came out as more of a peep.

"Because it's hot, and because the wind will blow away some of your idiocy."

Eve turned the car on.

"Ooh, it sounds like a lion that's just fed."

"How do you know what a lion that's just fed sounds like?"

"I watch nature shows on-screen sometimes to further my education."

"Because you never know when we're going to have to track a lion through Midtown." She ordered the top down, and Peabody executed a quick seat wiggle.

"If you're finished with your vehicular orgasms see if you can make any connections between Dudley and Intelicore." Eve activated the GPS on her wrist unit, read in Urich's address.

"We are so freaking high-tech!"

"I'm just seeing if it works." She shot out of the lot. Peabody let out a joyous, "Whee!"

"There's just not enough wind."

"You're going 'Whee,' too. Inside."

Maybe, Eve thought.

"If the killer isn't Urich — and nothing's that easy — then he has to look enough like him, or have made himself look enough like him to fool the vic. He could change his hair, add weight, take it off, do some face

165

work, but there should be at least a surface resemblance. The killer's probably Caucasian or looks it, likely in the neighborhood of five ten and a hundred seventy like Urich. Unless he's just randomly hacking IDs for his kills, we'll find a connection between Sweet and Urich."

"He's picking the top in their field for his victims," Peabody said as she worked. "Sweet and Urich both work for important companies, and have important positions in them."

"It's more," Eve said with a shake of her head. "When you think of the top companies, the wealthiest corporations, the biggest businesses, what comes to mind first?"

"Roarke."

"Yeah, but this guy's taken out two without crossing into Roarke's businesses."

"The amusement park."

"Yeah, which Roarke has a piece of, and a part in. But it's hard to pick a company without bumping into one of Roarke's, and the killer didn't go there for his cover either time. There's going to be a connection between the men and/or their companies. It's not random. Neither are the vics. They're not personal, but they're specific. We'll run a search to see if there's any connection between Houston and Crampton, but it's going to be the men, the companies, not the victims."

"I don't find anything on this first round. None of the subsidiaries are connected or even in direct competition. They do have offices in some of the same cities, but that's a stretch. They do each have long-running charitable foundations, but again, they veer off into different areas of interest and support."

"It's in there somewhere," Eve noted.

Peabody put her head back, closed her eyes. "Maybe employees who crossed over, or interbusiness marriages, relations. So the killer has at least some data on both."

"Possible."

"Or somebody who knows and has a hard-on against Sweet and Urich."

"A lot of trouble to go to, and pretty fucking extreme to take a punch at somebody. But we'll be looking for connections between Sweet and Urich. The methods aren't random either. They're planned well in advance, so they're deliberate. A bid for attention. He's showing off. Send an alert to Mira's office," she said referring to the department's top profiler and shrink. "I want a consult tomorrow. Send her the files so she can take a look."

When she pulled up in front of the dignified old brownstone, she smiled at her wrist unit. "Bastard really works."

She got out of the car, took a moment to study the townhouse, the neighborhood. "Nice spot. Quiet, established, monied but not flashy. Urich was married once and did it in a twelve-year stretch. He's worked for the same company for close to twenty years. He sticks. Got a little garden going here that looks all tidy and organized. Everything all nice and settled."

She passed through the short wrought-iron gate, to the walkway between a small, structured front garden, and up the stairs to the main door.

"Locks down at night." She nodded toward the steady red light on the security pad before pressing the buzzer.

This residence is protected by Secure One, *the computer informed her.* The occupant does not accept solicitations. Please state your name and your business.

"Lieutenant Dallas and Detective Peabody." Eve held up her badge for the scanner. "NYPSD. We need to speak with Foster Urich."

Your information will be relayed. Please wait.

Good security, Eve thought, but Urich kept it simple and straightforward.

It took several minutes, but the security light switched to green, and the door opened.

Urich stood in loose pants and T-shirt, his feet bare. His hair looked sleep tumbled and curled around a sharp-featured face. Fear lived in his eyes.

"Has something happened to Marilee? My daughter. Is my daughter —"

"We're not here about your daughter, Mr. Urich."

"She's okay? Her mother —"

"We're not here about your family."

He closed his eyes a moment, and when he opened them the fear died. "My daughter's at camp. It's her first time." He let out a breath. "What's this about? Jesus, it's after three in the morning."

"We're sorry to disturb you at this hour, but we need to ask you some questions. Can we come in?"

"It's the middle of the night. If I'm going to let you in, I want to know what this is about."

"We're investigating a homicide. Your

name came up."

"My — a murder? Who's dead?"

"Ava Crampton."

His face creased in puzzlement. "I don't know anybody by that name. All right, come in. Let's get this cleared up."

The long entrance hall opened on the side to a living area with deep colors, oversized seating, a wide wall screen. On the table in front of a long high-backed couch sat two wineglasses and a bottle of red. A pair of high-heeled sandals sat under the table.

"Who's Ava Crampton, and how did my name come up?"

"Are you alone, Mr. Urich?"

"I don't see that's any of your business."

"If you've had company this evening, it may clear up some questions."

He was blushing, Eve noted.

"I'm with a friend. I don't like being inter-rogated about my personal life."

"I don't blame you, but Ava Crampton lost her personal life."

"I'm sorry about that, but it has nothing to do with me. And I'd really like to know why you think it does."

"Elegant Transportation took Ms. Cramp-ton to Coney Island tonight."

He looked both irritated and baffled. "Lieutenant Dallas, if you're questioning everyone who routinely uses Elegant Transpo, you're in for a really long night."

"The reservation for the limo was in your name, and secured with your credit card."

"That's ridiculous. Why would I order a limo for a woman I don't even know?"

"That's a question," Eve said.

Irritation increased enough to smother the bafflement. "When was it booked?" He snapped out the question. "What card was supposedly used?"

When Eve told him, he took a moment before speaking. "That's my company card. I use that transpo service routinely for both business and personal, but I know neither I nor my admin reserved transportation for tonight."

"Let's get this part out of the way. Where were you between ten P.M. and one A.M.?"

"Foster?"

The pretty woman wore a man's robe miles too big for her. Her short, bark-colored hair fell to her jaw. Like Urich, she hadn't thought to comb it.

"I'm sorry. I got worried."

"It's all right, Julia. It's just some sort of mix-up. Julia and I spent the evening together." His color came up again. "I, ah, picked her up about seven-forty-five. We had an eight o'clock at Paulo's. Then we, ah, came back here. I don't remember the time."

"It was a little after ten," Julia supplied. "We've been in since. What's happened?"

He walked to her, ran a hand down her arm. "Someone's been killed."

"Oh, no! Who?"

"I don't know her, but there's some confusion about the use of my company card. I need to straighten it out. I can't think straight," he added. "I'm going to make some coffee."

"I'll do it. No, I'll do it, Foster. You sit down. Would you like coffee?" she said to Eve and Peabody.

"That'd be great," Eve answered.

"Foster, sit down with the police. I'll just be a minute."

"Sorry," he said when Julia went out. "Sit down. This has just thrown me off. I don't know how my company account could've been used. We change the code every couple of weeks."

Eve took the ID photo out of her bag. "Do you recognize her?"

He took a good look at the picture, then scooped back his untidy hair and took another, longer study before he shook his head. "No. And I don't think that's a face I'd forget. She's beautiful. Coney Island, you said," he added when he handed the photo back.

"Yes. You've been there."

He smiled. "I've taken my daughter there several times since it re-opened. She's going to be nine next month. I'm divorced," he said quickly. "Her mother and I have been divorced for several months."

"Understood. Do you know an Augustus Sweet?"

"I don't think so. It's not a familiar name. I meet a lot of people, Officer —"

"Lieutenant."

"Sorry, yes, Lieutenant Dallas. In my work . . . You already know what I do, where I work. You'd have checked."

"Yes. Who'd have access to your account information?"

"My admin. Della McLaughlin. She's worked with me for over fifteen years. She wouldn't be involved in this. Her assistant, Christian Gavin, would also have the information, but I have to say the same. He's been with us nearly eight years. Julia." He smiled again when she came back with a tray, and rose to take it. "Thank you."

"You're welcome." She stood as he set down the tray. "Should I go?"

"No, please. Lieutenant, I need to go put a block on that account, and initiate a search for use. I may be able to tell you who used it once I do."

"Go ahead."

He grabbed coffee, dumped creamer into it. "I'll only be a couple minutes."

Julia sat, tugged on her robe. "This is strange and . . . just strange."

"Can I ask how long you and Mr. Urich have been involved?"

"Involved? I guess about a month, but we've known each other for three years. Since our daughters became friends. They're at camp together. Kelsey's father and I divorced several years ago. Since Foster and Gemma divorced, Foster and I . . . Well, we spent some time together with the girls, playdates and parks and that kind of thing. And we'd talk. He needed someone to talk to who'd been there. Then . . . it sort of evolved. This is actually the first time we've . . . Anyway, I don't suppose any of that's relevant."

You'd be surprised, Eve thought.

"Difficult divorce for Mr. Urich?" Peabody asked, picking up the theme.

"They're all difficult. But it was civilized. They both love their daughter very much. Gemma just wanted something else. I think that's what was hardest for Foster to understand. It wasn't any one thing. She just didn't want what they had."

"Is she involved with someone else?"

"I don't think so. That's part of the something else. She just didn't want a relationship. Not now anyway. She didn't leave for someone else, if that's what you mean. She's a very decent person."

Urich came back, stood on the other side of the coffee table. "It's my code. Whoever reserved the transportation knew my code, my password. I don't know how that could be. I've ordered a sweep and sniff, to confirm we were hacked. It's the only explanation I have."

"Can you think of anyone who'd want to cause you trouble?" Eve asked. "Want the cops at your door at three in the morning?"

He didn't answer immediately, but frowned into the distance. "When you hold a position with a company like Intelicore as I do, you do generate some resentment, some anger, some hard feelings. People get fired or transferred, or written up. I can imagine there are some who wouldn't mind seeing me hassled or inconvenienced. There are probably some who'd enjoy hearing I'd been questioned by the police. But this is more than that. This is using my name in connection with murder. No, I can't think of anyone who'd do that."

"I'm going to send e-detectives to your office and your home to do their own check of your equipment. Any problem with that?"

"No. I want answers on this, and quickly. I'll have to tell The Third," he muttered.

"The Third?"

"Sorry." He shook his head. "The head of the company. I'll need to inform him there's been a breach, and that there's a criminal investigation connected to it." He dragged a hand through his hair.

"He can't blame you," Julia began.

"It's my account. At some point, someone's head's going to roll. So believe me, Lieutenant, when I say I want answers. I don't want that head to be mine."

"We appreciate your cooperation." Eve got to her feet. "If he's the head of the company, why do you call him The Third?"

"Sylvester B. Moriarity the Third. His grandfather started the company."

She had that information already, but circled around it. "And he takes an active role in the company."

"He's involved, certainly. I'll walk you out."

"They were sweet," Peabody said when she got into the passenger's seat. "Well, they were," she insisted when Eve said nothing. "Him all blushy and flustered about having a woman there, and her making coffee and wearing his robe."

"More to the point is he has a solid alibi, and he's just not part of this. We check the admin and the admin's boy. Cross-check them, and their family, tight friends, with Dudley. We run the weapon. Who buys a freaking bayonet? The same kind who buys a crossbow. A person who has access to high-tech jammers, and the shielding to get them through a scanner. Gotta have skills, or money, or both."

"Probably have to be whacked, too. Killing two people, and it's looking like those two people were pulled out of a hat — if you're right and it's not about the victim as much as the method and the killing."

"Who hires the most exclusive LC in the city, then doesn't take time to bang her? She gets paid a hefty deposit in advance, so it's somebody who doesn't mind pissing several thousand dollars away."

"Not his money anyway, since it came out of Intelicore's coffers."

"Yeah." Eve turned it over in her mind as she drove to Central.

"Back-to-back murders," she said, crossing the underground lot to the elevator. "Both planned out, set up, both using somebody else's ID, and both expensive whoever gets dinged for the cost. Big-ass corporations would probably be insured against this sort of fraud."

"I don't know. Maybe."

"Bet they are. Sweet and Urich will take some heat, but if it can be proved they didn't authorize the payment, they could squeak out of it — and the company probably will. The insurance company takes the hit. Let's find out who insures these people."

They switched to a glide. "Start the runs. I'm going up to EDD, see if they've got anything for us."

For once EDD was almost peaceful. Only a handful manned the cubes and desks at this hour. They paced and pranced, snapped gum and fingers, but there wasn't so much of a crowd. Noting McNab wasn't at his station, she veered off to the lab.

She saw him behind the glass, prancing and snapping — and sucking down a jumbo drink — probably something so sweet it caused the teeth to ache. Roarke sat manning keyboard and screen, his hair tied back, what she assumed was a sensible coffee on the counter.

To her surprise, she saw Feeney, EDD's captain and her former partner. His hair, an explosion of ginger and silver, looked as though he'd been struck by lightning. His face looked saggier than usual, probably because he'd been called into work in the middle of the night. He wore a white shirt more wrinkled than his brown pants.

She stepped in. "Geek report."

Feeney glanced her way. "Kid, can't you catch something normal? Freaking bayonets and crossbows?"

"Keeps me from getting bored."

"Rich people get bored. Working stiffs don't have time to." He took the drink out of McNab's hand, slurped some down. "Security discs got shaked and baked. Solid system for an amusement, but it's compromised. We'll get back what we can."

"It won't be much. Bloody buggering hell." Roarke shoved back. "The system wasn't simply jammed — and in a pinpoint manner at that — but wiped with a shagging virus tossed in for good measure. The device used had to be very sophisticated, possibly military."

"So it's a wash? You can't do anything."

His eyes narrowed, blue lightning, as she'd expected. "It's early days yet, Lieutenant."

"What about general park security? Have we picked her up there?"

"I'm all over that." McNab plopped down, swiveled to a unit. "We've got her coming in. Limo pulls up here, see? Driver gets out."

"Yeah, got her name. We'll talk to her."

"Vic gets out — some legs. Walks straight to the entrance for scan."

"She's looking around for him," Eve added. "Waiting just past the scanners, looking around. There, she spots him. See how she puts on the big smile, gives the hair a toss, starts forward."

"Yeah, and we hit another blip. Just a few seconds. Zap, zap. I've run through with her image as focal, picked up a couple more blips. When you cross them with the layout, you can basically follow them straight to the spook house."

"He didn't waste any time."

"And he knew the layout," Roarke added. "Of the park, and its security.

"But he missed just a nanosecond. Going into the spook house. Switching from jamming the outer cam and the inner. We've got a piece of him."

She saw the partial profile, the shoulder, the side of the body as the killer stepped in, one hand lifted, palm on the back of the white dress Crampton had worn, the other in his pocket.

"Just the face, enhance it."

McNab ordered the computer.

"Facial hair — you catch the side of a

beard. Wearing the hair long. Looks heavier than Urich. A few pounds. It's not him, but from what we can see there's enough resemblance to his ID shot to have fooled her. She's expecting this guy, and he's likely told her what he'd be wearing, maybe how he'd grown the beard, the hair, gained a little weight. She saw what she'd been prepped to see. How much more can we get from this?"

"I'm working on a composite. We can get a solid spec from this. We've got the shape of his face, part of one eye, basic jawline."

"The beard's going to be fake. He's got to convince her he's Urich, so he's got to have something to mask some features. Get me a composite with and without."

"On it."

"Tiny little mistake. He's excited, and he slipped up, just a little bit. He's going to be about Urich's height. Could be wearing lifts, but he's going to be about his height. He could be wearing some padding to add weight, but that doesn't play for me. He'd want to be as close to Urich as possible, so he's a little heavier, carries more pounds. Give me the shoe."

McNab blinked, shrugged. "Okay."

"Enhance."

She narrowed her eyes. "They're — what

do you call them — loafers. Dark brown, look expensive. Let's get a make on them."

"Taught her everything she knows," Feeney said to Roarke. "Nice play."

"He likes good shoes," Eve continued, "and he can afford them. Why wear expensive shoes to a murder at an amusement park?"

"Not everyone is as dismissive of good footwear as you, darling."

She turned a beady eye on Roarke. "No darlings from civilians. Sneaks or skids make more sense. You can move faster if you have to. It's Coney freaking Island. It's a playground. But he wears good shoes. He's vain, and he likes expensive, exclusive. Or maybe he's just used to them. He's going to kill her, but he wants her to notice he's got good taste and the dough to float it.

"Keep at it," she told McNab. "I need a minute with you." She crooked a finger at Roarke as she walked out.

When he'd followed her out, Roarke wrapped a light grip around the finger she'd crooked. "Try to remember I'm your husband, not a subordinate."

"Jeez, sorry. If I'd thought of you as a subordinate I'd probably have told you to get your ass out here. Or words to that effect."

"Most likely true. Still." He gave her finger a quick squeeze. "Let's have a walk. I'm hungry."

"I don't —"

"If I have to settle for something from the pitiful vending choices around here you can walk and talk."

"Fine, fine, fine." She shoved her hands in her pockets as he turned down a corridor toward the pitiful vending choices. "While you're at it, remember you're the one who jumped on board with this."

"I'm well aware." He stood in front of one of the machines, scowling at the offerings. "I suppose the crisps are the safest."

"Just use my code. It's —"

"I know what your code is." He ordered five bags.

"Jesus, I guess you are hungry."

"You're having one, and you'll toss one to Peabody. The others are for my lab mates."

While the machine, which was never quite so cooperative with her, jingled out the data on the soy chips, Roarke studied her. "What do you need?"

"I just have a couple questions. Does your control-the-global-economy corps have insurance against hacking and fraud?"

"Of course."

"Yeah, so if Sweet or Urich worked for

you, and this went down, you'd be covered."

"There'd be an investigation, which would take time, and possibly some legal wrangling, but yes. That's good," he added as he gathered up the bags. "I hadn't gotten that far yet."

"Makes you the subordinate."

He pinched her. "Makes me focused on the trees — or the data and imaging — rather than the forest. It would cost the companies time and some money, but it's relatively small change. The publicity could cause more damage, but they'll have their spinners working on that. Cooperating with the authorities, full internal investigation. And they'll likely chop a head or two."

"Yeah, that was Urich's take. As emperor of all you survey, do you know or have access to the codes and passwords of your employees?"

"If you mean as head of Roarke Industries do I have full access to that data, yes."

"Because you can out-hack the hackers, or because of your position?"

"Both. Isn't this interesting?"

"Maybe. What do you know about Winston Cunningham Dudley the Fourth?"

"Friends call him Winnie."

"Seriously?" She shook her head. "Do you?"

"No, but then I don't know him, particularly. We've met, certainly, at charity events, that sort of thing, but don't have anything in common."

"You're both really rich."

"There's a difference between multigenerational wealth and wealth more recently and personally acquired."

"So he's a fuck-headed snob?"

He laughed. "You do whittle things down. I have no idea. What I do know, and that's more impression and passing commentary, is he seems to enjoy his privilege and socializes with his own kind. Dudley and Son is solid and run well. If you're considering he's gone on a murderous rampage, folding in one of his top people, I'd have to ask why would he?"

"That's another area. I'm just trying to get a feel. What about the other company, Intelicore, and the other guy. Sylvester Bennington Moriarity the Third. And where do they come up with these names?"

"I think the fourth speaks for itself. Given our background and lineage, when we have children, we'll have to make up impressive names. Like Bartholomew Ezekiel."

"If we have a kid, I hope I like him better than to do that to him."

"That would be a factor." He turned back

to the machine and ordered a citrus power drink.

"You have coffee."

"Which is, thanks to this consultation, cold by now. I want something to wash down these crisps. I don't know Moriarity any better than the other — I believe friends call him Sly. If memory serves, they're both in their forties, grew up in the lifestyle one expects on that level. They play polo or squash or golf, I imagine."

"You don't like them."

"I don't know them," he repeated. "But no, not particularly, and that would be mutual. Their type has a built-in distrust and disdain for my type. Money polishes up the street rat, darling, but it doesn't exterminate it."

"Then I don't like them either." When he raised his brows, she poked him in the belly. "It's pretty clear one or both of them dissed my man. That's my job."

"Hold this?" he said and pushed the drink into her hand. Then he used his free hand to poke her in the belly in turn. "Thanks for that. But even if we deem them fuckheaded snobs, it's a long distance to murder."

"Gotta check the angles. Here." She pushed the drink back at him, took the two bags of soy chips. "Go do what you do, and I'll do the same. Thanks for the chips," she said as she walked away.

"You bought them."

"Right." She turned, walked backward a moment. "You're welcome."

9

Eve tossed Peabody the bag of chips as she walked into the nearly empty bullpen.

"Hey, thanks!"

"Did you earn it?"

"I've got a series of runs and searches going. So far, I can't find any connection between Sweet and Urich. They both belong to health clubs, but different ones. Sweet has a cabin deal upstate. Urich has a summer place in the Hamptons, but the wife got that in the settlement anyway. They didn't grow up or go to school anywhere near each other. They have different doctors in different areas of the city. They don't even shop in the same areas."

"Check out the exes. Might as well be thorough."

"I got that started, too. So far, zip. Did a secondary run on the driver tonight. Nothing there, either. She's worked for the service seven years, clean slate, no intersects

I've found with Sweet. She has driven Urich a number of times, but that's to be expected. I'm looking at Urich's admin and her assistant. Not hitting anything yet."

"McNab's going to send down data on a pair of shoes. I want to know venues for purchase."

"Shoes?"

"We got a partial image from park security. It's not much, but we can get the shoe. I'm going to check out the vic's place, get her appointment book."

Peabody opened the chips, took a deep sniff. "You don't want me along?"

"We need to get this drone work done. When you've got a good handle on it, take an hour — two if you need it — in the crib."

She fueled up with coffee, then headed out. She started to leave the top up, just as a matter of principle, but decided what the hell. Who was going to see her zipping around topless at four in the morning?

Added to it, when she pulled to the curb in front of the shiny building on Park Avenue, the droid doorman didn't sneer at her. Instead, he hustled up, respect in every circuit to open her door.

"Good morning, miss. How can I help you?"

"By not calling me miss." Pleased, she

pulled out her badge. "It's Lieutenant. I'm leaving my ride here. Nobody touches it. I need access to Ava Crampton's unit."

"Miss — Lieutenant. Ms. Crampton hasn't returned home this morning."

"And she won't be, seeing as she's dead."

He got that blank droid stare while he processed the unexpected information. "I'm sorry to hear that. Ms. Crampton was a valued tenant."

"Yeah. Code me in."

"I'm afraid I'll need to verify your identification before admitting you."

She held the badge up again, waited while its eyes scanned, while they processed. "Has anyone else tried to get into her place tonight?"

"No. Ms. Crampton occupied the penthouse triple, west corner, and there has been no exit or entrance to that unit since Ms. Crampton herself left at . . ." It got that droid stare again. "Twenty-two-thirty-two. At which time she took a private transportation, with driver, to an unknown to me destination. Do you require data on the transportation and/or driver?"

"No, I've got that."

"I'll pass you through to Ms. Crampton's unit. Will you require my assistance?"

"All I require you to do is make sure my

ride stays like it is, where it is."

"Absolutely."

Crampton had lived the high life, Eve thought as she rode a private elevator to the sixty-first floor. Three-level corner penthouse, with roof garden, on an exclusive piece of real estate.

More than sex, she mused. It took more than acrobatics and a good body to earn what it took to maintain this lifestyle.

The triple opened up into a sweeping foyer with an intricate chandelier of tangled and glinting silver draped with diamond-clear glass. Dark wood floors provided a canvas for rugs in bold colors and complicated patterns. Art maintained the theme, slashing hot, mixed colors and strange shapes against warm cream walls.

Furnishings, she noted as she wandered through the main level, managed to marry that complex style with sumptuous comfort. Deep, deep cushions and plenty of them, sparkling lights, mirrored tables, countless pillows.

A silver dining table held a huge clear vase of flowers someone with an artist's eye had arranged — and recently. Over an ebony fireplace in that room reigned a pretty spectacular portrait of its former occupant, boldly nude as she reclined on a bed draped in red.

So, she hadn't been the shy, modest type.

Eve swung through kitchen, powder rooms, a separate living area, admired the views more out of curiosity than necessity. It helped give her a sense of the woman. Lived full, she thought, lived well and enjoyed the fruits of her labors.

She took the clear curl of stairs rather than the elevator to the second floor.

The master — or mistress — bedroom was massive, and needed to be to accommodate the bed. Eve estimated it could sleep six, and wondered passingly if it had. She'd gone for gold tones in here, warm rather than glossy. And had spread the bed with what looked to be an acre of textured gold silk. Curvy sofas, more pillows, carved tables, lamps dripping with beads, and another, less massive arrangement of flowers continued the indulgent, sink-into-it style.

In the many drawers of the bedside tables, Eve found an expansive and efficiently organized arrangement of sex toys and enhancements.

She estimated the dressing room/closet combo to be about the size of her bullpen at Central, and also strictly organized. Full of rich fabrics, she noted, pricey labels, and enough shoes to outfit the population of a small country.

A tall, drawered case was locked and bolted to the floor. Jewelry, she decided. She'd get to that.

For now, she took a look at the bathroom, decided Crampton might just out-Roarke Roarke in some areas, then wandered the second floor.

Two guest suites, both generous and well outfitted, a second lounging area with a small, efficient kitchen . . . and an equally well-outfitted S&M room. Plenty of black leather, velvet ropes, a selection of whips and crops, restraints. Another bed, this one draped in black satin, a jeweled case of small knives with ornate handles.

She went to the third level. Here, she mused, was the business center. A CEO's office, luxurious certainly, but designed for serious business. A full wall of screens, organized file discs, a muscular data-and-communications center. It boasted another small kitchen with a stocked AutoChef and full-sized fridge, a bar holding several bottles of good wine, liquor, mixers.

She expected the computer to be secured and passcoded, and it was. Leaving that for the moment, she rifled through drawers until she found the appointment book. She found the entries both businesslike and discreet.

On the day she died, Ava Crampton spent the afternoon in her salon for what Eve assumed was the works. At five she'd scheduled a Catrina Bigelo for two hours at the Palace. Roarke's hotel, Eve thought. Why not fuck in the best?

She had Foster Urich listed, with a ten-thirty P.M. pickup by Elegant Transportation, for the meet at Coney Island. A four-hour date, with the option for overnight held open.

Costly, she mused.

Ava had a notation after his name. New Client, vetted and cleared.

Eve used her com to schedule an EDD team to pick up the electronics, but there was little else. The answers, she thought, weren't here in the victim's space. Still, they'd have to look through that space, at her, at all of her secrets.

She pressed her fingers to her eyes, rubbed hard, tried to will her second wind to kick in. She glanced with longing at the Auto-Chef thinking of coffee. She'd bet the vic sprang for real.

But copping a cup was disrespectful.

She pushed herself to her feet. She'd just

have to choke down whatever she could find on the street, get the boost if not the flavor.

By the time she came out of the building, New York was changing shifts. Those who played or worked by night started home, or to wherever they hoped to flop for the night. Those who lived by day switched on lights in their apartments, hurried to catch the early train or tram. Sanitation crawled down the streets, clanging dully about its work.

But along with the scent of garbage she caught the perfume of bakeries, pushing the sugary, yeasty smells outside through their venting to lure in that change of shift.

She remembered the chips she'd tossed on the passenger seat, and had them for breakfast as she drove to the morgue. There, she settled on a tube of cold caffeine, much safer than what passed as coffee.

She didn't expect anyone to have started the PM on Crampton. She simply wanted another look at her victim before she went back to Central.

She walked into Morris's suite, and there he was, putting on his protective gear with the body already prepped and on his table.

"Did you catch the night shift?" she asked. Then she saw it, the sadness, the signs of a sleepless night.

He wore black again, stark and unrelieved.

"No. But I see you did." He sealed his hands as he studied the body. "She was particularly beautiful."

"Yeah. Top-tier LC."

"So I saw in your report. I don't have anything for you. I haven't started."

"I was in the field, and wanted another look at her before I went in." She hesitated, but the unhappiness on his face twisted her up. "Bad night?"

He looked up, met her eyes. "Yes." Now he hesitated while she tried to figure out what to say, or if to say anything.

"There are times I miss her more than seems possible, or bearable. It's better. I know it's better because it's not every moment of every day, or even every day, every night. But there are times I realize, again, there is no Amaryllis Coltraine in the world, in my life, and it chokes me."

She didn't think about what she could or should say now, but only said what came through the heart and into her mind. "I don't know how much better it gets, Morris, or how long it takes. I don't know how people get through it."

"Minute by minute, then hour by hour, then day by day. Work is solace," he said, "friends are comfort. Life is for the living.

You and I know that, even though we spend so much time with the dead — maybe because of that we know we have to live. Chale has been a great help to me."

"That's good," she said, thinking of the priest she'd suggested Morris talk to. "You can . . . you know, anytime."

"Yes." His lips curved. "I know. You're work, and a friend, so have been both solace and comfort." He sighed, looked at the body again. "So."

"I'll let you work."

"Tell me about her," he said before she turned away. "What's not in your report."

"She lived well. She took care of herself, of her business. I think she was smart, and I think she took pride in her work, and I think she must have enjoyed it. I don't think you can be really good at something, not for the long haul, if you don't enjoy it. I guess she liked people, and making them feel important and desirable, and she knew how to do it. Not just the sex, I don't see how that's enough. She was a native New Yorker, working-class family, parents split when she was a kid. She got her first-level license at nineteen, kept her record clean, took the classes and tests for higher levels, worked her way up. I think she lived just the way she wanted to live, for as long as she had."

197

"What else is there? Thank you."

"I've got to get back." She started for the door, stopped when she reached it. "Listen, Morris, maybe you could come over for dinner or something." When he simply watched her, smiling, she shrugged. "You know, Roarke could play with that grill he got last year. We could do a summer deal, some friends, some cow meat."

"I'd like that."

"Well, I'll fix it up, let you know."

As she walked out, she heard him speak into the record. "Victim is mixed-race female."

She pulled out her 'link as she walked outside, and set for message only on the tag.

Even so, Charles Monroe answered. "Good morning, Lieutenant Sugar."

"What, is everybody up at dawn today?"

"We are. Louise had night duty at the clinic and just got home. I'm making breakfast. Want an omelet?"

"I was going to leave you a message, see if you could give me a little time today."

"For you, any . . ." The smile faded from his face. "I wasn't thinking. You call at this hour, someone's dead. Someone I know?"

"I'm not sure. Ava Crampton."

"Ava?" He dragged a hand through his

hair. "Yes, I know her. What happened? Can you tell me?"

"I'd rather not over my pocket 'link. I'm out in the field, not that far away. I could —"

"Come over."

"On my way."

The garden Louise had planted in the days before she and Charles married thrived. More sweet than elegant, with just a touch of wild, it added another layer of personality to the townhouse they shared.

Louise met her at the door, her blond curls still a little damp from her shower. She took Eve's hand, drew her in to kiss her cheek. "I wish somebody didn't have to die for you to come by."

"You look good." Still sun-kissed from the honeymoon, Eve thought, and still glowing from the happiness marriage brought her. "Sorry to cut in on your personal time."

"We're having breakfast. Charles is cooking — really cooking. His omelets are incredible. So you'll eat with us while you talk to Charles."

Louise walked her back to the kitchen as she spoke. Charles stood over the stove, shaking a skillet back and forth. "Just in time," he said. "Have a seat."

"Is your AutoChef broken?"

"I like to cook when there's time and a reason."

"It smells good." Louise put a mug in her hand, and Eve drank automatically. "Oh, this is real coffee. This alone is a reason to believe in God."

"Wait till you taste my omelet. You'll testify. What happened to Ava?"

"I'm sorry about your friend."

"We were friendly, but not really close. I liked her, you had to. She was charming and bright and just interesting. I can't believe it was a client. She was so careful."

"It was and it wasn't. He set her up, used false ID, covered himself thoroughly from the way it looks. She met him at the amusement park on Coney Island. Public place. She'd vetted him. I don't see she'd have had anything to question."

"You're saying she didn't even know him?"

"It looks that way. Like I said, she vetted him — or so it reads in her appointment book. How would she go about that?" With a skill that surprised Eve, Charles slid a fluffy omelet onto a plate, then poured more egg mixture into the skillet.

"Eat that while it's hot," he told her. "She'd have done a background check, similar to what police or private investigators would do. She'd access his criminal record, if he had one, his employment, his marital status."

"Basic data?"

"Yeah. Then she'd do a search for articles on or by him, mentions in the media. Then, I have to assume she'd run a program that would extrapolate all the information she'd gathered and give him a rating. By the time she met him, she'd have a good idea who he was, what his habits were, his lifestyle. It's a matter of protecting yourself, but also a method to give the LC a sense of what the client may be looking for."

"So she'd be careful," Eve said, "but at the same time, she was a risk taker. I saw the S&M room in her place."

"I worked with her once or twice." He completed another omelet. "But not in that area."

Eve drank her coffee, and wondered how Louise could sit, eating an omelet, while her husband talked about his experiences in group sex.

When he finished the last omelet, he sat to join them.

"Charles, this is wonderful." Smiling at him, Louise topped off his coffee from the pot on the counter. "You never said how she was killed, Dallas."

"She was stabbed," Eve said and left it at that for now.

"And her killer was masquerading as this other man, the man she vetted?"

"That's right."

"He must have looked enough like him to fool her."

"Yeah, we're working on that. Would she have kept the appointment, gone on with it, if she'd known this wasn't the man who'd booked?"

"No." Charles shook his head. "She'd have risked her license, and that she'd never have done. And going with someone you haven't checked out is just too dangerous. She did like the edge, but not enough to put herself in that kind of situation. She liked variety in the work, but she followed the rules. When a client hires someone at Ava's level, he or she — or they — aren't just paying for sex. They're paying for an experience relatively few can afford. She'd provide that, but she'd stay within the law and she'd have taken every reasonable precaution to protect herself."

Maybe, Eve thought, but it hadn't been enough.

When Eve got back to Central, Peabody wasn't at her desk, but most of her detectives were. Baxter, looking sleek as a fashion vid, glanced up from his.

"Took her crash time," Baxter told her. "She's been down about fifteen."

"Fine."

"Mira's in your office."

"Oh."

"My boy and I are heading out. Got a floater in the pond in Central Park. Couple of kids found it."

"Nice way to start the day."

"Fun never ends."

Mira sat in Eve's ugly visitor's chair in her pretty pale pink suit. She'd matched the suit with heels several shades deeper and a multi-chain necklace with tiny little pearls and colored stones. Her rich brown hair curled around her lovely face in a way both stylish and flattering.

Her quiet blue eyes tracked up from the screen of her PPC to meet Eve's.

"I was just rereading your data. I had some time now so thought I'd wait for you here."

"I appreciate you getting to it so fast." It threw her off, just a little. Consults were usually in Mira's airy office, and included cups of flowery tea Eve pretended to drink.

Which reminded her to offer.

"You want some tea or something?"

"Actually, I'd love some of your coffee. Dennis and I were out late last night with friends. I could use the boost."

"Sure."

"Have you slept?"

"Not yet. I'll get some in when I can." Sometime between the vic's apartment and Central her second wind had settled in.

Maybe it was the omelets.

"He's hit fast," Eve said as she took the steaming mugs from the AutoChef. "Two for two. Both risky, organized, and planned."

"Yes. He's organized, controlled enough to spend time with, and interact with, his victims and maintain his prepared persona. Clients, both times."

Eve turned with the coffee in her hand. "He buys his kill."

The smile lit Mira's face. "You could have gone into my line of work."

"No thanks. You have to be nice to the whacked. Buys his kill," she repeated. "That's an interesting angle. Does he figure since he's paid for them, they're his to bag? Like a hunter. But you don't hunt with a bayonet, so the hunting thing's thin."

"I'm not sure. We think of a bayonet as a wartime weapon, when man certainly hunts man. The killer has chosen the ground, established the rules — his — selected the weapon. All in advance."

"But in Houston's case, he couldn't know, not for certain, who he'd get for prey. No, that's not right," Eve corrected. "You don't know which furry animal you're going to shoot in the woods. It's just the species — the type. You go after a type. He likes the rush."

"In both cases, it was a fairly close-in kill, and in a location where discovery was a factor — and likely part of the excitement. He's mature, and the esoteric nature of the weapons tells me he's interested in the unique — in showing his knowledge and his skill."

"Showing off, that's how it hits me."

"Yes. God, this is good," Mira murmured over her coffee. "He has wealth or access to it. Excellent e-skills, or again access to them. His choice of the men whose identification he used tells me one of two things: He either resents those in authority, specifically in the corporate world, or he considers them subordinates, those to be made use of."

Mira angled her head. "Why does that make you smile?"

"It fits in with this theory I'm playing with, which seemed a long reach. You just shortened it. We've looked at people who work under Sweet and Urich, particularly the immediate staff, ones who'd either know the codes and passwords or would be able to get them. As it is I've got one asshole I'm bringing in today on another deal just because he fits. So I thought, maybe look up instead of down."

Intrigued, Mira nodded and gave herself the pleasure of just breathing in the scent of coffee. "Higher up the corporate level?"

"Might as well start at the top. Let's play this." Eve sat on the corner of the desk so she faced Mira. "He buys his kill — boy, I like that one — he feels entitled to them. They're expensive, exclusive. They're indulgences only people with enough scratch can have, so buying them makes him important. Now he wants more bang for the buck, isn't that the expression? And he wants to show off his smarts, his skills, his . . . creativity. He doesn't mess them up, no smacking around, mutilation, no sexual assault."

"Time would have been a factor," Mira pointed out.

"Yeah, but if you can plan it out that well, you could plan more time if you wanted to mutilate, to rape or humiliate. He doesn't, as far as I can tell, bother with souvenirs. Crampton had a lot of jewelry on her. It only takes a second to rip off a necklace, pull off a ring."

"He doesn't care about what's theirs," Mira said. "I agree."

"It's not personal, it's not passionate, it's not even a little pissed off. It's just plan it out, play it out, and walk away. But he leaves the weapon so we can see how frosty he is."

"You're considering these thrill kills. No motive other than the kill itself."

"We haven't found a connection between the vics. Nothing. We'll keep digging, and when he kills the next one, we'll look there. But we won't find it. They're just part of the package."

"He'll be mature, as I said. Educated, well spoken, able to assume roles and adapt to situations. He had to convince his two victims he was who they expected. A man of certain means planning to surprise his wife with a romantic gesture. A man, again of certain means, looking for sex and companionship after the failure of his marriage. Different types, different dynamics. He had to assume both personas long enough to position his quarry in the kill zone."

Mira sipped more coffee, shifted so her pretty necklace caught some of the light through Eve's narrow window. "He's certainly outlined and researched the next victim type, location, method. The time and timing. He most likely lives alone, or with someone he dominates. Both killings took place late in the evening and took considerable time to set up. It would be difficult to do that if he has a spouse or cohab unless he isn't questioned in the home, or manufactured careful reasons to be absent. He made no attempt to disguise what he'd done by the pretense of robbery. So I'll add confident, and arrogant."

Mira checked the time. "I need to go."

"Thanks for the time."

Mira rose, handed Eve the empty cup, then, smiling, laid her palm on Eve's cheek. "Get a little sleep, Eve."

"Yeah, I'll work it in."

But when Mira left, she turned to the work. And she smiled grimly when she scanned Peabody's update. She and McNab had made the shoe.

"Emilio Stefani, leather loafer, high shine, sterling silver buckle detail. Retails for . . . you have got to be kidding me. Three thousand for a pair of knock-around shoes?"

It simply offended her sensibilities. But she moved on.

"This many outlets carry this bastard? What is wrong with people? Still, it's a good lead."

She read further, nodded again. McNab might dress like a psychotic clown, but he had a cop's brain. He'd done some comp magic and estimated the shoe size as between ten and ten and a half, leaning toward the ten.

Now it was a damn good lead.

She ordered background checks on both Dudley and Moriarity, ordered the computer to analyze the shoe vendors and produce the three most exclusive. With that running, she arranged for a couple of uniforms to bring Mitchell Sykes and his cohab in for questioning.

Her incoming signaled, so she read Morris's preliminary report. No surprises. She considered snarling at the lab for more information on the bayonet but decided she was too fuzzy in the brain to deal with the new, improved Dickhead.

It seemed the second wind — or the omelets — had worn off.

Thirty minutes down, she told herself, and locking her door, stretched out on the floor. "Computer, set wake-up alarm for thirty minutes."

Acknowledged.

It was the last thing she heard.

Minutes later, Roarke bypassed her locks

and stepped in to find her. Facedown on the floor, he thought, sprawled out like the dead she stood for.

He thought surely there was a better place for a nap, but reengaged the locks before stretching out beside her.

He fell into sleep in seconds.

Dallas, your thirty-minute rest period has ended.

"Crap. I'm up." She opened one eye, then jerked awake. "Jesus, Roarke."

"You're entitled to a larger office, you know. One big enough to accommodate a couch. And I much preferred what we did together on the floor yesterday to this."

She rubbed her gritty eyes. "Didn't I lock that door?"

He only smiled. "I need to go into my own office for a few hours, and wanted to kiss my wife good-bye. Why didn't you go up to the crib for your thirty-minute rest period?"

"It's disgusting. You don't know who's going to walk in, or who was in there last, or what they were doing with whoever else might've been in there."

"That's a point." He sat up so they were face-to-face. "But I'm not sure this is better." As Mira had, he laid a hand on her

210

cheek. "You need more sleep."

"Skillet, pan."

"What?"

"You know, the skillet says the pan's the same deal."

He thought a moment. "I believe that's the pot calling the kettle black."

"Whatever, kitchen stuff can't talk anyway. McNab and Peabody made the shoe."

"Yes, I know."

"Three large for something you wear so your foot's not walking on the ground."

He decided against telling her how much he'd paid for the boots she was currently wearing. "You should be pleased. They'll be easier to track than something you could pick up for a hundred at Discount Shoes."

"True. I've got to screw with the little bastard — the drug pusher — then I'm going to go have a chat with The Third and The Fourth."

"You have fun." He leaned in to kiss her. I'll see you at home when we get there." He stood, pulled her to her feet, then pleased himself by drawing her into his arms. "We'll catch up on all this, and each other, over dinner."

"Yeah, I . . ." She leaned back, met his eyes with a smile in hers. "That's it."

"Is it?" he murmured and rubbed his lips to hers.

"Not that it. I went by to see Charles to talk to him about the second vic. And he's making breakfast for Louise because she pulled an all-nighter at the clinic. I mean cooking, like with eggs and that skillet thing. And we're sitting there eating omelets —"

"You had an omelet, and I get a bag of crisps."

"It just worked out that way. He's talking to me about LC stuff, and how he worked with the vic a couple times. And I'm thinking isn't this weird for her, for Louise to sit there and eat breakfast while we're talking about sex and S&M and clients? But it's not. It's their deal, that's all it is. It's kind of like you and me talking murder over dinner. It's just part of the package."

"I like our package." He tapped her on the chin. "Try not to work my cop until she falls down."

"He's going to kill again, and soon," she said when Roarke walked to the door. "He's already booked the appointment, or at the very least keyed it into his schedule. And it won't matter who it is, but what they are. He'll enjoy it, and that really pisses me off."

"Then think how pissed off he'll be when

212

you stop him."

"I'm counting on it. See you later."

10

Eve gathered what she needed before walking out of her office into the bullpen.

"Peabody, with me," she said, and kept walking.

Peabody scrambled to catch up. "We nailed the shoe."

"Good work. The top — when you're talking important and exclusive — vendor in the city is the designer's boutique on Madison. We'll need a list of people who bought that shoe in the size range."

"Shopping! Even if I couldn't afford the toe of a pair of socks in a place like that."

"Field work," Eve corrected. "First we're going to ruin Mitchell Sykes's day. He's in Interview A, and he's mine. You've got the cohab in B."

"I get to work her solo." Peabody rubbed her hands together.

"I want you to go in like this is in the bag. We got everything we need to put her over, but the PA wants to save the taxpayers some money, and offer a deal. First one to lay it all out, verify the skim and scam, gets to plead to misappropriation of prescription drugs and a lighter sentence."

"Because we want her to roll on Sykes."

"We do."

"And I get to be disgusted the PA isn't fully backing our play because it's all politics and crap. So here's the deal, sister, and you better grab it before your playmate does."

Eve rubbed her ear. "See where it takes you. If you get a sense she's as much an asshole as he is, change your tactic. We'll get them both on the whole shot. But I want to put this away fast. We've got bigger fish to bake."

"Fry. Fish to fry."

"Jesus, why would you care how metaphorically fish is cooked?"

Eve peeled off, stepped into Interview A. "Dallas, Lieutenant Eve, entering Interview with Sykes, Mitchell. Hey, Mitch, how's it going?"

"I don't have time for this."

"Who does?"

"Look, I told you what I know about all this already. I don't have to be here, but Mr. Sweet's directive is for full cooperation with the police."

"Sweet," she said, to amuse herself. "Have you been read your rights?"

"No. Why would I —"

"It's routine, Mitch, everybody knows that." She reeled off the Revised Miranda. "So, do you understand your rights and obligations?"

He let out a long, windy sigh. "Of course I do."

"Excellent. So, since we're both busy, let's get right to the point. You and your cohab are deep in shit. My partner's got her down the hall and is, right now, giving her a deal. I don't want to give you one because I just don't like you."

His shoulders jerked the instant Eve mentioned his cohab. "I don't know what you're talking about, but I don't have to listen to this."

"Yeah, you do, because you're under arrest. You and your girlfriend have been procuring drugs from Dudley and Son, and selling them on the open market. I know this, have solid evidence of same — that secret account of yours isn't a secret anymore."

She smiled pleasantly while a thin line of sweat formed over his top lip. "Basically what we're doing here is just a formality, and more about my personal satisfaction."

She spread her hands. "I've got to squeeze in some fun now and again, right?"

"You . . . you're making all this up."

"Got you cold, Mitch. You and Karolea Prinz stole from your own company, then profited on the weaknesses, needs, and sickness of others by distributing what you stole."

She leaned on the table, inching a little closer to his sweaty face. "You split the profits and set up a couple of offshore accounts under the name Sykpri Development." She watched his face go paler, paler. "The tax guys are going to have their fun with you on that deal later. But for now, it's all mine. Prinz is confirming the details right now with my partner in another interview room."

"I — I don't have anything to say. I want to talk to Karolea."

"You don't have to talk to me, but you won't be talking to her either. She's busy saving her own ass at the moment. Now we can move on because it strikes me that anybody who'd steal and sell drugs, who'd have the skill to set up an account that isn't flagged by the usual regulations, wouldn't have any problem screwing with his boss's ID and credit, using that to cover his sorry ass when he killed."

"I'm not a killer!" This time his voice squeaked, just a little ratlike sound that warmed Eve's heart. "Good God, I never killed anyone."

"Well, let's see. You're a thief, a liar, an illegals pusher, as well as being a complete dick." She sat as if weighing the notion. "Yeah, it's just a short step to murder. Maybe it went like this: You used Jamal's company and services to reach a higher-income client base, then he wants a bigger cut. Or maybe has a change of heart. Can't have that, so you have to take him out, don't you? And why not frame your own boss — get a twofer. Maybe a nice promotion. Then —"

"No!" He leaped out of the chair, then dropped straight down again as if his legs couldn't hold him. "I didn't even know that man, that Jamal person. I'm not a murderer!"

"Just a thief, liar, illegals pusher, and complete dick?" She shrugged. "Convince me, because I've got things to do, Mitch, and this one's looking all wrapped up with a bow on it."

"You're crazy." His eyes bulged and wheeled. "It's crazy."

"That's not convincing."

"Listen . . ." He tugged at the knot of his

218

tie, wet his lips. "Okay, fine, we skimmed some inventory."

"Inventory, as in drugs. As a rep for Dudley, Karolea could access them."

"Yes. Yes. All we had to do was doctor the logs, tweak the invoices. It's not a big deal. The company builds that kind of loss into the budget. We just wanted the money. I'm entitled to some perks considering the hours I put in. Do you know how much my education cost? And I'm stuck running errands for Sweet? We didn't hurt anyone. We . . . we provide a service. We sell at a discount."

"You steal drugs from Dudley —"

"Karolea acquires the merchandise," he said quickly. "She handles that area. I'm in sales."

"I see. So she acquires the drugs, and you sell them."

"Yes. We have regular customers. It's not as if we're peddling Zeus on street corners to children. These are safe medications. We're helping people."

"Like the guy who's addicted to painkillers and buys from you instead of going to the medicals for rehab or assistance. Or the one who ODs on tranqs, or the ones who mix the chemicals to get high. Or the ones, you fuckhead, who resell to kids on street corners."

"We're not responsible for —"

"Cut the crap. You've confessed, on the record. I don't need your sob stories and justifications."

"You can't seriously believe I killed that driver."

"Oh, hell no. I just said that so you'd spill your guts on the rest. Good job." She checked the time. "Now we can both get out of here. Me to work, you to your cell."

"But . . . I want a lawyer."

"No problem. They'll let you contact one on your way to booking. Thank you for your cooperation. Interview end."

She rose, opened the door, and hailed the waiting uniforms. "Walk him through, let him contact his lawyer."

She walked into Observation and watched Peabody wrap up a weeping Karolea Prinz.

"She cried a lot," Peabody said when they headed down to the garage. "I mean a lot. She says, or thinks, she's in love with the asshole. Didn't want to roll, but —"

"Push comes to shove, love goes down."

"I guess, except when it's really love. Do we get to go look at shoes now?"

"We're not looking at shoes. We know the shoe already. I want to make this quick."

"Shoes are fun." Peabody gave a little bounce of enthusiasm on her own. "It'll be good to have the side benefit of fun after all that crying. See, it's a nice combo. Shutting down a small, yet profitable prescription drug scam, running down a lead on the investigation, and getting to gaze longingly at shoes I'll never be able to afford, but imagining I could."

"You know what happens to people who longingly imagine having things they can't afford?"

"Happy dreams?"

"A life of crime."

As she drove, Eve considered that possibility as applied to the case. "Maybe this guy gazes longingly at fancy limos and high-priced LCs, and it just pisses him off he can't order them up like pizza. So he vents the anger and frustration by killing them. Which isn't bad as theories go except for the shoes. When you've got three thousand to spend on a pair of designer loafers, you're not hurting."

"Maybe he stole them," Peabody suggested. "Or got them as a gift, or blew a wide chunk of his savings just to have them for his own."

"All possible, and ors that shouldn't be dismissed. But he'd also have to spend a chunk on a crossbow and bolts — pricey ones, and an antique bayonet. Unless he scammed someone else's ID to acquire those. He still has to connect somewhere to the two corporations. Otherwise, why go through all the layers on the security there?"

It kept coming back to the companies, Eve concluded. "If he's just a homicidal hacker, he could've accessed any IDs and credit lines — and he could afford all the fancy limos and high-priced LCs he wanted anyway, so it doesn't jell."

Eve twitched her head toward the dash comp when it signaled incoming data.

"It's from the lab," Peabody told her. "A report on the weapon. Antique is right. It's mid–twentieth century. Dickhead's got make, manufacturer, even a serial number. Pretty thorough."

"You be thorough, start a search. Find us the owner."

It gave Eve a few minutes of quiet. Who was next on his list? she wondered. What type? Maybe a top-drawer salon tech, private shuttle pilot, some hot, exclusive designer.

She thought of Leonardo, her oldest friend's husband. And Mavis herself, Eve thought with a clutch in her belly. Famous music vid star. She'd make a point of checking in with them, putting them on alert.

No private gigs until she cleared it.

"It's not registered." Peabody looked up as Eve hunted for a parking spot. "It hasn't been sold by any legit vendor in the last twenty years. Something that old could've been bought twice that long ago, before weapons of that kind had to be registered. It could've been passed down through a family or something. It's military, and there's no way to trace the original owner back a hundred years. There's no records on that kind of thing."

"Okay." She hit vertical, causing Peabody to yelp, and squeezed into a second-level spot. "So he already owned it, skipped the registration — thousands do — or he picked it up on the shady side. More thousands do."

They walked down to street level, and the half block to the shoe boutique. As they passed the display window Peabody let out a distinctive yummy noise.

"Don't do that. For God's sake, you're a cop on a homicide investigation, not some tourist window-shopping."

"But look at the blue ones with the silver heels with the little butterflies."

Eve gave the shoes a narrowed stare. "Ten minutes on the feet, two hours in traction." She pushed through the door.

The air smelled like the sort of flowers shoe butterflies probably rocked on. Shoes and bags were displayed under individual sparkling lights, like art or jewelry. Seating spread in chocolate-colored low-backed sofas and cream-colored chairs.

Customers or lookie-loos browsed while others sat, a few surrounded by colorful rivers of shoes. Some of the few wore expressions that put Eve in mind of chemi-heads on a high.

One woman strutted from mirror to mirror in a pair of towering heels the color of iridescent eggs.

The staff stood out from the browsers and strutters as everyone was stick thin and dressed in snug urban black.

Eve heard the gurgle sound in the back of Peabody's throat, and snarled.

"Sorry." Peabody tapped her collarbone. "It's reflex."

"You'll have another reflex when you're on the ground with my boot on your neck."

"Ladies." The man who strolled over boasted a blinding smile and a jacket with sleeves that ended in points as sharp as razors. "What can I do to make your day special?"

Eve pulled out her badge. "Funny you should ask. You can give me the customer list on this shoe, size ten or ten and a half." She held up the printout.

"Really? Is it evidence? How exciting!"

"Yeah, we're thrilled. I want to know who bought this shoe in either of those sizes."

"Absolutely. What fun. How far back would you like me to go?"

"How far back is there?"

"That particular shoe debuted in March."

"Okay, go back to March."

"This store or citywide?"

Eve gave him a cautious stare. "Aren't you the cooperative shoe guy."

"Are you kidding? This is the most fun I've had all day."

"Citywide to start."

"Citywide it is! Give me a few minutes. Have a seat. Would you like some sparkling water?"

"No, we're good."

"That's why people who can afford magilicious shoes shop in these places and pay the full freight." Peabody nodded after the salesman. "You get offered fizzy water by people who look like vid stars."

"And who are so freaking bored they're delirious with joy when you tell them to do a customer search."

"But that's good for us."

"Yeah, it is."

Peabody clasped her hands together. "Please, you don't need me until he comes back. Five minutes is all I ask to worship at the altar of the shoe."

"Don't drool on any of them." Eve turned her back, and for the hell of it, tried out her wrist unit in a tag to EDD.

"Any progress?" she asked Feeney.

"We're going to be able to give you that projection on the rest of the killer's face. But there's nothing on the other discs at this point." He pursed his lips. "You got a new 'link."

"Sort of."

"Trans is crystal."

"It's my wrist unit."

"Get out. Those kinds of toys have crap trans."

"New model."

"Roarke didn't mention it. I want a look at that when you come in."

"Maybe." She saw the salesclerk walking back, a little spring in his step. "Gotta go."

"And here we are." He handed her a disc. "We sold a pair in that color choice in size ten last March, by the way, and another pair in a ten and a half just last month. In Raven, we sold —"

"I didn't ask about Raven. You sold two pair of those in four months?"

"In those sizes, in that color, in this store. Citywide includes several department stores and boutiques."

"The ones bought here? Regular customers?"

"As a matter of fact." He nodded. "So I'm afraid they're probably not who you're looking for. Sampson Anthony — the producer — last month, and Winston Dudley, the pharma king — in March."

"Just for fun, because my partner's getting juiced drooling over the shoes in here, who sold those two pair?"

"Patrick's down for Mr. Anthony. And Mr. Dudley only works with Chica."

Eve made a show of glancing over at Peabody. "I can stall another couple minutes. Why don't I take a run at Chica while I'm here, it'll give me something to put in the report and jibe the time she's having a little fun."

"You bet. She's right over there, just finishing with a customer. Aubergine hair."

Aubergine, Eve thought. It looked purple to her. "Appreciate it."

She walked over, sat, gestured.

"And what can I slip on you today?"

"I'll stick with what I got." She held up her badge.

"Okay. Those are good boots for a cop. A

227

good investment, and classic style."

"If you say so. What can you tell me about Winston Dudley?"

"Winnie? Size ten, medium. Slightly high in the arch, but a nice easy fit. He likes what's right off the runway. Favors classic styles, but he'll get crazy now and then."

"Does he come in a lot?"

"It depends on his schedule. Sometimes I take a selection to him."

"You make house calls with shoes?"

"Shoes, belts, ties, bags, other accessories. It's a service we provide to our upper clientele."

"Are you booked to see him anytime soon?"

"No. He was just in, actually, a few days ago. Bought six pair. I probably won't see him, either way, until next month, and then only if he's in town."

Eve took out a card. "Do us both a favor. If he contacts you for an at-home session, you get in touch."

Chica studied the card and for the first time looked concerned. "Why?"

"Because I'm a cop with good boots."

Chica laughed, but turned the card in her hands. "Listen, he's a really good client. I get a nice commission and a generous tip with the at-your-door service, and I'd really hate to do anything to mess that up."

"It won't mess that up."

"I guess it's no skin off mine."

"Good enough." Eve rose, started out. "Peabody, dry your adoring tears. We're done."

"Oh, God!" Peabody beamed as they climbed to the car. "That was the best time. Did you see those —"

"Do not describe a pair of weird-looking, overpriced shoes to me."

"But they were —"

"You'll be crying tears of pain and misery any second. Dudley bought that shoe, right in that store, in March. Size ten."

"No shit?"

"Not a single scoop of shit. We'll run the other name — just one other sale — on the list — and the others citywide, global, too, just to cover bases, but that's just too damn good. Circumstantial, but damn good. Let's go screw with his day. Verify with his HQ he's there. If not, find out where he is."

This time when they arrived at Dudley's, they were met in the lobby by a woman in a dark, pinstriped suit that showed a lot of leg and showcased excellent breasts. She wore her hair pulled back in a long, curly tail from a face boasting a perky, pointed nose, full lips, and wide, deep blue eyes.

"Lieutenant, Detective." She shot out a hand. "I'm Marissa Cline, Mr. Dudley's personal assistant. I'll escort you directly to his office."

"Appreciate the service," Eve said.

Marissa gestured, and began to walk, briskly, on her candy-red heels. Eve wondered if she considered them a good investment.

"Mr. Dudley's very concerned with the situation," Marissa continued, "and the company's indirect involvement in a crime."

She palm-printed a pad, swiped a card in the security slot, then again gestured for Eve and Peabody to step into the elevator.

"Marissa, carrying two, to sixty."

Verified, *the computer responded.* Proceeding.

"So, is Mr. Dudley active in the running of the company?" Eve asked.

"Oh, yes, of course. When Mr. Dudley's father semi-retired three years ago, Mr. Dudley took over the reins, primarily from this HQ."

"Before that?"

Marissa smiled, blankly. "Before?"

"Before he took over the reins?"

"Oh, ah, Mr. Dudley traveled extensively

230

to various other HQs and outlets, gaining a wide range of experience in all levels of the company."

"Okay." Eve wondered if that was corporate speak for Dudley's getting shuffled around, enjoying a variety of travel and partying while his father kept him on the payroll. They stepped out of the elevator into a spacious reception area, stylishly decorated with white lounging chairs equipped with miniscreens. Among the flowers, the refreshment bar, the conversation areas, three attractive women busily worked on comps.

Marissa knocked briskly — brisk seemed to be her mode — on one of the center double doors before tossing them both open.

Winston Dudley's office was more along the lines of a snazzy hotel suite — lush and plush, staggering view, sparkling chandeliers.

A great deal of furniture helped fill the space, artfully arranged in conversational groups. He rose from behind a desk with a black mirrored surface.

He was more attractive in person than the ID shot. Eve put it down to what people called charisma — the way he smiled as he looked you directly in the eye, the way he moved, smooth as a dancer. Just a hint of flirtation in that move, that smile, those eyes, she thought — the sort that said, you're a desirable woman, and I appreciate desirable women.

Avid eyes, she mused, that made her wonder if he'd recently sampled some of his own products.

His hair, so blond as to be nearly white, was swept back from a delicately boned face. Almost feminine, she mused. The features weren't quite as sharp as Urich's, but close.

His suit fit perfectly in a color she thought of as indigo. Old-fashioned links glinted at the cuffs of his pale blue shirt. His ID data, and her visual scan, put him at five feet ten and a half inches, weighing in at one-seventy.

Again, in Urich's ballpark.

His shoes were as black and shiny as his desk, and sported no silver trim.

He took Eve's hand, a firm grip, soft skin, and held it two flirtatious seconds after the shake.

"Lieutenant Dallas. I hoped we'd meet, but under different circumstances. I hope Roarke is well."

"Yeah, he's good."

"And Detective Peabody, a pleasure." He

took her hand. "I recently finished Nadine Furst's book. I feel I know both of you. Please sit down. Black coffee," he said as Marissa lifted a tray, "coffee regular." He tapped the side of his head. "Those details from the book stick. Thanks, Marissa. We'll let you know if we need anything else."

He sat on one of the wide chairs, laid his forearms on the wide arms. "I know you're here about the murder of the driver, and our own Augustus Sweet. It's very distressing. What can I do to help?"

"You can tell me where you were on the night in question."

His eyes widened, briefly, then lit with fun. "Really? I'm a suspect?"

"It's routine, Mr. Dudley —"

"Please, Winnie."

"It's routine, and just helps us cross things off the list."

"Of course. I was at a dinner party with a number of friends in Greenwich — Connecticut, that is. I believe my date and I arrived at just before eight, and left around midnight. I'll have Marissa give you the names and location. Will that do?"

"Works for me. How'd you get there?"

"My driver. I have a private car and driver. I'll get you that information as well."

"Good enough." She walked him through

233

a few standard questions — did he know the victim, had he used their services, tossed in a few more relating to Sweet.

"I have to tell you we've just arrested and charged two of your employees."

"Good God, for the murder? Who —"

"No, on an unrelated matter. Mitchell Sykes and Karolea Prinz. They've been skimming some of your products, selling them."

He sat back, arranged his face into sober lines. "I'd like more information on this. It's very upsetting. This shouldn't have been possible. Obviously, I need to have meetings with my department heads, Security, Inventory. I owe you a debt."

"No, we did our job. Another unrelated matter, just crossing off. Are you acquainted with Sylvester Moriarity?"

"Sly? Yes. He's a good friend of mine. Why?"

"Just covering bases. Was he at this dinner party?"

"No. He's not particularly friendly with the hosts, and it was a close-knit group."

"Okay. Thanks for the time, the coffee." She got to her feet, smiled as he rose. "Oh, just to tidy up. How about last night? Can you tell me where you were?"

"Yes. I had drinks with a friend about five,

then went home. I wanted a quiet evening, and very much wanted to finish the book. The Icove case. Just fascinating."

"So, nobody came by?"

"No."

"Did you talk to anyone?"

"Just the opposite. It was one of those nights I wanted to myself. I'm curious as to why you'd want to know?"

"I'm nosy. Part of being a cop. Thanks again."

"You're more than welcome, both of you. Let me walk you out, and have Marissa get you the information you need. I hope we'll see each other again, when it's not work related."

Marissa had the data at her fingertips — almost, Eve thought, as if she'd been told to have it there. In the elevator, Eve shook her head before Peabody could speak.

"Good coffee."

"Ah, yeah."

"It helps when you get that kind of co-operation." Eve leaned negligently against the side wall. "Saves time. I want you to check out the driver, and the dinner party, just so we can put it aside. We have to log it in, even though it's obvious he didn't book that limo or kill Houston. So . . . what're you and McNab up to tonight?"

Peabody's mouth dropped open in shock. "Ah, well, we thought we might catch a vid unless we're on OT."

"Probably wrap up shift on time."

She moved across the lobby, outside. She didn't speak again until she was behind the wheel and driving away.

"Slick bastard."

"Yeah, I was going to say —"

"And if that elevator isn't monitored, eyes and ears, I'm having an affair with Summerset."

"You're — oh. Damn, sure it is."

"Lobby might be, too."

"You didn't really want to know what McNab and I were doing tonight?"

"Why the hell would I care? He's slick," she repeated.

"He is, but he didn't kill Houston. And he didn't have an alibi for The Night of the Shoe."

Eve snorted out a laugh. "Good one. That's right, and he's also five ten, and a little heavier than Urich. What else did we get out of that?"

"The connection you wanted between the two companies. Just call me Winnie and Sly. Good pals. It's the first real link we've found."

"That's right. Top-level connection. What

else did we get?"

"Okay, what?"

"Who wasn't at the famous dinner party two nights ago when Jamal Houston was getting a crossbow through the neck?"

"Sylvester Moriarity? You're thinking . . . Like that case a while back. Where the two women killed the other's husbands? They each took one? But why?"

"Don't know. But it's an interesting angle. Track down Sly, and let's go see if he's as slick as Winnie."

11

While the tone of Dudley and Son hit modern and angular on the nose, Intelicore adorned itself in the heavy and ornate. Lots of curves and curlicues, Eve noted, big-ass urns, plenty of gilt.

Contacting the company en route had paved the way, and pretty damn smoothly, straight to the hallowed halls of Sylvester — The Third's — offices.

Like his counterpart at Dudley, he reigned on the top floor, or floors in this case, as a sweep of marble steps joined the office space to what Moriarity's admin explained were his private quarters.

They were served coffee from a silver pot and invited to wait while The Third concluded a meeting. Left alone with Peabody, Eve scanned the office area.

Fancy taste, a love of excess — well, that could have described Roarke, she mused. Except he went in for that more at home than at work. The big, carved desk held court in front of triple windows — privacy screened — and held the expected data-and-communication center as well as mementos, an antique clock, a painted box.

Thick rugs, age-faded, spread over the floor while lights with colorful glass shades adorned tables with curved legs. Art, likely worth a mid-sized fortune, covered the walls.

Moriarity strode in, exuded the aura of a busy man — sharp movements in a sharp suit. His angular, thin-lipped face held a golden tan, and with his sun-streaked hair tousled, his eyes of bright, bold green, he gave the impression of action, athleticism.

He offered Eve a firm, perfunctory handshake, then nodded to Peabody.

"I apologize for keeping you waiting. Last night's incident required a departmental meeting. I hope you have an update on the event."

"The Crampton murder is an open and active investigation. Evidence supports that Foster Urich's identification and credit line were compromised by the person responsible for Ava Crampton's death."

"Then he's not a suspect."

"At this time we believe Mr. Urich was at home, in the company of a friend, when

Crampton was killed."

Moriarity nodded. "If Foster says he was home, he was home. I can and do vouch for his honesty without hesitation. He's a valued part of this company."

"For the record, Mr. Moriarity, where were you last night between nine P.M. and one A.M.?"

His jaw went tight, drawing those thin lips into a harsh frown. "I fail to see how that could be of interest to you in this matter."

"It's a matter of routine and information gathering. Your employee's identification was used, your company car service was used, your company credit line was used, all in connection with a homicide. You are head of the company, are you not, Mr. Moriarity?"

"My position hardly —" He cut himself off, held up a hand. "It's not important in any case. I entertained a small group of friends in my box at the opera. We had cocktails prior in a private room at Shizar, then walked the two blocks to the Met for the performance. Afterward we gathered for a late supper at Carmella. This would have been from approximately six-thirty last night to after one this morning."

"It would help our records if we could have the names in your party."

His eyes bored into hers. "It's difficult enough to have any sort of connection with a murder. Now you'll contact my personal friends to verify my word? It's insulting."

"Murder's a nasty business for everybody."

Now the muscles in his jaw twitched as he reached into his pocket for an appointment book. "I don't care for your demeanor, Lieutenant."

"I get that a lot."

"No doubt." He rattled off a series of names and contacts while Peabody scrambled to key the information into her notebook.

"Thank you. Do you have any idea, any speculations as to how Urich's identification was compromised?"

"I just completed a meeting on that subject, and have ordered a full company screening and internal investigation."

"You believe the compromise came from inside the company."

He took a sharp breath in and out of his nose. "If it didn't our security is lacking, and security is the core of my company. If it did, our employee screening is lacking, and we are in the business of screening. So either way we require our own investigation."

"I hope you'll keep us informed of your

progress and findings."

"Believe me, Lieutenant, when we find how this was done, and by whom, we will notify you. I will not have Intelicore's reputation smeared in this matter. Now, I have another meeting, with our public relations division. We have a media crisis on our hands with this. So if there's nothing else at the moment . . ."

"Thank you for your time. If you could take another moment of it, and verify your whereabouts night before last, between seven P.M. and midnight, it would be very helpful."

Color flared in his cheeks. "That's simply outrageous."

"It may seem so, Mr. Moriarity, but we're pursuing a line of investigation, and it would benefit us as well as you and your company if we had that information on record."

"I was at home that evening, if you must know. I had a headache, took some medication, and went to bed early. Am I under arrest?"

Eve answered in kind. "Not at this time. I apologize for the inconvenience, and the intrusion, but we have a body in the morgue with a connection to your company. We owe it to her to be thorough. Again, thank you for your time. Peabody, with me."

In the elevator, Peabody cleared her throat. "I guess it's understandable he's upset, but we're just doing our job."

Eve shrugged. "He can be an asshole, as long as we have the information. Check out the alibi so we can cross him off."

"Yes, sir. So . . . what are you and Roarke up to tonight?"

Amused, Eve cocked an eyebrow. "No plans. I'll probably be working late anyway. I'm going to sit hard on EDD. We've got a hacker out there somewhere who likes to kill people. They need to find the source."

Outside, Peabody slid into the passenger's seat. "He's not going to like you calling him an asshole, if he was listening."

"Oh, he was listening, and he expected the asshole, or some similar insult. He played for it. Dudley goes slick, this one goes sharp."

"You think that was an act."

"At least some of it." She tapped her fingers on the wheel as she drove. "If they're in this, and if they're in it together, what's the point? What's the purpose? I tell you this, they're too clever for their own good. Each of them alibied tight for one night, home alone on the other. Switch-off. But why? What's the root?"

"What if Houston driving that night was

rigged. It looks random, but what if the killer knew, or maybe played the odds it would be Houston?"

"It doesn't feel that way, but okay." Flip of the coin, Eve thought, but then again fifty-fifty odds weren't bad. "Keep going."

"One of these guys has some connection to Houston. Could be way back when the vic was getting in fights, in trouble. Could be more recent. Houston sees something he's not supposed to see, hears something he's not supposed to hear. He's a driver, an overheard conversation, an exchange of money for illegal goods. Whatever. With the LC, it could've been jealousy, unrequited passion."

"Neither of them are in her book."

"Well, we know they — if it's they — can diddle with ID. Maybe one or both of them used her services with a false ID. And okay, it's all reaching way out," Peabody admitted, "but why do a couple of really, really rich guys without any priors hook up to kill a couple of complete strangers?"

Damn good question, Eve thought. "Maybe they're bored."

"Jeez, Dallas."

Eve glanced over at the dismay in Peabody's voice, saw it reflected on her partner's face. "You've been a cop for a while now, and in Homicide for a couple years. And you still don't get people are just fucked up?"

"Boredom as motive is more than fucked up. I'll buy maybe for the thrill, in part, but it just seems there has to be something under that. Jealousy, revenge, profit."

"Then look into it. Seriously," she added when Peabody frowned at her. "Maybe you're right, and there's some concrete motive here, some connection between killer or killers and victims we haven't found. Find it. If you do, it opens things up. If you don't, it narrows the focus. Either way it's progress."

"My own fork in the investigative road?"

"Whatever. Work on it, at Central, or take what you need and work at home. Carve out some downtime before your brain goes to mush."

"Is that what you're going to do?"

"I'm going to try to grab Mira, run some things by her, then I need to take what we have to Whitney. After that, yeah, I'm thinking I'll work at home."

They separated at Central, with Eve heading toward Mira's office as she contacted the commander's with a request for a report meeting. She geared herself up to confront Mira's fierce gatekeeping admin but found

245

a young, perky woman in the dragon's place.

"Who are you?" Eve demanded.

"I'm Macy. Doctor Mira's administrative assistant is out today. What can I do for you?"

"You can give me five minutes with Doctor Mira."

"Let me see what I can do. Who should I say would like to speak with her?"

"Dallas, Lieutenant Eve."

"Oh!" She bounced a little in her chair, and actually clapped her hands as if one of them had won a prize. "I know who you are! I read Nadine Furst's book. It's all just amazing."

Eve started to dismiss it, rethought. "Thanks. Being able to consult with Mira made a huge difference in the Icove case. I'm working on a pretty hot one now. I could really use that five."

"Give me one minute!" She all but sang it as she turned to her com. "Doctor Mira, Lieutenant Dallas would like five minutes with you if you're available. Of course, yes, ma'am." Macy beamed at Eve. "You can go right in."

"Thanks. Ah, how long are you on the desk?"

"Oh, just for a couple days. I wish it was longer. It's fun!"

"Yeah."

Mira started to rise from her desk when Eve came in. "No, don't get up. Five minutes tops. Could there be two?"

"I'm sorry?"

"No, my sorry. I'm thinking ahead of myself. Two murders, two killers. My cases."

Mira frowned. "With the pattern, the repeat of element types, I have to conclude these murders are connected."

"Connected, yeah, but two killers, working in tandem, working a set pattern."

"Interesting. Again, the elements, the executions are so very similar, even the tone."

"Yeah, and that could be deliberate. Involve number one through an employee, but you're alibied because number two's on that one. Then repeat, switching off."

"A partnership."

"Maybe even a business deal. I don't know, not yet, but both Dudley and Moriarity ring my bell. They're different types." Despite telling Mira to stay seated, Eve paced the pretty office. "At least they projected different types when we interviewed them. But under it, they're not that different. Rich, privileged, inherited wealth, inherited positions in major, long-standing corporations. And they're friends."

"Are they?" Mira queried.

"Yeah. Dudley confirmed that. Friends, but neither of them mentioned discussing this very similar situation they find themselves in with the other. That's bogus. Both are alibied tight for the night of the murder connected to their company, and home alone on the other."

"Mirrors then." Mira pursed her lips, nodded. "And perhaps reflecting too close, which raised your instincts to suspect."

"Even the alibis rang the same. Out with friends, multiple, covering the entire evening. Smarter if one of them had a woman over, or a business meeting, some wider variation. But they've stuck with the same pattern throughout. And they're smug. I don't like smug." She shrugged it off. "I'm about to report to Whitney. I wanted your take before I did."

"What you're theorizing is certainly possible. I would have to conclude that, if this is the case, the two men have a deep and strong level of trust or mutual need. If either one of them had failed or changed his mind, or otherwise impacted the partnership, the other would suffer the consequences as well."

"Okay. I'll look into that. Thanks."

"Eve, if you're right, they could be finished. Each has done their part."

"No." She thought of the sparkle in Dudley's eyes, the hard, superior gleam in Moriarity's. "No, they're not finished. They think they've done their parts too well to be finished."

Organizing her thoughts, Eve made her way to Commander Whitney's office. She recognized the low throb behind her eyes as caffeine buzz warring with fatigue. Peabody wasn't the only one who could use a little downtime.

She stepped off the glide, turned to switch to the next, barely registering the weeping behind her. Crying, cursing, whining, shouting were all ambient noise in a cop shop. But she caught the move, the man directly in front of her drawing a hand from his pocket. She saw the eyes, the baring of teeth, the hot rage.

She laid a hand on her weapon, shifted to block him.

The knife was out of his pocket before she could clear her weapon, and slicing out at her. She felt the sting of the tip across her forearm. Heard the weeping turn to high, terrified screams.

She said, "Goddamn it," and kicked the assailant hard in the balls even as she yanked her weapon clear. "You son of a fucking bitch."

Since he was curled on the floor, retching, he didn't respond.

"Lieutenant. Jesus, Lieutenant, he cut you."

"I know he cut me. I'm the one bleeding. Why is she screaming?" Eve demanded as she lowered, put a knee in the small of the retching man's back, then restrained him. "Let me repeat: I'm the one bleeding."

"He was going for her when you got in the way. Way it looks. Detective Manson," he said, "Special Victims. The asshole on the floor is her ex, who paid her a visit last night, beat the crap out of her, raped her, and told her he'd cut her heart out if she left. He went out for brew, she left. He must've trailed her here or something. We'll find out."

"How the hell did he get a knife through?" As she asked, Manson used a pair of tweezers to pick it up off the floor.

"Christ, it's one of those plastic deals from the Eatery. He sharpened it with something. I'd say he was waiting out here to go at her. In goddamn Cop Central. Crazy bastard."

"Get him the hell in a cage. Make sure you charge him with assault with a deadly on a police officer." She crouched down to push her face close to the knifer's. "You can

250

get life for that, asshole. Put in the other charges, and you're done. You cost me a pretty nice jacket."

"You need to go to the infirmary, sir."

Eve looked down at the ripped sleeve, the blood. "Crap."

Instead, she slipped into a restroom, ripped the sleeve off the jacket, and fashioned a quick field dressing. Then, with some regret as it had been a nice, serviceable jacket — shoved what was left of it in the recycler.

The steady pulse of pain from her arm joined the head throb. Home, she thought, as soon as she gave Whitney her report, she was going home, cleaning up, shutting down. Two hours' sleep would do the trick.

At home.

At his desk when she walked in, Whitney held up a finger for silence as he finished reading a report. Eve stood where she was while behind his window a blimp lumbered through the sky with its flashing ad, a couple of shuttles zipped in a crisscrossing path, and a tram carried a payload of tourists.

Whitney tapped the index finger of his big hand on the screen, then shifted his eyes, dark, intense, to her.

"How were you injured?" he asked her.

"It's just a scratch."

"I asked how."

"Sir. Some mope on the tenth level, east, lying in wait for his ex, who'd come in to SVU after he beat and raped her. He'd copped a plastic knife from the Eatery, sharpened it up. I got in the way. A Detective Manson has him in custody."

"That's not a proper dressing."

"I'll get one. I was on my way to give you my report, so —"

Again, he held up a finger, turned to his com to tag his admin. "Send a medic in here for the lieutenant. She has an injury, left forearm. Knife wound."

"Sir, I really don't need —"

"Report."

"Sir." Damn it.

She reviewed the facts, the steps taken, the various avenues of investigation addressed.

"You've yet to find any connection between the victims."

"No, sir, we've found nothing that intersects them other than the killer."

"And you believe both victims were killed by the same individual."

"Detective Peabody and I have just completed first interviews with Winston Dudley and Sylvester Moriarity. I believe the result of those interviews opened another avenue of investigation. I consulted with Doctor Mira on the —"

She broke off at the knock on the door.

"Come," Whitney ordered.

Eve eyed the medic with instinctive distrust. "Commander, if I could conclude before —"

"Sit down. You can give me the rest while he works on you."

"Carver, sir," the medic said cheerfully. "Let's have a look-see."

She didn't care for the idea of a medic named Carver, but under direct orders sat.

"Good field dressing," Carver told her as he removed it. "Nasty little slice. We'll fix it up."

Several sarcastic remarks came to mind, and she swallowed them as Carver began to clean the wound she'd already damn well cleaned in the bathroom.

"There's a connection between Dudley and Moriarity," she began. "They're friends, of the same social strata, and both head large corporations that came down to them through birth. Each has a — shit."

She jerked a little, and aimed a hard glare at Carver as he replaced the pressure syringe in his kit.

"Always a little sting, but it's better than

an infection."

"Each," Eve said through her teeth, "has a strong alibi for the night his employee's ID was used to lure the victim. And each has no alibi for the alternate night and time."

"You think they're working together? For what reason?"

"Motive may come to light as we shift angles, take a closer look at the vics with the alternate company, company head, both personally and professionally. Or it may be exactly what it appears to be on the surface. Thrill kills."

She did her best to ignore the faint buzz of the suture wand, the vague and persistent discomfort of her skin drawing back together.

"The pattern comes through," she continued. "The victims represent wealth, position, indulgence, the weapons unusual and showy, the kill sites public and risky. In both cases false ID was utilized, and sprang from one of the companies run by these men. An outside hack is, of course, possible, but it feels like an inside job. It plays as one."

"And Mira's profile?"

"They both fit. The interviews, sir? It felt like theater, in both cases. Rehearsed, with each taking a specific type of role. They're arrogant and smug, and enjoying the fact that they're in the middle of this. We have an additional piece of evidence from a partial image EDD was able to enhance from the Coney Island security. From it, we can estimate the height of the killer, and we were able to identify the designer and model of his shoes, and the approximate size. It's made by Emilio Stefani —"

As he bandaged, Carver let out a low whistle. "Those'll cost ya."

"They retail for three thousand, to confirm Carver's statement. Dudley bought a pair of that shoe, in the color and the size we have, in March. Only one other pair was purchased in the city, in that color and the size Detective McNab ascertained from the security image. That individual is currently in New Zealand, and at the time of the murder was on a location shoot for a major vid. That leaves Dudley."

"That's good, but it won't get you an arrest warrant much less a conviction. If you're set on this line of investigation, get more."

"I intend to, sir."

"You're all set." Carver rose. "Want a pain pop?"

"No, I don't want a pain pop."

"Your choice, but it's gonna ache for a while. I can take a look at it for you tomorrow, change the dressing. You should only need me to slap some NuSkin on it by then."

"I'm fine. It's fine." Relieved it was done, Eve got to her feet.

"Thank you, Carver." Whitney sat back as the medic tapped a finger to his temple as salute and left.

"If the bayonet was military, and you've got the era, check to see if either of your suspects had an ancestor who served, and would have been issued the weapon, and push on the crossbow. One or both of them could be licensed."

"If Moriarity used the bow, as I believe, he's practiced. Even at that distance, he had to be confident in his shot, first time. The second killing runs the same. It was dead in the heart, which kept the bleeding light, reduced the spatter. They took time to work on their skills, or already had those skills."

"Get more," Whitney repeated. "And take care of that arm."

"Yes, sir. Thank you, sir." Recognizing the dismissal, Eve walked out.

As she made her way back to her office, she started the search on her PPC for the military connection. That was a line she'd missed, she admitted, and shouldn't have. It might have something to do with being up for around forty hours, but reasons weren't excuses.

Once again, the shift was changing as she passed through the bullpen. She spotted Baxter just pushing back from his desk.

"Here early, here late. What have you done with Baxter?"

"Ha ha. Just finished the case from this morning. PA dealt it down to Man One, but it's closed. Report's on its way to you."

"Good enough."

"Sent the boy home. He's still dating the cutie in Records. But we're clear if you need more hands on your double."

"I'll let you know."

"Heard you took a little slice," he said with a nod toward her arm.

"Word travels."

"Oh, and I sent you the monthly eval on Trueheart. He's going to make a good detective. Needs a little more time, but if you give me the green light, I'm going to tell him to start boning up for the exam."

"That's a pretty fast track, Baxter."

"He's quick, unless you're talking about with women." He grinned at that. "He's got good instincts, and he thinks things through. Plus, the kid's got me for a trainer. How can he lose?"

"I'll look over the eval, think about it."

"He's made for Homicide," Baxter added as Eve turned away.

She stopped. "Because?"

"He looks at a DB and sees a person. We can forget that, just see the case. You know how it is. But he doesn't, and not just because he's still a little green. He's wired that way. This is his place, that's what I'm saying, even if you figure he needs more time in uniform."

"I'll think it over."

She got what she needed from her office and joined the end-of-shifters on the exodus.

She set her vehicle on auto so she could let her mind drift.

Baxter and Trueheart, she thought. Some would have seen it as an odd pairing, the slick, often brass detective and the shy, sweet-natured rookie.

She hadn't, and that was why she'd assigned Trueheart as Baxter's aide. She'd believed they'd complement each other, and that Baxter's style would ripen and toughen the rook.

It had, but the partnership had also . . . softened wasn't the word, she thought. Maybe opened was better. It had opened Baxter. He'd always been a solid cop — smart, smart-mouthed, competitive. And, in her opinion, mostly out for number one.

Trueheart had changed that so that now they were much more partners than trainer and aide.

They understood each other, communicated with and without words. They trusted each other. A cop couldn't go through the door with a partner unless there was absolute trust.

A man didn't kill with a partner unless there was absolute trust. Trust, knowledge, understanding, and a common goal.

What was the common goal?

How had they developed the trust and understanding? How and when had they decided to kill?

Friendships, she thought, took all kinds of forms, and formed for all kinds of reasons. But they stuck, didn't they, out of genuine affection, genuine need, or the solid base of common ground?

Considering, she used the dash 'link to contact Mavis Freestone.

"Dallas! Belle and I were just talking about you!"

Since Belle was about six months old and mostly said "ga!," Eve figured it had been a short conversation. "Yeah? Listen, I —"

"I was just telling her all the things she could be when she grows up. You know like president or goddess of all she surveys, or a vid star like Mommy, a designer like Daddy. How she could be the total of totality like Roarke or a kick-ass supercop like you."

"There you go. I was just . . . are you wearing a crown?"

Mavis lifted a hand to the sparkly gold crown perched on a mountain of hair — currently a bold grass green. "We were playing dress-up."

"Mavis, you're always playing dress-up."

Mavis laughed, a bright, happy giggle. "Being a girl is the frostiest. Oh! Oh! Look. You've got to see!"

Eve blinked when Mavis swung the 'link screen — in that second or two the world was a swimming blur of color and shape. Then in the middle of it, the chubby blond baby motored across the floor on all fours toward some sort of red animal. A bear, a dog, a species of undetermined origin, Eve wondered. In any case, Belle zeroed in like a blaster stream, grabbed the animal, then plopped down on her butt and chewed on it vigorously.

"Is that mag or what?" Mavis demanded. "Our Bellamia is growing up so fast."

"Don't cry. Jesus, Mavis."

"It just makes me go all fountain. She's crawling already and see how she knows just what she wants and goes for it? This morning she crawled over and picked out her pink sandals with the stars all by herself."

"Amazing." Maybe it was — how would she know? One thing she did know, common ground wasn't the base of her friendship with Mavis. The grifter and the cop hadn't had anything in common, not on the surface. Eve supposed what had cemented them was a kind of recognition.

"Where's Leonardo?"

"Oh, he had a fitting. He's picking up some yums on the way home."

"With who, a regular client?"

"Ah, yeah." Mavis bent, scooped up Belle and the red mammal. "Carrie Grace, the screen queen. You need him?"

"No. But I'm working on a case —"

"Shockamundo! Right, Bella?" Bella giggled, much like her mother, and waved the red thing in the air by its drooled-on ear.

"The thing is somebody's killing people who provide what we'll call fancy or exclusive services. Expensive services, and at the top of their line."

"I don't — oh. Oh! Like my honey bear?"

"Yeah, like your honey bear, and like you, Mavis. Just do me a favor, and don't take any solo appointments or meetings until I close this up. Same for your honey bear. No new clients."

"You got that squared. Our Bellarina needs her mommy and her daddy. I've got that gig in London at the end of next week. We were kind of thinking about adding on some hoot time."

"Hoot time?"

"Time for having a hoot. Fun. Vacation."

"Why don't you do that? Go have a hoot. Let me know one way or the other."

"Hell, I'm packed five minutes from now. Do you really think somebody could try to hurt us?"

"Probably not. But I don't take chances with you guys."

"Aw, I love you, too."

"Why is that? Why do we love each other?"

"Because we are what we are, and we're both okay with it."

And that, Eve thought as she drove through the gates, pretty well nailed it.

When she opened the car door, the heat knocked her back on her heels. And when she had to brace a hand on the door because her head spun, she had to admit sleep had to be the first order of business. She steadied herself and walked inside to the blissful, quiet cool.

"Have you been brawling again?" Summerset wondered. "Or is this some kind of fashion statement?"

She remembered the bandage on her arm, and the lack of a jacket to conceal it. "Neither. I lost a bet and had to get your name tattooed on my arm. So I carved it out with a penknife."

A little lame, she thought as she went upstairs, but the best she could do when her brain wanted so desperately to check out.

Two hours, she told herself. Two hours down to recharge, then she'd go at the whole thing fresh.

In the bedroom she didn't bother to remove her weapon and harness but simply dropped facedown on the bed. She barely felt the thump on her ass when the cat landed there.

Forty minutes later, Roarke came home.

"The lieutenant's sporting a bandage on her left forearm," Summerset reported. "It doesn't look serious."

"Ah, well."

"You need sleep."

"I do. Block the 'links for the next couple of hours, would you? Unless it's an emergency or her dispatch."

"Already done."

Roarke went up, found her crossways and

facedown on the bed, a position that signaled exhaustion. From his perch on Eve's ass, Galahad blinked.

"I'll take over now if you've something else to do," Roarke murmured. He peeled off his suit coat, his tie, his shoes. When he pulled Eve's boots off, she didn't budge an inch.

Much as he had that morning in her office, he lay down beside her, closed his eyes, and slept.

12

She hunted. With a bayonet sheathed at her side, a crossbow in her hands, she stalked her prey through richly appointed rooms, glittering light, velvet shadows.

The fragrance was drowning floral, so thick it felt like breathing blossoms. On the ornately carved desk she'd seen in Moriarity's office, two men — hooded, stripped to the waist — turned a screaming woman on the rack.

"Can't help you," Eve told her. "You're not real, anyway."

The woman paused mid-scream to smile wearily. "Who is? What is?"

"I haven't got time for philosophy. They've already picked out the next."

"The next what? The next who? The next what?"

"Do you mind," one of the hooded men said. "You're interrupting the program."

"Fine. Carry on."

She moved into the next room, sweeping her weapon, right, left. In the sleek black-and-white drama, the bold red on the floor was blood, and on the blood floated a chauffeur's cap.

Leaving signs, she thought. They liked leaving clues. Liked thinking they were too smart, too insulated, too rich to be caught.

She stood in the center of the room, studying it. What was missing? What had she missed?

She stepped through and into her own office at Central where her murder board dominated.

Was it there? Already there?

Limo driver, crossbow, transpo center.

LC, bayonet, amusement park.

Who, what, where.

But why?

She eased out the door, turned toward the bullpen.

But rather than the cops, the desks, the smell of bad coffee, she stepped into what she imagined to be a room in some exclusive club. Big leather chairs, a simmering fire though the heat was fierce, deep colors, paintings on the wall of high-class hunting.

Hounds and horses.

The two men sat, swirling amber-colored brandy in balloon glasses. Long, slim cigars smoked on the silver tray on the table between them.

They turned to her as one, and their smiles were sneers.

"I'm sorry, you're not a member. You'll have to leave or face the consequences. It takes more than money to belong."

"I know what you did, and I think I know how. But I don't know why."

"We don't answer to you and your kind."

It was Dudley who lifted the gun, an enormous silver weapon.

She heard the snap when it cocked.

She jerked, and her eyes flew open. She swore she heard — even smelled — the explosion of gunfire.

"Shh." Beside her Roarke pulled her closer, wrapped her in. "Just a dream."

"What's it telling me?" she mumbled. When she tried to shift, an annoyed Galahad dug his claws into her butt. "Ow, damn it." She maneuvered him off, and ended up face-to-face with Roarke. "Hi."

"Again." He trailed his fingers lightly over her wounded arm. "How?"

"Idiot with a plastic knife sharpened to a shiv, right in fucking Central. The worst was Whitney made me get a medic on it while I gave him my report."

"Why the bastard, forcing one of his cops

to have a wound tended."

"I'd field-dressed it. Jacket's toast."

He snuggled her in on the remote chance they'd both just drift off again. "There's more where that came from."

"I don't like Dudley or Moriarity."

"Isn't that handy? Neither do I, particularly."

"Dudley comes up smarm and charm, with that 'I just love women' light in his eyes, and the other's all 'I'm a busy and important man so move this along, peon.' And maybe that's what they are, on top of it. Maybe it is. But under it they were smirking."

He watched her face as she spoke, and decided that remote possibility didn't exist. "I know that look," he murmured. "You think they did this — together."

"It's a theory." She scowled at nothing. "It's the right theory. And not just because I don't like them. I didn't like that little bastard Sykes either, but I didn't look at him for murder."

"All right, so you know who. How?"

She took him through it, the alibis, the lack of them, the friendship.

"It's not a hell of a lot, but there was . . . a tone, a feel, a sense that they'd been waiting to play those scenes. And . . . I know what I missed. Family. Family firms, right?"

When she started to sit up, he just kept his arm hooked around her waist. "Let's just lie here a bit. I'm listening."

"Well, why wasn't there anything of or about family in their offices? They've got huge spaces, all fancied up. No family photos, or photos at all. No, there's the cricket mallet my —"

"Bat. It's a cricket bat."

"It doesn't look like a bat. Or mallet either, but it doesn't matter. Here's the cricket whatzit my dear old dad gave me on my tenth birthday, or yes, that's my great-grandfather's pocket watch. They're generational firms without any generational tokens in their spaces. Nothing. Neither of them. They're running a company passed down from father to son, and so on, and there's nothing."

"Devil's advocate. It might be a deliberate show that they're their own men."

"That's part of where I'm going. Legacies are a deal with those types, even if it's for show. And family weighs. Mira's got her family all over her office. Whitney's got stuff, Feeney, like that, and maybe that's a different kind of thing, but there ought to be some sort of show. It's off, isn't it, that neither of them has anything, at least visibly, that connects them to their family but the company itself?"

"You think they resent being put in their positions?"

"Maybe. I don't know. Or they figure it's their due so who gives a fuck about dear old Dad or whoever. And maybe it's nothing. It's just odd it's both of them. Common ground. I think that's how it started. They have all this common ground."

"It's a long step from a similar background to a murderous partnership."

"There's more than background between them."

"Sex?"

She considered. "Maybe. That would certainly add a layer of connection and trust. It could be sex, even love. Or just the bond of like minds, like interests. People find each other."

"We did."

"Aw." She exaggerated the sound as she grinned at him. She kissed him lightly, then nudged him away. "I've got to update my board, and do some runs. I have to keep looking for a connection between the vics, and between the vics and the company, even though I don't think there are any. And I've got one that should be done on military ancestors who might've owned the bayonet."

"Red meat."

"Huh?"

"We'll have steak. We could both use the boost."

"You're not tired anymore. I'm looking right in your eyes, and I'd see if you were. It's annoying."

"I still want steak."

"Now I want it, too. But first I want a shower. Wash off this day and a half." She sniffed at him. "How come you smell so good?"

"Could be I'm simply blessed that way, or it could be the shower I had at the office. Go on then." He gave her ass a friendly pat. "I'll set up the meal."

She felt better, after the shower, another hit of coffee, a change of clothes. And when she walked into her home office, she smelled grilled meat, and felt better yet.

And it reminded her of her early-morning conversation with Morris.

"Ah, I sort of said how we might have a thing, you know with that big-ass grill of yours, and people."

Roarke lifted the bottle of wine he'd opened. "You want me to grill people?"

"Only some people. But that should be

done privately. Just half a glass of that for me."

He poured. "You're after having a cookout."

"I'm not really after it, but I saw Morris this morning, and he looked so damn sad, and I said something about it before I actually thought about it, then I forgot about it until I smelled the steak."

He crossed to her, handed her the wineglass, then caught her chin in his hand, kissed her. "You're a good friend."

"I don't know how the hell that happened."

"Saturday evening?"

"I guess. Unless —"

"There's always an unless, but as we'll be entertaining cops or those associated with, it's a given for all."

"You're okay with it?"

"Eve, I know this continues to astound and baffle you, but I actually like to socialize."

"I know. If it wasn't for that, you'd be perfect." When he laughed, she walked over, lifted the cover of a plate. "God, that really does smell good. I'm getting that boost and I haven't even eaten it yet."

"Let's see what happens when you do. How's the arm?" he asked when they sat at the table by the window.

"It's okay." She rolled her shoulder, flexed. "Hardly feel it."

"We should have a contest," he decided, "to see if you can go, say, two weeks without an on-the-job injury."

"I was just switching glides." She cut into the steak. "Minding my own business. And what kind of idiot thinks they're going to get away with stabbing their ex with a plastic knife in the middle of Cop Central?"

"One who's only thinking of the satisfaction of the act, not the consequences."

"Probably toked up," she muttered. "But not enough he didn't feel it when I kicked his balls until they tickled his tongue."

It made him smile to picture it. "Is that what you did?"

"It was the quickest and most satisfying action."

"That's my girl." He toasted her.

"What are you going to do? Asshole with a plastic knife in Cop Central. It's like . . ."

He knew that look as well, and said nothing to interrupt her train of thought.

"Make that Asshole's Ex with a plastic knife in Cop Central."

"All right."

"Could that be it? Is it just that sick?"

"I can't say." Watching her, he sipped his

wine. "You tell me."

"It's Major Ketchup in the bathroom with the laser scalpel."

"Hmm." He sliced a delicately herbed spear of asparagus. "Obviously we were meant for each other as I can interpret that as you meaning something more like Colonel Mustard in the conservatory with the candlestick."

"Whatever. It's that game — who was it — McNab or Peabody said something about that game sometime back."

"Clue."

"You always know this crap. But yeah, and it sounded interesting, so I brought it up on the comp one day to check it out. And that doesn't matter."

"You playing a game on the comp is big news, but I'd say your brainstorm on this is bigger. You're speculating that Dudley and Moriarity, if indeed they're in this homicidal partnership, are in fact playing a game."

"The elements are all screwy — the methods. The weapon, the vic, the kill site. They come off as random kills, connected by the type of each element, which still strikes me as random. So what if it is, what if it is fucking random because they're elements of a contest, a game, a competition? Or, if not that sick, some sort of deeply disturbed agreement?"

"If so, the question would be why."

"Why does anyone play a game, enter a contest, compete? To win."

"Darling, while that viewpoint is one of the reasons you're not much of a player, many play because they simply enjoy the game or the experience."

She stabbed another bite of steak. "Losing sucks."

"I tend to agree, but nonetheless. Your hypothesis is: two respected and high-powered businessmen, with no previous criminal record or reputation for violence have partnered up, not merely to kill, but to kill for . . . sport?"

"Sport." She jabbed a finger at him. "Exactly. Look at the vics. Jamal Houston. Neither of the men or their companies used his transpo service. Nothing we've uncovered shows any previous connection to him. Peabody's looking into the remote possibility one of them did use him on the QT — which isn't probable or logical — and he saw or overheard something, then one or both of them decided to eliminate him. But just look at that convoluted mess. First, one or both had to use a service they didn't routinely use, which limits their security. Then one or both have to do or say some-

thing incriminating, illegal, immoral, whatever, in front of a driver they don't routinely
use."

She scooped up some of the baked potato
she'd already drowned in butter, sampled,
then kept talking while she — to Roarke's
mind — buried it in salt.

"Then one or both have to decide to kill
him, and chose a method that highlights the
crime when, shit, they could've hired the
hit."

"Why don't you just salt the butter and
eat it with a spoon?"

"What?"

"Never mind. All right, I agree that scenario doesn't make sense. It's too complicated and illogical."

"That doesn't even get to Crampton.
Neither of them are in her book. Now,
maybe one or both of them used her services
with another ID, but it's hard for me to
swallow she wouldn't have made one or
both in her vetting process. And if they were
using fake ID and getting away with it, why
kill her? I've got no evidence of blackmail,
as in she learned who the client was and
tried to shake him down. Which would be
stupid and risk her very valuable rep for
money when she was already flush, and risk
her license when she didn't have a single

blemish on it. Add the method and location, and it's too showy."

"Can't argue. Eat your vegetables."

She rolled her eyes but ate some asparagus. "There. So, simplify it, break it down to its elements."

"And you have a game of Clue."

She circled a finger in the air as she chewed more steak. "Or their version of that sort of thing. Maybe their version of some urban hunt for really big game."

"Which winds back to why. It's murder, Eve, and by your supposition the murder of innocent and personally unknown people."

"People important in their field. People in business or services for the upper rung of the social and financial ladder. I think that's an element. Maybe that's part of the why. I don't know yet."

"Because anything less isn't worthy."

Eve paused with a liberally salted forkful of potato halfway to her mouth. "Worthy."

"Just trying to follow the trail you're breaking. You've described them both as arrogant, smug, wealthy, privileged, and from my limited knowledge of them I don't disagree."

He poured more water in her glass as he expected she'd need to drink like the dying with that much salt in her system.

"They've been steeped in that privilege all their lives," he continued, "and have known only the best, have been able to select the best in every area. That can be a heady experience when you come from nothing. Conversely, it could be a matter of considering what you deserve is only the best, and less isn't to be tolerated."

He lifted his wine, gestured before he drank. "Why murder a sidewalk sleeper, for instance? Where's the shine in that, where's the prestige? And you've no truck with that sort in any case. They're too far beneath you."

"But a tony chauffeur service, or the best LC in the city, while beneath you, are still people you would or could utilize."

"It's logical."

"It damn well is," she agreed. "An unusual weapon, or unique weapon, it adds to the shine."

"And perhaps the challenge."

"So does the location. Makes it challenging, and worthy."

"They've each completed their round, if that's what this is," Roarke pointed out. "Or bagged their trophy. Maybe that's the end of it."

"No. It's a tie, isn't it? A tie doesn't cut it, not in games, in competition, in sports. Ties suck for everybody. There has to be a winner. They have to go to the next round."

He turned it over in his mind. "They know you're looking at them, checking alibis, doing background checks. That would add to the flavor, the buzz of it all, if that's what this is about."

"They were ready for me." She nodded to herself as she looked back at both interviews. "See that's what struck me when I talked to each of them. They were ready with their performance, their script, their play. It was like another kind of round, wasn't it? A level. Okay, we each qualified in that round, now it's Beat the Cop time for bonus points. They had to factor that in when they used employee IDs. They had to want that element, too."

"A bigger bonus that it was you, with your reputation."

"Add my connection to you. A little more — what's it — panache."

"As you're talking me into it, consider the timing. We're just back from holiday. It's very easy to verify we'd both be back to work. And if any research had been done, a good bet that your name would come up on a fresh homicide when you're just back. I'd say they wanted, hoped, and did their best to ensure it would be you. Only the best."

"He brought up the book. Dudley," Eve remembered. "Nadine's book, the Icove case. A lot of shimmer on that right now. Damn it, maybe I should tell Nadine to watch her back. She's riding a big, shiny bestseller. And the bastard made a point of mentioning it."

"I can't see her as a target, but you'd feel better if you contacted her."

"Why not a target?"

"Both victims have been service providers. Some would even consider them a kind of servant."

"Maybe, yeah, maybe, but I'm going to tell her not to do anything stupid. Then, damn it all over again, she's going to push me for a one-on-one on this, try to wheedle more out of me on the investigation."

"Friendship's complex and layered."

"It's a pain in the ass." But she pushed away from the table and walked to her desk to contact her friend.

She was pumped, Roarke thought as he lingered over his wine. Pumped and ready. It was more than the sleep, the meal, though God knew she'd needed both. It was the mission. She saw it now, and maybe that's what Sinead had meant by Eve's gift. She could see, and feel, both her victims and their killers.

He rose now, walked to her murder board.

He could hear her arguing with Nadine over making an appearance on *Now* to discuss the case, over giving a straight interview for Channel 75, but he paid little attention.

That, too, was a kind of game, he supposed. They each played their parts, pushed their agendas, and respected each other's skill. A fine trick between two hardheaded, strong-willed women who believed absolutely in their duty to their profession.

When Eve broke transmission, muttered: "Coffee," he said, "I'll have some as well."

He waited until she came out, handed him a cup. "They look through you."

"What?"

"People — some people — with this level of social and monetary privilege. Those who can have whatever they wish whenever they wish it, and have chosen not to care, or simply haven't the base in them to care about those who can't. They don't see you, the ones sweating out a day's pay to meet the rent, or those begging on a street corner with empty bellies. They don't see those who provide the services they use as they're no more than droids in the world of that tunnel-vision privilege. I'll wager they don't know the names much less the situations of those who work for them outside their admins or PAs — and then only the names."

"You see, you know. And you could probably buy and sell both of them."

He shook his head. "It's a different matter, not only in that base, but in the background. I've been the one looked through. It was one of the things I determined to change. And I've killed. There's a weight in that for most of us. I can see, I think, how they might kill without that weight."

"Because the victims aren't people to them. They're like a chair or a pair of shoes, just something they buy. They pay for the kill, that keeps coming around for me. They bought them, then own them."

"And it's a new thrill, the killing."

He could, now that she'd opened the window to it, see them sitting in their fine homes over fine brandy, discussing that new thrill.

"It's fresh and fascinating," he went on. "When you can have anything you like, there can be little that feels fresh and fascinating."

"Do you feel that way?"

"Not a bit." He smiled a little as he turned to her. "But in my way, it's the business itself, the angles, the strategies, the possibilities that are fresh and fascinating. And I have you. Who do they have? As you said, they keep nothing on display that connects them to family, to a loved one."

"It's one of the things I'm going to look at. Their exes, their family connections, the people they hang with. What do they do with their leisure time?"

"They don't play polo or squash, but I had it right on golf. You'd made me curious," he said when she frowned at him. "So I looked into it a bit. They both belong to the Oceanic Yacht Club, quite exclusive, as you'd expect, and have participated or sponsored quite a number of races and events. They both enjoy baccarat, high stakes. They each own majority shares in racehorses, which often compete."

"Compete," she repeated. "Another pattern."

"When not in New York tending to their companies' HQs — or in my opinion after a bit of digging, sitting in as the symbolic head — they tend to follow the seasons and trends. They sail, they ski, they gamble, attend parties and premieres."

"Together?"

"Often, but not always. They do have separate interests as well. Dudley enjoys tennis, playing and attending the important matches. Moriarity prefers chess."

"Nonteam sports."

"So it seems."

"They compete with each other in several areas. That's part of their dynamic. Separately they go for activities where you compete head to head rather than suit up with a team." She nodded. "It's good data. Now I need to get more. Do you want in on that?"

"I have a little time I can squeeze in." He traced a fingertip along the dent in her chin. "For a price."

"Nothing's free."

"There's my motto. What can I do for you, Lieutenant?"

"You could go back further. See if these two went to school together at any point, or have any relatives in common. Basically I'd like to pin down when they met, how, that sort of thing."

"Easy enough."

"And keep it on the straight line."

"You do know how to spoil my fun. That may cost you double. You can start with the dishes," he said and strolled away.

She scowled, but she couldn't bitch since he'd put the meal together.

"I bet these guys don't expect their bed partners to dump stupid dishes in the machine," she called out.

"Darling, you're so much more to me than a bed partner."

"Yeah, yeah," she grumbled, but gathered up the dishes, dumped them in the machine.

She sat, input all the information Roarke had given her, added various elements of her own into the file.

"Computer, run a probability on Dudley and Moriarity killing both victims while working as competitors and/or partners, considering these acts part of a game or sport."

Acknowledged. Working . . .

"Yeah, take your time. Chew it over. Computer, simultaneous tasking. Background check on former spouses and co-habs of Dudley and Moriarity. Addition," she thought quickly. "Search and find any official announcements of engagements for either subject, run background check."

Secondary task acknowledged. Working . . .

"Computer relay the data on previous search regarding military service for ancestors of both subjects. Screen one display."

Acknowledged. Data on screen one . . .

She sat back, began to scan — and thanked God she'd limited the search to between 1945 and 1965, as there were dozens of names in each family.

She sipped coffee as she read, and found another pattern.

"Computer, separate commissioned officers, major and above, from current list. Display that data, screen two."

Acknowledged. Working . . . Primary task complete. Probability is fifty-four-point-two that subjects Dudley and Moriarity killed both victims as competitors or partners as a game or sport.

"Not bad, but no cheers from the crowd." She studied the remaining names on screen one. "Only five. Okay, computer, run a full background on the individuals on screen one, highlight military service."

While it worked, she rose to update her board, to circle it, to consider it until the computer announced her secondary task complete.

She studied the composites Feeney had sent her from the partial image on the amusement security.

Could be Dudley, she mused, sporting a fake goatee and long brown hair. Could be

Urich. Could be an army of other men. Which is just what the defense team would point out.

The shoe was a better bet. But she'd have the composites as weight, she'd have them to help tip those scales if she needed them, and when she was ready.

She ordered the names on screen two saved and removed, and replaced with the new data.

One ex-wife each, she noted, and each from prestigious, wealthy families. Same circle again. Barely two years for Dudley, shy of three for Moriarity. Just over two years prior to his marriage to one Annaleigh Babbington, Dudley's engagement to a Felicity VanWitt had been announced and its dissolution announcement had come some seven months later.

"I thought that was my job."

"Huh?" She glanced back, mind elsewhere, as Roarke came in.

"The relations."

"This is something else. What?"

"Felicity VanWitt, engaged to Dudley for slightly more than half a year, is first cousin to Patrice Delaughter." He nodded toward the screen. "Moriarity's ex-wife."

"Fucker."

"When I can, and only with you, darling."

"Not you." But she laughed. "Delaughter married Moriarity right after Dudley and the cousin broke it off. Moriarity would've been twenty-six, Dudley twenty-five. They met through the women. I want to talk to the women. Hold on," she snapped when the computer interrupted with another completed task.

She took a breath, cleared her head again. "On-screen."

Pacing, she read the data on each name. "See this one? Joseph Dudley, good old Joe. Great-uncle to our current Dudley. Joe gets tossed out of Harvard, drops out of Princeton, gets a couple knocks for drunk and disorderly. Then he joins the regular Army as a grunt. He's the only private, regular Army of the bunch, and he's the closest relation. Not a cousin six times removed or whatever it is. But the great-granddaddy's brother."

"He served during the Korean War," Roarke added. "Earned a Purple Heart."

"I bet he had a bayonet. I bet you my ass he did."

"I already have your ass, or intend to."

"Cute. I raise that bet with Joe bringing that bayonet home as a memento, where it ended up being passed down to Winnie."

"Difficult to prove."

288

"We'll see about that, but even if I can't, it's another strong probable. We're loaded with them."

"By the way, they didn't attend the same schools. But the fiancée and the ex-wife — the cousins — both attended Smith — as did a female cousin of Dudley's at the same time."

"Okay, so they go back. They go back, ran in the same pack, at least in their twenties. And they're still running in the same pack. Both had marriages that failed. Neither had offspring, and both remain unmarried and unpartnered. Lots of common ground. Like minds? Competitive."

She blew out a breath. "Murderous, that's a different matter. Look at the fiancée. She's married now, married for eleven years, two kids. Lives in Greenwich, that makes it easy. Worked as a psychologist until the first kid. Professional mother status until last year."

"The youngest would have started school."

"She's the one I want to talk to first. Tomorrow. They're not going to hold off the next round too long. Not too long."

She sat, went back to work.

13

Eve woke in the quiet, in the stillness, and for an instant thought the waking a dream. But she knew the arms around her, the legs tangled with hers. She knew the scent of him, and drifted into it as her mind waded through the thinning fog of sleep.

She barely remembered going to bed. He'd carried her, as he often did when she conked out over her work. Reams of data, she thought, and nothing solid in that fluid stream to push the investigation beyond theory.

She'd run it all again, picked at it and through it, re-angled it. Connections to connections always meant something, so they'd conduct more interviews.

Swim in the stream long enough, she told herself, you'd rap up against something solid.

"You're thinking too loud."

She opened her eyes, looked at Roarke. It

was rare to wake with him on a workday as he habitually rose well before she did. She often thought he conducted more business in the hours just before and after dawn than most did in a full day.

Did they live their work or work their lives? And boy, her brain wasn't ready to tackle that kind of question at this hour. Better just to know whichever it was — or maybe it was both — they did okay with it.

In the normal course of things, by the time she got up he'd be checking the stock and other financial reports on-screen, drinking coffee, fully dressed in one of his six million perfectly fitted suits.

And why did men wear suits? she wondered. How and why had it worked out so men wore suits and women wore dresses, unless you were talking about trannies? Who decided these things? And how come everybody just went along so guys said, "Sure, I'll wear suits and tie a colorful noose around my neck," and women said, "No problem, I'll wear this thing that leaves my legs bare, then stick these shoes with stilts on the back on my feet"?

That was something to think about, she decided. But some other time because right now it was nice to wake this way, all warm and soft and naked together, as they had on vacation.

"Still too loud," he murmured. "Mute your brain."

It made her smile, the slurry voice, the before-coffee irritability. That was usually her job. She tried to judge the time by the soft gray light sliding through the sky window, tried to calculate how much sleep they'd managed to catch.

He opened his eyes. Like a blue bolt of lightning, she thought, in the soft gray.

"Not going to shut up, are you then?"

The hell with the time, she decided. If he was still in bed, it was pretty damn early.

"I guess I could think about something else." She stroked a hand down his flank. Watching his eyes as she glided it up again between their tangled legs. "Since you're up anyway. It's funny, isn't it, how a guy's dick wakes up before he does. Why is that?"

"It doesn't like to miss an opportunity. Such as now," he added when she guided him inside her.

"Nice." She sighed, and when she began to move, it was just as slow and easy.

Soft, sweet — this aspect of his cop, his warrior never failed to dazzle him. His mind and body woke to her, roused to her in a long, quiet rise while day took its first breath in the sky above them.

Her whiskey-colored eyes intoxicated, but more, in them was the light he'd yearned for all of his life. She was his daybreak, his sunrise after the long, hard shadows of night.

Wanting more, needing more, he shifted to bring her under him, pressed his lips to the curve of her neck. And with the taste broke his fast with her.

She sighed again, but longer, deeper with a catch in her throat as pleasure saturated every pore. Her mind emptied so all those circling thoughts drifted away under the blissful hum of sensation. That steady beat that was heart and blood and breath belonged to them in this still and hazy moment before dawn. With it there were no questions, no cases, no sorrows, no regrets.

She gave herself to it, and him, let herself open on that slow ride.

When her breath quickened, when it all coalesced inside her, burgeoning on that thin line between need and release, she framed his face in her hands. She wanted his face in her eyes when the line dissolved.

For a long, lovely moment the world slid away so the morning shimmered to life with quiet joy.

With the jump start to the day, she didn't

feel guilty about loitering over a breakfast of berries and a bagel. While the morning reports scrolled on-screen, she indulged in a second cup of coffee.

"Ninety-six." She nodded toward the forecast. "And look at that humiture."

"The city'll be a steambath."

"I like steam." She bit into her bagel as the cat watched her with hope and resentment. "And we'll be out of the city for a while anyway. Connecticut," she reminded him. "I spent a lot of time getting the skinny on Dudley's former fiancée, and his ex-wife, and Moriarity's ex. Nobody knows you like an ex, and generally, nobody's happier to share the crappier sides of you."

"Then I'd better keep you."

"Be a fool not to. Neither of them's been able, or maybe it's willing, to maintain a serious long-term relationship. Except, the way it looks, with each other." She plucked a fat black raspberry out of the bowl. "That's telling. I burned my eyes reading society squibs, articles, gossip shit. They've dated a lot of the same women, and that's interesting, too. Another kind of competition maybe."

She scooped up more berries. "And another thing I found interesting. There's all these little bits about one or both of them being at some bullfight in Spain, some big premiere in Hollywood, or skiing the Matterhorn or whatever. Doing the shiny spots when other people in that strata do the shiny spots. Would we be doing that if I wasn't such a bitch about it?"

"Absolutely. Pass me that coffee, bitch."

She snorted out a laugh. "Remember your crappier side, ace, and my knowledge thereof. Anyway, what was interesting was none of the exes were in any of the shiny spots at the same time as they were. Not once that I could find a mention of. They still occupy that same strata, and the ex-wives in particular run the same kind of loop, but they never seem to hit the same spot at the same time. Running with that, I scraped a little more off. Ex-Moriarity has a second ex, but they do. Hit the same spot at the same time, often. I want to get her to tell me why that is."

She paused. "Did you know there are all kinds of write-ups and little features on us, on our vacation?"

Roarke pointed a finger at Galahad who'd begun his crouch toward the berries. The cat turned his head toward the screen as if suddenly enraptured by the financial news.

"I expect there would be."

"Doesn't it bother you?"

"No, it's just what is." He watched her drink some of the orange juice he'd fortified with a vitamin supplement. "And none of those who write up that sort of thing have any idea I'm sitting here having breakfast with my bitch of a wife after some very pleasant morning sex."

She shifted her gaze. "The cat knows."

"He'll keep his mouth shut if he knows what's good for him. We have home." He touched a hand briefly to hers. "Outside of it? Privacy isn't as important, or as possible."

"I get that, mostly. Some of these people, and I think these two are in that type, they seek out that kind of attention. They want to read about what they were wearing when they had pizza in some trattoria in Florence."

Apparently she'd been wearing cropped celadon pants and a white, sleeveless float. She shrugged that off.

"They like attention," she continued. "I think that plays into why they chose this sort of murder game, with the attention-getting elements. They like hearing the media buzz about it."

"Another reason they may have timed it so it favored the odds of you being called in as primary."

"Maybe." She downed the rest of the juice having no idea how much that pleased him. "I need to get going. I'm going to swing by and pick Peabody up at her place, save some time."

"Will you spread the word about Saturday, or should I?"

"Saturday?"

"Your gathering of friends."

She stayed blank another moment. "Oh. Right. I'll do it."

He pulled out a memo cube. "A reminder." He took her chin, drew her over for a kiss. "Try not to come home with any more slices or holes."

She trailed a finger down his side, where he'd had a slice of his own. "Same goes."

She used the time she poked along in traffic to send e-mails for what Roarke called the gathering of friends, got it off her plate. And promptly forgot about it.

Attention, she thought. Her killers enjoyed it. Considered it their due? Possibly. A different matter from the killer who sought attention because on some level he wanted to be caught, wanted to be stopped, even punished.

If it was, as her line of theory followed, some sort of contest or competition, getting caught wasn't an issue. Winning was — or if not winning, the competition itself.

However, competitions had rules, she concluded. Had to have some sort of structure, and in order to win, someone else had to lose.

How many more rounds of play? she wondered. Was there an endgame?

Questions circled in her mind as she stopped at a light, idly watched pedestrians cross. Ordinary people, she mused, off to their ordinary day. Breakfast meetings, shops to open, marketing to deal with, jobs waiting to be done.

People with a direction to keep, chores to be done, lists in their heads, duties to perform. Most people, most ordinary people, ran by the clock. Work, school, family, appointments, schedules.

What did these two run by? They weren't ordinary people, but two men born into the top level of privilege. Men who could have whatever they wanted whenever they wanted it, and ordinary people served it up for them, ran on their schedule, even their whim.

Power and privilege.

Roarke had both, and, yeah, she thought, maybe part of the reason he was who and what he was was due to the fact he'd grown up hard, and grown up hungry. But that wasn't the sum of it.

She thought of him and Brian Kelly, that long, strong connection, affection, trust. Brian owned and ran a successful pub in Dublin, and Roarke owned and ran half the damn world. But when they came together, as they had at the park, at a murder scene, at a family farm, they were simply friends.

Equals.

It was more than what you had, even more than how you'd come by it. It was what you did with it, and with yourself.

Power and privilege, she thought again. Just another excuse for being an asshole.

Two blocks from Peabody's, Eve tagged her partner. "Five minutes. Get your ass down."

She cut transmission without waiting for a response.

When she pulled up, double parking while other vehicles objected bitterly, she scanned the building where she'd once lived.

Ordinary again, a squat tower like so many others in a city jammed with people who needed space to eat, sleep, live. A hive, she thought, honeycombed with those spaces, those people, all living on top of each other. Now she lived in a home far from ordinary, one Roarke had built through ambition, need, style, wealth — and which she was still faintly embarrassed to admit was a mansion.

Maybe she wasn't exactly the same woman she'd been when she'd lived in the hive, and maybe she'd come to understand that she was better for it. But the core remained, didn't it? She still did what she did, still did the job, lived the life.

Maybe you just were what you were, she considered. Evolving, sure, changing as your life changed. But that core was still the core.

She watched Peabody come out, her dark hair pulled up and back in a short, bouncy tail; a thin, loose jacket swinging at her hips; short, summer pink gel boots on her feet. A long stretch from the square helmet of hair, the buffed and polished uniform she'd worn when Eve had taken her on as aide.

Changes, and Eve admitted she wasn't always comfortable with change. But pink shoes or not, Peabody was a cop right to the bone.

"Money doesn't make you an asshole," Eve said when Peabody opened the door, "it just makes you an asshole with money."

"Okay."

"And people who kill for thrills? They always had the thirst for it, the predilection for it. Just maybe not the stones."

Peabody wiggled her butt to settle in.

"And you think we're going to see that about Dudley when we talk to the ex-fiancée?"

Cop to the bone, Eve thought again. "I'm going to be pretty damn surprised if we don't."

"From the background I ran, she seems like the solid type. Volunteers as a counselor at the local youth center and he coaches softball. They belong to the country club, and she chairs a committee here and there. Feels like sort of the usual bits for that social and financial lifestyle."

Ordinary people, Eve thought again, with money.

"She'd have been a lot higher on the ladder if she'd married Dudley." Peabody shrugged. "But she's not exactly scraping bottom. Anyway, with what you dug up last night she's connected to Dudley and Moriarity with the cousin thing, the college pal thing. Makes you wonder, if we're right about these two, how far back they've been into the nasty."

"That kind of partnership requires absolute trust — or stupidity. I don't think they're stupid — or not completely stupid." Eve considered. "And that kind of trust has to build over some time. Because if one of them cracks, it all cracks, if one talks, they both go down. And still . . ."

"Still?"

"If it's competition, one has to lose. Losing would be not making the kill, or getting caught, or screwing up. I can't turn it any other way."

"Maybe neither one of them believes he can lose."

"Somebody has to," Eve countered.

"Yeah, but when McNab and I play, for instance, I'm always sort of shocked and pissed off if I lose. I go in knowing I'm going to win. Every time. It's the same with him. I think because we're pretty well matched in the games we get into. And separately we usually destroy whoever else we're playing against."

"It's a thought." Eve squeezed it a little harder. "It's a good thought," she decided. "They're arrogant bastards. Maybe the concept of losing isn't on the table." She rolled it around in her mind, let it bump against the other elements. "The killings are planned. They're orchestrated, and so far we know two were orchestrated back-to-back. There's no impulse about it. Someone plots and plans and basically choreographs murder, there's something in there that wants the kill. You can hide it, spruce it up with coats of polish, but that something's going to eke through off and on."

Peabody nodded. "Especially with or around someone who's close enough to see it. So they, you could say, recognized each other."

Recognition. Wasn't that the same term she'd come to when considering her long friendship with Mavis?

"Yeah. I would say recognition's a factor. What we need is to find other people who recognized them. We need to build on that until we have enough to bring them in, sweat them some. Or enough to get a search. Because they have to be communicating after a kill. There's no way either of them would or could wait until the media hits to confirm the round."

"On my fork, I haven't found any connection between the vics, between the vics and Sweet or Foster, between the vics and Moriarity or Dudley, or any combination thereof, except for the known company connections."

"Might still be there, something more subtle, or something that just doesn't show."

Connecticut was different, Eve mused. The space people could claim for their own purposes spread, with lots of green, lots of trees, gardens manicured as luxuriously as any society matron after a salon session.

Vehicles showed off their style and shine on paved driveways — and as those private spaces increased in size, she caught glimpses of red clay tennis courts, the Caribbean blue of swimming pools, the dark circles of helipads.

"What do people do out here?"

"Whatever they want" was Peabody's opinion.

"What I mean is, you can't walk anywhere. There's no deli on the corner, no handy glide cart, no buzz, no movement. Just houses."

"I guess that's why people live out here, or move out here. They don't want the buzz. They want the quiet, and the space. You get to have both," Peabody pointed out.

Using the navigation on her wrist unit, Eve turned into a driveway that circled to a house on a small rise. VanWitt had gone for a modified U-shape with the center two-story leg connecting the long, single-story juts in a mix of stone and wood and glass.

Flowers were cheerful and plentiful, trees tall and shady.

She angled where the drive widened into a small lot, and pulled in beside a spiffy little topless number in stoplight red.

"It's pretty." Peabody looked around as they walked to the main door. "Probably a nice place to raise kids with all this room. Low crime area, good schools."

"You thinking of moving?"

"No. I want the buzz, too. But I can see how people aspire to places like this."

A woman in cropped pants and a tucked white shirt answered the bell. "May I help you?"

"Felicity VanWitt." Eve held up her badge. "Lieutenant Dallas and Detective Peabody, NYPSD. We'd like to speak with her."

"The children." The woman's hand rushed up to slap against her heart.

"It has nothing to do with the children."

"Oh. Oh. They're on a field trip in New York today, with their youth club. I thought . . . Sorry. Doctor VanWitt is in session. Can you tell me what this is about?"

"Who are you?"

"Anna Munson. I'm the house manager."

"We'll need to speak with Doctor VanWitt directly."

"She should be done in about ten minutes." Still she hesitated. "I'm sorry. I don't want to be rude, but we're not used to having the police at the door."

"There's no trouble," Eve told her. "We're hoping the doctor can give us some insight regarding an investigation."

"I see." Clearly she didn't, but she stepped

305

back. "If you don't mind waiting. I'll let the doctor know you're here as soon as she's out of session."

The house was as pretty and spacious inside as out, managed, Eve supposed, very well by Anna. Flowers looked to have come straight from the gardens, and had been arranged without fuss. Anna showed them to a sitting area with views of those gardens, and a pretty little house that served a sparkling swimming pool.

"Can I get you something cold to drink? I was just thinking about iced coffee."

Eve couldn't understand why anybody wanted to screw good coffee up with ice, and shook her head. "No, thanks."

"I'd love some, if you're making it, anyway."

Anna smiled at Peabody. "It gives me an excuse to have some. Please, sit down, be comfortable. I'll only be . . . did you say Lieutenant Dallas? Eve Dallas?"

"That's right."

"In the book? The Icove investigation? I read it last week. Oh, it's so exciting — horrible," she added quickly. "But I couldn't put the book down. Dallas and Peabody. Imagine that. Doctor VanWitt's reading it now. She'll be thrilled to meet you."

"Great," Eve said and left it at that. She

306

didn't roll her shoulders to shift off the discomfort until Anna hurried out. "How long do you figure that's going to happen? Ooh, the Icove book. Crap."

"I don't know, I think it's pretty frosty. And you've got to admit, it changes attitudes. She was polite but suspicious, now she's juiced we're here."

"I guess there's that." Eve wandered the room. Flowers, some family photos, nice paintings, comfortable furnishings in soft and serene colors.

Given the size and layout of the house, she suspected this was a kind of company room rather than a family hangout.

Anna was back quickly with a tray holding Peabody's iced coffee, a second glass, and a cup of hot black. "I remember from the book you like coffee, Lieutenant, so I made some just in case. The doctor will be right with you. The other iced coffee's for her. Is there anything else I can do for you?"

"No. We're set. Thanks for the coffee."

"It's no problem at all. I'll just . . ."

She trailed off as Felicity came in, another glass in her hand. "Anna, you left your coffee in the kitchen." Felicity passed the glass, then walked straight to Eve. "It's a pleasure to meet you. Both of you. I'm absolutely riveted by the Icove story, and desperately

307

hoping you're here to ask me to consult on some fascinating murder."

She laughed when she said it, bright and easy, and obviously not at all serious. She wore her hair short and brightly red, and her eyes, a deep, dark green, held warmth and ease.

"Actually, Doctor VanWitt, we'd like to ask you some questions about Winston Dudley." And Eve watched that warmth and ease die.

"Winnie? I don't know what I could tell you. I haven't seen him in years."

"You were engaged at one time."

"Yes." The smile remained in place, strained at the corners. "That was practically another life."

"Then you can tell us about that life." Deliberately Eve picked up her coffee, sat.

"I'll just be in the kitchen," Anna began.

"No, please stay. Anna's family," Felicity said. "I'd like her to stay."

"That's fine. How did you meet Dudley?"

"At a party, at my cousin's — at Patrice Delaughter's. She knew him a little. She was seeing Sylvester Moriarity, and in fact became engaged shortly after the party. Winnie and I started seeing each other, and were engaged for a short time."

"Why short?"

"I wish you'd tell me why this matters to anyone. It was nearly fifteen years ago."

"I wonder why it's difficult for you to talk about it, after almost fifteen years."

Now Felicity sat, picked up her coffee for a long, slow sip as she studied Eve. "What has he done?"

"What makes you think he's done anything?"

"I'm a psychologist." Both her face and her voice sharpened. "You and I can play cryptic all day long."

"I can only tell you he's connected to an investigation, and my partner and I are conducting background checks. Your name came up."

"Well, as I said, I haven't seen or spoken to him in a very long time."

"Bad breakup?"

"Not particularly." Her gaze shifted away from Eve's. "We simply didn't suit."

"Why are you afraid of him?"

"I've no reason to be afraid of him."

"Now?"

She re-angled in her chair. Stalling, Eve noted, trying to pick the right words, the right attitude.

"I don't know that I had any reason to be afraid of him then. You're not here because you're doing simple background, because he's connected to an investigation. You're investigating him. I think it's reasonable for me to know what and why before I tell you anything."

"Two people are dead. Is that enough?"

Felicity closed her eyes, lifted a hand. Without a word, Anna moved over to sit on the arm of the chair, take that hand in hers.

"Yes." She opened her eyes again. They stayed direct and steady as they met Eve's. "Do I have any reason to be afraid of him, for myself, for my family?"

"I don't believe so, but it's hard to say when I don't have the background between you and Dudley. He was at a dinner party in Greenwich a few nights ago," Eve added. "A few miles from here. He didn't contact you?"

"No. He'd have no reason to. I'd like it to stay that way."

"Then help us out, Doctor VanWitt." Peabody kept her voice low and soothing. "And we'll do everything we can to make sure it does stay that way."

"I was very young," Felicity began. "And he was very charming, very handsome. I was absolutely dazzled. Swept off my feet, cliché or not. He pursued me and courted me. Flowers, gifts, poetry, attention. It wasn't love on my part, I realized that after it ended. It was . . . thrall. He was, literally, everything a young woman could have wanted or asked for."

She paused a moment. Not stalling now, Eve noted, but looking back. Remembering. "He didn't love me. I realized that sooner than I realized my own feelings, but I wanted him to. Desperately. So I tried, as young women often do, to be what he wanted. He and I and Patrice and Sly went everywhere together. It was exciting, and God, so much fun. Weekends at Newport or the Côte d'Azur, an impromptu dinner trip to Paris. Anything and everything."

She took a deep breath. "He was my first lover. I was naive and nervous, and he was very considerate. The first time. He wanted other things, things that made me uncomfortable. But he didn't push, not overtly. Still, the longer we were together, the more I felt something off. Something . . . as if I'd catch a shadow or movement out of the corner of my eye, then turn and it would be gone. But I knew I'd seen it."

She drank, cleared her throat. "He enjoyed illegals. Many did, and it was recreational. Or it seemed so. Then again, recreation was what he did, what we did, so there was always a little boost of something. And he did pressure me to use, to have fun, not to be so closed in.

"When he and Sly were together, there was a kind of wildness. And it was appealing at first, exciting at first. But then it got to be too much. Too fast, too hard, too wild because, at the core I wasn't what I was trying to be."

She paused, breathed, and on the arm of the chair Anna continued to sit. A silent wall of support.

"He started hurting me. Just a little, little accidents — accidents that left bruises, and I started to realize he liked to see me frightened. He'd always soothe me after, but I could see on his face he enjoyed frightening me — accidentally locking me in a dark room, or driving too fast, or holding me under just a bit too long when we went to the beach. And the sex got rough, too rough. Mean."

She stared into her iced coffee for a long moment — remembering again, Eve thought — but her hand stayed steady as she lifted the glass to drink.

"He was so charming otherwise, and so smooth. For a time I thought it was me, that I was too closed in, not open enough to the new or the exciting. But . . ."

"You didn't want what he wanted," Eve

prompted. "Or to do what he pressured you to do."

"No, I didn't. It just wasn't me. I started to realize, more to accept, I was pretending to be something I wasn't to please him and I knew I couldn't keep it up. I didn't want to keep it up," she corrected. "Once I overheard him and Sly talking about it, laughing at me. I knew I had to break it off, but didn't know how. My family adored him. He was so charming, so sweet, so perfect. Except for those movements out of the corner of the eye, except for the accidents. So I picked a fight with him, in public, because I was afraid of him. And I maneuvered him into breaking it off. He was so angry, and he said horrible things to me, but every word was a relief because I knew he didn't want me, and he wouldn't bother about me. He'd walk away, and I'd be free. He never spoke to me again."

She shook her head, let out a short, surprised laugh. "I mean that literally. Never another word. It was as if all those months hadn't happened. We both attended my cousin's wedding to Sly, and he didn't even speak to me, or look at me — not, if you understand me, in a way that was a deliberate snub. It was as if I were invisible, didn't exist. Never had. I was just no longer there for him. And that was an even bigger relief."

They look through you, Roarke has said, and Eve understood exactly what Felicity meant.

"Is that what you wanted to know?"

"Yeah. You have a nice place here, Doctor VanWitt. I bet you have nice kids, and a good husband, work you're good at and enjoy, friends who matter."

"Yes, I do. Yes."

Eve rose. "Maybe you were young, maybe you were naive and dazzled and swept. But you weren't stupid."

"He's a dangerous man, they both are. I believe that."

"So do I. He won't bother you or your family," Eve promised. "You're not in his world, and he has no reason to hurt you. I'm going to talk to your cousin."

"Will it help if I contact her, tell her some of this?"

"It might."

"Then I will." Felicity got to her feet, held out a hand. "I hope I helped, but I have to tell you this sort of thing is a lot more exciting, and a lot less emotionally wearing, in a book than it is in real life."

"You got that right."

14

Peabody stayed quiet for several miles while the lushly green landscape whizzed by.

"You really don't think there's a chance Dudley will go at her, or her family?"

"Not now, not while he's into this competition. If he'd wanted to pay her back for dumping him, or maneuvering him into dumping her, he'd have done it before this." She wanted to talk to Mira, but . . .

"She wasn't worthy of him. He was just using her as a toy, then he got tired of her. That's how it plays in his head. So, just as she said, she stopped existing in his world. She's not even a blip at this point. If they keep at it, continue to rack up points or however they're scoring this deal, either one of them could decide to make it personal. But not now."

"If it is a competition, how do two men like these two come up with it? Does one of them just say, 'Hey, let's have a murder

tournament?' I can almost see that," Peabody added. "Too much to drink, hanging
out, maybe add in some illegals. Things you
say or do under the influence that seem so
brilliant or funny or insightful, and you're
never going to follow through with clean
and sober. But they do, and if this is a
contest, they go forward with it, with rules,
with, like you said, structure."

She shifted, frowned at Eve. "It's a big
deal. Even if it's just a game to them, it's a
big game. Not just the killing itself, which is
way big enough, but the selections — vics,
weapons, timing, venue, and cover-your-ass.
Do you go into that cold? I mean, if you're
going to compete in a major competition —
sports, gaming, talent, whatever, you don't
just jump in, not if you want to win. You
don't jump on a horse to compete for the
blue ribbon if you've never ridden before,
right? Because odds are pretty strong for
not only losing, but humiliating yourself in
the bargain. I don't see these guys risking
humiliation."

"Good." Excellent, in fact, Eve noted.
"Neither do I."

"You think they've killed before?"

"I'd bet your ass on it."

"Why my ass?" Eyes slitted, Peabody
jabbed a finger in the air. "Because it's big-

ger? Because it has more padding? That's hitting below the belt."

"Your ass is below your belt. I'd bet mine, too, if it makes you feel better."

"Let's bet Roarke's ass, because really, in my opinion, of the three of us his is the best."

"Fine. We'll bet all the asses on it. They've killed before. Together most likely, impulse, accident, deliberately — that I don't know yet. But I'd bet Mira's shrink's ass that the kill is what turned this corner for them. That, and getting away with it."

"Mira has a really nice ass."

"I'm sure she'd be thrilled to know you think so."

"Jeez, don't tell her I said that." Peabody's wince included a defensive hunch of shoulders. "I was just following the theme."

"Follow this theme," Eve suggested. "Probability is high, factoring the prevailing theory is correct, that Dudley and/or Moriarity killed, by accident or design, within the last year. I got an eighty-nine-point-nine when I ran that last night. Take it further into the theme, and assume this is also correct, it's very likely the kill took place when they were together, and they conspired to cover up the crime. With this success, they opted to create a competition so they could revisit the thrill of that experience."

"As whacked as it is, it makes more sense than the 'Hey, let's go out and kill people' idea."

"They might've been traveling, business, vacation. Both of them spend more time bouncing around than pretending to work in New York. I want to track their travel over the past year, then search for missing persons or unsolved murders, unattended or suspicious deaths in the location during that time frame."

"It's possible they killed someone who wouldn't be missed."

"Yeah, but we start with what we can do. I think there will be two."

Peabody nodded slowly. "One for each of them. They'd need to start even. Jesus, it just gets sicker."

"And the next round's coming up."

Roarke had no particular fondness for golf. He played rarely, and only as an overture and addendum to business. While he appreciated the mathematics and science of the game, he preferred sports that generated more sweat and risk. Still, he found it simple and satisfying to entertain a business partner with a round, especially when he'd arranged it to coincide with Dudley's and

Moriarity's morning tee time.

He changed from his suit to khakis and a white golf shirt in one of the private dressing areas, then waiting for his guest in one of the lounge sections, passed the time with golfing highlights on the entertainment screen.

When he spotted Dudley stepping out of a dressing area, he rose and strolled toward the refreshment bar at an angle designed to have their paths crossing. He paused, nodded casually.

"Dudley."

The man's eyebrows rose. "Roarke. I didn't know you were a member."

"I don't get in often. Golf's not really my game," he said with a shrug. "But I have a business associate in town who's mad for it. Do you play here often?"

"Twice a week routinely. It pays to keep the game sharp."

"I suppose it does, and as I haven't when it comes to golf, I doubt I'll give Su much of a challenge."

"What's your handicap?"

"Twelve."

Roarke watched Dudley smirk, an expression of derision the man didn't bother to mask. "That's why it pays to keep the game sharp."

"I suppose so. You?"

"Oh, I run at eight."

"I think that's what Su hits. I should send him along with you. He'd have a better time of it."

Dudley let out a short laugh, then signaled. Roarke turned, gave Moriarity another casual nod as he approached.

"I didn't know you played here," Moriarity said when he joined them.

"Rarely."

"Roarke's entertaining a business associate with a round, though he claims golf isn't his game."

"It's the perfect way to mix business and pleasure," Moriarity commented, "if you possess any skill."

"What's one without the other? David." Roarke turned again, drawing the lean man with the silver-speckled black skullcap of hair into the group. "David Su, Winston Dudley and Sylvester Moriarity. David and I have some mutual interests in Olympus Resort, among others."

"A pleasure." David offered his hand to both. "Would Winston Dudley the Third be your father?"

"He would."

"We're acquainted. I hope you'll give him my best."

"Happy to." Dudley angled, subtly, giving his shoulder to Roarke. "How do you know him?"

"Other mutual business interests, and a shared passion for golf. He's a fierce competitor."

"You've played him?"

"Many times. I beat him the last time we played by a single stroke. We have to make arrangements for a rematch."

"Maybe I can stand as a surrogate. What do you say, Sly? Shall we make it a foursome?"

"Why not? Unless Roarke objects."

"Not at all." And that, Roarke thought, couldn't have been easier.

Shortly, they stood outside in the breeze surveying the first hole. Dudley smoothed on his golf cap.

"I met your wife," he said to Roarke.

"Did you?"

"You must have heard about the murder. A limo driver, booked by someone who, it appears, hacked into one of our security people's accounts. A terrible thing."

"Yes, of course. I caught a mention of it on a screen report. I hope that's not causing you too much trouble."

"A ripple." He dismissed it with a flick of the wrist as he took his driver from the caddy. "She did me a service when she uncovered a scam being run by two of my employees."

"Really. Not connected to the murder?"

"Apparently not. Just something she came across while looking into the compromised account. I should send her flowers."

"She'd consider it her job, and nothing more."

Dudley took a few practice swings. "I assumed, from reading Nadine Furst's book, you were more involved in her work."

Roarke flashed an easy grin. "It plays well that way in a book, doesn't it? Still, the Icove business had some real meat, and certainly interest in it has proven to have considerable legs. A dead limo driver, even with that loose connection to you, isn't quite as . . . sensational."

"The media seems to find it meaty enough." Turning his back on Roarke, he set at the tee.

Annoyed, Roarke thought, and wasn't surprised to find himself largely ignored by both men. Su was more of an interest to them as his blood was bluer and truer than an upstart from the Dublin alleyways.

He had no doubt they'd never have spoken above two words to him, much less arranged a golf foursome, if not for their belief he had the inside track on Eve's investigation. Now that he'd indicated otherwise, he was of no particular interest.

The space they provided gave him the opportunity to observe them.

They cheated, he noted, and by the fifth hole he'd deciphered their codes and signals. Smooth and subtle, he concluded, and very well practiced.

They were a bloody pas de deux, he thought.

Midway through the course Roarke and Su opted to send their cart ahead and walk to the next hole.

The temperatures hadn't yet reached their peak, and on the tree-lined green in Queens, with the occasional breeze to stir the air, the heat was pleasant enough.

And the walk, as far as Roarke was concerned, provided more entertainment than bashing at a little white ball with a club.

"They're disrespectful to you," Su said, "in the most polite of ways."

"That doesn't concern me."

But Su shook his head. "They wear their rudeness as comfortably as their golf shoes."

"I expect they put more thought into the shoes. The rudeness is simply second nature."

"So it appears." He gave Roarke a curious

look as they walked. "In the years we've done business together, you've indulged me in a round of golf, which you dislike, but this is the first time you've arranged a foursome in this way. Which you did," Su continued, "by maneuvering Dudley into suggesting it."

"One of the reasons I like doing business with you, David, is you see clearly no matter how thick the bullshit."

"A skill we share. And so seeing, I think you have other concerns here."

"You'd be right. It was an opportunity to ask your opinion, as you know Dudley's father. What do you think of the son?"

"That he and his friend aren't the sort I would play golf with as a rule."

"Because they cheat."

Su stopped, narrowed his eyes. "Do they? I wondered. But why would they risk censure by the club for a casual game? We have no bet."

"For some, winning's more important than the play."

"Will you report them?"

"No. That doesn't concern me either. I'm happy to let them win this game, in their way, as there's a bigger one they'll lose. This game was, for me, a way to observe, and a chance to add to their sense of entitlement, overconfidence. Should I apologize for drawing you into it?"

"Not if you'll give me more details."

"As soon as I can. How well do you know Dudley's father?"

"Well enough to tell you the father is disappointed in the son. And I see now he has cause." Su sighed. "It's a pity you don't put more time and effort into your golf game. You have a natural ability and an excellent form, without the interest. If you had it, I think even with the cheating we could beat them."

Well then, Roarke mused, he was here to entertain an associate. "I can make it harder for them to cheat."

"Is that so?"

"Hmm." Roarke slipped a hand into his pocket, tapped his PPC, which boasted a number of off-the-market modifications. "In fact, it might be more to the point of the exercise to do just that. The game itself, David, will be mostly on you, but I'll put myself into it with more . . . interest from this point."

Su's smile spread sharp and fierce. "Let's bury the bastards."

Eve turned toward the bullpen at Homicide as Baxter and Trueheart walked out.

"You've got a Patrice Delaughter looking for you," Baxter told her. "We put her in the Lounge."

"Huh. Word spreads fast."

"It does. Such as looking forward to Saturday."

"Appreciate the invitation, Lieutenant," Trueheart added.

"Right. Good. Peabody —"

"Listen, Trueheart's too shy to ask, but I'm not. Can the boy bring a date?"

"I don't care," Eve said as Trueheart turned light pink and hunched his broad shoulders. "I guess that means you want to bring one, too."

"Actually no." Baxter grinned. "A date means I'd have to pay attention to somebody, and it's going to be all about me, brew, and cow meat. We're due in court." Baxter tapped a finger to his temple and strode toward the glide.

"Thanks, Lieutenant. Casey's going to be really excited about Saturday. Um, can we bring something?"

"Like what?"

"A dish?"

"We have dishes. We have lots of dishes."

"He means food," Peabody interpreted. "Don't worry about it, Trueheart. They've got plenty of that, too."

"Why would somebody bring food when they're coming to your place to eat?" Eve wondered when Trueheart hurried after Baxter.

"It's a social nicety."

"There are too many of those, and who started them? It's like dresses and suits."

"It is?"

"Never mind. I'll take Delaughter. Write up the interview with VanWitt, and start digging into the travel."

"All over it."

Eve headed into the Lounge with its simple, sturdy tables, vending offerings, and smell of bad coffee and meat substitute. A scatter of cops took a short break there, or conducted informal interviews.

No one would mistake the woman at the corner table for a cop. A mass of wavy red hair with golden highlights spilled past her shoulders in a fiery waterfall. It tumbled around a porcelain face dominated by bold green eyes, such was the family resemblance to her cousin.

It ended there.

She wore a snug, low-cut tank over very impressive breasts and a snug, short skirt over fairly stupendous legs. A multitude of thin chains of varying lengths sparkled around her neck, over the impressive breasts, and to the waist of that snug, short skirt.

She looked . . . indolent, Eve thought, as if she had all the time in the world to sit there — all sparkle and flame in the dull room — and was mildly amused at where she found herself to be.

"Ms. Delaughter?"

"That's right." Patrice did one quick up-and-down sweep, then offered a hand. "You'd be Lieutenant Dallas."

"I'm sorry you had to wait. I was expecting to go to you at some point."

"Felicity contacted me. I was in the city, so I decided to come here. It's a fascinating place. That's a fabulous jacket. Leonardo?"

Eve glanced down at the blue jacket she'd put on to cover her weapon. "Maybe."

"Simple lines in a cropped length matched with a strong color in that Nikko blue, and the interest of the Celtic design on the buttons, which match the one on your ring. Clever. And the fit's perfect."

Eve glanced down again. She'd just thought of it as the blue jacket.

"Leonardo's one of the reasons I'm in the city. He's designing a gown for me."

"Okay. Do you want something to drink?"

Patrice's smile went from beautiful to breathtaking. "What's safe?"

"Water."

With a laugh, she gestured. "Water it is."

Eve crossed over, scowled at the vending machine, and mentally warned it not to give her grief. She plugged in her code, ordered two bottles of water, and to her surprise the machine spit them out without incident.

When Eve came back to sit, Patrice held up a hand. "Let me just say, before we start, that I knew some of what Felicity told you today, but not all. We're friendly, and we love each other, but we tend to drift in and out of each other's lives. I wish, back when she got involved with Winnie, I'd taken more care with her, that I'd taken care of her. We were both young, but she was, always, softer than I. Sweeter, and more easily hurt. So I suppose I'm here because of that, because I feel, in some ways, responsible for what happened to her. How he treated her."

"She came through it."

Felicity smiled again. "Softer and sweeter, and in some ways stronger. The woman he ended up marrying was neither soft nor sweet, and came out of it richer. Maybe a bit harder."

"You know Annaleigh Babbington?"

"I do, though we're not particularly close. I dated her second husband for a while."

Patrice flashed that smile again. "We're colorful, playful fish in an incestuous little pond. From what Felicity said, I imagine you're going to talk to her at some point. It may have to be a later point, as she's vacationing on Olympus for the next couple weeks. I can tell you, as it's common knowledge in our little pond, there's no love lost between Leigh and Winnie."

"Is there any lost between you and Sylvester Moriarity?"

"None."

"Why don't you tell me about it? About him."

"Sly." She sighed, sipped her water. "No woman forgets her first — husband I mean. You're still on your first."

"Planning to stay there."

"We all do. I was crazy about him. Maybe I was a little crazy altogether, but I was young and rich and considered myself invulnerable. He was exciting, maddeningly aloof, and a little dangerous under all that polish. It attracted me — the undercoating, you could say."

"Dangerous how?"

"Everything was immediate, and harder, faster, higher, lower than everyone else. It had to be or we'd be like everyone else, and that we would never be. We drank too much, did whatever illegals were in style, had sex anywhere and everywhere." She angled her head. "Did your mother ever pull out that chestnut about if your friends jumped off a cliff, would you jump, too?"

Eve had a flicker, very brief, of her mother's face, and the loathing in her eyes for the child she'd borne. "No."

"Well, it's an old standard. We had to be the first to jump off the cliff. If there was a trend, we were going to set it. If there was trouble, we were going to make it. God knows how much money our parents pulled out of the coffers to keep us out of jail."

"There aren't any arrests on your records."

"Greased palms." Patrice swept her fingers over her palm. "It's also a standard and works in every language. We were self-indulgent and reckless, then I did the most reckless thing of all. I fell in love. I believe he had feelings for me, which I thought were love — and might even have been, for a while, in some strange way. Then he met Winnie, and though it took me a long time to see it, Sly loved him more.

"Not romantically, exactly, and not sexually," she added. "Sly likes women. But what I came to realize after we were married, after it became clear we couldn't remain so, was he and Winnie weren't like two sides of the same coin. They were the same side. They didn't want anyone, not long-term, on that other side."

"Did he ever hurt you, physically?"

"No, never. I think there might have been others, other women he did hurt, but never me. I was his wife, and that was, again in a strange way, a point of pride — for a while. Still, it was after we were married, a year or so after Winnie and Felicity broke up and Winnie was out and about with women, that Sly asked me if I'd be agreeable to experimenting with a third bed partner."

She paused, sipped, studied Eve. "Felicity told me she felt you were very nonjudgmental."

"I have no reason or cause to judge you, Ms. Delaughter."

"Do me a favor, considering the topic. Call me Pat." She set down the water, said nothing for a moment as conversations murmured around them, as people came in, as others walked out. "This takes me back. God, I really was crazy about Sly. I thought he was everything I wanted. Exciting, handsome, daring. And at that point in my life I was completely open to trying everything. Except initially I thought he meant Winnie, and that I wasn't open to."

"Why?"

She leaned forward. "I came to understand Sly wasn't everything I wanted, and there was something in there that would doom or damn me, but Winnie? After Felicity broke things off, he was, again under that polish, vicious. There was something in his eyes, in his voice, in his body that sent alarms out. I don't really know how to explain it to you, but young and adventurous as I was, I wasn't willing to share a bed with him. And on that point I was very clear, very firm."

"How'd he take that?"

"He barely spoke to me for the next two weeks, and in fact, took off without me for a few days to spend some time . . . God, I don't remember where. It hardly matters. When he came back, and we made up, he told me he'd been angry because of my attitude, because I'd insulted his closest friend, and put restrictions on our own relationship."

She smiled a little. "It didn't change my mind about those restrictions, but I was relieved when he told me that wasn't what he wanted either. He didn't want another man, even his good friend, in bed with us, but another woman. And I thought, what the hell, that could be fun, and I had been pretty harsh about Winnie. So why not?

"He suggested hiring a pro, which would keep things very level. No emotional involvement. I liked the idea, I admit it. And at first it was very sexy, very exciting, strangely intimate. She was skilled and truly beautiful, and seductive. Patient with me as it was my first time with a woman or with more than one lover."

Eve felt the buzz. "Do you remember her name?"

"I'm sorry. I don't. I'm not sure I knew it, or if she used her name. Is it important?"

"It might be. Do you remember what she looked like?"

"Perfectly. It's etched." Patrice didn't smile as she tapped her forehead. "Sly enjoyed watching us together for a time, and having us with him, around him. But then he began to hurt her, he was so rough, so unlike himself — or what I expected. I didn't like it, but it didn't seem to bother her. In fact, she soothed me. I remember drinking buckets of champagne, smoking some zoner, doing what I thought was Exotica. Then it all went a little mad. A lot mad. It turned frantic and mean. I had no control, no boundaries. And I have very little memory of the rest of the night, into the next day."

"He slipped you something."

"He gave me Whore and a chaser of Rabbit. My husband did that to me." She pressed her lips together for a moment, gripped the chains around her neck as if they were an anchor keeping her in place. "I like sex. I like a lot of sex, but this wasn't voluntary. Do you understand?"

"Yes."

"I thought, when I surfaced, we'll say, that I'd just overdone it with the alcohol and drugs, with the experiment. Physically I felt sore and sick and blurry for days, enough that Sly had the house droid keep me in bed and bring me soups and teas until it passed. But worse, I had flashes for months after, where I swore I saw Winnie's face over mine, heard his voice, felt his body. Sly never asked me to repeat the experiment, and told me I imagined things, so I let it go. But part of me knew, from the way Winnie looked at me, I hadn't imagined it."

When Patrice lapsed into silence, Eve leaned forward so their eyes met. "Do you need a break?"

"No. No, let's just get it done. One day I was waiting for a friend at Chi-Chi's. We were going to have lunch and do some shopping, and the pro slipped into the chair across from me. I was surprised, to say the least. She said there were lines, and my

335

husband had crossed them, but she would deny ever having spoken to me if I told him. She told me he'd given me drugs, and he'd let his friend have me when I was under them."

Her voice faltered, but she took a long drink of water and came back stronger.

"Maybe I didn't care, and that was my business. She could lose her license if she engaged with a client who used illegals, so she would deny that, too, if it ever became an issue. But I had a right to know he'd abused me. She told me they'd recorded it. Recorded taking turns with me. That she'd said and done nothing because she was afraid of them, because she was new, because my husband was her client. And she left before I spoke a word, before I could think of a word to speak. I knew she told me the truth."

"Do you want more water?" Eve asked her.

"No, I'm fine. It was a long time ago. I'm over it." But she took a deep breath. "I waited. It took weeks. I had to search when he was out of the house, when I knew I'd have plenty of time. But eventually I found the disc. I made a copy, which I still have. Which he knows I still have. I confronted him, and I suppose — technically — I blackmailed him. I got one hell of a settlement in the divorce." She breathed again, sat back. "I suppose that was cold and mercenary."

"Personally, I think it was fucking smart."

That spectacular smile shone again. "Thanks. I've never told anyone. Not even my husband — my third — whom I do love, very much. I married a second time before I was over what had happened, and that was a mistake. But Quentin and I have a good marriage, a good life, and I'd rather, even now, he didn't know. But Felicity thought it was important, vital even, that you understand who these men are."

"It is. Very. Excuse me a minute." Eve rose, pulled out her communicator and stepping away contacted Peabody. "My partner's going to bring in some pictures for you to look at. Is that okay?"

"Yes, all right." Her fingers closed over her chains again, twisted them, untwisted them. "Should I get out of town?"

"I don't think there's a problem for you, but I understand you often travel in the same circles — same place, different times. I'd keep to those different times."

"That's easy enough."

"Are they usually together — in that same place, same time?"

"Often, from what I read, what I hear. They like to gamble and compete, and preen. Well, we all preen, it's part of what we do. I do see them a bit here and there, and make it a point — it's pride — to speak to him when I do. But it's show. We don't really socialize, we don't have mutual friends who are actual friends. I think you understand."

"Yeah."

"Oddly, I've never been afraid of either one of them until now. I figured I had the upper hand, and it was all so long ago. It hardly seems real. Then Felicity called today, and suddenly it was very real, and I'm afraid."

"Do you want protection, Pat?"

"I can get my own, and I think I will, but thank you. Do you really believe they've killed two people?"

Eve kept her gaze steady so Patrice could see the truth in them. "At this point Moriarity and Dudley are persons of interest in my investigation. I have no evidence against either of them at this point." She waited a beat. "Do you understand?"

"Yes. Yes, I understand perfectly."

When Peabody walked in, Eve gestured her over. "This is Detective Peabody. Patrice Delaughter."

"Thanks for coming in, Ms. Delaughter."

She smiled, but it lacked some of the earlier brilliance. "It's been an experience."

"I'd like you to look at these pictures." Eve opened the folder, began to spread out the shots. "Tell me if you recognize anyone."

"Her." Eve had barely set out the ID photos when Patrice laid a finger on Ava Crampton's. "That's the pro Sly hired. She's older, of course, but I know her."

"This is the licensed companion Sylvester Moriarity hired when you were married, and who subsequently spoke to you regarding the night you were her clients?"

"Yes. There's no question about it. She's stunning, isn't she? A face that's hard to forget. She did me a very good turn. I remember her."

"Okay. Thank you."

"Wait." Patrice grabbed Eve's wrist. "Felicity said there'd been two murders. Is she one of them?"

"Yes. Here's what I want you to do. Stay out of his way, off his radar. He's got no reason to think about you, and we'll keep it that way. I may need you down the line, but I'll try to keep the information you gave me out of it."

"He killed her."

"I can only tell you she's dead."

Patrice closed her eyes. "I'm going to ask my husband to come to New York. I'm going to tell him everything. If you need to use what I've told you, use it. She helped me, and she didn't have to. If he's responsible for her death, it must go back to that night, mustn't it?"

"I'd say so. Where's your husband?"

"Right now he's in London on business."

"Leave me your contact information and go there. You'll feel safer. I can have a couple of officers escort you where you need to go, to stay with you until you're on your way."

"Do I look that shaky?"

"You did what was right. Why should you look shaky?"

"I'm going to give you my card. I'm going to take your officers and I'm going to take your advice. And I'm going to contact Felicity and ask that she and her family join us in London."

"I think that's a good idea. Peabody."

"I'll take care of it. You can wait right here, Ms. Delaughter."

"I've always thought of myself as intrepid," Patrice murmured. "Now I'm going to ask if you could stay here with me until this is arranged."

"No problem. Do you know if either Moriarity or Dudley owns a crossbow?"

"I don't, sorry. I do know they both have an interest in weaponry and war. We have some mutual acquaintances that have been on hunting parties with them, or have gone on the same sort of safaris. Quentin and I aren't really interested in that sort of thing. I could ask around."

Eve considered. "When you're in London, maybe you could contact someone you know who's been out with them. Without mentioning them specifically."

"Just asking about the experience," Patrice said with a nod. "Quentin and I are thinking about trying a safari or a hunting trip. What's it like, what do you do, any gossip, any stories? Yes, I can do that."

She leaned forward, looked hard into Eve's eyes. "I think you know the answer to this, and I think I need to know it. Why her and not me? Why kill her, a hired pro from so long ago?"

"She was the best," Eve said simply. "You were just his wife, and then you weren't. But she'd become the best in her field, and the former connection made it — I think — irresistible."

"Just his wife." Patrice let out a weak laugh. "Well, thank God I didn't matter."

"You will. When this is done, you'll matter. And, to my way of thinking, that's the

341

kind of payback money can't buy."

Eve rose when Peabody came in with two officers.

15

Connections, Eve thought as she watched Patrice walk away flanked by two burly uniforms.

"You picked big males so she'd feel safer."

"I thought it would add to it," Peabody admitted. "She nailed Crampton's photo. It's been better than twelve years, but she nailed it."

"Some faces stay with you." Her own father's, Eve thought, over hers in the dark while he pushed himself inside her. She understood, too well, how some faces, some moments, some nightmares never quite faded away.

"So Crampton wasn't random."

Eve shook her head, gave a come-ahead gesture as she started back toward her office. "What she was, was unlucky. And your instinct that there were some links in the whole mix was on target."

"Yay, me. Even if I couldn't find what I

thought should be there."

"It wasn't going to show, and that's something they counted on. The odds of us talking to any of their exes had to be long from their perspective. And if we did, neither of them would consider the women would talk, relive old humiliations."

"We got lucky."

"No," Eve corrected. "We worked the case and got lucky. Ava Crampton's not only a connection, but probably a sore spot for Moriarity at last. And that added a little bonus to the contest. The random isn't altogether random, and that's where I've been off, and you were on."

"Again, yay me. Woot! Sorry, just needed the moment."

"And the moment's gone."

"Okay. So contest structure demands there be some connection between killer and vics. And maybe in both cases, it's back a ways, and that's why it's unlikely the vics recognized their killer."

"Dudley killed Crampton," Eve pointed out, "and while he probably fucked her that night, the connection's with Moriarity. He hired her. His wife. His place."

"Another kind of switch-off."

"Yeah, or," Eve considered as she kept moving, "another flag of friendship. Let me

344

do that for you, pal."

"It's not friendship, it's . . . Mira would have a word for it. A fancy word."

"Whatever the word, there's going to be some connection between Dudley and Houston. Maybe back a couple decades, too. Probably where you were going before, when Houston was getting in trouble. Illegals," Eve said when she turned into Homicide. "Dudley and Moriarity used and I'm betting Dudley, at least, still does. They had to buy them somewhere. Houston used and sold, and they're all of an age. They might have done a few deals before Houston straightened out."

She angled it, turned in. "Patrice said their families spent a lot of money greasing palms, keeping them out of jail, off the books. Houston maybe gets busted for a deal, and the deal's with Dudley say. Dudley's father has to pony up to keep his son out of it, but he was probably pissed, punished the son some other way."

"It plays for me. Another pay-it-back factor. Both the vics serviced them in some way," Peabody proposed, and followed Eve into her office. "Then became successful, got the cache, but still offered services."

"It could be enough. Both vics played to what Delaughter called their underlayment." Eve stood, studying the board. Saying nothing, Peabody moved to the Auto-Chef, programmed two coffees. "Who they are beneath the surface, and now what they can and do command. They bought them then, they buy them now."

Eve took the coffee, eased a hip onto her desk, continued to study the board. "Who's going to put them together with an LC they booked in their twenties? That's what they think. They're not in her book. And who'd put them together with a limo driver who dealt illegals when they were all hardly more than kids?"

"Even connecting them this way doesn't lock it in."

"No, but it will. Another mistake of arrogance — their little private joke."

"And maybe, like you said, they still use."

"No maybe about it. Dudley's got the whole toy store, and he'd never resist taking samples. And with this twisted relationship they have, I'd say Moriarity would share."

"The sex is another angle. They weren't in the vic's book, but they might be in someone else's."

Again, Eve shook her head. "Too much ego to pay for sex or more to risk anyone finding out they did. They're above that, too high on the food chain to have to pay at this stage. Women are supposed to be eager to give it to them. It's not about sex anyway. It never was. It was, and is, about power, dominance, violence, privilege. Expensive thrills. A man drugs his wife so he can watch his best friend rape her? That's not about sex. It's about their own amusement, and still is. About their connection to each other. She was just another knot in the rope that ties them together. They're fucking soul mates."

"If they drugged Delaughter so they could share, they could have done it again. If they use sex as a kind of bond."

"Yeah. They'd be a lot more careful since she found them out. What have you got on the travel?"

"Enough to tell you they're all over the damn place. They may be based in New York, but they're not here half the time. Maybe less than half. I'm putting together trips they've either taken together or ended up in the same place but traveled separately. They've both got private transpo — multiple transpos — so it's tricky. Added to it they've each got homes or villas or pieds-à-terre or however you say it all over. We're going to have a lot to go through, even keeping it to a year."

"Send me a chunk of it, and I'll start

scrolling for missing persons or unsolveds."

She sat at her desk, considered her board. Then contacted Charles Monroe.

"I just sent you an e-mail," he told her. "We're looking forward to seeing everyone on Saturday."

"Saturday . . . right." What the hell had she done? "Good."

"And this isn't about asking if we'd bring potato salad."

"No. It's about Ava Crampton. Did she ever mention an incident from her early days. Hired for a threesome, husband and wife. Young, rich. During the book, the husband slips the wife a Whore/Rabbit combo, and adds a friend to the mix. Husband and pal take turns with the wife."

"No, and she wouldn't have. She could've lost her license, or had it suspended for not reporting the illegals use, particularly if the wife wasn't aware or in full prior agreement. That would've added rape, and Ava could've been charged. And that's a career ender. Reporting it afterward would have covered her, as she'd have had a strong case for participating under duress or out of fear, but it would've gone in her file."

"That's what I thought."

"If this happened, how did you find out about it?"

"She told the wife."

On-screen, he smiled. "That sounds like her. Direct and clean."

"Give me a quick overview of the husband's motives. Just a general opinion."

"Without having the background or dynamics I can't be anything but general. The use of a rape drug indicates a need or desire to control and debase. By bringing another man into the event, without the wife's prior knowledge or permission, he expands that control, deepens the debasement while at the same time demonstrating to the other male the female is his property. He can do as he pleases to or with her. Basically he's saying use her, that's what she's here for. By sharing her they make her a kind of commodity, little more than a platter of meat they might split for dinner. It may also be a way of releasing latent homosexuality."

"By fucking her in tandem, they metaphorically fuck each other."

"You could put it that way."

"Interesting. Thanks."

"Anything I can do."

For a few moments she sat, letting pieces settle in her mind. After updating her notes she streamlined them into a report, including both interviews, her impressions, the generalized opinion from a sex therapist, and the directions she intended to pursue.

She sent copies to Whitney and Mira.

She updated her murder book, her board, then sat with her feet on her desk, another cup of coffee in her hand, and let it all settle again.

Tonight, she thought, or tomorrow. Not much time before the next round. If the pattern she was seeing was a pattern, Moriarity would be up, which meant the vic would be connected most closely to Dudley's past, and the lure would be through Dudley and Sons.

"And it could be anyone," she said aloud.

No, not accurate. The anyone had to be in New York, as both Dudley and Moriarity were in New York. So the target lived here or worked here or was currently visiting here.

The target was important in his or her field — some field of service most probably. Humble beginnings? she considered. Both vics had that in common, starting low on the ladder and climbing high.

Did that play?

Still active in their field. Someone who could be hired or called in, consulted, booked.

Shit.

Someone was going to die because a

couple of arrogant whacked-out assholes wanted to bond over blood, and she couldn't prove it.

No point obsessing about what had yet to happen, she reminded herself. Better to dig into what already had. Opening the file Peabody had sent her, she began a slow, systematic search for death.

She had grids of data on-screen when Peabody stepped back in.

"Dallas."

Eve looked over in time to catch the Power Bar Peabody tossed at her.

"These are disgusting."

"Nah. A num-nummy treat. Vending says so. Besides if you've generated as many missings and unsolveds as I have, you need the boost."

"Maybe." With some reluctance Eve tore the wrapping. Focus had smothered the low-grade headache that now made itself known behind her eyes. She took a bite, winced. "Jesus, what do they put in these things?"

"It's really better not to know. If we're not going to clock any more field time, I'm going to take the files home and put some time in on them."

"Why are you going home?"

"Because it's already past end of shift, and

I want my man and real food."

Eve scowled at her wrist unit. "Dammit."

"I can stay if you want to work it here."

"No. No, go. I lost track. Send whatever you've put together to my home unit, and I'll . . ." She trailed off as she saw she'd lost Peabody's attention. Her partner had shifted, was currently brushing at her hair and smiling a dopey smile.

"What's Roarke doing here?" Eve demanded even as she heard his voice.

"Hello, Peabody. I like your hair. Cool, efficient, and feminine all together."

"Oh." She fussed some more. "Thanks."

"The lieutenant working you late?"

"She's going," Eve snapped. "Go."

"Have a nice evening," Roarke said. "See you Saturday."

"We'll be there."

"Do you have to do that?" Eve muttered when Peabody scurried away.

"Which that is that?"

"Make her go gooey-eyed and stupid."

"Apparently I have that power, though she didn't look either to me." He came in, sat on her desk. "You, however, look tired and cross." He picked up the PowerBar. "And this is likely part of the reason."

"Why are you here instead of home?"

"I took a calculated risk that my wife

352

would still be at her desk. Now she can drive me home after we stop and get a meal."

"I really have to —"

"Work, yes. It can be pizza."

"That's fighting dirty."

"Fighting clean always seems like such a waste." He two-pointed the PowerBar into her recycler. "Gather up what you need and we'll eat while I tell you about the round of golf I played today."

"You hate golf."

"More than ever, so you owe me. You buy the pizza."

"Why do I owe you?" she asked as she organized her file bag.

"Because I played eighteen holes with your suspects."

She stopped dead. "You did what?"

"I arranged to take a golf-mad business associate to the club where Dudley and Moriarity play. We made a foursome."

She actually felt the temper spurt up from her center to her throat. "Damn it, Roarke, why did you —"

He cut her off by poking a finger in her belly. "You don't want to start on me after I spent a morning hitting a ball toward a hole in the ground with a club. Which admittedly I'd likely have done anyway, as David

353

loves the bloody game, so it seemed efficient to maneuver it into a little field work. I do occasionally run into your suspects here and there."

"Yeah, but . . ." She thought about it, and had to admit the spurt ebbed. "Yeah. What did you —"

"Walk and talk," he interrupted. "I've put myself in the mood for that pizza now."

"Fine, fine, fine." She grabbed the bag, shut down her computer. "You've never played golf with them before?"

"And never will again," he vowed as they started out. "Though we did end up beating them by three strokes, which didn't put either of them in a cheery mood. Masked it well enough," he added and with resignation squeezed into an elevator with Eve and a dozen cops.

"They don't like to lose."

"I'd say winning is a kind of religion for them. They cheat."

"Seriously?" She narrowed her eyes. "Not surprising really. You mean they work together — team cheating?"

"They do. I can't say how they compete with each other, one-on-one, but with others, they have a system."

The elevator doors opened. Two cops crowbarred out, three more muscled in.

Summer sweat clogged the air like cooking oil.

"How do you cheat at golf?"

One of the cops, obviously a golfer, snorted. "Sister, it ain't that tough."

She spared a glance over her shoulder. "Lieutenant Sister."

"Sir."

"They use signals, code words."

Roarke got a wise nod from the uniform. "Bribe a caddy, he'll maybe shave a couple strokes off. I played a guy who carried balls in his pocket. Dropped them down his pants legs. Asshole."

"They were a bit more high-tech." Roarke spoke directly to the uniform now. "They used doctored balls programmed to pocket directional devices."

"Fuckers. A man who'll cheat at golf will scam his own mother outta the rent money."

"At the least," Roarke agreed, amused enough to tolerate the rest of the ride down to the garage.

"They know the course," he continued as they walked to her car. "Have obviously mapped out each hole, programmed various lies. They signal each other as they study their positions, the angles and so on. One takes his turn; the other engages the device. They're smooth about it. I'll drive since you have a headache."

"I don't have a headache. Exactly." When he cocked his brow at her, she dropped into the passenger seat. "I have an eye ache. That's different."

He walked around the hood, slid behind the wheel. "They're careful not to play so well it causes undo attention. Solid players, is what they come off as. And having a very good game today, a few strokes under their handicap. Until the tenth hole."

"I don't know what that means and don't want to."

"Neither do I, particularly."

"Successful businesspeople are supposed to like golf. It's some sort of rule."

"Well, by your rules I'm an abysmal failure." He said it cheerfully, with a definite tenor of pride. "In any case, we started closing the gap on the tenth."

"How did you beat them?"

"David's a superior player, and you can say I got into the spirit of the thing, put myself into it more."

"They were cheating. It takes more than having a good game to beat a cheat."

"They're not the only ones who know how to manipulate a game. I screwed up their devices with one of my own. Every time they used one, they sliced or hooked."

"What, like a fish?"

"I adore you. I do." Unable to resist, he leaned over and kissed her cheek. Noisily. "You make me feel like a duffer."

"Okay. If you want."

"Actually, not at all." He streamed through traffic. "I'd send their ball far right or left, into a trap or the rough, which added strokes or points to their scores. In golf you want the lowest."

"I know that much."

"In any case, by the thirteenth hole, bad luck for them, we were even, and they couldn't risk using the devices. So we played it straight."

"Really?"

He turned his head to smile at her. "I was tempted to add an edge, just to rub their faces in it. But I had brought David in for the entertainment, and he got more pleasure out of beating them without it." He paused a moment, nipped through an intersection. "And the truth of it, so did I."

"How'd they react to losing?"

"Oh, they were well and truly pissed, masked under hearty laughter and gracious congratulations. Even bought us a round at the nineteenth hole. Dudley's hands shook, and that was rage. He had to keep them in his pockets until he'd controlled it. And I believe he controlled it with whatever he snorted or swallowed on a trip to the loo."

"Yeah, I'm betting he snorts, swallows, or smokes a lot. But I meant losing to you in particular."

Nothing got by his cop, he thought. "I'd say they've gone from disdain to loathing, which is also satisfying. If I were the sensitive type, I'd have scraped off their loathing with a putty knife, as it was thick and sticky, but the fact is I enjoyed it quite a lot."

"That's because by drinking on their dime and joining their hearty laughter you were actually giving them the finger."

"And with a modest, just-had-a-run-of-luck smile."

"You milked it," Eve concluded.

"Like they were a couple of cows with engorged utters."

"Eeww."

"Maybe you had to be there. You'd be interested, I think, to know that Dudley had a bit of a rage in the locker room when we weren't around and ordered his clubs destroyed."

"How do you know?"

"I bribed the butler, naturally."

"Naturally, and naturally locker rooms in your world include butlers."

"He also smashed his transmitter. I found

pieces of it on the floor of the dressing room he used."

"Temper, temper. That's good. I can use that."

"I thought so. He mentioned you. Made a point of telling me he'd met you, and tried to find out how involved I am in your investigation. I made it seem as if this case wasn't of any particular interest, just a driver and an LC, hardly worth my notice, and not all that important to you from my perspective. That didn't please him either."

She said nothing for a moment as he maneuvered through the sluggish river of vehicles. "That was good. That was a pretty good play. It gives him an emotional investment, makes him want to create more importance, more notice. It can't be ordinary, that's the whole point. If you were right, and they wanted me in particular, and likely you, it's no good if you aren't interested, and it's just another day of work for me."

"The Icove case was huge — investigatively, in the media, in the public's attention. You said he mentioned the case, the book to you when you interviewed him. He did the same with me."

"Fuck." Now she scrubbed her hands over

her face. "It could've been part of the inspiration."

"They'd have come to this sooner or later. What I do think is the case, the book, the upcoming vid made him, or them, consider how exciting it might be to become a book or vid. To have their competition, then generate all the interest, the notoriety of a major case."

"The thrill would last a long time. Might be able to play that, too," she mused. "Just maybe."

He pulled into a private underground lot, the sort she, on principle, refused to pay the price for.

"You could've found a street spot."

"Live a little, darling. There's a place a few blocks from here. It's a nice evening for a bit of a walk, and I can guarantee the pizza's excellent."

He took her hand as they walked outside.

"You own the place."

"Since my wife tends to live on pizza half the time, it seemed a good idea to have a spot close to home that serves exceptional pie."

"Hard to argue."

The bright evening sun brought people out in droves. Strolling tourists hauling shopping bags and gawking up at the buildings and sky traffic. And getting in the way, Eve thought, so the people with somewhere to go weaved, dodged, and kept moving. It was a kind of weird and chaotic ballet, she decided, punctuated by the blare of horns, the chatter of the sidewalk hawkers, the pips and pings of 'links and headsets.

A couple of kids surfed by on airboards, laughing like hyenas. And on the corner, the glide cart vendor broke out in song.

"I guess this was a pretty good idea," Eve decided.

"It's cleared your headache — sorry, eye ache." And he paused, selected a sleeve of flowers in bold red and blue from a sidewalk display. He passed the price to the merchant, handed the flowers to Eve while the cart operator's voice soared in some Italian aria.

It was a damn nice moment, Eve thought. A damn nice New York moment.

"I guess this makes it a date."

Roarke laughed, circled her waist, and tugged her in for a showy kiss that had the flower vendor applauding. "Now it's a date."

A half block down he showed her to a little sidewalk table outside a bustling pizzeria. She tapped the Reserved sign. "You booked ahead."

"It pays to be prepared. I also ordered

ahead, so they'll know what to bring us. Now that I've told you about my day, you can tell me about yours."

"It was a little rough."

"I don't see any bruises."

"Not that kind of rough."

She started with the interview in Greenwich. Before she was done, a waiter brought a bottle of red, another of sparkling water, and an artful tray of antipasto.

"I'd say she made a wise decision, and had a lucky escape."

"She had this little pocket of fear tucked away, away deep enough I expect she forgot about it for long stretches of time. Then something reminded her, or she just had a bad day and it opened up. But there was something about him, once she got close enough to see it — and I think she's wired with that shrink circuit — to create that fear."

"Well, he's a monster, isn't he?"

"Why do you say that?"

"Your man who abducted women and tortured them to death was a monster. The Icoves with their twisted egos and science were as well. He's no less of one. He uses his position, which he's never earned, to intimidate or humiliate or frighten because it makes him feel more important. And now he's escalated that and kills for sport, for amusement. He's been handed his wealth and position, and rather than do something with it, or simply coast on it for that matter, he uses it as a weapon and considers the weapon his due, and the killing his right."

"And again, hard to argue." She studied the pizza the waiter set between them. "That looks pretty damn great. The second interview was rougher than the first. Are you sure you want to hear about it over dinner?"

"That's our way, isn't it?" But he saw something in her eyes. "It can wait if you'd rather."

"I guess I'd rather not. Wait, I mean."

So she told him, over pizza, of betrayal and cruelty and rape. It was better, really, to get it out, say it all with the city buzzing around them, with the comfort of food, with his hand reaching over to cover hers in a gesture of absolute understanding.

"You feel a connection to them, especially Patrice Delaughter."

"Maybe more than I should."

"No." He covered her hand again. "Not more than you should."

"They didn't have to tell me, neither of them. They chose to. Like Ava chose to tell Patrice what had been done to her when she could've just walked away from the whole deal. They did the right thing, and it couldn't have been easy."

"For the two who are alive and well and with their families, I think it will be easier now. I think when you're done, those pockets of fear you spoke of will be empty."

She drank some wine, and thought: *No, fear pockets are never really empty.* But she didn't say it.

"They're both monsters. Killers aren't always," she added. "Some kill, and for terrible and selfish reasons, but they aren't monsters. The idiot in Ireland was stupid and selfish and ended Holly Curlow's life because what, she hurt his feelings? Because he was drunk and pissed off? But he'll never really get over what he did. He'll replay those moments in his head the rest of his life, because he's not a monster."

And you'll remember her name, Roarke thought, *and her face.*

"Some kill because they're misdirected, bent, scared, greedy. But these two kill because, I think in some way, they feel entitled. More, under the polish is the monster, but under the monster is a kind of spoiled, ugly child."

"You know them better now."

"Know them," she agreed with her eyes

364

cop-flat. "Know some of their weaknesses, the flaws in the polish. Their next target . . . there'll be a connection somewhere, some-time — Peabody was right about that, and we'll find it. I don't know if it'll help us stop them, but it'll help me lock the cage door after we do."

"I'll help you when we get home. We'll divvy up those searches and see what we can make of them." He poured her a little more wine. "I think you're right. They've had practice."

"I can't do anything about the ones they've done, except use them to stop them from killing more. But, Roarke, I don't have enough to stop them before the next. I know in my gut I'm already too late. Someone's clock is ticking down right now."

She looked around at the bustle, at the tourists, at the others sitting at pretty outdoor tables drinking wine.

"Maybe they're having dinner, too, maybe some nice wine. Or they're working late, or getting ready to go out for the evening. They're probably doing something ordinary, just what they do on a summer evening in New York. They don't know how little time they have left. They don't know the mon-sters are at the door, and I'm going to be too late."

"Maybe that's true, and I know you'll suffer for it if it is. But, Eve, the monsters don't know you're even now breathing down their necks. They don't know their clock is ticking down as well. That's for you to remember now, for you to know."

He lifted her hand, kissed it. "We'll go home, and maybe, just maybe, we'll get to the door first."

16

Luc Delaflote arrived at the elegant home on the Upper East Side at precisely eight P.M. He was, after all, a man who prided himself on precision. The dignified droid met him at the door, escorted him and the driver, who carried carefully packed ingredients, to the spacious kitchen with its views of the patio, little koi pond, and gardens.

Delaflote carried his own tools, as he believed it demonstrated their import and his own eccentricity.

Fifty-two years before, he'd been born Marvin Clink in Topeka. Through talent, study, work, and towering ambition young Marvin had formed himself into Delaflote de Paris, maître cuisinier. He'd designed and prepared meals for kings and presidents, sautéed and flambéed for emirs and sultans. He'd bedded duchesses and kitchen maids.

It was said — he knew, as he'd said it

himself — that those fortunate enough to taste his pâté de canard en croûte knew how the gods dined.

"You may go." He dismissed the driver with a single turn of his wrist. "You." He pointed at the droid. "You will show me now the pots."

"One moment, please," the droid said to the driver. The droid opened several deep drawers holding a variety of pots, pans, and skillets. "I will show the driver out, then come back to assist you."

"Assistance I don't want from you. Keep out of my kitchen. Shoo."

Alone, Delaflote opened his case of knives, spoons, and other tools. He took out a corkscrew, and opened the bottles of wine he'd personally selected. After opening, he searched the polished steel cabinets for a worthy wineglass.

Sipping, he studied his temporary realm, the stove, ovens, sinks, prep counters, and deemed it would do.

For the client who had paid him handsomely for the trip to New York to prepare a romantic, late-night supper for two, he would create a selection of appetizers highlighted by the caviar he'd chosen and served on a bed of clear, crushed ice. When the appetite was whetted, the fortunate pair would enjoy an entrée of salmon mousse along with his signature baguettes and thin slices of avocado. His main, poulet poêle de Delaflote, would be served with glazed baby vegetables and garnished with generous sprigs of fresh rosemary from his own herb garden.

Ah, the fragrance.

This he would follow with a salad of field greens harvested only an hour before he'd boarded his private shuttle, then his selection of well-aged cheeses. For the finale he would prepare his far-famed soufflé au chocolat.

Satisfied, he set up his music — romantic ballads — in French, *bien sûr,* for a romantic meal. Donning his apron, he got down to business.

As he sometimes did, he acted as his own sous-chef, chopping, slicing, peeling. The shapes, the textures, the scents pleased and excited him. For Delaflote, peeling a potato could be as sensuous and pleasurable as peeling the clothes from a lover.

He was a man of small stature and trim build. His hair, a dramatic and carefully styled mane of glossy chestnut, flowed back from a face dominated by large, heavily lidded brown eyes. They gave him the look of a romantic, a dreamer, and were often the first element in the seduction of women.

He adored women, treated them like queens, and enjoyed having several lovers revolving through his life at the same time.

He lived life fully, wringing every drop of flavor from it and savoring every morsel.

With the chicken in the oven, the mousse chilling, he poured another glass of wine. Enjoying it, he sampled one of his own stuffed mushrooms, approved.

He cleaned his area, washed the greens, vegetables, and herbs for the salad, then set that to chill. This he would lightly toss with a tarragon dressing while his client and the fortunate husband dined on the main course. Pleased with the scents perfuming the air, he basted the chicken with sauce — the recipe a secret guarded as fiercely as the Crown Jewels — added the pretty little vegetables.

Only then did he step out into the walled garden where, according to the client's wishes, the meal would be served. Again he approved. Lush roses, big-headed hydrangeas, arching trees, starry lilies rose and spread and speared around the paved courtyard. The night held clear and warm, and he would see that dozens of candles were arranged and lit to add the sparkle of romance.

He checked the time. The servers would be arriving any moment, but in the meanwhile he would call the droid, have it set out the table, show him the selection of linens and dinnerware.

He took out one of his herbal cigarettes to smoke while he set the scene.

The table just there, little tealights glittering in clear holders. Roses from the garden in a shallow bowl. More candles ringing the courtyard — all white. He would send one of the servers out to get more if there weren't enough on hand.

Ah, there, nasturtium. He'd toss some of the flowers with the salad for color and interest.

Crystal stemware, *mais oui.*

The sounds of the city, of traffic crept over the garden walls, but he would mask that with music. The droid would have to show him where the system was kept so he could make the appropriate selections.

He turned a circle, stopped when he saw a man step out of the lights of the kitchen into the shadows of the garden.

"Ah, you are arrived. There is much work to be . . ." He stopped, eyebrows lifting when he recognized the man.

"Monsieur, you I was not expecting."

"Good evening, Delaflote. I apologize for

the subterfuge. I didn't want it known I was your client tonight."

"Ah, so, you wish to be incognito, *oui?*" Smiling a knowing smile, Delaflote tapped the side of his nose. "To have your rendezvous with a lady, what would it be, on the q.t. You can trust Delaflote. I am nothing if not discreet. But we are not complete. You must give me time to create the ambience as well as the meal."

"I'm sure the meal would be extraordinary. It already smells wonderful."

"Bien sûr." Delaflote made a slight bow.

"And you came alone? No assistants?"

"Everything is prepared only by my hands, as requested."

"Perfect. Would you mind standing just over there a bit? I want to check something."

With a Gallic shrug he'd perfected over the years, Delaflote moved a few steps to the right.

"Yes, just there. One moment." He backed into the kitchen, retrieved the weapon he'd leaned against the wall. "It does smell exceptional," he said as he stepped back out. "It's a pity."

"What is this?" Delaflote frowned at the weapon.

"It's my round." And he pulled the trigger.

The barb went through the heart as if the organ had been ringed like a target. With its keen, merciless edge, it continued out the back to dig into the trunk of an ornamental cherry tree.

Moriarity studied the chef, pinned there, legs and arms twitching as body and brain died. He stepped closer to take the short recording as proof he'd completed the round.

With the ease of a man who knew all was in place, he walked back inside, replaced the weapon in its case. He opened the oven for a moment, breathed in the rich aroma before shutting it off.

"It really is a pity."

So as not to waste the entire business, he rebagged the wine, found the champagne Delaflote had chilling. He took one last glance around to be sure all was as it should be, and satisfied, walked back through the house and out the front. The droid he'd programmed for the event waited in a black, four-door sedan.

He checked the time, smiled.

The entire business had taken hardly more than twenty minutes.

He didn't speak to the droid; it already had instructions. As programmed it pulled into Dudley's garage.

"Put these in Mr. Dudley's private quarters," he ordered, "then return the car. After you return to base, shut down for the night."

In the garage, Moriarity retrieved the martini he'd left on a bench less than thirty minutes before, then slipped out the side door. He strolled toward the house, circled, and joined the loud, crowded party already in progress.

"Kiki." He chose a woman at random, slipping an arm around her waist. "I was just telling Zoe how wonderful you look tonight, and had to track you down to tell you myself."

"Oh, you darling."

"Tell me, is it true what I heard when I was inside a few minutes ago? About Larson and Kit?"

"What did you hear?" She looked up at him, all eyes. "Obviously I'm not mingling enough if I'm not getting the gossip."

"Let's both get another drink, then I'll tell you all."

As he walked with her, his gaze met Dudley's through the sea of people. When he inclined his head in a faint nod, they both smiled.

Eve rubbed a hand on the back of her neck to ease the crick.

"People go missing, or end up dead. That's why we have cops, but . . ."

"You have something?" Roarke worked at the auxiliary in her office rather than in his own so they could easily relay impressions.

"About nine months ago, the two of them went to Africa, a private hunting club. It costs a mint and a half, and you're only allowed one kill of an animal on the approved list. You have guides, a cook, assorted servants, various modes of transpo, including copters. You sleep on gel beds in big, white, climate-controlled tents that other people haul around, eat on china plates, drink fine wine, blah blah. The brochure here hypes it as adventurous elegance. You can have a gourmet breakfast, then go out and shoot an elephant or whatever."

"Why?" Roarke wondered.

"My thought, but some people like to shoot things, especially if the things can't shoot back. Melly Bristow, a grad student from Sydney, working on her master's — wildlife photog — signs on as a cook. One fine morning she isn't there to whip up that gourmet breakfast. They figure she's gone off on her own to take pictures and vids, which she's done occasionally according to the statements I've got here, and her camera shit's gone, and so's her daypack. But she doesn't answer the 'link everyone's required to carry at all times. Everybody's a little ticked because she's holding up the hunt."

Eve swiveled in her chair. "Somebody else makes breakfast, and when she still isn't back, they triangulate her 'link, and one of the guides heads out to bring her back. All he finds is her 'link. Worried now, contacts camp, and we've got a search party forming. They find her camera stuff, or most of it, and they find a blood trail. Eventually they track a pride of lions, and the female and young are snacking on what's left of her."

"Christ, that's an ugly end. Even if she'd been ended beforehand."

"I think she was spared being eaten alive or mauled while she was still breathing." Though Eve had to agree. Even if, it was ugly.

"You think Dudley and Moriarity killed her, then framed the lions?"

"That's a gambit you don't hear every day," Eve mused. "But here's the thing. When they recovered her she was still, more or less, wearing her belt. And the stunner everyone's required to carry was still in the holster. This was her third trip out with this company, so she wasn't altogether green, especially if it's true everyone on staff has to go through training before going out with a group. She has time to get her 'link out of its holder, drop it, but she doesn't go for her stunner? And there weren't any photos taken that morning in her camera."

Didn't play, she thought. Just didn't jibe.

"She wanders a mile away from camp, but doesn't take any pictures?" Every step of it sent out a buzz for her. "They found what they determined was the kill site, trampled brush, the blood, drag marks, and so on. A mile from camp, and they'd missed her just after dawn. She goes out in the dark — flashlight was in her daypack — when according to the data on this site that's when a lot of the animals with really big teeth go hunting."

"What are the locals calling it?"

"Death by misadventure. Her neck was broken. Apparently lions go for the throat, rip it open, and/or break the neck of their prey. Mama lions with young cubs will drag the prey back to the den or lair or the old homestead so the kids can eat."

"A mile's a considerable clip, even if she panicked — and who wouldn't? — and ran away from camp rather than to it."

"And in a footrace, I'm betting on the lion. Now, maybe she was stupid, maybe she was, but I'm reading her data, and she doesn't strike me as stupid. She spent time in the Australian bush, did another stint at some preserve in Alaska, hit India. She had experience, and knew how to handle herself.

"Look at her." She ordered the ID shot onto the wall screen.

"Very attractive," Roarke remarked. "Very."

"It could be one of them felt he was entitled to her, and she didn't agree. Or she did and it got too rough. Got a dead woman on your hands, what do you do now? You call in your best pal, and you figure it out."

"They work together well," Roarke commented, thinking of the golf outing.

"Same side of the same coin. That's how Moriarity's ex described them. Partner up. Get her dressed, get her stuff. They knew where the pride was, and the basic hunting ground of the female because they'd seen it the day before, and the guide gave a spiel on it. Carrying deadweight a mile's not easy, but not so bad if you're taking turns. Dump the body, maybe slice it up a little hoping the cat scents the blood and comes to chow down. Toss her camera, toss her 'link, go back to camp. If the cat doesn't cooperate, well, you alibi each other. It still looks like she went out on her own and got attacked. Just by a two-legged animal."

She picked up her coffee mug, scowled when she found it empty. "Anyway, this could be where it started. It's all there. Or possibly there. A kill — an accident or impulse — the cover-up, working together. The excitement of that, then the aftermath. The search, and you two are the only ones who know — more excitement. Then, wow, it worked just as you'd hoped. You're untouchable, and wasn't that fun?"

"How long had they been out?"

"Three days. This would have been day four."

"Had they had a kill?"

"Ah . . ." She turned back to her comp screen, scrolled through statements and reports. "No."

"Then it might be even more than you've laid out. They paid to kill, and hadn't."

She said nothing for a moment. "What time is it in Africa?"

"That would depend on which part. It's a big continent."

"Zimbabwe."

"Well . . ." He glanced at the time. "About five in the morning."

"How do you just know that?"

"It's math, darling. You don't worry your pretty head about it."

"Bite me."

"Considering the topic of conversation, that was in poor taste. Hmm. So was that. And before you call the hunting club trying to dig out more, I might have another for you."

"Where?"

"Naples, Italy, or off the coast of. They were in a sailing tournament, and in and around that area for a couple weeks. During that time Sofia Ricci, age twenty-three, went missing. She'd been at a club, and had been drinking, as one would. She had a row with her boyfriend, and left."

"Alone?"

"Alone," Roarke confirmed. "Under quite a head of steam according to witnesses. The last anyone remembers seeing her was about half-midnight. She didn't make it home, and her roommate didn't worry, as she assumed she was at the boyfriend's. She didn't work the next day, so again, no one noticed she was missing. Until Sunday when the boyfriend went by her flat to make amends. He told the police, who looked at him hard and long, that he'd gone home about a half hour after she had, and he'd tried her 'link twice the next day — which was verified on his own outgoings — and assumed she was still not speaking to him. They've never found her. That was seven months ago."

"It's a big ocean," Eve commented.

"It is, yes. Your suspects stayed on Dudley's yacht or in Moriarity's villa during that period. Both of them, along with several others from their sailing club, joined in the initial search."

"More of a thrill. Another woman," she considered, "on the young side. Could've started that way figuring women are easier game — two men, one woman. Most women wouldn't stand much of a chance."

"The police cleared the boyfriend, but he was their focus for the first seventy-two hours. They're looking at it as an abduction. She had friends, family, stability, no major troubles, a good job, and so on."

"Two months between. Peabody tossed out they might have practiced on people no one would miss, but I think no. It's a bigger rush if there's an alarm, a search, media reports. Ricci might be their second. Two months gives them time to congratulate each other on getting away with murder, ride on the juice, lose the juice. Want that again."

"Time to plan," Roarke agreed. "Working together requires deciding who's responsible for what, coordinating schedules."

"Time to talk it through, work it out, pump it up. Away from their base again,"

Eve noted. "And they either figure out they don't want to be involved with another dead body or decide to switch it up, so they can use the location to dump it where it won't likely be found, at least not while they're in the area. Maybe they trolled awhile, and they got themselves a pissed-off, little-bit-drunk woman."

"A very pretty one," Roarke added and put the image on-screen.

"Yeah, that might've been part of it at first. Use her, share her, kill her. But they didn't need the sex. It was the kill that got them both off. They'd need to do it again, maybe mix it up a little, see what happens."

"Was it already a game, do you think? Already a competition between them?"

"It's intimacy. It's . . ." She shifted to look over at him, to meet his eye. "It's what we're doing here, looking for the missing and the dead. It's you and your aunt saying a few words — words that matter — in Irish. It's Charles making omelets for Louise when she's pulled the night shift."

She stopped, hesitated. "That sounds lame. I don't know how —"

"No, it's perfectly clear. It's more than teamwork, shared interests, partnership. You see it as a terrible kind of love."

"I guess I do. If I was going to pull a Mira,

I'd say they found each other, recognized each other. Maybe if they hadn't . . ." She shrugged. "But they did. And in that terrible way, they complete each other."

"Yes, I see. There might have been others, Eve. Before Africa. Others, who as Peabody theorized, wouldn't have been noticed."

"Easing into it," she considered even as her stomach tightened at the idea. "Perfecting that teamwork before they tried someone who'd show, who could even be connected to them." She raked a hand through her hair. "Let's work from here, sticking with victims who show. Let's start with six to eight from Italy. These kinds of killers generally start to escalate. They need their fix."

She ordered the computer to factor in her suspects' whereabouts for that time frame, and refined the search.

"Son of a bitch. Son of a bitch. I knew it! Data on-screen, goddamn bastards. Look at that," she snapped at Roarke. "Seven weeks almost to the damn day after the woman in Italy. Quick gambling trip, Vegas. Closer to home now. They don't travel together, but meet up there. Dudley arrives a day ahead. Big baccarat tourney, which is a stupid game."

"Actually, it's —"

"Don't interrupt."

"Yes, sir."

"Smart-ass," she muttered. "Twenty-nine-year-old female, found dead in her own car on the side of the road in the desert north of Vegas. Stun marks on her chest. Beaten to death with a tire iron left at the scene. No defensive wounds, no sexual assault. Put her out first, then killed her. No bag, no jewelry. Played at making it look like robbery. Smashed her car up, too. Cops look at that, think illegals. Some chemi-heads, drifters with bad attitudes, along those lines. Get her to pull over, stun her and the rest.

"But here's the kicker. Our vic, Linette Jones, tended bar at the casino holding the tourney. She had the next two days off, her pay, and a boatload of tips, and was heading off to Tahoe to meet up with her boyfriend. Everyone within hearing distance knew where she was going and when because it was like an anniversary thing, and she had this ring she was going to give him — also not found at the scene. She was going to propose."

"They gave statements," Roarke observed, reading the data.

"Fucking A. I bet they couldn't wait. Just loved watching the cops go off in the wrong direction. Here's where they started getting

384

more and more full of themselves, put the connection back between them and the vic. I'm going to tie them up with this, tie them up and choke them."

"I don't doubt it, but it's all what you people insist on calling circumstantial."

"As you people say, bollocks to that."

He let out a delighted laugh that only got a snarl from her. "I wonder how it is that hearing your use of the idiom of my youth makes me both sentimental and aroused at the same time."

"Idiom-smidiom. It's to the point. I can put this together, show a pattern. I just have to make it shiny enough to convince a judge to give me a search warrant. I need the next. Three to four months out now."

She found the next, three and a half months out. A male this time, older than the other victims.

"An architect," Eve read, "considered one of the best in his field, killed while vacationing at his secondary home on the Côte d'Azur. Found floating in his swimming pool by his wife the next morning. He'd been stunned, then garroted — weapon left on the body — before falling into or being dumped in the pool."

"And the wife?" Roarke asked when Eve ran it through.

"Heard nothing. They had a kid, six, and he'd been restless and feverish, so it says — and medical confirms — so she bunked down in the kid's room. No motive for the wife they could find. No trouble in the marriage, no outside affairs unearthed. She has money of her own and plenty of it. She cooperated fully, including opening all financials without a blink. She wouldn't have had the strength to do what was done to him with that wire, even with him stunned. And there's no evidence she bought a hit."

"The first male victim you've found," Roarke observed. "And a family man, one who left a wife and a son."

"I know her — the wife." Eve narrowed her eyes as she searched her memory. "How do I know her? Carmandy Dewar. I know that damn name. Computer, search for Carmandy Dewar in files and notes on Dudley/Moriarity."

Acknowledged. Working . . .

"Both of them were there at the time?"

"Yeah they were." Juiced up, she thought. Completing each other. "Hanging out with a bunch of people who hang out at places like that. I've got media reports, gossip — That's it," she said even as the computer responded.

Task complete. Carmandy Dewar appears in files from society articles involving Dudley and Moriarity. Most specifically Moriarity, who escorted her a number of times to —

"I got it, cancel task. He dated her," she said to Roarke. "Before she married the architect, Moriarity dated her. She's old money, runs with that crowd. Or did before the kid. You can bet your ass they went to her to offer support and condolence, went to the funeral looking shocked and sad. Cocksuckers. Smug, self-important cocksuckers."

"You'll want this one then, though it breaks the pattern. Two months ago," Roarke told her. "Another woman. Larinda Villi, considered in her day the greatest mezzo-soprano of her generation, and others come to that. A luminary, and at seventy-eight one of the most important and influential patrons of the arts in the world. She was found at the doors of the opera house in London, stabbed through the heart. While they were both there — Moriarity purportedly on business, and Dudley to attend the London premiere of a major vid he'd invested in — neither of them had a connection with Villi or any association."

"That showed," Eve corrected. "It's not breaking pattern. It's establishing the current one — and just what I'm looking for. We dig, there'll be something. One of their grandfathers boned her, or their mothers made them go to the opera to hear her sing when they wanted to play slap the monkey. There'll be something."

She paced back and forth, remembered she hadn't had coffee in much too long. "I need a hit."

"I'll get it. I could use one myself."

"What time is it in Africa now?"

"An hour later than the first time you asked," he called back.

"I could contact them now." She paced again. "No, write it up, shine it up, get it all down to the steps, the patterns." Add onto the board, she thought. All the other victims, the data on them. Then she'd start with Africa, expand the picture, and work her way right up to now.

"Thanks." She took the coffee Roarke offered, gulped some down. "I've got them. It's going to take some work, some finessing, but I've got enough to start pushing. You saved me a lot of time tonight."

He skimmed his knuckles down her cheek.

Pale with fatigue, he thought. "And you'll thank me for that by working several more hours."

"I've got to lay it all out so I can pull it all in, so I can talk Reo into talking a judge into giving me search warrants on two really rich men from really important families who have alibis on alternate homicides. I have to convince her, and Whitney, that all this plays — and that I can make it stick. If I can't make it stick, we can't go with it. Not yet. And —"

"Someone's clock is ticking down." He leaned in to brush her lips with his. "I know. I can update your board with these new victims. Don't look so surprised. I know how your mind works."

"I guess you do. But . . . I have to do it."

"Superstitious, are you then?"

"No. Maybe. Probably. Anyway, I have to do it. It'll help me get it set in my head."

Because they were hers now, too, he thought. That was yet another kind of intimacy.

"I'll tackle some work of my own for a bit."

"This is going to take a couple hours. You should go to bed whenever you —"

"I like going to bed with my wife, whenever possible. I can fill a couple hours."

Though he expected, as he went into his own office, she would be longer than that.

She forgot what time it was in Africa by the time she contacted the hunting club, but she knew damn well she'd hit two in the morning in New York.

She considered finessing — lying — then decided against. If one of the guides or the owners or anyone else chose to contact Dudley or Moriarity and tell them of her interest, that was fine.

She was ready to give them something to worry about.

When she'd finished, she looked down at her notes. The guide had been cautious at first, then more and more open. He'd been fond of Bristow, and that had come across clearly.

Never understood how or why she would stray so far from camp.

Never understood how or why she would cross into known hunting territory for the female lion.

Could never reconcile in his mind why she would have been so careless or why she would have set out before light.

Dudley a braggart, rude to staff. Demanding, impatient. Suspected he'd brought illegals into camp.

Moriarity cold, aloof. Rarely spoke to staff

except to order or demand.

She tried her luck with the local investigators next, and managed to flesh out — a little — what she'd pulled out of media reports.

She worked her way forward in the time line, to Naples, to Vegas, to France, to London, gathering crumbs and bits, putting those slivers and pieces in place with the whole.

She used the back of her board, making a chart of that time line, pinpointing locations, adding each victim's photo, linking all with more notes. With fact and with supposition.

Seven dead, she thought as she stepped back from the board. She knew those two pair of hands carried the blood of seven people.

Maybe more.

She continued to stare at those faces as Roarke stepped behind her, laid his hands on her shoulders, rubbed at the aches there.

"All those lives cut off. An adventurous woman, girl with a boyfriend who wanted to make up, a husband and father, a woman about to start the next phase of her life, an old woman who'd spread beauty and culture around the world. And then to another husband and father who'd turned a bad beginning into a solid now, and a woman who'd once given another woman the chance to escape a monster.

"All on this board because they decided they wanted a new thrill. A new form of entertainment. The same as somebody else turning on the screen or going to a vid."

"No. It's like a new, stronger drug."

"Yeah." Exhausted, sickened, she rubbed her eyes. "You're right, it's more that. And that's going to help me stop them. That need, that addiction, it'll push them."

"Come to bed now. You need to sleep." He turned her, slid an arm around her. "Let it rest a few hours, Eve, so you can."

"Can't think anymore, anyway." She walked out with him.

It was after three hundred hours, she realized, and no call from Dispatch. Maybe she wouldn't be too late. Maybe she wouldn't put another face on her board.

17

At first, she thought the lion gnawing greedily on her leg woke her — which was bad enough. But when she struggled through the surface of the dream, her communicator sent out its sharp, insistent beep.

"Fuck. Just fuck."

Roarke's hand ran up and down her arm in comfort as she pushed up in bed. He ordered lights on at ten percent.

"Block video," she said as she snatched the communicator from the night table. "Dallas."

Dispatch, Dallas, Lieutenant Eve.

As Dispatch ordered her to report to the house on the Upper East Side, relayed the basics, she shifted to sit on the side of the bed, dropped her head in her hands. And acknowledged.

"Before you beat yourself up," Roarke told

her, "tell me what else you could have done."

"I don't know. That's the problem. If I knew what else I could've done, I'd've done it. Then I wouldn't be going to look at a body." She scrubbed her hands over her face before she lifted her head. "And I guess I knew I would be."

"You're tired, and you're pissed off. I'm right there with you. We haven't had a decent night's sleep since we got back from holiday." He raked a hand through his hair as he shoved himself up to sit. "I had a dream there was a bloody lion prowling through the house looking for a handy snack."

She turned her head, pointed at him. "He found it. I had a dream the bitch was chowing down on my leg." And for some odd reason, the solidarity of their unconsciouses made her feel better. "I've got to grab a quick shower, clear my head. Fucking lions."

"I want one, too. The shower, that is, not the fucking lion."

She slitted her eyes at him.

"Please. I think I can resist you. This once. I'll go with you. Your scene's not far."

"We barely clocked three hours down," she pointed out. "You can go back to sleep. You're not —"

394

But he was already sliding out of bed. "I'll be your Peabody until the real one gets there. She's a lot farther to go than we do."

She dragged a hand through her hair, considered. "I could use a Peabody until Peabody shows up. And some freaking coffee."

"Then let's get moving."

When they went downstairs fifteen minutes later, Summerset stood, dressed in his habitual and spotless black suit. Eve wondered if he slept in it, like a vampire in a coffin. But she refrained from saying so as he held a tray with two go-cups of coffee and a bag that smelled like cinnamon bagels.

"Perhaps, at some point in the future, the two of you might consider actually living here."

"In this dump?" Eve snagged a coffee before he could change his mind.

Roarke took the other coffee and the bag. "Thank you. If you'd contact Caro. She can handle the eight o'clock holo. I'll be in touch with her if anything else needs to be shifted."

"Of course. Perhaps I should suggest she put 'police assistant' on your official bio."

"Well, that's just mean."

But Eve grinned widely as she walked out the door, and glanced back at Summerset, and the cat who squatted at his feet. "Thanks."

Her vehicle was, as expected, waiting. How did he manage it all? she wondered. "Maybe I need a Summerset. God, did I just say that?"

"I hesitate to point out you have a Summerset. He just provided us with coffee and bagels."

"I don't want to think about it. I'll drive. You can start being Peabody and find out who owns the house we're going to, and what the connection is to Dudley. It should be a Dudley connect this time."

She dug out half a bagel, crunching as she drove, washed that down with coffee.

"A house this time. That's not particularly public. Gotta be an angle on that. Maybe there were other people around when it went down, or —"

"The house belongs to Garrett Frost and Meryle Simpson. Simpson is the CEO of Marketing for Dudley."

"Well, they're still playing by the rules. Vic's a male, so it's not her. Could be her housemate."

"Husband," Roarke corrected. "Married nine years."

"Probably not him, either, unless they're shifting pattern a bit. What does he do?"

"Corporate law. Solid firm, and he's been with them twelve years. Full partner, but nothing that pops out as special, according to the contest rules."

"So they're probably still breathing, and have no connection to the victim. I bet Dudley's been entertained in that house plenty. He'd know the setup."

"But you think Moriarity did the killing."

"His turn at bat." She swung around a maxibus lumbering its way east with its load of sleepy passengers. "And yeah, that means Dudley would have to give him the layout. They want the kill as much as the win — more," she corrected, "so they keep the playing field even. It's logical in a really screwed-up way."

As Eve pushed her way across town, Roarke continued to play Peabody, in his own way. "Frost and Simpson have owned and lived in the house for six years. They also have a place on Jekyll Island, off Georgia. And two children, one of each, six and three. Simpson's also a loose family relation on Dudley's maternal side. A niece of his mother's second husband."

"Interesting. Increasing the connection, adding another link. It just adds to the supposition he knows the house."

"More interesting is that Frost and Simpson bought the house from Moriarity."

She flashed a look at him as she blew through a yellow light. "You're kidding?"

"I'm not, no. He owned it prior, and for five years. I'd say he already knew the basic layout without his friend's assistance."

"They don't actually give a shit about the risk of tying themselves to the murders. No, they want to."

"It adds levels and layers to the contest," Roarke commented. "Gives it a more complex structure."

"Yeah, adds a bigger rush. It's part of the rules, part of the contest rules," she said. "They have to select a target that has some connection, and facilitate the kill by using another connection. It ups the stakes. What are the stakes? What does the winner get?"

She swung in at a gate, studied the house behind it as she held up her badge for the uniform at guard.

Mansion, she corrected. It didn't come up to Roarke's level, but what did? Still, it boasted three stories, took up an entire corner, sat prettily behind a low wall.

When the uniform cleared them, she drove through, pulled up behind a pair of black-and-whites.

"There's going to be good security here." Even as she climbed out of her vehicle she tracked the cams and sensors. "Maybe they kept the system Moriarity had. He just had to break their codes."

"Body's in the back, LT," a uniform told her. "There's a patio garden deal back there. Gardener's who found him." The uniform gestured toward the work truck. "Said he was here to do some work, and said how the people who live here are away, down in Georgia. Been gone all week.

"House was locked," he continued as he walked them in and through. "No signs of break-in, no signs of struggle. Got plenty of valuables right out in plain sight. It doesn't look like anything's been taken."

"Did you clear the house?"

"Yes, sir, we did a walk-through. The place is empty, and in order. Except for the kitchen." He gestured as they entered. "Somebody was cooking. There's a whole damn chicken mostly cooked from the looks of it in the oven, and all this other stuff — food and cooking junk — on the counters."

"Oven on or off when you got here?"

"Off, LT. The lights and the music were on, just like now. The vic's wearing an apron, and I gotta say, he's a sight to see."

"Where's the gardener?"

"We got him, and his kid — bad day to bring his kid to work — in there." He gestured. "Looks like a maid's or mother-in-law's quarters."

"Get started on the knock-on-doors. Anybody saw anything I want to know. Keep the wits secured until I send for them."

"You got that."

She stepped outside, and had to agree. It was a sight to see.

She sealed up, tossed the can to Roarke, but continued to stand where she was a moment. Just taking it in.

"Garden area. Walls, sure, but it's outdoors, people walking or driving by beyond the walls. Buildings, too. People maybe looking out the window. So it fits the rules."

She turned her attention to the victim. "He's got to be a cook, right? An important cook."

"Chef. If I'm not mistaken that's Delaflote of Paris. And yes," Roarke confirmed, "he's important. One of the top chefs in the world. He owns a restaurant by his name in Paris, and occasionally cooks there. Primarily he serves private clients. Heads of state number among them."

"It fits. So Moriarity gets him here, likely using either Frost's or Simpson's ID and info. We'll want to check how he got here, and —"

"He travels on his own shuttle. It's easy

enough to confirm."

She only nodded. "Got him here, even got him to cook — or start to. Lured or forced him out here, then . . . The chef in the garden with the — what the hell is that pinning the poor, sorry bastard to that tree."

"Some sort of spear?"

She frowned at him. "What kind of spear? You're the weapon guy."

"Well, for Christ's sake, whatever propelled it isn't here, is it?" But challenged, he moved closer, studied what he could see in the early-morning light. "It would have to have some velocity to go all the way through him and into the bloody tree far enough to hold the body weight. I wouldn't think it could be done by hand. It's metal, not wood, and coated. Thin and smooth, and . . . I think it's a harpoon."

"Like for shooting whales?"

"Smaller mammals in this case and designed for spearing game fish, I would think. It's not thrown, but propelled from a kind of gun. But that's best guess."

"The chef in the garden with the harpoon. It fits, so there's the hat trick."

She walked over now, reopened her field kit. "Be Peabody."

"Peabody wouldn't have recognized a harpoon spear."

She had to give him that, but simply pointed to the kit. "TOD and ID."

He'd seen it done often enough, and he had been the one to put himself into the Peabody substitute position. So he worked while Eve examined the body.

"No other visible marks on him. No defensive wounds." She looked down, tagged a cigarette butt for the sweepers. "Probably his. Even Moriarity isn't arrogant enough to hand me his DNA on a butt. What's he, about five seven? Spear goes right through the chest, another heart shot. You want to make it count, don't want the vic wounded so he could scream. Yeah, about five seven, and right through the chest, almost dead-fucking-center of this tree trunk. Like he had a target on his chest."

"It's Delaflote," Roarke confirmed. "Luc, age fifty-two, dual citizenship, French and American, primary residence in Paris. Unmarried at the moment, with three children from various prior relationships."

"I don't need all that yet."

"I'm being Peabody, and our girl is nothing but thorough. Time of death appears to be twenty-two-eighteenish." He pointed when Eve frowned at him. "As it's my first day on the job I'd like a bit of slack, Lieutenant."

She waved that away, walked into the kitchen, back out again. Studied the body. Repeated everything.

"Somebody had to let him into the house, or give him the codes so he could let himself in. What kind of client would give somebody the codes to their house? More likely, somebody let him in. There's all the food stuff. So either the vic brings that in or the killer had it."

"From what I understand Delaflote insisted on bringing in his own supplies."

"Fine, probably no chance tracking down any fancy ingredients and nailing Moriarity with the purchase. If Moriarity let him in, did the vic know him, was he expecting him? Wouldn't he have checked, just like any other service provider, on the client? But he had to get into the house, so somebody let him in. If it's Moriarity, why wait so long for the kill? How long does it take to cook a chicken?" she demanded.

He simply stared at her. "How in bleeding hell would I know?"

She sent him a thin smile. "I bet Peabody would."

"Bloody hell. Wait. How many pounds?"

"I don't know." She scowled, held out her hands. "It's about like this."

"Hmm." He fiddled with his PPC. "Maybe two hours, according to this."

"You're a pretty good Peabody. Have to figure the killer turned it off before he left. Don't want to start the smoke or fire alarms and have the fire department here. It looks pretty much done to me, but I guess it would, like roast in the heat after it's turned off. And it's got to take some prep time. So it's likely the vic was here a couple hours. Cooking and mixing and chopping away. There's a lot of knives and cleavers and really sharp shit in there, and a fancy case for them."

"That would be Delaflote's, I imagine."

"Moriarity doesn't let this guy in, hang around for two hours while the cooking's happening. It's a waste of time, and too risky." She circled the patio, considered the angles. "Maybe he lets him in, leaves, comes back. We'll check security, but I don't know why he'd leave anything on it. It had to be light out when the vic got here."

She walked in and out again. Seeing it, Roarke thought, letting herself see it in different ways until one clicked.

"Late supper deal," she said when she came out. "Had to be. There's not enough food for a party. It looks like a fancy dinner for two, late supper. There's an open bottle

404

of wine, and a glass. That'll be the vic's, too. So where's the wine for supper? Where's the champagne? There's none in the fridge in there, chilling. The owners probably have a wine cellar, or a wine bar somewhere in there. But . . ."

"Delaflote likely selected and brought the wines he wanted for the meal," Roarke finished.

She nodded. "So this guy's doing his private chef thing, having some wine while he's at it. Gets some of it prepped. There's some sort of fishy-smelling stuff in the fridge, sealed up. But I'm not buying the owners left fishy-smelling stuff in there, then took off for vacation. Even I know better than that. So he's made some of the stuff, got the chicken in the cooker, he's got salad crap washed and in this draining thing. Takes a little break, comes outside here into the garden to catch a smoke.

"Wait, where's the staff? Don't fancy cooks like him have minions to do the grunt work? Peel, chop, like that?"

Roarke glanced toward the unfortunate Delaflote. "It's a bit late to ask him."

"We'll check on that. Anyway, he's out here, having his break. Moriarity's either with him or comes out. He's got the weapon hidden somewhere . . . No, he comes out because he's got the weapon with him. If he'd hidden it, somebody — the gardener maybe comes by a day early — might find it. He gets the vic to stand in front of that tree. Step back, pal, or step over. Has to be fast at that point because the vic didn't run. No way anybody makes a dead-on shot like that, through the middle of a tree, when the target's running."

Eve stepped over, angled herself outside the kitchen door, lifted her hand as if holding a weapon. She shifted a couple inches, then nodded. She'd bank the computer simulation would put the killer where she was standing.

"Then he checks, just to make sure he's scored his points, won his round. Does he tag Dudley to confirm? Take a picture, a short vid, something to bring his pal in. Share the moment. He goes in, shuts off the oven, and the fucker decides what the hell and takes the unopened wine, and he walks out."

"In and out, through the gates, without anyone seeing him. That's a risk, too."

"Dudley wore a disguise at the amusement park. Moriarity would have one. Something that makes him look like what he's not. Unless he's an idiot, he doesn't bring his own transpo close, take a service or a cab from right here. He has to walk awhile, put some distance in. He's got to have the propeller thing — the mechanism for the spear — with him. He's carrying some kind of case or bag for that, another for the wine. We can use that."

That was a break, she thought. A man walking carrying a case and a bag. That could be a break.

"He'd look like some guy carrying stuff home from the market, but we can use that. He should've left the wine. Smug, greedy bastard."

"There's a garden gate," Roarke pointed out. "Smarter to use that, slip around the side, out the corner, than to go out the front and through the main gates."

"Yeah. Good thought."

"Sorry it took so long." Peabody hurried out, puffing a little. "The subway was . . . oh, hi, Roarke."

"You can be you," Eve said to Peabody. "And you can be you," she said to Roarke.

"While I'm being me, I'll give you a few more minutes," Roarke suggested. "I'll find the security system, see if there's anything on it of use to you."

"You could do that. The vic is Delaflote, Luc." Eve began to catch Peabody up. "Fancy private chef, top of his field."

"Same pattern. What is that pinning him to the tree?"

"We believe it's a harpoon spear."

"Like for whales?"

Eve couldn't help herself. "Does that look big enough to bother a whale?"

"But a harpoon's for whales, right? Like in that book with the crazy guy and the ship and the whale. With the other guy named Isaac or Istak or . . . wait a minute . . ." She squeezed her eyes shut, then popped them open. "Ishmael. Call me Ishmael."

"Any guy who goes out in a ship with a spear to take on a whale's automatically crazy. And I'm going to stick with calling you Peabody. This deal is, most likely, from a harpoon gun, which propels it. It's used for fish and for killing fancy French chefs."

Lips pursed, Peabody studied Delaflote. "It works."

"TOD," Eve began again, and ran it through.

"Cold" was Peabody's opinion. "Having the vic come all the way from Paris, spend all that time cooking, then zap, impale him before the chicken's even done."

"I think the chicken's the least of the vic's problems right now. He probably brought the supplies with him, probably bought them in Paris because he's a French chef and would likely prefer his own suppliers. Run that down. I want to ID the wines he brought with him. No way it's just the one open bottle. Also run down his travel. Did he come alone? How did he get here from the shuttle? I want the times. We need EDD to scope out the security, and we might as well bring in the sweepers and the ME. The owners need to be notified. We'll —"

She broke off when Roarke stepped out. "Lieutenant? You should see this."

"Is he on the fucking system?"

"No," he said as she strode over. "But there's something else that is."

She followed him in and to a small, well-equipped security station.

"There's no activity until this point. Seventeen-thirty hours."

As he'd already cued it up, he simply hit the replay.

Eve watched the car stop at the gate. "Late-model sedan, New York plates. Peabody, run it."

The gates opened smoothly. "He had the code, or a bypass, rode right in." House security picked up the car in front of the house. The driver stepped out, walked to the front door, and coded in.

"That's not Dudley or Moriarity. Back it up, enhance. I want a better look at . . ."

She trailed off again, leaned in to the screen. "It's a damn droid. Okay, that's smart. They're not idiots. Use a droid, program him with the codes. He goes in, waits for the vic, lets the vic in. He's programmed to be there, to be . . . who or whatever they want him to be. Staff most likely."

"No other activity until Delaflote arrives at twenty hundred, on the dot, with a driver." Again, Roarke ran it through. "You can see the droid does indeed let them in. And fifteen minutes later, the security was turned off. Cams, alarms, locks. Shut down, which should have alerted the security company if they'd been informed the owners were away. I'm going to assume the owners had the good sense for that, so they'd need to use a bypass, a clone that would run on an alternate and make it appear there was no interruption in service."

"Intelicore's in the data-and-security business," Peabody commented. "Moriarity could get his hands on a clone."

"And with the security off, Moriarity can walk right up to the door and never risk being captured by the cams. He doesn't even have to code in because the door's unsecured."

Eve paced one way, then the other. "And he'd leave by the vehicle, not on foot. Why

410

walk when you can slide into the backseat and have the droid take you where you want to go? We'll still check, but that possible break just closed."

"The vehicle belongs to a Willow Gantry," Peabody told her. "I'm doing a run."

"It's going to be stolen." Eve watched the break cement shut. "They only needed it for a few hours, and they've got the droid to snag a vehicle for them. They didn't even bother to take the disc or try to screw with the hard drive. They didn't care if we made the vehicle or the droid. The vehicle's back where it came from or ditched elsewhere, and the droid's dismantled and recycled."

"I can do a diagnostic on the system here, see if I can find the bypass."

Eve looked at Roarke, shook her head. "I'll get EDD on it."

"Well then, I need to go. A moment first, Lieutenant. Good luck, Peabody."

"See you tomorrow."

"What's tomorrow?" Eve demanded as Roarke drew her out of the room.

"Saturday."

"How can it be Saturday already?"

"Blame Friday." He laid his hands on her shoulders, rubbed there until her eyes met his. "You couldn't have saved him."

"I know that in my head. I'm working on

getting the rest of me there."

"Work harder on that." He tipped her face up, kissed her.

He knew what was inside her, in her head and in the rest of her. Because he knew, some of the sorrow eased. Eve framed his face, kissed him back.

"Thanks for the help."

She walked back, found Peabody in the kitchen studying the chicken in the oven.

"You know, that looks like it would've been really good. So, Willow Gantry, sixty-three-year-old child-care provider. No record. I went ahead and checked with the day care company she works for. She and her husband of thirty-eight years left two days ago to visit their daughter and her husband, who are expecting baby number two any minute. They drove to the transpo station themselves."

"Busted it from long-term parking. Probably left it parked on the street somewhere when they were done. Go ahead and have airport security try to locate it," Eve told her. "If it's not there, let's do the Gantrys a solid and put out an alert on it. We can get it back to them."

"It would suck to come home, find your car stolen."

"Worse things happen, but why should

this? Let's take the gardener and his kid."

"There's a kid?" Distress jumped into Peabody's eyes. "A kid saw that?"

"Yeah, there's a kid. Did I leave that out?" Grateful Peabody was there to deal with the kid factor, Eve opened the door.

Eve tagged it as staff quarters, probably a live-in housekeeper or Summerset type. Nice, attractive living area, roomy, nicely appointed.

The uniform sat in one of the oversized chairs, talking to the kid about baseball. A good touch from Eve's point of view, and had her second grateful in a row when she saw the kid was about sixteen.

He sat with his father on a high-armed sofa, arguing with the cop over a call at third base in the previous night's game.

The kid was spare and trim, with skin like rich, creamy cocoa and just an inch away from beautiful. She imagined girls' hearts fluttered if he aimed those liquid brown eyes in their direction.

The father, also spare and trim, held a ball cap in his hands, and turned it round and round with nervous fingers. He didn't have the kid's beauty, but a weathered, sculpted face, and dark glossy hair that sprang in tiny ringlets.

He looked up as Eve stepped in, that face

both pained and hopeful.

"Officer, I'll need the room."

"Yes, sir. A Mets fan." The uniform shook his head in mock pity as he rose. "You meet all kinds."

"Ah, come on!" The kid laughed, but his eyes darted to Eve, too, and he inched a little closer to his father.

"I'm Lieutenant Dallas." Eve gestured them down when both father and son started to stand. "This is Detective Peabody."

"I'm James Manuel, and my son, Chaz."

"Hard day for you," she said, and sat in the chair the uniform had vacated. "You work for Mr. Frost and Ms. Simpson."

"Yes. I do their gardens, tend the pond. I have several customers in this neighborhood. They're away. They weren't here when . . . this happened."

"So I understand. Why were you and your son here this morning?"

"We were going to refill the fish feeder — koi need to be fed more in hot weather — and freshen the mulch, deadhead —"

"Sorry, do what?"

"You need to cut the dead blooms from the plants, the shrubs. You don't want them to go to seed. This —"

"Okay, I get it."

"And we were to add food to the soil. My son came with me today, to help. We have — had — a job nearby. Some planting, and a small build. We came early to do this maintenance since the owners are away and wouldn't be disturbed. It was just before dawn when we came. The lady, she gave me a code for the gate. I've had this code for five years, since I began to work for her. And this also allows us to come through the gate to the garden. Not into the house," he said quickly. "We didn't go inside."

"I understand. So you came to do your job, through the gate. You parked your truck, then you and your son came in through the garden."

"Yes." He took a long breath. "Yes, ma'am, this is just what we did."

"We were laughing," the boy said. "I told a joke, and we were laughing. I went through first. We didn't even see, not at first. We were laughing, and Papa turned to lock the gate, and I saw him. I saw the man, the dead man."

"You must've been scared." In the way she had, Peabody moved over, leaned on the high arm of the couch by the boy.

"I yelled." Chaz looked down. "I think I screamed, like a girl. Then I laughed again, because I thought it wasn't real. I didn't

415

think it could be."

"What did you do then?" Eve asked.

"I dropped my tools." James shuddered. "It sounded like an explosion, in my head anyway. And I ran to the man. I think I was yelling. And Chaz grabbed me, pulled me away."

"It was the tools. It was so loud when Papa dropped them. Like a slap, I guess. And he was going to try to pull the man off the tree. God." The boy pressed a hand to his belly.

"Do you need a minute?" Peabody laid a hand on his shoulder. "Do you want some water?"

"No. Thanks, no. I know you're not supposed to touch anything. It always says so on the cop shows. I watch a lot of screen, and it always says so. I don't know how I remembered. Maybe I didn't. Maybe I just didn't want my father to touch. It was . . . awful."

"We left. I mean we didn't stay in the garden. I was afraid someone might still be there, and my boy . . . my son."

"You did right. It's okay," Eve told him.

"We got the tools. I don't know why, except I always get the tools. And we ran to the truck. We called nine-one-one and said what we saw, and where we were. And we locked the doors and stayed until the police came."

"Had you ever seen the man before?"

"No, ma'am." James shook his head. "I don't think so. Ma'am, Ms. Simpson, Mr. Frost, they're good people. I've worked for them for five years. They have children. This isn't them. They didn't do this. They're not even here."

"I know. Don't worry about them. Where is the staff? Where's the person who lives in these rooms?"

"Oh, that's Hanna, Ms. Wender. She's with them in Georgia. And so is Lilian who helps with the children. They go for a month in the summer to their other house."

"Do they have a droid?"

"No, I don't think so. I've never seen one here. They have Hanna and Lilian, and cleaning people who come twice a week. And me."

"And do others have a code to access the gate and the garden?"

"I don't know. I think Hanna would, and Lilian. Lilian takes the children to the park, so they have to go in and out. And Hanna markets and does other things, so she would go in and out. But they're not here. This was someone else. I don't know why that man was here, how he got here. Why would

417

someone kill him here? This is a good place, a good home. These are good people."

"That's what I'm going to find out. You did everything right, both of you. We'll take it from here."

"We can go now?"

"Yeah. Did the officer get your contact information, in case we have to talk to you again?"

"Yes. He has everything. Should I tell Mr. Frost? Ms. Simpson? Should I tell them what we found?"

"We'll take care of it."

They rose as Eve did, and Peabody moved to walk them out. The boy turned, met Eve's eyes. "It's not like it is on-screen. It's not really like that at all."

She thought of Sean standing over a young girl's body in the Irish woods. "People are always saying that. They're right."

18

Eve did a walk-through herself, to get a feel for the house, the people who lived there. And to make absolutely certain there were no droids in residence.

She found the wine cellar, well stocked and secured. She'd have EDD check the log, determine the last time a bottle had been removed, but she held the opinion they'd confirm the vic had brought the wine with him from France, and the killer had taken it with him.

She went back to the kitchen. What she knew about cooking wouldn't fill a teaspoon, but she could gauge the general concept.

She imagined herself back in the kitchen of the farmhouse in Ireland, watching Sinead fix breakfast.

There was an order to these things, she mused

"What would he do first? Take out his supplies, that's what I'd do. Supplies and tools. Some of the stuff must need refrigeration, so he'd put that in the chiller until he needed it. Put his music on, maybe pour a glass of wine.

"Get everything all organized. Has he worked here before? We'll want to find out. If he already knew the lay of the land, it wouldn't take him as long to get set up."

She opened the oven, studied the fatal chicken. "Roarke said the bird would take a couple hours. It's probably the longest deal, so he'd do that first."

"Roarke knows how to roast a chicken?"

"No. He looked it up."

Peabody poked her head in the oven again, nodded. "A good ninety minutes anyway, less for the veggies, so he'd arrange them in the pot a little later. I actually know how to roast a chicken, but not so fancy. It's got this sauce, and see he's trussed it up?"

"Yeah, it's real pretty. How long to get it in the oven?"

"Hmm. He's a pro, so maybe not as long as your average. Or maybe longer due to fancy. Maybe half an hour. He'd have to peel and chop the veggies, so that's a little more time once the bird was in."

"He's got this fishy thing in here." Eve

opened the fridge.

Peabody poked in again, sniffed. "It's like a mousse deal. That probably took some time. And there are artichokes. I guess he was going to do something with them. Caviar, too — mega-fancy. And all those greens over there. It's too bad they're all wilted now."

"Put it all together, and he worked here at least two hours. From the looks of the bottle, he had a couple glasses of wine. ME can confirm."

"You know what else?" Hands on her hips, Peabody took a long survey. "It's tidy. No spills, no jumble. When my granny cooks it's like a hurricane's been through. So either he or the killer cleaned up."

"I think we can eliminate the killer. No point, and wiping off a counter or sticking something in the washer isn't something Moriarity would consider his job."

But Peabody's observation helped her see it more clearly. "The pro liked an organized workspace, so he cleaned or had the droid do it. We're going to feed all this into the computer, get the most probable timing. Which is likely what Moriarity did. Then, with the security down, all he has to do is have the droid drive him away, and wherever he wanted to go.

"Didn't drive himself here." Eve shook her head. "He wouldn't want to deal with two vehicles. Maybe the droid again. Otherwise he'd have to walk, at least for several blocks. So he'd have to disguise himself somewhat. Carting that harpoon in some sort of case or bag. If it went that way, the droid lets him in through the gate, and he sends it out to the car."

She shoved her hands in her pockets. "That's just sloppy. Why walk when you've got a droid and a stolen car at your disposal, and you'll be the one with an alibi according to the pattern? He wouldn't want to waste time."

"Vehicle gives him cover, saves him the disguise," Peabody added.

"And there's a nice safe place to go, just about five-six minutes' drive from here."

"Dudley's primary New York residence."

"That's the one. Droid picks him up there, brings him here. He'd figure the vic's busy in the kitchen, or taking a break in the garden. All Moriarity has to do is walk through the house. If the vic's in the kitchen, he just has to talk him outside. If the vic's outside, which he was, having his smoke, Moriarity just walks out, gets the vic in position, and spears him. Puts the mechanism back in the case, bags the wine, walks out, and the droid drives him away.

"The kill didn't take more than five or ten minutes from the time he came through the gates."

She circled one last time. "I want the timing locked down, and we're going to find out where Moriarity was last night, if they have the nerve to start alibiing each other. Let's go see Dudley."

"He's connected to the owners," Peabody pointed out. "So, sticking to pattern, he'll have an alibi."

"Yeah. I want to know what it is. I want to contact them first, the owners. We need to confirm they didn't hire the vic. The vic's got to have an admin or assistant. Track them down, get the setup. How he was hired, how it was arranged, how he traveled. And the supplies. Did he bring them with him, and if so, where he got them. Lock down the wine. It's going to be key."

"Then what?"

"Then we put it all together, every step, every layer, every angle." She felt her anger struggle to rise up, and hardened it into sheer resolve. "We're going to put on a fucking show, Peabody, because we have to convince Whitney, the PA, and anybody else who needs convincing to issue search warrants. I want to tear these bastards' houses, offices, playgrounds, clubrooms, and pieds-à-goddamn-terre apart."

It was probably small, and hardly relevant, for Eve to feel such cold satisfaction when she noted Roarke's house could've swallowed Dudley's whole, then spit it out again.

It was nothing to sneeze at. From the looks of it, it had likely been a smallish hotel pre-Urbans. Someone with vision had redesigned it and turned it into a mini estate too sleek and modern for her taste.

Or, she supposed, the taste she'd developed over the past few years.

The windows, coated with a silver sheen for privacy, tossed back shimmering reflections of the city Dudley could smirk at from the other side. He'd opted for stone and metal sculptures rather than plantings at the entrance.

She supposed they were somebody's idea of high art, but that somebody wasn't her.

Security put her through the usual paces before a young, shapely woman in a snug red uniform opened the door.

"Lieutenant Dallas, Detective Peabody. Mr. Dudley will be with you shortly. He apologizes for the wait. He entertained last night, quite late."

She gestured them into the wide foyer

done up in silvers and red, slashes of black, and into a large living space where the walls alternated between glossy white and glossy black, and the floor formed a kind of chess-board of the same colors.

Furniture, and too much of it, gleamed in jewel tones Eve decided would make her eyes ache after twenty minutes.

"If you'd wait in here. I've already ordered coffee. Mr. Dudley will be with you as soon as possible."

"So he had a party last night?"

"Yes." The woman smiled brightly, show-ing perfect and whiter-than-white teeth. "A garden party. Such a lovely night for it. I don't think the last guest left till nearly four this morning."

"Some people just don't know when to go home."

Red Uniform's laughter was as bright as her smile. "I know what you mean, but Mr. Dudley didn't mind, I'm sure. Mr. Moriari-ty's such a dear friend."

Eve's answering smile edged thin. "I bet."

"I'll just go check on your coffee."

Eve shook her head before Peabody could speak. "I got about two hours of sleep last night myself," she said and wandered to the windows, let out a yawn. "Couldn't that gardener have started work at a decent hour? It's not like the dead French guy was going anywhere."

"I didn't tell you about the subway deal this morning," Peabody said, playing along. "Some sort of snafu, so I had to get off a station early and hoof it the rest of the way to the scene."

"Screwed-up days always seem to start early. The media's going to be all over this last murder, and the commander's going to want us to toss them something."

"At least the media hasn't connected the first two. Maybe they won't go there yet."

"We've been lucky. Luck doesn't last."

Another woman, again young, curvy, dressed in red, wheeled in a coffee service and a silver basket of muffins.

"Please help yourself. Is there anything else I can get you?"

"No, we're good."

"Be sure to try a muffin. Celia baked them this morning."

Eve eyed the basket when the second red uniform clipped out. "I guess Celia didn't go to the party."

"I can have a muffin," Peabody decided. "I had a morning power walk."

As she chose one, Dudley came in.

He looked bright-eyed, in Eve's opinion. Maybe just a little too bright, the sort that came from a little chemical boost. No suit today, she noted, but a rich guy's casual wear. And the fucker was wearing the loafers, the shoes he'd worn when he'd killed Ava Crampton.

"This is an unexpected morning treat." He beamed at them. "I hope you're here to tell me you've found whoever killed that driver the other night."

"Unfortunately, no."

"Ah, well. I suppose these things take time."

He poured himself coffee, added three little squares of brown sugar, then sat comfortably on a chair the color of a nuclear sapphire.

"What can I do for you, ladies?"

"I'm sorry we've disturbed you so early in the day," Eve began, "and after, we're told, you had a late night."

"Wonderful party. Actually, I'm feeling very up this morning. Evenings like that are so stimulating."

"That kind of thing wears me out, but it takes all kinds."

"Doesn't it?"

"I'm afraid we have some disturbing news," Eve continued. "Would you object if I recorded this? And I'll need to read you your rights. It's official, a formality, and it would keep the record clean."

"Not at all."

"I appreciate that." Eve engaged her recorder, and noticed Dudley's eyes got just a little brighter. "Dallas, Lieutenant Eve, and Peabody, Detective Delia, in interview with Dudley, Winston, the Fourth, in his home." She read off the Revised Miranda. "Mr. Dudley, you employ a Meryle Simpson, correct?"

"Yes, she's our CEO of Marketing. And a family connection . . . convolutely. No, don't tell me something's happened to her. I thought she and her family were away for a while."

"They are. However, her ID, her company credit information, and her home were used in a homicide."

"This just can't be." He braced his head in his hand, closed his eyes. "Not again."

"I'm afraid it can be. It's possible her information was compromised before your recent security checks. If not, you still have a problem."

"It's a nightmare." He breathed it out, brushed a hand over his white-blond hair. "I have to assure you Meryle couldn't be involved. She's not only a trusted member of the Dudley team, but family."

"We have no reason to believe she's involved. I spoke with her and her husband this morning, and informed them of the incident. Also I advised them there's no need for them to return to New York at this time, but I believe Mr. Frost intends to do so, to reassure them both their house is in order."

"Yes, he's a very responsible sort. What a terrible thing." He aimed a sorrowful look in Eve's direction. "Their home, you say?"

"That's right. Ms. Simpson's name and information were used to engage the services of a private chef. A Luc Delaflote, from Paris."

"Delaflote!"

Dudley pressed a spread hand to his heart. Eve wondered if he'd practiced the gesture and the shocked expression in the mirror.

"No. My God, was he the victim? Is he dead?"

"You know him?"

"Yes, I do. I certainly do. The man's an artist, a genius. We've — myself, friends, family — hired him many times for events, for special occasions. Why, I dined in his restaurant the last time I was in Paris. How did this happen?"

"I'm not free to give you the details, as yet. As the employer, and a family connection, and now with your personal acquaintance with the victim, I have to ask for your whereabouts last night between the hours of nine and midnight. Obviously you were entertaining," Eve continued. "If I could have your guest list, even a partial, to verify, it would put that matter aside so we can focus in on viable lines of investigation."

"Of course, of course. This is such a shock. I'm going to contact our security, and have this checked yet again."

"I think that would be wise. Again, we're sorry to disturb you at home, and with such distressing news. Thank you for your time."

"I'm more than happy to give you my time under these tragic circumstances. This is a terrible business."

He chose a grim expression this time, and Eve thought he selected his facial reactions the way a man might pick the correct tie.

"I want to contact Meryle, offer my support and sympathy. That won't be a problem, officially, will it?"

"Not at all. We won't keep you any longer. If we could have that guest list, or even a handful of names, we'll get out of your way."

"Let me just tell Mizzy to make you a copy." He rose, walked to a house 'link.

"Nice shoes," Eve said with a casual smile. "The silver accessory gives them some jump, but they look comfortable."

"Thank you, and they are. Stefani invariably marries comfort and style. Mizzy, would you make a copy of last night's guest list for Lieutenant Dallas? Yes, dear. Thank you."

He walked back, picked up his coffee again. "It won't take a minute. Have you ever dined on Delaflote?" he asked her.

"I couldn't say."

"Ah, if you had, you could and would say." He forgot to look grim or sorrowful as delight twinkled over his face. "I'm surprised Roarke wouldn't have indulged you."

"Yeah, it's too bad since we've missed our chance there. Still, I lean toward Italian," she said, thinking of the pizza she'd shared with Roarke the night before.

Mizzy, yet another red uniform, strode in, brisk on toothpick heels. "Here you are, Lieutenant. The guest list, with contact data. Is there anything else I can do?"

"This should cover it. Thanks again." Eve rose, held out a hand to Dudley. "Shoot, sorry, lost track. Interview end."

"Mizzy will show you out. Please keep me up to date on these matters."

"You'll be first in line."

After they'd walked out, gotten into their vehicle, Eve let her own smirk free. "You caught the footwear?"

"Oh, yeah, and now we've got them on record, with his murdering feet in them."

"Murdering feet?"

"Well, he's a murderer and the feet are attached to him. Solid alibi," Peabody added. "And the first red-suited bombshell mentioned Moriarity was at the party, so it's looking like he'll have one, too."

"Easy drive from here to the Simpson place. I clocked it at six minutes. Maybe shave off a minute that time of night, but stick with twelve for the round-trip, ten to do the kill, add another two at most to gloat and pack up the wine."

Eve gave a last glance at the Dudley house in the rearview as she drove away. "Big party, drinks flowing, people wandering around outside, in the house. Who's going to notice one guest slipping out for under a half hour?"

"It's a little squishy. But they're all really rich people, and people of the same type tend to stick together. I bet more than half the people who were there will swear Moriarity was."

"Then we'd better prove he wasn't, for at least the time needed to skewer Delaflote. Next, there's going to be a past connection between the vic and Dudley. We find it. The vic's got about ten years on him, so they didn't go to school together. We'll search the society and gossip shit first. And we dig into the vic, see what he had in common with Dudley. If they traveled to the same places, had any common interests."

She engaged the dash 'link, contacted Feeney.

"Yo," he said.

"I've got an image of Dudley in the same fucking shoes he wore on Coney Island. Can you compare images, get me a match?"

"Bring it in. Amusement park's image isn't pristine, but we ought to be able to give you a solid probability."

"Heading in now. I'm going to need you and that match later today. I need ammo, and plenty of it, to talk my way into search warrants."

"We'll take our best shot. What time later?"

"I'll let you know as soon as I do."

She clicked off. "Book us a conference room."

"For when?"

"For starting now until I'm damn well finished with it. I need more room to spread this out. I need a bigger board while you're at it and a second comp, and I need Baxter and Trueheart."

"I need a million dollars and a smaller

433

ass. I was just throwing that in the pot." Peabody shrugged off Eve's snarl, and got to work.

A block from Central her communicator signaled. She used her wrist unit to answer.

Dispatch, Dallas, Lieutenant Eve.

"No fucking way."

Obscenities over official communication can result in a reprimand. Report to Central Park, Great Hill Jogging Track. See Detectives Reineke and Jenkinson.

"On what matter?" Eve demanded.

Possible homicide, possible connection to previous ongoing investigations. Urgent request for you from your detectives. Acknowledged.

"Acknowledged. Goddamn it," she said as soon as she cut off the transmission. "Tag one of those guys now." Eve cut west, cursing all the way, then headed back uptown.

"Reineke," Peabody told her, on dash 'link.

"This better be damn good," Eve warned him.

"We think it's one of yours, Lieutenant. It looked like a suicide first glance, then when we got here, took a better look, it smelled of homicide. We ran the vic. Adrianne Jonas. She was what they call a facilitator for the rich. They want it, she finds a way to get it. She's number one, get it?"

Yeah, she thought as her stomach sank. She got it. "Keep going."

"She's hanging from a tree right off the track here, by a freaking bullwhip. You don't see bullwhips every day, and you don't usually see some skirt in a party dress hanging by one. We figured it fit your vic profile pretty much down the line. Public place, vic considered the tops, screwy weapon."

"Keep the scene secure." She swung toward the curb, ignored the blare of horns. "Get the recording to Feeney, get the rest set up. Get what you can started. Run the list, Peabody. Work it. I'll take this with the detectives on scene."

"Dallas, how the hell did he do it? How'd he —"

"Just work it. Out. Out, now."

Peabody had barely slammed the door before Eve hit the sirens, swung out, and headed uptown running hot.

She imagined Adrianne Jonas had been a

beauty, but hanging victims just didn't stay pretty. The whip had bloodied her throat, and she'd had time to claw at the constriction before she'd been yanked off her feet.

She'd lost her shoes, probably from her body jerking, twisting, legs kicking. They lay sparkling in the grass.

"Couple early joggers spotted her, called it in." Reineke wiggled his thumb toward a pair of women huddled together talking to Jenkinson. "They said some woman hanged herself, and were pretty hysterical. Hard to blame. Uniforms got here, took a gander, and sent out for Homicide to take our sweep. Once we ID'd the vic, got the skinny on her, got a good look at what she's hanging by, we figured, well, fuck us sideways, this is Dallas's."

"Yeah, you figured right. TOD's going to be early this morning. Not last night. Last night was Moriarity's round. Dudley just hit his early."

"You're on it. About three A.M. We went ahead and established TOD. You wanna talk to the wits? I can tell you we've gone round with them. They jog here three times a week, together for safety. They're both clean. Live in the same building over on Hundred and Fifth."

"No, if you've got their information,

spring them. Give me five here, Detective."

"You got it, LT."

She pressed her fingers to her eyes a moment, ordered herself to clear everything else out of her head. Work it, she ordered herself just as she'd ordered Peabody.

Lured her here, she thought. Hired her, false ID to keep his name out of her books. Facilitator. That sort would be used to going to odd places at odd times. Catering to the rich and eccentric. He'd be here first, waiting. She probably knows him, yeah, probably he's used her before. His sort would. She'd be surprised to see him, wouldn't she? Not expecting him, but not worried.

She circled the body. No tears in the clothing, she noted. One lash of the whip then, he'd practiced. One lash wraps it around her throat. Painful, shocking, strangling.

Frowning, Eve crouched, studying the ground.

She fell . . . maybe hands and knees. Eve detected what looked like faint grass stains on the heels of the victim's hands, on the knees just below the skirt of her suit.

"But he's got to get the whip over the limb. It's not high. It doesn't have to be. She's what, five three in her bare feet?"

"Five two and a half on her ID. Sorry, Lieutenant." Jenkinson shrugged when she turned to frown at him. "I thought you were talking to me."

"Just thinking out loud. He's got to hoist her up. He's in good shape, and he's tall enough to manage it. But that takes some solid muscle. Or some chemical help," she considered.

Zeus made gods out of men — or at least gave them the adrenaline rush to think so.

"He's a user. A couple tokes to get his juices up. Maybe he brought a collapsible ladder. Hell, maybe he told her to bring one. Drag her up while she's choking, kicking, clawing. Secure the butt end of the whip, wait until she stops kicking. Wouldn't take long, then go home and tell your pal it's a tie."

"We got word there was another one last night."

"Yeah, they're all revved up."

"Me and Reineke want in, Dallas. These fuckers need some ass-kicking."

"You're in. Get her to Morris. Have crime scene go over this area like it was sprinkled with diamonds. Let me have her address. Where's her purse?"

"There wasn't one. Might be some mope came by and snatched it. People will do any

438

damn thing."

"And leave those shoes? I bet you could sell them for a grand easy. He took her bag. She'd have a bag. For face stuff, credit, 'link. Probably had some sort of repel spray, panic button, too. He took the bag, like his pal took the wine. Sloppy, getting sloppy," she murmured. "Cocky bastards."

"She's got a place on Central Park West. Didn't have to come far to die. You want one of us with you?"

"No." She took the address. "Finish up here. Dot every 'i.' And write it up. Work with Peabody on this. Sylvester Moriarity is going to have some past connection to her. You need to find it. Peabody will bring you up to date. If you've got anything else hot, pass it to another detective. This is priority."

"No problem."

She stood another moment, looking at the no longer pretty Adrianne Jonas, then turned her back and walked away.

Walking across the park, she pulled out her 'link. She just needed to talk to him for a minute, she told herself. Thirty seconds. Maybe she just needed to see his face.

God. She needed something.

"Hello, Lieutenant." Caro, Roarke's admin, smiled out of the screen. "If you'd just hold one moment, I'll put him on."

"He's into something." Or he'd have answered himself. "It's not important. I'll get back to him later."

"I'm under orders to put you through anytime you call today. I . . . Are you all right?"

Jesus, did it show? "Yeah."

"Hold on," Caro said.

Stupid, Eve berated herself. Stupid to have interrupted him. Stupid to have needed to. What she needed to do was the job — but if she broke transmission, he'd tag her right back. Then she'd feel stupider.

"Eve? What's wrong?"

"I shouldn't've . . . doesn't matter because I did. They got another one."

"Today?"

"Three this morning, Central Park. I just . . . God. He hung her in the park. Used a bullwhip. And I just . . ."

"Where are you now?"

"I'm leaving the park, going over to the vic's place. I have to check it out, find out how she was booked. I have to work it."

"Give me the address. I'll meet you there."

She felt her throat burn and realized emotion was shoving against the resolve that held the anger underneath. "That's not why I got you out of some meeting. I'm sorry

440

about that."

"If you don't give me the address, I'll just get it by other means, which you won't like. Let's avoid the fight over something unimportant when we're both tired and frustrated."

"Look, I've got my work, you've got yours. I'm sorry I —"

"Last chance to avoid the fight. You're a little more beaten up than I am, so I'll win."

She cursed, but she gave him the address. "I'll clear you with building security."

"Now, that's just insulting. I'll be there shortly."

So he'd be Peabody again, she thought as she got into her vehicle. What the hell. She could use all the eyes, ears, hands, and brains she could muster.

19

The doorman took one look at Eve's vehicle and, wincing, left his post to stride over. He plastered a smile on his face, she had to give him that.

"Something I can do for you, miss?"

She held up her badge as she got out of the car. "Couple of things. First, make sure my ride stays where I put it. Second, clear me up to Adrianne Jonas's place. Third —"

"I'll have to check with Ms. Jonas before I clear you. Ah —" He took another look at her badge. "Lieutenant."

"Good luck with that. She's on her way to the morgue."

"Oh, come on!" The sincere shock and distress made her wish she'd been slightly more tactful. "Ms. Jonas's dead? What happened to her?"

"You knew her pretty well?"

"Nicest lady you'd ever want to meet. Always had a word, always had a smile. Did she have an accident?"

"No, somebody made her dead on purpose."

"Oh, come on!" he repeated. "You mean somebody killed her? Why would anybody want to kill a nice lady like that?"

"I'd like to find that out. You need to clear me." As he had with her badge, she took another look at his nameplate. "Louis. I have a consultant on the way. You'll need to clear him when he gets here."

"I gotta take a minute."

He removed his spiffy, silver-trimmed red hat, lowered his head, closed his eyes. The simplicity threw Eve off, had her slipping her hands in her pockets and giving him his moment of silence.

He let out a breath, replaced his hat. Squared it, and his shoulders. "I need to log your badge in." He moved to the door, opened it into a quiet and pristine lobby area. "And I'll need the name of the consultant."

Eve pulled out her badge again. "Roarke."

The doorman's head snapped up. "Oh." He gave her badge yet another, closer look. "I didn't realize. Sorry for holding you up, Lieutenant Dallas."

"No problem." So Roarke owned the building. Big surprise.

"You just take Elevator Two right up to fifty-one, then . . . God, I'm not thinking straight." He rubbed a hand over the back of his neck, shook his head. "Ms. Wallace is already up there. She got in about a half hour ago."

"Ms. Wallace?"

"Ms. Jonas's assistant, and Maribelle — that's the housekeeper — she left a little before that to do some morning errands. Should I tell Ms. Wallace you're coming up?"

"No. Does anyone else work for her, or live in the unit?"

"There's Katie. I guess she's what you'd call a gofer, but she's not here yet today. Maribelle has her own apartment next to Ms. Jonas's."

"Okay. Thanks."

"She's fifty-one hundred, Lieutenant," he said as she crossed to the elevator. "I don't mean to tell you your job or anything, but if you could maybe gentle it up some with Ms. Wallace? It's going to knock her back pretty hard."

Eve nodded, stepped into the elevator. Murder was supposed to knock you back, she thought. She keyed the names the doorman had given her into her notes as the elevator rode silently, smoothly up fifty-one floors.

As she pressed the buzzer beside the wide double doors of 5100, she wondered what constituted "gentling it up."

The woman who answered had about five pounds of madly curling black hair and skin the color of Peabody's coffee regular. Her eyes, a spring leaf green, held Eve's for a long beat. Long enough Eve understood she didn't have to worry about the gentle.

"I know you." The smoky voice was breathless. "I know who you are. It's Adrianne. Something's happened." Her lips trembled, her hand squeezed the edge of the door. "Please say it very fast."

"I have to inform you Adrianne Jonas is dead. I'm sorry for your loss."

She swayed, but even as Eve braced to catch her, she toughened up. Tears sheened those soft green eyes, but didn't fall. "Someone killed Adrianne."

"Yes."

"Someone killed Adrianne," she repeated. "She wasn't here when I got here. She's not answering her 'link, and she always answers her 'link. Someone killed Adrianne."

Just because the woman wasn't going to faint or scream or rush into hysterics didn't mean she wasn't in shock. Gentle, Eve supposed, had different levels.

"I'd like to come in. Why don't we go inside and sit down?"

"Yes, I need to sit down. Yes, come in."

The entrance foyer led to another set of doors, open now, that connected to a large, high-ceilinged living space with a wide ribbon of windows. Seating had been cleverly built in beneath the windows, with more glass doors worked in between.

The woman chose a scroll-armed chair, lowered into it slowly. "When?"

"Early this morning. She was found in Central Park, near the Great Hill. Do you know why she would have been there?"

"She had an appointment. At three o'clock this morning."

"With whom?"

"Darrin —" Her voice broke. She shook her head, cleared her throat. "Darrin Wasinski. A client. He wanted to arrange for his daughter to be married there, at that time of the morning. She and her fiancé had gotten engaged there, at that time."

She put her fingers over her eyes, breathed and breathed. "I'm sorry. I'm trying to think clearly."

"Take your time. Do you want something? Some water?"

"No. He wanted her to meet him there, to

get an idea of the terrain, the look of it at that hour. His daughter wanted romantic, but unique. Something nobody else had done. He wanted Adrianne to handle the logistics. Oh, God, was Darrin killed, too? Oh, God."

"No. Is he a new client?"

"No. He's used us before, personally and professionally. He's CFO for Intelicore, New York operations."

Of course he is, Eve thought.

"I should have gone with her." Her breath tore and wheezed as she fought for control. "Adrianne's so self-sufficient, and God knows she can handle herself. But I should have gone with her. We were at a party last night, and she was going straight from there."

"Where was the party?"

"Winston Dudley's home. It was still going strong when I left, about one-thirty. I don't know what time she left. Did Darrin meet her? Do you know if —"

Eve interrupted. "Did he personally book the appointment?"

"Yes. He e-mailed her yesterday afternoon. Lieutenant, Darrin wouldn't have hurt Adrianne. I can swear to it. He's a very lovely man, devoted to his family — which is why he'd go to such lengths to make this

447

brainstorm of his daughter's happen."

"Did either you or Ms. Jonas or anyone else on staff actually speak to him about the arrangements?"

"Just by e-mail. It was very last minute, and nothing we'd have taken on except Darrin's a regular, long-term client."

And a booking by a regular, long-term client when Jonas would already be out — at the party Dudley had invited her to — ensured she'd be where they wanted her, when they wanted her.

"I'd like copies of the e-mails. Has Ms. Jonas ever facilitated for Mr. Moriarity, Mr. Dudley?"

"Yes. They're very good clients. Was it a mugging?"

"No."

"I didn't see how it could be. She's trained in self-defense, a black belt in several martial art disciplines, and she carried repel spray and a panic button."

"In her purse?"

"The spray, yes. Her wrist unit had the panic button. It's very much like mine." Wallace tapped her wrist. "Adrianne gave everyone who works with her one. We go into unusual places, often at unusual times. We all take self-defense courses. She wanted us safe," Wallace added, and the first tear spilled down her cheek. "Can you tell me what happened to her?"

It would be out soon enough. "She was hanged."

"Oh, God, my God." She blanched as her hands gripped together in her lap. "Can any of this be happening?"

"I know this is hard, but I need to see those e-mails. It would help if I could go through the apartment. Did she have work-space here?"

"Yes. Yes. We work in the adjoining unit, primarily. It spills over, of course, into the living space."

"You and Ms. Jonas, and Katie?"

"Oh, Jesus, I have to tell Katie. She's not due in until noon today. I should contact her. And Bill and Julie."

"Bill and Julie?"

"Her parents. They live in Tulsa. She's from Tulsa."

"We'll notify her parents. Maybe you can contact them later today after I've spoken with them."

"All right. Yes. All right. I was worried, a little worried, when she wasn't here this morning. But I thought maybe she went back to the party after her appointment, and maybe she went home with someone. It's not usual, but she and Bradford Zander

— one of the other guests last night — saw each other occasionally. But she didn't answer her 'link, and she was fierce about always answering, or at least acknowledging a contact. But I told myself it was nothing, to give her a few more minutes, that she might be in the shower or . . .

"Then I saw you at the door, and I knew. We have a whole file on you."

"You what?"

"Oh, that sounded wrong." She rubbed her damp face with the heels of her hands. "Adrianne believes in being prepared. You might be a client one day. So we keep files — articles and basic data. She admired you. She believed, strongly, in women leaving a deep mark doing what they were meant to do. And as soon as I saw you, I knew why she wasn't home, why she didn't answer her 'link. She's my best friend in the world, and I knew you were here to tell me she was dead."

Wallace wiped another tear away, blinked the rest back. "You'll find who did this to her. She'd have expected that from you. I'll take you through to the offices."

As they rose, the buzzer sounded.

"Will you excuse me a minute?"

As Wallace went to the door, Eve angled herself to keep it in view. She watched

Roarke step in, take Wallace's hands. He kept his voice low, so all she heard was the comfort in the tone.

When she turned back, Eve saw the tears had won again.

"I'll take you both over. I'll get a printout of the e-mails you wanted."

"It would be helpful if you'd get me a list of anyone who knew Ms. Jonas was going to the park, and when." Busywork, Eve thought, but it would give the woman something to do.

"All right." She walked them back through the foyer and through already open doors to another large unit.

Another living space designed to Eve's eye to keep clients comfortable. Stylish, sunny built-ins that likely housed entertainment and refreshment equipment.

Later, Eve decided, she'd need to go through the rest of the space, the more personal spaces.

"Can you tell me if she had trouble with anyone? A client who was unhappy or dissatisfied? A personal problem with anyone?"

"She never left a client unhappy. She'd find a way, and if it wasn't exactly what they were after, she had a talent for making them think it was, or that it was better than they'd expected. On a personal level, she kept things casual. She wasn't ready, she said, for a serious relationship. I honestly don't know of anyone who'd do this to her. People liked her — it was part of her success. Giving people what they wanted, and being likable."

She stepped out into another, smaller living space, then turned into an office. It reminded Eve of Mira's. Not in the decor, she realized, but in that it struck her as feminine, pretty, and efficient all at once.

"I can put those e-mails on disc for you, unless you'd prefer a hard copy."

"Both wouldn't hurt."

"All right." She sat, engaged the computer. When she'd finished, she handed Eve a thin paper file, and a disc in a case.

"I'd like to scan some of the other correspondence, some of the files."

"I feel like I have to say this business runs on privacy and discretion. But I'm not in the mood to care about that right now. And I know Adrianne would be pissed off by what happened — that sounded stupid."

"No, it didn't. It sounded accurate."

Wallace managed a weak laugh. "She'd also want you to have whatever tools you needed to do your job. I'd like you to tell me if you make copies or transfer any files."

"No problem."

"If you don't need me to stay, I could really use a few minutes."

"Go ahead. Ms. Wallace?" Eve added as she started out. "It strikes me Ms. Jonas had good judgment in friends."

"That was a kind thing to say," Roarke murmured.

"I'm not feeling very kind. Adrianne isn't the only one pissed off right now. I told you I could handle this."

"Do I interpret that as you're pissed off at me?"

"Not especially." Eve sighed. "A little, but mostly because you're here and I could punch you if I needed to."

"If I hadn't come, you wouldn't be pissed off at me, but then I wouldn't be here to punch."

"Don't try to logic me right now. They had a really big night, splashy party, with their private entertainment on the side. Figured on using that party, and each other, for alibis — with the bonus of having a lure for Jonas. One slips out, skewers the chef, then later, the other slips out, hangs the facilitator. And they cover each other.

"You didn't tell me you owned the building."

"The majority share, but that wasn't on my mind when you gave me the address. I knew her a little. Adrianne."

"Were you a client?"

"No." He slipped his hands into his pockets, wandered the room. "I can facilitate for myself. And if I don't have the time, or don't want to spend the time, I have Caro and Summerset. But she had a sterling rep."

He touched the frame of a photo where both Adrianne and Wallace smiled, arms around each other's waist.

"A lovely woman with a lot of style and charm," he added, "and a talent for fluid thinking. I do know several people who were clients, and worked with her, or with her through Bonita — Wallace," he added at Eve's blank look. "How did they get her into the park?"

She ran it by him as she scanned the hard copy of the e-mails.

"This guy, Wasinski, won't know squat about this. I'll have to check him out, but he's the same as the others. Just the dupe — the difference being unlike the others he knew the vic."

"Adding more connections," Roarke said.

"Yeah, upping the stakes every time now. Look here, right in his e-mail to her it asks her not to contact him via 'link as he's in meetings most of the day. Not to leave voice mail, as he wants this to be a surprise and his wife might check his messages, blah blah. Just to use this e-mail account he's set up — not his regular account — to keep it on the down-low until they check it all out."

"And she didn't question it."

"He's a client, one she's known awhile. He uses his daughter's name, his wife's name, works in just enough personal stuff. He even mentions he knows she's been invited to Dudley's garden party. Why would she question it? It's probably not the weirdest request she ever got."

Eve sat on the desk, began to scroll through the most recent correspondence. "Since you're here and I'm not punching you, maybe you could check out the desk 'link."

"I'll do that, on one condition. You stop blaming yourself, right here, right now."

"I'm not doing that. Exactly."

She looked at the photo, and noted she'd been right. Adrianne Jonas had been a very pretty woman in life.

"I feel like I'm lagging behind in this contest, and because I am two people are dead. But I also know the contest is rigged. It's set up so I can't know who's a target, and so I have to spend time checking out their dupes and alibis."

"Why spend the time when you know

they're dupes, and you know the alibis are bollocks?"

"Because I can't play by their rules. I have to show a judge, and eventually a judge and jury, that I investigated and verified and eliminated. That I compiled the evidence. Maybe this Darrin Wasinski got a wild hair, was carrying on an affair, or wanted to, with the vic. Maybe he decided to try to do a copycat and killed her because she wouldn't run off to Mozambique, or because she threatened to tell his wife they did the dirty in Mozambique when he was supposed to be in Albuquerque on business."

"None of which you believe for an instant."

"Not a nanosecond, but it has to be checked out, verified, eliminated. When I take the dupe out of the picture, leave no wiggle room there, it goes back to the pattern. It goes back to establishing enough probable cause and circumstantial for a search warrant, for me to bring them into the box."

And, God, she thought, she wanted them there. Wanted those smug, smirking faces in her house.

"These bastards think they're so fucking smart, so goddamn clever, and more — they think they're insulated because they're rich and important, and because I have to play by the rules. But it's the rules that'll tie them up and choke them at the end.

"Computer, attempt reply to account on-screen, no message."

One moment please . . . the account has been terminated. Do you wish to use an alternate?

"No. Cancel. First step — the account he set up for this lure is now closed, and you can bet it was closed by remote. We can work with that."

"We can." The steps and time factor of her rules might frustrate him, but he could admit mitering those corners rather than cutting them did the job. "Very good. Anyone in EDD can find you the location of the computer used to set up, then close the account. And they'd certainly know that."

"So they used another dupe's comp, or a public with false ID. But it leaves a trail. So far they're ahead on the trail, but they're leaving a lot of cookie crumbs to follow."

He had to smile as he brushed a hand over her hair. "That's bread crumbs."

"I'd rather have a cookie. And I pick up enough crumbs I can make a damn cookie.

But you're right about EDD. I'll get them in here to deal with this."

"I can get your locations in less time than it would take you to arrange that."

She hesitated. "We have permission. Go ahead. I'm still getting EDD in. They can do what they do, and I can work my way back to Central via the morgue. They're having a two-for-one sale."

"Sick," he commented.

"Yeah, but it helps keep me from being sick. If you'll get the locations — and keep the work right down the line, no blurs, I'm going to get the go-ahead to check out the vic's other spaces. You never know."

She found nothing in Adrianne's private spaces that applied, but she verified through the files that both Dudley and Moriarity had used her services in the past. With Wallace's permission, she used the vic's office 'link to notify next of kin.

When she was done, Roarke leaned over the chair to kiss the top of her head. "Devastating for them. Painful for you."

"I can't think about it now." Couldn't let herself feel it, not now. "He used a remote, likely a disposable 'link, you say, both times. To set up and to close."

"The same device, both times," Roarke

confirmed. "As were the e-mails. We have various locations. I've listed them for you."

"I've got to go finish putting this together. You saved me some time, so I won't be punching you."

"My face is relieved, yet strangely disappointed."

"I don't know when I'll be home."

"Neither do I, as when I've cleared up some business I need to clear up, I'll be coming down to Central to see if I can be of use to Feeney."

"I'd tell you Feeney can handle things, but with nine dead, I'm not turning down any help. No point, is there, in telling you not to buy a bunch of food for a bunch of cops?"

He sent her a cheerful grin. "None at all if I'm hungry."

When they were out on the street, he cupped her face in his hands. "No point telling you to catch an hour's sleep, even if it's on the floor of your office."

"Probably not today." Her 'link signaled. "Hold on. Dallas."

"Tell me you love me."

"I can't. My husband's standing right here. He might get suspicious."

"He'll understand," Peabody claimed, "when you both hear what I found. Guess whose mommy had a scorching affair with a dead French chef before he was dead. Like twenty-five years ago."

"Delaflote boned Dudley's mother?"

"That's the word, mostly in French. It was a BFD in Europe back then. The vic was younger, and she was still married to the father. She left him — the husband — and set up house with Delaflote. Didn't last more than about six months, but it broke the marriage, and, according to the gossip back in the day, caused serious embarrassment for the Dudley family."

"That's worth a 'very fond of.'"

"Aww, I'm all about the love."

"Find me a connection between Adrianne Jonas and Moriarity, more than he was an occasional client, then we'll talk love. Status with the shoe?"

"I've been buried in illicit affairs, fashion, marital high jinks, and celebrity scandals. I'll check."

"I'm heading to the morgue. When I'm done, I'll be in. Polish it up, Peabody."

"I think it's starting to shine. I really do."

Eve clicked off. "I have to go."

"What about the shoe?" he demanded as she jumped in her car.

"The bastard was wearing the same shoes we caught on security when I interviewed him this morning. Cookie crumbs."

He watched her go, and decided he'd pick up a few dozen cookies before he met her at Central.

Peabody tagged her back as she strode down the white tunnel of the morgue. "I'm still at 'very fond,' " Eve said.

"You may be ready for 'sweet on,' at least. Unofficially, McNab says if it's not the same damn shoe, he'll eat it with barbecue sauce."

"He'll eat anything with barbecue sauce. I need official."

"Feeney just confirmed, officially, that the shoe Dudley was wearing this morning is the same size, the same make, the same color as the shoe on the amusement park security."

"Close but not sweet enough."

"He can't state unequivocally it's the same shoe. He can give that an eighty-eight-point-seven probability."

"I want ninety plus. See if he can enhance the images any more, or squeak that out. Ninety's better than eighty-eight."

"I'll relay."

Eve stuck the 'link in her pocket, and pushed through the autopsy suite's doors.

Morris looked up from his work. "Well, Dallas, we're having a hell of a summer."

"It's going to be hell for two smug bas-

461

tards before it's done."

"Before we get into this, I want to thank you for arranging this gathering tomorrow."

"Oh. I think —"

"I find myself pulling back, too often, from friends. It's easier, and more self-indulgent, to be alone. I need a nudge out of that cycle from time to time."

"Yeah." And there went her very rational, reasonable plan to postpone the whole deal. "Well."

"Can I ask a favor? I'd like to bring someone."

Her jaw nearly hit the floor. "Ah, sure . . . I didn't realize you were . . ."

"Not that sort of someone. Chale — Father Lopez. He's a good friend now, and I know you think highly of him. He's fond of you."

A lot of fondness going around, she thought. A priest at a cop party. Mostly cops, she corrected. What the hell. "No problem. It'll be good to see him again."

"Thanks. And now for your double-header."

"Ha. I called it a two-for-one sale. We're both sick."

"How else do you get through a hell of a summer? Our Frenchman is actually from Topeka, by the way. Born Marvin Clink."

"No shit?"

"Peabody did the run, which included the full data, and legal name change. In any case, your supposition on scene was correct. Death by harpoon. It's been identified as such, and you've had the weapon — the gun, I think it's called — ID'd by the lab."

"That's not your usual line. You verified with Dickhead?"

"We're all pulling a bit more. And I was curious. He's in love, you know."

"Yeah, I heard."

"It's a bit disturbing."

"Yes!" She gave him a shove of solidarity. "Thank God. It gave me the serious creeps."

Humor lit his dark eyes, and gave Eve her first lift of the day. "Which is unkind, but I confess to the same. You have the weapon ID on your office unit by now. This was another heart wound. In simple terms the barb pierced the chest, ripped straight through the heart and out the back. Your spear's been removed, as you see, logged and sent to the lab. There are no other wounds. He had consumed just shy of eight ounces of white wine. I'm having the type analyzed."

"I have the bottle."

"And we'll confirm. He'd eaten a light meal several hours before death. A salad, grilled shrimp, asparagus in wine sauce, and a small amount of vanilla bean crème brûlée."

Despite the circumstances, her stomach yearned. "Sounds pretty good."

"I hope it was. He did have more current stomach contents that from the variety and amount I'd say came from sampling what he was cooking, along with a little cheese, a couple of crackers. There were no drugs in his system. He was a smoker."

"It all fits."

"He's had some face and body work," Morris continued. "Minimal. He kept in good shape, his muscles are nicely toned."

"What about her?" Eve moved to Adrianne's body.

"She didn't die as quickly. She'd consumed about sixteen ounces of champagne, and neutralized the effects with Sober-Up. We'll get you the timing on that. Some party food in her stomach. Caviar, toasted bread, some berries, some raw vegetables, and so on — very light amounts — consumed over a period of two to four hours before death. No sign of sexual activity, forced or consensual."

He lifted her hand. "There's some light bruising on the heels of her hands, on her knees, consistent with a fall, these deep scrapes on her throat — consistent with the blood and flesh under her own nails. She'd clawed at her throat, and you see she broke three of her nails, snapping two below the quick."

"Dragging at the whip."

"It circled her neck three times, and with force. Tearing the skin in these patterns here, constricting her airway, bruising her larynx."

"She couldn't have screamed."

"No. And if you look . . . Do you want goggles?"

"No, I can see." But she bent down closer. "He jerked her — maybe even pulled her off her feet. Then jerked again, but upward — that would be dragging her up, hoisting her on the branch. Her neck's not broken." She glanced at Morris for confirmation, got a shake of the head. "So it would've been painful and terrifying, and endless. Just a minute, maybe two, but endless."

"Yes, I'm afraid so." With Eve, he looked down at the body. "She would have suffered."

"Her parents will be contacting you."

"I'll tell them it was quick, and she didn't feel any pain." He touched a hand to Eve's arm briefly. "They'll want to believe me, so they will."

As she walked back down that white tunnel, she wished she could believe it.

20

Eve hit the bullpen at Homicide like a blaster.

"Trueheart."

He jolted in his seat, then knocked a short stack of file discs to the floor as he sprang to attention. "Sir!"

"Whatever you're doing, stop doing it. I'm going to send you a list of weapons — images, makes, models, ID numbers where applicable. Run them. I want a complete list of vendors, outlets, collectors, and licenses. Cross-reference same with Dudley and Moriarity, personally, through their companies — Dudley and Son and Intelicore, respectively, all arms and locations — and family members, living and dead. Include ex-wives and their family members, living and dead.

"Questions?"

While his eyes were wide enough to swallow Pluto, he shook his head. "Ah . . . no, sir."

"Good. Baxter."

He sat as he was, smiled a little. "Yo."

"Same weapons list. I want names and locations of hunting clubs, hunting and/or fishing venues that allow the use of crossbows and/or harpoon guns. Stick with first-class venues, extreme first-class. On and off planet."

He straightened now. "You want every one of them in the universe?"

"And when you've got them, get the member list or client list. Find Dudley and/or Moriarity. They've practiced. More, they're show-offs. They've used those weapons somewhere, sometime."

"Reineke, Jenkinson, I want your report on the Jonas homicide on my desk ASAP. You're going to work this case like Adrianne Jonas was your beloved mother. If Dickhead hasn't tagged the whip yet, chew on his ass until he does. When he does, pass it to True-heart and Baxter. Meanwhile find bullwhip experts."

"Experts?" Jenkinson echoed.

"If I hand you a freaking bullwhip are you going to know how to wrap it around somebody's throat? And do it strong enough to hang her by it? He had to learn somewhere, from someone. Experts, venues, trainers. Find them, contact them, dig until somebody remembers Dudley or Moriarity. Or both. Dig. Got it?"

"Got it," Jenkinson answered as Reineke gave a thumbs-up.

"Carmichael." As Eve turned, two voices answered.

"Detective Carmichael," she specified, and the uniform Carmichael looked faintly disappointed. "I'm going to give you a list of names, invites to Dudley's alibi party last night."

"Lieutenant, I'm not caught up with the details and particulars of this investigation."

"Catch her up," Eve ordered Peabody. "When you are," she continued, "contact the names. Both suspects left the premises at some point: Moriarity most likely shortly before twenty-two hundred and likely returned before twenty-three hundred; Dudley between two and two-thirty, returning sometime after three hundred hours. Dudley may have been in the company of the last vic. Find somebody who noticed, somebody who missed them. When you're done with the guest list, start on the staff, permanent and any hired for the event.

"New guy." Eve pointed at a young, broad-shouldered man who'd transferred in the days before she'd left for vacation.

"Detective Santiago, Lieutenant."

"Right. Work with Carmichael." She tried to think what went into it when Roarke threw a fancy party. "Dudley probably had some valets for parking. Some of the guests likely came and went with private car services. He'd have had catering, servers, people who don't have any particular reason to be overly loyal. Service providers are invisible to these people, and that's a vulnerability because they don't consider those service providers to have the wit to notice, or the balls to talk. Find somebody with wit and balls."

With one glance she targeted uniforms.

"Newkirk, Ping, the other Carmichael, do whatever the detectives need you to do. Anything pops, anything even breaks the most discreet of wind, I hear about it. Full briefing and all reports in two hours. Conference room . . . Peabody?"

"C."

"Conference room C, two hours. Sweat," she ordered. "These cocksuckers are killing people the same way a kid steps on ants. Because they want to see them squish. More, they think we're stupid, too stupid to bring them down. We're going to prove them wrong. Peabody, with me."

Eve headed straight to the AutoChef in her office for coffee, then jerked a thumb at the machine.

"I better not." Peabody's voice signaled sincere regret. "I was fading so I took a boost. Now I feel like my eyes are glued open and my nerves are all twitchy. I haven't found the connection to the last vic and Moriarity."

"Pass it to Carmichael. Uniform Carmichael. And why do they have to have the same name? One of them needs to change it. Anyway, he's a vicious bastard on details. And, yeah, you'd find it," Eve added before Peabody could protest. "But he'll come with a fresh eye, and without the twitches. Plus I need you on other angles. Hold on a minute."

She sat, copied the relevant files, and transferred them to the relevant cops.

"French guy's wine and supplies."

"Bought in gay Paree." With so many details crowded in her head, Peabody took out her notebook to keep them straight. "He got the booking five weeks ago."

"Five weeks. That's good, that's a confirmation of long-term planning. Dudley would know Simpson and her family would be in Georgia. She'd have to clear the vacation time in advance, and this is an annual family summer thing. They'd want to lock Delaflote in, had to suss out and plan the alibi, the timing. Probably practiced that, too."

"Booking was done by e-mail, through what I've already checked was a temp account, assigned to Simpson for billing. The vic's assistant has it listed as a surprise for the husband, for Frost. Intimate, romantic dinner for two, alfresco."

"The garden. All set up for the garden," Eve added, nodding.

"Late supper," Peabody continued. "Delaflote's travel fee — and he came in on his own shuttle — paid early this week, through Simpson's account. Delaflote personally shopped for the food supplies and the wine on the day of departure. He has a major interest in a vineyard, and selected three bottles of Pouilly-Fuissé, a bottle of Sauternes, three bottles of champagne. All from the Château Delaflote label. I have the vintages for all of them, as the vic kept a kind of spreadsheet for jobs."

She paused, and pleasure moved onto her face. "And Dallas, as the client hyped this as such a special deal, expense no object, the champagne's from a limited edition label and vintage. They're freaking numbered. He took numbers forty-eight, forty-nine, and fifty from the private reserve he kept back for special clients."

Eve's smile spread slowly, a reflection of Peabody's pleasure. "Maybe I do love you."

"Aww."

"We find one of those bottles, we'll nail them with it. Clean that report up. You'll be presenting that to the ADA and the commander in a couple hours."

"Oh, jeez."

"Tag Feeney, and tell him when and where. I want a solid report from him for same. I want everybody ready and in the conference room on time. No excuses. I'll set the commander and Reo for ten minutes after. Brief Carmichael — both of them. I'll send you a report on Jonas as soon as I put it in order. Now go away. Shut the door."

Before it shut, she was contacting Whitney's office. She locked him in, then Reo, then moved onto Mira. If she'd had time, she'd have cheered when the temp came on-screen.

"Oh, hi, Lieutenant. Gee, the doctor's in a session right now."

"I'm going to send her a number of files, starting now and over the next hour. I need her to give them her immediate attention, and report to conference room C, Homicide Division, with her conclusions, at fourteen hundred and fifteen."

"Oh, well, golly, I think she has an appointment at —"

"This is priority one. Commander Whitney and an ADA will also be attending. Doctor Mira's presence is mandatory."

"Oh, gosh. I'll cancel her appointment, and —"

"Good. If she has any questions, she can contact me."

Cutting the temp off, Eve shot Mira the report Peabody had written on Delaflote, the reports her other detectives had written on Jonas. She pushed through the ME's reports, the labs, the prelim from the sweepers.

Then she cleared her head and began to write her own on each.

Twice she rose for more coffee, to check her time lines, to consult the computer on the time required to travel the distances from Dudley's home to each crime scene — on foot, and by transpo. She brought up her map, studied it, then confirmed with the computer the most direct routes to and from each.

With nearly an hour left, she loaded up everything she could carry to take it to the conference room. She turned out of the office just as Jenkinson turned toward it.

"If you've got something, walk and talk."

"Let me give you a hand."

"I got it. It's balanced."

"Okay." He fell into step with her. "We checked with the vic — our vic's — usual car service. They took her to Dudley's, and she told the driver she'd contact them for a time of return, which was booked to include travel home, then to the park location and back, or — depending on the time — straight to the park. She left it open."

"Figuring if the party was a dud, she could take off, go home awhile before her appointment. Okay."

"Yeah, but what she did was cancel pickup altogether, about two A.M."

Eve felt that slow smile cross her face again. "Because she copped another ride."

"We checked with every freaking legit cab company in Manhattan. Nobody picked up a fare at that location between two and three A.M. And nobody dropped off a fare between those times at the logical entrance to the park for the Great Hill. We gotta figure —"

"She got a lift," Eve finished, and jerked her head at the conference room door, "with Dudley."

"That's our take." He opened the door, followed her in. "So far Carmichael and the new guy haven't hit on anybody, but they're asking if anybody saw the vic and Dudley hanging together between the two A.M. and the two-thirty mark."

"Okay." She dumped her things on the conference table. "She sure as hell didn't walk from the party to that point in the park in those shoes. No reason to cancel her pickup unless she had alternate transpo, and we've covered she didn't book alternate transpo."

A lot of other guests at the party, she thought, a lot of other alternatives for a lift. That would be the argument, but she would damn well knock it down.

"We're going to push for a warrant to search all Dudley's vehicles for her DNA. We find her prints, a stray hair, it adds more weight."

"I think the other Carmichael hit something, because he started making those noises in his throat like he does."

"Yeah, the grunting. Good."

"Reineke gave Dickhead a shove, and Dickhead came through. It's an Australian deal — the whip — made out of freaking kangaroo."

"The hopping things, with the pouches?"

"Yeah. Freaking kangaroo. It's seven feet long, eleven with the handle or grip, and that's lead-loaded steel. Dickhead said it had a coating of some sort of leather cream, and he's working on IDing the brand, and he's still working on dating it, but says it ain't no antique or anything. He's saying the sucker's handmade. So we've got Trueheart checking out Aussie whip makers. Dickhead comes through with the rest, that'll narrow it.

"You know that fuckhead's in love?" he added.

"Yeah, yeah."

"It's creepy."

"So say we all. Get back to it, Jenkinson."

Alone, she began with the murder board.

She'd worked her way halfway through the time lines when the other Carmichael came in, making grunting noises in his throat. "Boss, I got something."

"Give it to me," Eve said and continued to work.

"Jonas used to work as a concierge at the Kennedy Hotel on Park. Started as an assistant right out of college. Moriarity's grandfather owned the hotel along with a couple partners. They had a lot of events there like business stuff and private stuff, and put up important accounts and whatnot."

Eve glanced up long enough to acknowledge the pop.

"When he croaked he left his share to Moriarity — the grandson — and he sold it off about ten years ago. The vic was still working there. She didn't go out on her own until about a year after the sell. She got a write-up in *The New Yorker* back before she left, about how the girl from the Midwest became one of the top concierges in New York."

"And used that capital to parlay into her own business. Smart. Good work, Carmichael. Write it up tight, attach the article and any other media."

Coming together, she thought, crumb by crumb.

When her boards were complete, she sat at the computer to check the images and data she'd want on-screen.

"Lieutenant? Sorry to interrupt."

"If you've got something, Trueheart, you're not interrupting. If you don't, go away."

"It's about the harpoon gun."

"Spill it."

"They've been running tests on it in the lab. On the mechanism and the spear, and checking on regulations. It turns out the projectile . . ."

"You're trickling, not spilling."

"Um. Both the spear and the gun required to shoot it exceed the limits accepted by sport fishing regulations here in the U.S. and in Europe, as well as several other countries. Baxter's research corroborates when it comes to tours and clubs and organizations. Mr. Berenski —"

"Jesus." She shoved back in her chair to goggle at him. "You don't actually call him that?"

Trueheart pinked up. "Well, not always. He concludes the weapon was manufactured prior to regulations, as it's American-made. Or that it was made in violation of the regulations, and he leans there because he believes it's between five and ten years old. Some of the internal parts carry a manufacturer's mark, and I traced that to a company in Florida. It's one of Moriarity's subsidiaries, one of its companies under its SportTec arm."

Her legs stretched out, she smiled, and her eyes stayed flat and cold. "Is that so?"

"I have the data, sir, if you'd like to verify."

"That was a rhetorical is that so. Keep digging. I want to put that weapon in Moriarity's hands." She frowned when Baxter strolled in. "I haven't finished with your boy yet."

"I have something to pump up what he just brought you. Both suspects did belong to both a sport fishing and a scuba club, though they've let their memberships lapse. But they've twice — five years ago, and just last winter — hosted a private island party for fifty-odd of their closest friends. A party that included scuba, sport fishing off your choice of yacht, and spear fishing. Among other assorted water sports. Several celebrities dropped in — vid stars and the like. It got a lot of play in the media."

"Fucking A."

"Ditto. I've got some lines out to bullwhip experts and instructors. There's more of them than you'd think."

"Go to Australia."

"Thanks. I've always wanted to."

"On the C&D. The whip was kanga-fucking-roo. Maybe Dudley took his lessons from whoever made the bastard. Add in handmade kanga-fucking-roo bullwhips."

"I'll run a search now, but it's going to be close, Dallas, if you want me in here for the briefing."

"Get it started, but be here. Put everything you've got together, and make it succinct. We've got some selling to do."

When they left she rose to go to the room's AutoChef for another hit of coffee and remembered she'd neglected to load it with the real thing she'd become spoiled by.

"Shit. Sometimes you just got to suck it

up. Or down."

She programmed an extra large, black. And when the scent hit, she smiled. It was loaded with her brand. "Peabody, it really must be love."

She gulped some down, ignored the jitter in her belly from caffeine overload, as Feeney came in. "Got your ninety percent. Ninety-point-one, and you ain't going to get better. Give me that."

He grabbed the coffee, drank it like a camel at an oasis. And he eyed her over the rim. "Maybe you need this more than I do. You don't look like you've slept in a week."

"Four dead, Feeney, in less than that. And those?" She gestured to the side of the board where she'd put the other victims. "All of those, too, from before. Their practice sessions. There could be another face up there tonight, or tomorrow. And what've I got?"

She pushed at her hair, pressed on her eyes. "It's like weaving cobwebs together. A few strands of . . . whatever's stronger than cobwebs. What I've got points to motive, method, opportunity, but it doesn't hit the bull's-eye. And I have to convince the PA and Whitney that it does, that it will."

"You believe you can make it stick?" When she hesitated, he jabbed her shoulder.

481

"Ow."

"You better fucking believe it or they won't. Don't waste my time here, or everybody else's."

"I know it. I know it. I'm tired. Half punchy, half twitchy."

"I'd tell you to take a booster but you've probably had a cargo hold of coffee already." He took a long, merciless study. "Go . . . do something with your face."

"Huh?"

"Whatever it is your kind does. It's one thing to look overworked, and another to look wrung out when you're trying to pull a warrant this way."

"You think because I have a vagina I cart around face enhancers?"

"Jesus, Dallas, you don't have to use language like that. Borrow some, for Christ's sake. You don't want them looking at you thinking, 'Man, Dallas needs some sleep.' You want them focused on what you show them."

"Fine. Fine. Crap." She yanked out her communicator. "Peabody, put this on private."

"What? Is there a break?"

"Are we private?"

"Yeah, what —"

"Do you have any face gunk?"

"Ah . . . sure. I got a supply in my desk for — what's wrong with my face?"

"It's for me. And if you say a word, if you breathe a syllable, I'll rip your tongue out with my bare hands and feed it to the first rabid dog I find. Meet me in the bathroom, and bring the crap." She clicked off. "Satisfied?" she demanded of Feeney, and stomped out.

It only took about five minutes, and that with Peabody trying to offer advice and instruction. The first thing she did was put her head in the sink, grit her teeth, and turn the water on full and cold.

It shocked the edge of fatigue away.

She toned down the circles under her eyes, added some color to cheeks she had to admit looked pasty and pale.

"That's it."

"I've got some nice lip dyes, and this mag eyeliner, and some —"

"That's it," Eve repeated, and raking her fingers through her wet hair, headed back to the conference room.

The scent of food hit the empty pit of her stomach. In the few minutes she'd been gone, someone had brought in another table and loaded it with paninis, subs, pizza.

Roarke picked up a panini, held it out. "Eat. You'll think more clearly. And later, you can have a cookie."

She didn't argue, but took a huge bite. And just closed her eyes. "Okay. Good. You got cookies?"

"It seemed apt. Now take this blocker. No point going into this with a headache. Just a blocker," he added, popping the little pill in her mouth, then handing her a bottle of water. "Hydrate."

"Jesus. Cut it out." She guzzled water, took another bite of panini. "I'm in charge here."

He tugged a damp lock of her hair. "And it suits you. Your bullpen's buzzing."

"I need five minutes of quiet before —"

"Food!" McNab, who probably smelled pizza in EDD, led the charge.

"Take your five," Roarke told her, and she nodded.

She settled for crossing to the windows, and blocking out the sound of cops pouncing on a bonanza of free food.

When she heard the commander's voice, she turned. Mira came in, walked straight to her. "I wasn't able to get away sooner."

"Were you able to review any of what I sent you?"

"I read all of it. You make a number of persuasive points. If we could take another hour, I think we could refine several of them."

"It's already midday on a Friday. In July, when half the people who live here go somewhere else for the weekend. I've got to lay this out for Reo, have her convince a judge to issue warrants. I want to get it down before the end of business. We're just waiting for her now, so . . . and there she is. I'm going to get started."

She moved to the center of the room. "Officers, Detectives, take your seats. If you're going to continue to gorge, do so quietly. Commander, thank you for taking the time."

He nodded, took a seat. He had two slices of pizza on a plate and looked . . . guilty, she realized, and wasn't sure what to make of it.

"The wife doesn't like him eating between meals," Feeney muttered in her ear.

"I thought I'd missed lunch." Reo chose a seat, nibbled on half a panini.

Eve let the murmurs, the shifting, the laughter run on for a moment. Let them settle. She glanced at Roarke. He hadn't sat, but stood leaning against the wall by the windows.

She walked over, shut the conference room door, then moved back to the center of the room.

"I'd like to bring everyone's attention to the board." She used a laser pointer, highlighting each photo. "Bristow, Melly, Zimbabwe, Africa," she began, and named them all.

"All of these people were killed by Winston Dudley and Sylvester Moriarity. I know that with absolute certainty, just as I know with absolute certainty that they will kill again if they aren't stopped."

She let that sink in, just two beats of silence.

"Detective Peabody and I have built a case that I believe is substantial enough for search warrants for the suspects' homes and businesses and vehicles. With the murder of Adrianne Jonas, Detectives Reineke and Jenkinson joined the investigative team. Earlier this afternoon, I assigned every officer in this room specific tasks relating to this investigation. Together, we've built a stronger, wider case. We've correlated with EDD, Doctor Mira, and the expert consultant, civilian.

"Bristow, Melly," she said again, and ordered the data on-screen.

It took time, but she couldn't rush it. She walked them through every victim, every connection, every overlap. She called on each member of the team to present his or her findings, then connected those.

"The shoes." Reo gestured. "How many sold, that size and color?"

"Peabody."

"Three pair, from New York merchants. I've verified one of the buyers was in New Zealand at the time of the murder. The other lives in Pennsylvania, is eighty-three years of age. Though I can't absolutely confirm his whereabouts at the time in question, he doesn't fit the height or body type from the image EDD was able to access from park security. He's six inches shorter, at least twenty pounds lighter."

"Okay, that's good. But worldwide there would be more, and that's what the defense would point out."

"Less than seventy-five pair sold as of the date of the murder," Eve said. "Peabody's already eliminated forty-three."

"Forty-six now, sir."

"I'll take those odds."

"The alibis," Reo began. As she and Eve debated, Baxter's 'link signaled. He glanced at the ID, held up a finger to Eve, and walked out of the room.

"Some people swear they were there the whole time," Eve continued. "Some state they don't remember seeing one or both of them for long periods. Others just don't remember one way or the other. If you can't break that flimsy an alibi, you're not doing your job."

"You don't want to tell me my job," Reo shot back. "I'm doing my job by questioning every aspect of this. If you go after these two before we're solid, they could slip through. My boss isn't going to go for arrests on this unless he believes he can convict. These are wealthy men, who can afford an army of very slick attorneys."

"I don't care if they're —"

"Lieutenant." Baxter stepped back in. "Sorry to interrupt. I need a minute."

She walked to him, listened, nodded. "Tell the room."

"I just got off the 'link with one of the most respected and renowned makers of whips — that's your bull, your snake, and so on. He verifies making the murder weapon for a Leona Bloom — who was buying it as a gift for a friend. Buying the whip and a package of lessons. The whip guy keeps very specific records as he takes large pride in his work. The lessons were given to Winston Dudley the Fourth six years ago, in Sydney."

"That's good," Reo said.

"Whip guy remembers Dudley," Baxter

488

continued. "Remembers he took the lessons seriously. He not only took the package, but added to it with another round of lessons. Whip guy says Dudley was damn good with a whip by the end of it."

"That's very, very good," Reo added.

"It's bull's-eye," Eve countered. "What do you need, to actually see them kill somebody? We can link the weapons to the men, the victims to the men. Moriarity's going to have the crossbow and harpoon gun, Dudley's still got the sheath he used for the bayonet. Believe it. A case for the whip. They'd want part of the weapon to keep, to gloat over.

"There's no way to know who they've targeted next, but there will be a target." She pressed that button, pressed it hard. "These are addictive personalities, and they won't stop. They can't stop," Eve insisted. "They like it too much, and they're at tie score. They won't stop until one of them misses, and even then, they won't stop. After an entire life of playing at work, at playing at sport, at just goddamn playing, they've found something they're really good at, something that they can share as intimately as lovers. The people they kill are only important because they're important — but every one of the victims lack what these men would see as their pedigree, their privilege to be important by birth.

"They're addicts," she repeated, "and won't give up this drug. And they're freaking soul mates, so they won't give up this union. They may take it elsewhere — Europe, South America, Asia, mix their pie a little when they're bored of New York."

"I think they'll stay until they've finished this particular contest." Mira spoke quietly. "I agree with the lieutenant's evaluation. These men need to feed their desires, their whims, their sense of intimacy with each other. They need to indulge themselves, and this is their ultimate competition, and partnership. They work together, even as they compete. Killing two people, one after another, using the same alibi would have been yet another kind of rush. A new thrill, and codependency. They may continue that pattern, or escalate. And once again kill together. I believe that's how they plan to indulge themselves with you, Eve."

21

He'd wondered if she'd followed those dots, but Roarke could see now she hadn't gone there. Oh, her ego was healthy enough, but it simply hadn't clicked how precisely she fit their victim profile.

She was the best at what she did, and well known for it, particularly well with the success of Nadine's book. She'd made herself what she was.

She wasn't for hire in a technical sense, but she served.

And the connection, well fuck it all, it was through him, wasn't it?

She was going there now, and bloody buggering hell she was considering how she could use it, use herself.

"It's your opinion I'm a target," Eve said to Mira.

"It's my opinion that you're not only a perfect fit, but would be, to them, the ultimate prey. Their timing of the first murder played the odds, and they were good ones, that you would catch the case," Mira reminded her. "If you hadn't, you would certainly have been involved in some manner by the second murder, which also connected to Roarke through its location. You fit their target requirements. You're known to be one of the best in your field, a field of service. You've gained notoriety for what you do."

"I don't have any past connection with them." But even as she said it, she glanced at Roarke.

"Of course you do," he said, equably, "because I do. My business dealings and theirs have crossed in the past. They have reason, if they take such matters personally, to resent me for some of those dealings."

She hooked her thumbs in her front pockets. "Why not go for you?"

He smiled. "Wouldn't that be entertaining? I don't fit," he added. "I don't provide a service, nor am I for sale. Protect and serve, Lieutenant, for which you draw a salary. And if you'd think as they do for a moment rather than grinding those gears wondering how you could set yourself up as bait, you'd see you're an indulgence. Mine. From their perspective, I bought and paid for you. Mind you don't sputter."

He felt her fury, the hot burst of it, and continued to lean against the wall and watch her.

She pulled it in — he had to admire the strength of will — and simply nodded.

"I'd like to give this some thought, discuss it further, but detailing the investigation, thus far, and getting the warrants are the priority and purpose here. Do you have enough to take to your boss, Reo?"

"I'll take it to him, and I'll push." Reo sat where she was, scanning the boards and screens. "You've got a mountain of circumstantial here that adds up to a solid argument for the search warrants. You're shy of arrest — and you know it," she added. "You've convinced me, and I'll convince the PA. Convincing a judge to issue the warrants to search the homes of two men with no priors, with their pedigree, their connections and influence, that's going to be work, and it's going to take time."

She rose. "So I'd better get started. It's damn good work, all around. I'll be in touch."

"Let's add to the mountain," Eve said as Reo walked out. "Dig, push, wheedle, finesse. We're going to pile it on, and we're going to bring them in. Get back to work. Doctor Mira," she continued as cops surged to their feet, "if I could have a few minutes. Commander, I'll keep you fully updated and informed."

"I believe I'll stay."

"Yes, sir. Peabody, coordinate the —"

"If my partner's thinking about sticking herself on a hook, I'm going to be in on the strategy session."

"Bait needs an e-team." Feeney chose a pickle from the food table, crunched in.

"I'm not, at this time, planning any such operation." She felt, literally, squeezed in. "It would be backup only, if Reo doesn't get the warrants. I believe she will, so everybody can just stop hovering. Apologies, Commander."

"Unnecessary."

"Doctor Mira, if I'm a target, it's likely they've already chosen the location and weapon, if not the time."

"I agree. It would be my belief that you would be their endgame, at least here in New York, and at least for this phase of the contest. Everything points to their enjoyment of the competition, its results, so it's unlikely they've positioned you for the last round. But —"

"If and when we get the search warrants, that would change the complexion of things." Eve nodded. "It would piss them off, and it would challenge them. They'd want to go at me sooner."

"I'd have to agree. They've left pieces of themselves at the scenes — the weapons. They've connected themselves to the murders, indirectly, to ensure you would have contact with them. While they compete with each other, they're competing against you, as a team."

"And they cheat." Roarke took a bottle of water from the table.

"And when they tried that on you, you beat them. A golf thing," Eve said with a shrug. "I'm not convinced you wouldn't be a more exciting target. You're not in service, fine, but you employ a universe of people who are. You're already a competitor, and one they dislike because you had the nerve to build a fortune instead of inheriting one. It's a pretty fair bet you've been involved with some of the women they've been involved with."

He took a slow sip of water. "I'll just say my taste has improved. Then point out what you should know very well. There's no better way to strike at me than by murdering my wife."

"The one you bought and paid for?"

Well now, that grated her ass, didn't it? he mused. And for some perverse reason her reaction banked the embers of his own temper.

"Yes, to their minds. They don't understand you, or me for that matter. And they certainly don't understand love. Would you agree, Doctor Mira?"

"I would. And they prefer killing women. You can judge the ratio." Mira gestured to the board. "They've killed men, and certainly will continue to if not stopped. But women are the preferred target, as both of them consider women something to be used, something disposable. Something less."

"Dudley particularly," Eve commented. "He surrounds himself with them. It's like a harem. Okay." She nodded again as her mind took a few leaps forward. "We'll need to put something in place. The search warrants may be enough to push me to the head of the line, but we can work something that ups that time frame."

"But if you wait for Reo to come through," Peabody protested, "we'd have more time to work out the strategy, the backup."

Feeney shook his head. "She fronts the play, they react. That puts them on defense. They have to rush their move, and while they're pissed off. They don't maneuver her into a situation, because she's maneuvering them. We can get eyes and ears on you."

"I've got this." Eve held up her wrist, and Feeney's eyes narrowed.

"Let me see that. Take it off," he told her when she held her arm out. "I'm not going to pocket it."

When she obliged him, he took it off to a chair to examine.

"I confront them. I'm pissed off." Eve tapped a hand to her chest. "All these bodies piling up, and two in one day. I'm the best, right, and they're running circles around me. I know they're involved," she continued as she began to pace. "I've got all these arrows pointing, but they're racking up the points while I'm spinning. Makes me look incompetent."

She could work this, she realized. Yes, she could work it.

"My commander's on my ass, my husband's getting testy with the hours I'm putting in. I'm starting to look like an idiot and I don't like it. I'm going to light some fires."

"How much will you give them?" Whitney asked her.

"Just what they've given me. The surface connections, but I need to make it personal. Them, me. Budget's stretched," she decided. "Yeah. I can't access the resources through the department, but I'll use my own money to get those resources outside the department. Don't you know who I am? Don't you know I've got more money than the two of you put together? That'll speak to them, won't it?" she asked Mira. "He bought me, but now I can get my hands on billions as long as I bang him when he wants it."

"A fool and his money," Roarke murmured, amused despite himself.

Mira let out a little sigh. "I would say it's their probable view of your relationship."

"And I'd say this no longer sounds like a backup plan," Roarke put in.

"Feeney's right, I front the play. I can time it. Hit them after I know, or am reasonably sure, we're going to get the warrants, but before we serve them. It's just adding incentive for them to move up their timetable. We sting them right," she insisted, and Roarke understood she was pushing to get him in her corner, "they go after me, they go after a cop, they're done. Their high-priced lawyers, their family fortunes, their goddamn pedigrees aren't going to keep them out of a cage for the rest of their lives."

"Is that what worries you?" he asked. "That even with the case you've built, even with the evidence you believe you'll gather with the warrants, they'll slip through the system?"

"They worry me." In one sharp move, she pointed to the board, to the faces of the dead. "The chance I'll have to put another up there worries me."

He watched her realize she'd let her emotions spike, let them show in front of her superior. And he watched her draw them down again, draw them in.

"They want me up there," she said in a tone both cool and flat, "so we'll make them want me up there sooner."

"You know, I've been working on something like this off and on." Feeney continued to study the wrist unit as his casual comment defused the charged air. "This one's nice and compact, got more bells and whistles than I'd worked out."

He glanced up, his gaze flicking over Roarke before homing in on Eve. "What would be prime is if you run into them — the both of you — someplace. Public place. Restaurant, club, like that. That's what fries you, see, trying to get a little downtime, and there they are in your face. Maybe you're already pissy, having a spat with Roarke, and that just shoves you over the line. That way it comes off impulse. Like you just lost it there for a minute."

"That is prime," Eve agreed.

"I've got moments." Feeney rose, handed the unit back to Eve, looked at Roarke. "That's nice work."

"Thanks."

"Peabody, see if you can find out where they're going to be tonight. At least one of them. Friday night . . . they're not going to sit at home playing mah-jongg."

"It'll be easier and quicker for me to find out." Roarke took out his 'link, walked away.

"Still want eyes and ears on you," Feeney told her.

"Fine." She stuck her hands in her pockets as she tracked Roarke out of the room.

"You keep them on, unless you're locked up in that fortress you live in, or you're working toward getting your hands on some billions."

"What . . ." It struck her. "Jesus, Feeney."

"You started it. I'll start setting it up."

"I want two officers on you at all times. That starts now," Whitney added.

"McNab and I will take tonight."

"They've seen you," Eve reminded Peabody.

"They won't make me."

Mira slipped out, waiting until Roarke put his 'link away.

"I'm going to apologize to you," she began. "I couldn't, in good conscience, keep my opinion to myself, even knowing how she'd react, what she'd do. But I'm sorry."

"I'm obliged to accept what she does. What she is," he added, reminding himself that she, in turn, accepted him. Hardly realizing he did so, he slid a hand into his pocket, found the button he carried there. That tiny piece of her. "That obligation started when I fell in love with her, and was sealed when I married her. Before you told her, I'd been engaged in a vicious internal debate about telling her myself."

"I see."

He held her gaze for a long moment. "I don't know which side of me would've won."

"I do. You'd have told her, then had your argument over her reaction in private."

"I expect you're right."

"What troubles you more? What she's planning to do, or the fact that she's in the position of doing it because her connection to you qualified her?"

"Toss-up. They have utter contempt for me, and enjoy letting it show. Just enough. I suppose they think I'd be insulted, or have my feelings hurt."

"As you said, they don't understand you."

"If they did, they'd have tried to kill her already. They think killing her will inconvenience me, certainly disrupt my personal and professional lives for a bit, cause me some distress."

He turned the button in his fingers. "They'd enjoy all of that. If they knew losing her would destroy me in levels they can't imagine, they'd cut her into pieces and bathe in her blood."

"No." Eve spoke from the doorway. "No, they wouldn't because I'm better than they are. They can't beat me, and they sure as hell can't beat us. Can you give us a minute?" she asked Mira.

"Yes." She touched Roarke's arm before she went back inside the conference room.

"Do you really think those two trust-fund fuckwits could take me down?"

Oh aye, he thought, her ego was healthy enough — so was her temper. But by God, so was his. "Think, no. But neither would I have thought those two trust-fund fuckwits could or would murder nine people or more, and have the NYPSD chasing their tails."

"Chasing our . . ." Fury erupted. He'd have sworn his skin singed in the hot flow of its lava. "Is that what you call this? Is that what you call putting a solid case together in under a week? Making connections that tie them up out of sweat and sleepless nights and solid, consistent police work? Chasing our tails?"

"So solid a case you're about to paint a target on your back rather than trust that solid case and police work."

"This is police work, goddamn it. This is the job, and you know it. You knew it from the jump, and if you can't back me when —"

"Stop there," he warned her. "I haven't said I wouldn't back you, but I won't be pushed into it."

"I don't have time to ease into it, to debate and discuss. I didn't put it together, and I should have. I didn't see it until Mira pointed it out, and it should've been flashing like fucking neon in my brain. I'll know who their next target is if it's me, and I won't have to stand over somebody else I couldn't save."

"I understand that, and you, very well." Christ, he was tired. He couldn't remember when he'd last been so bloody knackered. "Do you really expect me to have no concerns, no worries, no dark thoughts? Reverse it. I'm putting myself up as bait. What do you do?"

"I trust you enough to know you can and will handle yourself, and use the resources you have available to ensure your own safety."

"Eve, please don't stand there and shovel that bullshit at my feet. These are good shoes."

She hissed out a breath, but at the end of it he saw the chip on her shoulder tumble off. "Okay, I would trust you, but I'd also have some concerns, worries, and dark thoughts. And you'd be sorry I did. You'd hate that I did."

"All right."

She squinted at him. "All right? That's it?"

"I had a bigger and considerably more vicious fight with you before, in my head. It was passionate, fierce, and very, very loud."

"Who won?"

He had to touch her, just a skim of his fingertip down the little dent in her chin. "We hadn't quite got there, but since we've finished it here, I like to think we both have."

"I meant what I said in there, which I shouldn't have said in front of Whitney. I can't have another face on that board." He watched her face change, watched her let him see what was inside.

"The ones on there now, I couldn't stop it; I couldn't save them. But if there's another, I own it, because I know I have the tools to stop it. To make the best possible effort to stop it."

"And the warrants aren't enough?"

"I had to believe it to sell it, so I did. I still do, almost clear through." She looked away for a moment. "But there's that fraction, that percentage that maybe they've covered everything, that we won't find enough to charge them — or we'll charge them, indict them, and that fleet of high-priced lawyers will find enough little holes to spring them. I'm hedging my bets, and I've got a couple other ideas that should add more edge. You could help me with them."

"I suppose I could."

"Do you know where they're going to be tonight?"

"They're attending the ballet, at the Strathmore Center."

"Can you score us tickets?"

"We have a box. They are, however, meeting for drinks at Lionel's before the performance."

"That'll work even better." She took his hand, linked fingers. "Let me lay it out for you."

He had to admit, she'd slapped together an interesting and inventive scenario in very short order. He refined it a bit, and felt as confident as he could.

"I'm going to give Reo another thirty. She should've finished talking to her boss by then. I'll need to brief the team."

"They're meeting at seven. That gives you time for an hour's sleep. Not negotiable," he said before she objected. "And not on the damn floor. There have to be cots at least in your infirmary."

"I hate the infirmary."

"Suck it up," he advised.

"Mira has a big couch in her session room. I'll ask if I can use it."

"Make it we. I could use a lie-down myself."

She slept like the dead woman a couple of rich guys wanted her to be, then contacted Reo. Again.

"Tell me you've got it."

"I told you I'd contact you when I did. Didn't I tell you the boss thinks Judge Dwier's the best hit on this?" The testy edge of frustration came through loud and clear. "No known connections with either family, solid reputation, open-minded, and so on and so on, and didn't I tell you Judge Dwier is fly-fishing in Montana?"

"And didn't I say go with another choice?"

"Don't tell us our jobs. The PA's talking

to the judge right now. He's walking him through it, and my sense is we're nearly there. We're ninety percent there."

"Close enough. When you've got it, tag Baxter. He'll head up that end."

"Where are you going to be?"

"I'm going to meet a couple guys at a bar."

She clicked off as Feeney came in. "Gotta suit you up."

"I can do that." Roarke walked in behind him, carrying a silver garment bag. "She'll need to change anyway."

"Into what?" Eve demanded.

"Appropriate attire. Your con will be more convincing if you're dressed for an evening out."

"I'll test you out when you're attired." With a snort, Feeney strolled out.

"Strip it off, Lieutenant," Roarke told her. He shut and locked the door.

"I need to be able to carry my weapon."

"I said appropriate attire." He unzipped the bag.

The dress was short, simple, and black. But it came with a hip-skimming jacket that fastened up the front with a lot of fancy loops.

"Somebody could kill me five times before I got that jacket undone and drew my weapon."

Roarke simply demonstrated by tugging the jacket open. "The loops are for show."

"Not bad. Not bad at all." When she peeled off her clothes, Roarke fixed on the recorder, the mic, the earpiece. "Where'd the dress come from?"

"Your closet. I had Summerset bring it down. Along with the accessories." He held up diamond earrings. "They'll see these, believe me, and won't give a single thought to the possibility you're wired. And switch your wrist unit for the evening one."

She gave it, all that fire and ice, a dubious glance. "I haven't really played with that one."

"It works the same way as your everyday. You can carry a clutch piece in this bag — though not much else. Add the shoes."

They were hot murder red with heels that made her arches twinge when she looked at them. "How am I supposed to run in those?"

He gave her a quick, amused look. "Are you planning on running?"

"You never know." But she dressed, and added the murderous shoes. "Appropriate?"

"You're perfect." He framed her face with his hands. "Perfect for me."

"We're supposed to be pissed at each

other, remember. You need to get in character."

"I never have a problem acting pissed at you." When he grinned, he brushed his lips over hers. He laid his forehead to hers briefly at the knock on the door, then crossed over to answer.

"Peabody, you look lovely."

"Thanks." She lifted her hands, palms up to Eve. "Well?"

She also wore black, young and funky, with a brightly striped sleeveless vest that covered her sidearm. With her hair done in crazed corkscrew curls, her eyes lined in emerald green, and her lips as red as Eve's shoes, Eve was forced to agree.

"You're right. They won't make you."

"McNab and I are heading out now so we'll already be in place when the subjects get there. Detective Carmichael and the new guy will take the ballet. Baxter's waiting for the go, then he'll have both search units move in."

"Good work, Peabody."

"See you at the bar."

"She's juiced," Eve commented. "She took a booster earlier, but this is just juice. Because we're close, because we're going to bring them in before much longer. Bring them in, sweat them, break them. End it."

"Someone else is juiced."

"Bet your ass, ace." She did a couple of squats and pivots to see how the dress cooperated. "Can you tell I'm loaded? The weapon," she elaborated when he smiled at her.

"I can. They won't. You know, I'm starting to enjoy this whole business myself."

"Wait till I unload on them." She tore open the jacket, pulled her weapon. Slapped it back in its harness. "You're going to get a serious charge."

They walked into the elegant lounge with its deep ruby and rich sapphire tones in what appeared to be a low-voiced continuation of an argument. When Roarke cupped her elbow, she deliberately jerked it away, let her voice spike up.

"Don't try to placate me."

"I wouldn't dream of it. Two," he said to the hostess who, admirably, kept her face blank and polite. "Roarke."

"Yes, sir, of course. I have your booth ready. Just this way."

"You know the kind of pressure I'm dealing with," Eve continued, keeping her eyes on Roarke. "The commander's setting up permanent residence on my ass."

"It would be a lovely change of pace if we

could spend one bloody evening not discussing your commander, your problems. Whiskey," he told the hostess. "A double."

"And for you, madam?"

"Head Shot, straight up."

Roarke leaned into her as if murmuring something, and she jerked back. "Because I need it, that's why. Look, I'm here, aren't I? Which is more than you'll be tomorrow since you're leaving town. Again."

"I have work, and responsibilities, Eve."

"So do I."

"Yours don't put toys like this on your ears," he said and gave one of her earrings a flick of his finger.

"I earn those other ways, and don't you forget —" She broke off as if just spotting Dudley and Moriarity. "Oh, that's perfect. That's just fucking perfect."

"Keep your voice down."

"Don't tell me what to do. I'm sick of orders. I'm the top murder cop in this goddamn city, and I'm getting zip from the department on this, and less than zip from you. Well, fuck that. I'm getting some of my own, and right now."

She shoved out of the booth, and he timed his lunge to stop her seconds too late.

She had to admit striding the few short feet to the next booth in the killer red heels felt powerful.

"You think I'm stupid?"

"Lieutenant Dallas." All concerned charm, Dudley reached for her hand. "You seem upset."

"You touch me and I'll haul you in for assaulting an officer." She slapped her palms on the table between them, leaned in. "I know you killed Delaflote and Jonas, probably the others, too, but those I know."

"I think you must be drunk," Moriarity said, very quietly.

"Not yet. Believe me when I tell you I'll make a case. I don't care how long it takes or what it takes. You're not going to beat me at my own game. This is what I do."

"Eve." Roarke stepped up to her, gripped her arm. "Stop this. We're leaving."

"Your wife seems very upset and not a little deranged." Dudley smiled. "You don't appear to be able to control her."

"Nobody controls me, asshole. You want to leave." She turned on Roarke. "Fine. Go. Why don't you just go wherever you're shuttling off to right now instead of tomorrow and get off my back?"

"That's an excellent idea. Gentlemen, my sincere apologies. You can get yourself home," he said to Eve.

"I'll get there, when I'm good and ready."

As Roarke walked out, she spun back to the booth. "The department won't give me the money to go full-out on you two. Screw them. He'll give it to me." She jerked her head in the direction Roarke had taken. "I know how to get what I want. The PA may not have the balls to give me a go now, but give me time. I close cases. I'll close this."

She grabbed one of the drinks on the table, tossed back a swallow before slamming it down again. "Did you think I wouldn't see? Using your people as dupes, covering each other's ass while the other one gets the kill in? You both knew the last two victims, and I'll find how you knew the first two. I'm the hot breath on your neck."

"You're making a fool of yourself," Moriarity told her — but his gaze shifted to Dudley's.

"Like Delaflote made a fool out of the Dudleys when he was nailing Winnie's mommy?" She bared her teeth in a smile. "Oh, yeah, I know. I know a lot. Nearly there, boys. Nearly time to pay the bill."

"Madam." The hostess came over, eyes full of apologies for the men. "I have to ask you to leave."

"No problem. I can find better places to drink than a dump that serves scum like these two. Drink up," she told both men.

"They don't serve fancy liquor in the cages you're going to be in within forty-eight. And that's just where I'm going to put you. You can bet on it."

Eve almost wished she wore a cape so she could've swirled it as she stormed out of the room.

She kept storming a block north, turned, and kept the pace another half a block. Feeney opened the back of the e-van. She hopped in, yanked off the shoes. "How'd I do?"

"If I was married to you, I'd be divorced."

Roarke took her hand, kissed it. "She's a bitch, but she's my bitch."

She tapped her ear. "Peabody reports they're in intense conversation. It looks to her like Dudley's trying to convince Moriarity, is pushing a point."

"I can hear her." Roarke tapped in turn. "You're not the only one with ears."

"Oh. That was a good idea, putting it out you'd be gone tonight. They're going to want to make their move."

She turned her wrist when her com signaled. "Check this," she said to Feeney. "Dallas."

"Reo pulled it off," Baxter told her. "We got the warrants."

"Don't go in yet. Give them some time. If

this worked, one or both of them is going to show up at one of the houses or one of the HQs where they have private quarters. They need to get the weapon. Let them come and go. No longer than ten minutes in. It's over that, move in. I don't want to have spooked them into ditching any evidence, but if we take them in with a weapon, we're going to add attempted on a police officer. That's the icing on the cupcake."

"We're on hold."

"Seems a shame to waste the performance," she said to Roarke. "Damn it." She scowled at Peabody's voice in her ear. "They're ordering another drink. Maybe they're not going to bite after all. Stick with them," she ordered Peabody, then answered the com again. "What?"

"Movement at the Moriarity house. It's the droid, Dallas, the same droid we have going into the Frost/Simpson house."

She shook her head in wonder. "God, they are idiots. They didn't destroy the droid, and odds are he'll bring them the weapon. I want a team on that droid. I want to know where it goes, what it does. When it's clear of the house, move in. All locations."

She rubbed her bare foot. "They bit."

"I believe they did," Roarke commented.

22

Eve tried to ignore the fact that Feeney and Roarke were talking in e-geek. That was bad enough, but on the other side of her Mc-Nab and Peabody snuggled up together like a couple of sleepy puppies, and she was pretty sure the murmurs and giggles were some sort of sex talk.

If she didn't get out of the damn van soon, she'd commit mass murder. She'd use the ice-pick heel of one of the arch-throbbing red shoes to skewer geek and puppy brains.

They'd make a good weapon, she considered. With the right force, the right angle, you probably could skewer brains.

Maybe that's why women wore them, *as a just in case I have to kill somebody* tool. That, at least, made some sense. Except it would make more sense to wear them on your hands where they'd be right there if you needed —

Her homicidal thoughts scattered as Carmichael spoke in her ear.

"Subjects entering the theater."

"Copy that. Keep eyes on them."

"On them now. They're heading straight to the bar. Ordering a bottle of champagne for their box. Making a big show of it, a lot of loud, hearty laughter, drawing attention. They're heading in now. Staff's scrambling to get it up to their box before curtain."

Establishing the alibi, Eve thought. "Take positions. One of them goes to take a leak, you're with them."

"I think I'll leave that to the new guy. Out."

"Cutting it close," Eve said. "Getting there five minutes to curtain, ordering champagne. The bartender will remember them, and so will the servers and some of the people milling around."

Idiots, she thought, but not completely stupid.

"They'll need to wait until the performance starts to make any move. Wait until people are watching the stage, the house is dark. But soon. It has to be soon. Cut it out." She gave Peabody a shove. "You're making my eye twitch."

"We're just sitting here."

"I know sex giggles when I hear them."

"I wasn't giggling."

"Not you. Him."

McNab just grinned at her. "Those were manly chuckles."

"You're cops. Be cops."

She shifted, scowled. "What are you smiling at?" she demanded of Roarke.

"Why don't you sit here and I'll tell you." With a sparkling look in his eyes, he patted his knee. "And I might produce a manly chuckle of my own."

"Stop it. You're embarrassing Feeney."

"I'm past it," Feeney muttered and kept his head down. "Surrounded by a bunch of giggling, twitching, chuckling fools when we're on an op looking to take down a couple of crazy thrill killers."

"Didn't I tell them to cut it out?"

"You give them any attention you just encourage them." He said it mournfully, raising his gaze to hers. "Now I'll start twitching because you chipped the wall."

"What wall?"

"The wall I build in my head so I don't hear the sex giggles. Now you chipped it, and I'll hear them, and I'll be twitching."

"So it's my fault? Your wall's weak, that's what it is, if I can chip it just by mentioning — Shut up," she ordered, snapping to when her 'link signaled. "Everybody zip it." She looked at the display, and then she smiled.

"Showtime."

She scrubbed her fingers in her hair to disorder it, slapped her cheeks to pink them up, then brought the 'link close to her face. From Dudley. "The fuck you want, asshole?" she demanded, slurring her words.

"Lieutenant Dallas, thank God. You have to listen to me. I only have a few moments."

"Screw you."

"No, no, don't cut me off. I need your help. It's Sly. I think . . . dear God, I think he's mad."

"Speak up. It's noisy in this place. I can barely hear you."

"I can't risk speaking any louder." He continued to use dramatic hisses and whispers. "Listen to me, listen! I think he killed Delaflote, and poor Adrianne. The things he said after you left Lionel's . . . I can't believe it. He was so angry, and frightened, too. He said . . . I can't tell you all this over the 'link. He's drinking, too much. I think I can get away, soon. Make an excuse, or hope he passes out and get away to meet you. I need to tell you . . . please, you have to meet me."

"Where the fuck are you? I'll call it in, slap his drunk ass in restraints."

"No, no! What if I'm wrong? He's my oldest, dearest friend. Have pity. I'm asking for your help. Yours, Lieutenant, because you'll know what to do. If I'm overreacting, you'll know, and Sly won't be embarrassed. And if I'm right, you'll solve these horrible murders tonight before he . . . You'll be a heroine, again. You'll be credited for stopping this madness. You alone. I don't want my name involved. It's . . . painful. Please, please. I'm at the Strathmore Center. I can slip out. I can't go far. I'll have to get back before intermission in case . . . Our Lady of Shadows. It's only a block away."

Inside, her smile spread even as she scowled into the 'link. "A freaking church?"

"It's close, and we can talk without being interrupted or overheard. I have to trust you. I have to trust you'll know what to do. I'll be there in twenty minutes, and then I'll tell you everything I know. You're the only one I can tell."

"Yeah, yeah, fine. It'd better be good, Dudley. I've had a shitty day."

She cut him off, tapped the 'link against her palm. "They do think I'm stupid."

"Pissed-faced and stupid," Roarke added. "They'll double-team you."

"Absolutely. Feeney."

"I've got it."

"McNab, take the wheel while I bring in the teams. I want street level and I want no more than two blocks from the target site."

"You got it."

"What are you doing on that thing?" Eve asked as Roarke worked on his PPC.

"Bringing up the floor plans of the church again. You'll want to refresh your sense of the place."

"He thinks like a cop," she said to Feeney. "He hates when I say that, but what're you going to do? Dudley said twenty, so he'll be there in fifteen or sooner. I'll need to hoof it in those bastards for a block, from the east, in case one of them's watching for me. Dudley's using," she added. "His pupils were the size of dinner plates. Moriarity's likely had a few hits, too."

"Don't think that makes them less dangerous," Roarke said.

"No, I don't. But it's what's making them careless, what's pushing them as much — more, I guess, than the show we put on for them earlier." She took the PPC from Roarke, studied it. "Okay, as we laid out when Baxter's team reported the droid's movements, we put men here and here."

She looked at Peabody, got a nod. "Second team outside, covering the exits. I want them kept back until we know both subjects are inside, and I don't want anybody breaking cover until I give that go. Clear?"

"Yes, sir. I'll go in now, take this position. McNab —"

"I'll take the other."

Peabody started to speak, but subsided when she saw the look in Roarke's eyes.

"All right. The two of you take the inside positions." Eve would have offered Roarke her clutch piece but she knew damn well if Summerset had gotten the change of clothes for her, he'd have gotten a weapon to Roarke. She didn't want to know how he'd gotten one through security.

"I want inside, Dallas."

She glanced up at McNab as he maneuvered the van to the curb. He could irritate the hell out of her, but she trusted him to the bone. "You take position with Peabody. I'd better not hear any sex giggles."

She tapped her ear. "Copy that. Dudley's on the move. Stay where you are, Carmichael, until Moriarity makes his move. Give him room. Team A better get its asses to church."

Roarke leaned to her, spoke with his lips against her ear. "Think twice before you let them put a single mark on you if you want them in one piece and conscious for your arrest."

Before she could speak, he turned his head, pressed his lips firmly to hers. "Take care of my cop," he told her, and jumped out the back after Peabody.

Eve reached for the shoes, met Feeney's bland stare. "What?"

"I didn't say a word. We got some body armor if you want it."

"Makes me look fat," she said and made him laugh.

"Wouldn't help anyway if they try a head shot. Here." He reached in one of the drawers, pulled out a bottle.

"Christ, Feeney, I'm not going to drink that, and I'm sure as hell not going to drink before I run this op."

"You're going to swish it around in your mouth and spit it out." He held a glass out along with the bottle of Irish. "You want them to think you're drunk enough to fall for this crap, walk into their half-assed trap? You should smell drunk."

"Good point."

She took it, swished it, and while swishing dabbed some on her throat like perfume to make him laugh again. Then spat. Leaning forward she huffed out an exaggerated breath in his face. "How's that?"

"You'll do. Are we having cow meat burgers tomorrow?"

"Probably."

"I could go for a fat one. How about pie?

Is there going to be pie?"

"I don't know."

"Lemon meringue pie. That's what you want at a summer barbecue. Maybe strawberry shortcake."

"I'll get right on that — as soon as I avoid being murdered."

"My granny used to make lemon meringue pie. It got these little beads of sugar on the meringue. She could bake a goddamn pie, my granny."

"Yum. Dudley's heading toward the church." She rose, practiced pulling open the jacket, pulling her weapon. "That'll work. All teams hold positions. Dallas, on the move."

"You ought to wobble some, in case they get eyes on you."

She stepped out the back. "That's no problem in these shoes."

"Good hunting."

She shot him a grin as she shut the door.

She took her time, played her attitude in her head. She spotted her cops, but she knew where to look. She staggered into the church.

He'd lit some of the fake candles, she noted, so the light shifted and swayed. She took a couple more unsteady steps until she stood in the aisle formed by the back pews.

"Dudley, you asshole." Her voice echoed. "You better not be wasting my time."

"I'm here." His voice shook. She supposed he hoped it sounded fearful, but she caught the edge of laughter. "I — I wanted to be sure it was you. That he didn't follow me."

"Don't worry, I'll protect you. I get paid to protect the city's assholes."

"It can't be enough." He eased out of the shadows at the far end of the church.

"You're damn skippy. It's not the pay, it's the power. Nothing like watching suspects piss themselves when I lean on them. You got five minutes," she said as Carmichael murmured in her ear that Moriarity was on his way.

"You can't know what it means to me that you'd come like this. I know you're under terrible pressure."

"That's what drinking's for. And screw pressure. I close this one, I'll be on-screen for weeks. Maybe get another book out of it. Couple of rich assholes like you and Moriarity, the media's going to slather all over me."

"Sly's the one." He moved toward her, stopped again. "I covered for him, but I didn't know what he'd done. If I had . . . I didn't know, not until tonight."

"You're eating up your five, Dudley. Lay it

out or I'm going to haul you in for annoying an officer. Believe me, I'm not in the mood to haul your ass or mine down to Central."

Moriarity at the door, she heard in her ear, even as she caught the faint vibration from the 'link in Dudley's pocket. He slid his hand in.

"Hey, hands where I can see them!" She reached clumsily in her bag.

"I'm sorry." He tossed his hands up. "I'm nervous. I'm sick at heart. You have to help me!" He grabbed her wrists as if in desperation.

The door burst open behind her. She had to squelch her instinct to defend, staggered instead. Then felt the stunner press to her throat.

"Hold very still," Moriarity ordered.

"Not yet, not yet!" Dudley shouted it. "Damn it, Sly. No cheating."

"Just getting her attention." He slid the stunner down to her shoulder.

It would take her down, Eve thought, but it wouldn't kill her.

"What the hell kind of game is this?"

"Not a game, Lieutenant," Dudley told her. "Games are for children. This is adventure. It's competition. Drop that very attractive evening bag, or Sly will give you a very nasty jolt. Very nasty," he repeated when she hesitated.

"Let's all take it easy." She let the bag drop.

"I wish we had more time." Dudley walked down a few pews, bent down. "We'd hoped to have more time when we got to you. And we'd planned on using St. Pat's. Wouldn't that have been glorious?"

"It would've made a statement." She felt Sly shift slightly. "This place? It's nothing important."

"It will be after this." Dudley straightened, whipped the sword in the air. "We'll have made it important."

"What the hell is that?" Eve demanded.

"This." Dudley struck a fencing pose, tore the air with the blade. "It's a foil, you ignorant bitch. Italian, very old and very valuable. It's the blade of an aristocrat."

"You won't get away with this. My partner knows where I am, who I was going to meet."

"Lies won't help. You're so drunk you barely knew your own name when I talked you out of whatever bar you were in. And you came just like I told you to."

"You killed them. All of them. Houston, Crampton, Delaflote, Jonas. Both of you, working together, just like I thought."

"It wasn't work," Dudley corrected.

"It was pleasure."

"We had another round planned before you, but . . ."

"I knew it!" Still playing the helpless drunk, she swayed a little in Moriarity's hold. "The two of you conspired to kill four people."

"In New York," Dudley confirmed with a wide, wide grin. "But we've racked up more points elsewhere."

"But why? Who were they to you?"

"Old nobodies, new luxuries." Dudley laughed until he shook.

"Winnie, we have to get back."

"You're right. It's a shame we can't play with her awhile. It has to be at the same time, remember. At exactly the same time so the score stays tied. Your trigger, my blade. Let's say on three."

Moriarity leaned in, let his lips caress her ear. "Who's the asshole now?" he said to Eve.

"That would be you."

She knocked Moriarity's weapon hand with an elbow strike, slammed the sharp point of her left shoe into his instep. As she pivoted, Dudley charged. The blade skipped lightly over her biceps, jerked as she finished the turn. And ran Moriarity through.

Eyes wide, Moriarity looked down at the blood seeping through the snow white of his shirt. "Winnie, you killed me."

As he fell, Dudley let out a howl, a wild combination of grief and rage. While cops flooded the room, weapons drawn, she indulged herself with one short-armed, vicious punch to his face.

Roarke barely glanced at Dudley as he stepped over the man. "That's two jackets ruined this week."

"It's not my fault."

"Whose then, I'd like to know? And look here, you've bruised your knuckles."

"Don't —" She hissed it when he lifted her hand, and winced when he kissed her knuckles.

"You deserved that," he said, "for knocking him out when you knew I wanted to."

"Bus and wagon on the way." Peabody glanced back at Moriarity. "That was a nice move. It's too bad about the jacket."

Eve pressed a hand to the tear, in the cloth and her arm. "It was worth it. All right, people, let's finish this up. Peabody, book an interview room. Oh, and tell the MTs to try to keep that one breathing. It may be poetic if it turns out his pal killed him, but I'm not looking for poetry. I'm going back to Central to change, and update the commander."

"Not until the MTs have tended that wound," Roarke corrected.

"He barely nicked me — and he wouldn't have done that if I hadn't had to deal with these idiot shoes."

"Two choices. Sit and wait for a medic, or I'll embarrass you in front of your men and kiss you."

She sat.

Since Dudley demanded a lawyer with his first conscious breath, Eve had time to shower and change, update Whitney, debrief, and dismiss her team.

She stood in the conference room, alone, in front of the board, in front of the faces of the dead. She thought of Jamal Houston's wife, of his partner and friend, of Adrianne Jonas's weeping parents, the trembling control of her assistant, and of all the others she'd had to crush with news of death.

She would speak to them, all of them again, tell them the men who'd taken those lives, shattered those worlds had been stopped. Would, she was determined, pay for their actions.

She had to hope it would help the living, and continued to believe, for reasons she didn't fully understand, it gave solace to the dead.

"Eve."

"Doctor Mira." Eve turned from the board. "What are you still doing here?"

"I wanted to see this through." She stepped beside Eve, and studied those faces in turn. "So many. Such utter selfishness."

"There would be more. We stopped them tonight and we're sealing that cage door. A lot of that's because of you. If I'd clicked to them targeting me earlier, there might not be so many faces on this board."

"You know that's wrong, both in reality and in thinking. It could just as easily be said there would be more if you hadn't intuited the pattern so quickly. You worked the case, and tonight you'll close it. I'd like to observe your interview with Dudley."

"It may be a while yet. He's conferring with his bevy of lawyers."

"I can wait. I'm told you were hurt."

"Just a scratch, seriously. It was the shoes. They screwed up my balance. Still." She tapped her arm. "It was an antique Italian fencing foil. That's pretty frosty."

Peabody stepped in. "Hey, Doctor Mira. Dallas, Dudley's head lawyer's asking to talk to you."

"This ought to be good. I'll meet him outside the interview room."

■ ■ ■ ■

An imposing man with white wings flowing back from his mane of black hair, Bentley Sorenson nodded curtly to Eve.

"Lieutenant, I'm informing you that I intend to file formal complaints over your treatment of my client, and your use of excessive force, entrapment, and harassment. Additionally, I've already contacted the governor, who will be speaking with the prosecuting attorney about falsifying information for an improper search of my client's residence, business, and vehicles. I want my client released until these matters can be fully resolved."

"You can file all the papers you want. You can call the governor, your congressman, or the freaking president, but your client's not walking out of here. You can stonewall me, Mr. Sorenson." She added a careless shrug. "I'll go home to bed and have a nice relaxing weekend. Your client will spend his in a cage."

"Mr. Dudley is a respected and valued businessman from one of the premier families in this country. He has no prior record and has cooperated fully with you and this department. Additionally, he contacted you for help, and to offer his, and you abused him."

"You know it's a toss-up as to whether you're an idiot or just doing your job. I'm giving you the benefit of the doubt and going with doing your job. You're going to decide now if you're going to block this interview tonight — which means he'll chill behind bars until Monday — or if we go in there and talk."

"I can have a hearing before a judge set within the hour."

"Go ahead. I'll go take a nap while you set it up. It's been a long week."

"Are you seriously willing to risk your career over this?"

She shifted, stood hip-shot, hooked her thumbs in her front pockets. "Is that a threat, Counselor?"

"It's a question, Lieutenant."

"I'll tell you what I'm not willing to risk. Your client stepping out of that room unless it's into a cage before I've interviewed him. I'm not willing to risk him going poof because he has the money and means to do so. In or out. You know very well I can hold him until Monday, so let's stop wasting each other's time. I talk to him now, or I go home."

"Have it your way."

Eve used her wrist unit. "Detective Peabody, report to Interview. Frosty, huh?" she said when she noted Sorenson studying her unit. She opened the door, stepped in.

Dudley sported a bruised and swollen jaw and eyes red and puffy from weeping. He'd had enough time to come down from his high, she noted, and that could be useful. Flanking him were two other lawyer types. Young, female, attractive. One of them actually held his hand.

"Record on. Dallas, Lieutenant Eve, in interview with Dudley, Winston — the Fourth." She dropped a thick file on her side of the table. "Also present is Mr. Dudley's attorney of record, Sorenson, Bentley, and two other representatives. Would each of you state your name for the record?"

As they did, she simply delegated them to Blonde and Redhead. "Peabody, Detective Delia, entering Interview. So, the gang's all here. How's the face, Winnie?"

"You struck me. I saved your life and you struck me and dragged me in here like a criminal."

"Saved my life? Gosh, my recollection, and my recording, which was — as is proper procedure — engaged throughout our meeting, have a different take. As do the recordings and statements of the officers in Our

534

Lady of Shadows Church."

"And those recordings and statements will be questioned," Sorenson put in, "as we can document your vendetta against my client."

"Yeah, you do that little thing, see where it gets you. So let's start from there. You contacted me at just past twenty hundred hours."

"She was drunk," he said to Sorenson. "But I was desperate. She could barely speak coherently, and when she arrived, she could hardly stand up she was so inebriated."

Eve opened the file, pulled out a hard copy, tossed it on the table. "My tox screens, taken at hour intervals from nineteen hundred hours to twenty-one hundred hours. Clear and clean."

"Falsified, just like the rest! You were already drunk when you accosted me and Sly at Lionel's. A dozen witnesses would corroborate that, and your abusive attitude. Your own husband was disgusted with you."

"Roarke says hi, by the way. You might not have noticed him in the church." She smiled as fury reddened Dudley's face.

"You entrapped my client," Sorenson began.

"Bullshit. Your client contacted me, which is verified by both our 'link logs. I met him,

535

as he requested. My backup was not only within procedure, but recommended by departmental policy. You confessed, Winnie, during our meeting — when your pal had a stunner to my throat — that the two of you had engaged in a competition that involved killing selected targets."

She drew photos out of her file, lined them up.

"You misinterpreted my words. I was doing whatever I could to stall Sly." Tears, and she thought them sincere, sprang to his eyes even as he lied his murdering ass off. "I betrayed and killed my dearest friend for you."

She sent him a look, the same kind she'd seen him send Roarke in Lionel's. Civilized contempt. "You sure roll on your dearest friend quick and easy."

"I'm doing my duty. And God knows it can't harm him. He's dead. I killed him to save you."

"Oh, don't worry, you didn't kill him. He's actually doing pretty well."

"You're a liar. I saw him."

"You didn't see much of anything being souped up on Hype cut with a little prime Zeus. Your client's tox screen." Eve tossed it out of the file.

"I was frightened. Maybe I was weak, but

I was frightened, so I took something. You can charge me with using, but —"

"Be quiet, Winnie."

"I'm not a murderer!" He rounded on Sorenson. "It was Sly. And Sly's dead!"

"Not dead yet, and I'll be talking to him in the morning," Eve commented. "I'm betting he rolls on you just as quick and easy. The officer with him tells me he's pretty steamed you stabbed him."

"Saving you."

"Why did you bring an antique Italian fencing foil to church, Winnie?"

"I didn't. Sly did."

"Actually, no, he didn't. Your droid did. The same droid that the two of you used to pose as Simpson's house droid the night Sly murdered, and you conspired to murder, Luc Delaflote. We have the droid, Winnie, and are running his drives. You guys really should have destroyed that unit."

She nodded to Peabody, who went out.

"Detective Peabody exiting Interview. There are a lot of things you probably should've gotten rid of. Oh, look here, more pictures."

"I have no idea who those people are." But his hands began to twitch.

"Sure you do. You killed them."

"Lieutenant, if you're going to add more

ridiculous charges to those already levied against my client, I'll —"

"It's a pattern, Counselor, and I can connect each and every one of these people to your client. This one, the first one we've dug up. You're in Africa, it's hot, kind of wild. And hell, you're paying her, aren't you? She should do what the hell you want when you want it. And you've got that buzz on," she added, rising and circling the table. "Women are supposed to lie down when you say lie down, supposed to spread them when you say spread them. It was her own fault, really, and thank God you had Sly there to help you out."

She reached over, leaning over him, pulled the death photo of Melly Bristow out of the file.

Blonde gagged.

"Yeah, harsh, but, hey, she was dead already. Such a rush, getting away with murder. And they're all just people for hire anyway — like Sofia Ricci in Naples, like Linette Jones in Vegas."

She tapped each ID shot while Sorenson dismissed her accusations, and Dudley continued to twitch.

"But wouldn't it be more of a rush to kill people who've got some cachet?" she continued. "Why waste your time on nobodies?

Add some spice to the contest. What was the winner going to get anyway?"

"You're making things up."

"A high-class version of the classic game of Clue. Oh, wait." She pressed the recorder she'd already cued up, and Dudley's voice came out.

Games are for children. This is adventure. It's competition.

"How many points did you get for the LC in the amusement park with the bayonet?" she wondered. "Your great-uncle's bayonet. Or for the facilitator on the jogging trail with the bullwhip. The bullwhip custom-made for you in Australia. Detective Peabody returning to Interview. And, look, she's brought party favors."

"I was nowhere near either of those places. You know very well I was entertaining on the night Adrianne was killed."

"We've been talking to people on your guest list. Even better, to staff hired for that little soiree. The hired help, Winnie? They tend to see things because people like you don't really see them." She smiled. "We've already found a couple of guests who state they looked for you to say good night before they left, and gee, couldn't find you."

"I have a large home, an extensive estate."

"Yeah, and needed a lot of extra help, the kind who don't have any reason to lie about or for you. We've got a few who noticed you and Adrianne Jonas heading for the garage, a couple others who noticed you coming back, a bit after three A.M. Alone."

"You bribed them." Sweat coated his face like dew. "It goes back to this vendetta. It goes back to jealousy."

"Oh, of what?"

"You may have finessed marriage out of Roarke, may have money, but you'll never be anyone. Either of you. You'll never be what I am."

"Thank God for that. I've got statements, recordings, witnesses, weapons." She shrugged. "Oh, and you know what else? You had this in a locked drawer in your bedroom." She pulled out an evening bag. "It's Adrianne Jonas's."

"She left it at the party. I was keeping it for her."

"No, do better. We have those pesky hired help who saw her, with the bag, as she was entering your garage."

"She dropped it."

"And oddly, her 'link wasn't in it, though she was seen using it minutes before you walked her to the garage. Oddly, too, her

540

prints and several strands of hair were in your vehicle. Oh, and a couple of the valets you hired saw your vehicle leave the estate just under an hour prior to her time of death."

"She must have asked one of the servants to drive her. I can't keep track of everyone."

"Are these your shoes?" She pulled them out of the box, got a shrug. "I can save us time and tell you these were taken out of your shoe closet, tagged, and logged. You wore these same shoes the night you killed Ava Crampton. We have you, wearing them and a bogus disguise, entering the House of Horrors with her, less than thirty minutes prior to her time of death."

"You can't have. I took . . . I wasn't there."

"You were going to say you took care of it, jammed security with this." She drew out the jammer. "You did a pretty good job, Winnie. Credit where credit's due. But you didn't get them all. And before you say there are any number of people with this particular make of shoe," she said to Sorenson, "you should know they're a limited edition, and in this size and color, very few have been sold — and we've been briskly eliminating them as suspects. I really don't think your client's been fully forthcoming with you."

"I'll need time to confer privately with my client."

"Sure. We can do that. And given the time, I can postpone the continuation of this interview until Monday morning. I bet you're feeling a little tense and itchy, Winnie. Gee, you're all shaky and sweaty. I bet you wish you had just a little hit to smooth it out. It's a long time until Monday, a long time in a cage without all your usual indulgences."

"You can't keep me here."

She leaned forward, into his face. "Oh, yes, I can."

"Sorenson, you useless shit, deal with this."

"Lieutenant, if I could speak with you outside."

"I'm not going anywhere." In fact, she leaned back in her chair, crossed her booted feet. "Why don't you deal with me, Winnie? That was the plan. But Sly screwed up, he messed it up for you. He's the loser. But you, you're a screwup, too. Jesus, you're laughable. I beat both of you in under a week. Maybe I should have a victory drink."

She pulled a bottle of champagne from the box. "Fancy French stuff. Special vintage, numbered and signed and recorded in Delaflote's log for the Simpson job. It was in your wine cellar. That Delaflote, he had no business getting naked with your mother. Freaking French upstart."

"You shut your mouth."

"Oh, I got more. Lots more. So much I'm amazed the two of you had a nine-month run at this. The NYPSD judge?" She gestured to Peabody.

"Gives them a five-point-eight out of ten. But that's for creativity," Peabody added. "Execution drops to a four-point-six."

"That's fair. But it was fun, wasn't it, Winnie? That much fun, you do it for the love, not the score. And you loved it, just like you love your chemicals. What's life without some buzz and thrill?"

"Lieutenant, that's quite enough." Sorenson stood. "We'll end this interview here."

"I'm not staying here, going back to that cell. You moronic prick, do what you're paid to do! I want to go home. I want this bitch punished."

"Ouch, starting to jones some, huh?" Eve shook her head in sympathy as she checked her wrist unit. "It's been a while. Not that you're going home — ever — Winnie, but you wouldn't find any of your stashes there. We've got them, too."

He surged to his feet, backhanding Redhead out of her chair when she tried to soothe him down again. "You have no right to touch my things. I pay you. You're nothing but a public servant. I own you."

"You bought and paid for these people." Eve gestured to the photos scattered over the table. "You had every right to kill them for sport."

"You're damn right we did. They're nothing." He swept the photos to the floor. "Barely more than droids. Who cries when a droid's destroyed? And you, you're nothing more than a conniving, social-climbing nobody's temporary whore. We should've killed you first."

"Yeah, guess so. Missed that shuttle."

"Winston, I don't want you to say another word. Do you hear me, not another word."

"Going to listen to your paid servant, Winnie?" She put a taunting sneer into her voice. "Does he tell you what to do?"

"No one tells me what to do. I'm walking out of here, and I'll ruin you. You think because you married money you're safe? I have a name, I have influence. I can crush you with a word."

"Which word? Because I need more than one, and here they are. Winston Dudley the Fourth, in addition to the charges already on record against you, you are hereby charged with five additional counts of murder and conspiracy to murder the following: Bristow, Melly, a human being . . ."

Behind her as Eve continued the litany of names and charges, Peabody opened the door for two uniforms. Because she'd already decked him once, Eve stepped aside when he charged and left it to the uniforms to restrain him.

"Lieutenant!" Sorenson came after her. "It's obvious my client is emotionally and mentally distressed, and may be suffering from illegals abuse. I —"

"Take it up with the PA. I've done my job."

She kept walking, and as she passed Observation Roarke came out, fell into step with her. "Nice work, Lieutenant, for a temporary whore."

"That's saying something from a conniving, social-climbing nobody."

"What a good fit we are." He took her hand. "Ready for the weekend?"

"Oh, boy, howdy. I need lemon meringue pie and strawberry shortcake."

"Aren't you the greedy one?"

"Hey, sometimes you've just got to go for a little indulgence." She turned toward the conference room. "I need about thirty to deal with the paperwork. And I'm going to need a couple hours tomorrow morning on Moriarity."

He only nodded, and kept her hand in his as they looked at the board. "No more faces," he said. "Not tonight."

"No, not tonight."

He understood, she thought, that she'd needed to ensure that. And understood, as she did, there would be other faces on other nights.

But not tonight.

She turned to him, slid her arms around him, laid her head on his shoulder, and breathed clear.

He was right. What a good fit they were.

ABOUT THE AUTHOR

J. D. Robb is the pseudonym of *New York Times*-bestselling author Nora Roberts. In the spring of 1995, J.D. Robb's first book, *Naked in Death*, appeared. Robb introduced readers to New York City in 2058, as seen through the eyes of Eve Dallas, a detective with the New York City Police and Safety Department. The popularity of that first book built up through the release of the thirty subsequent Eve Dallas books including *Creation in Death, Strangers in Death, Salvation in Death, Promises in Death, Kindred in Death,* and *Fantasy in Death*. Nora Roberts is the number-one *New York Times*-bestselling author of nearly 200 novels. There are more than 400 million copies of her books in print in over 34 countries. Visit her website at www.noraroberts.com.